THE PRINCESS F DEATH

BOOK ONE
TANGLED FATES SERIES

LEONA REED

Copyright

The Princess of Death © 2024 by Leona Reed

All rights reserved.

Content Warning

This book addresses themes of mental illness, including panic attacks, anxiety, PTSD, and eating disorders. It contains graphic violence, gore, and explicit sexual content. Additionally, there are references to attempted sexual assault and child abuse as past, off-page events.
Reader discretion is advised.

Contents

Dedication

*For readers who crave that delicate kind of love
to fight the darkness in their head.*

Character Index

Main characters

- Nevaeh Blackburn (20) - Princess of Death
- Anxo Alarie (23) - Horseman of Conquer
- Harvey Adler (25) - Horseman of War
- Seiji Nakaya (22) - Prince of Famine
- Grace Blackburn (22) - Supernatural Bookkeeper
- Hazel Seagrave (26) - Conquer's Warriorhead/ Siren
- August Trevino (3) - Werewolf

Side characters

- Dean Blackburn (Horseman of Death) - Nevaeh's father
- Yua & Akihiko Nakaya (Horseman of Famine) - Seiji's parents
- Khatri - Death's Warriorhead
- Sage and Henry Adler - Harvey's parents
- Kiara and Luke Alarie - Anxo's parents

1. Terrific idea, terrible execution

Nevaeh

What do you do when the real nightmare begins *after* you wake up?

The chains bound to my limbs make a sharp clinking sound that echoes around the quiet dungeon as I force my weakened body to sit up. The hideous overall my abductors gave me is still damp with blood which only makes it harder to stop shivering.

The ice-cold cement wall against the fresh cuts on my back makes me wince and the memories of last night's whipping flash before my eyes.

My healing powers have all but vanished over the past week. Judging by the number of open scars littered around my numb body, it's clear my *Divine* is on vacation while I suffer in its absence.

Divine: A raw power source capable of creating and destroying worlds formed by the combined powers of The Almighty God and All-knowing Fates. Every supernatural has a small piece of this magic running in their veins.

The blood, ache, and stink of burnt flesh coming from a cell nearby is nothing new. For me, this is just another morning at *mi casa tortura,* except something is missing—*or someone.*

The absence of my cellmate is enough to pull me out of my daze abruptly. Fighting against my blurred vision, I frantically start patting the cold floor around me, but there are no signs of him anywhere. For months I have woken up to the toddler snuggled tightly against my stomach so where is he now?

Where's my little boy?

A whimper filled with terror sounds from afar, and my

heart stops at the familiar cry. Without thinking, my neck snaps in that direction only for the iron collar tied to my hair to pull harshly. The sudden sharp pain in my scalp completely blinds me briefly before dread creeps in.

They took him.

Bile claws at my throat when another small whimper echoes inside the dark walls of my cell. No, they can't take him. They haven't touched the boy in *months*. We had a deal. I've taken his share of daily punishments so they'll leave him alone.

Fear grips me entirely and his muffled scream rattles my insides. I'm still disoriented from my blackout, but the terrified cry from the kid has me pushing past the bone-crushing pain I'm in. Breathing rapidly through my nose, I try to stop my hands from shaking.

I'm wasting time just sitting here. I need to find the kid before they taint him. I can't let them break him like they broke me. I won't let him suffer in this nightmare any longer.

Being mindful of the collar around my neck, I keep my head tilted at an angle and start dragging my battered body to the far corner of this disgusting dungeon.

Stuffing as much of my tattered dress as I can under my scarped knees to act as a makeshift cushion, I start digging. The broken cement cuts through the skin on my fingers, but I invite the pain. It's helping me push past the dizziness.

When I hear the kid sobbing a few cells away, my mind blanks. Getting to him as fast as I can is now my sole focus.

I've been planning our escape for months. I carefully noted the days which had fewer guards on duty and marked the ones I thought would be easier for me to fight off in my current state. I was preparing to break my little guy out of here, but not like this. Not when I can barely remember what the day is or which warlock is in charge of security.

When I finally reach the dagger I had stashed in the ground a while back and try to pull it out, the cold metal digs into my palm and I have to swallow my gasp of pain before I make a sound.

Ignoring the stings, I crawl back with the dagger to where my chains are hammered in.

The dagger is rusted and probably wouldn't do much harm, but at least I have a weapon now. A weapon, I risked my life stowing away after they threw that little boy in my cell because I had a feeling I would have to put it all on the line for him one day.

With trembling hands, I stomp on the last shred of pride I have left and cut my hair free from the chain. The dark cell and my blurry vision makes it difficult to see much of anything so I blindly search the chain around my wrists for a weak point by pulling on every link.

When I finally find a hook ready to fall apart, I take a deep breath and center myself before pulling on it with all my remaining strength. It takes three hard tugs and scraped palms to free my wrists and two more for my ankles.

I wish I had more time to revel in being free of these damn chains for the first time in a decade, but time is not on my side today.

Fucking witches. I hate them and this entire fucking coven from the deepest corner of my heart.

The crescent moon is the strongest and most disgusting coven among supernatural's and I can't wait to burn it all to the ground. The overwhelming need for revenge chokes me until I push it down.

I need to save the kid first.

His life triumphs my thirst for blood.

Unfortunately for them, the deviant guards on shift are so focused on traumatizing my little boy that they won't see me coming until I'm right behind them.

Deviants: Undead human puppets with no working brains.

Witches created Deviants to do their dirty work and be fiercely loyal to them. They follow the Queen's commands like loyal puppies without remorse or hesitation.

The crescent moon coven has an ancient practice of

hunting down helpless humans on their deathbeds and offering them immortality for the small price of eternal loyalty.

Of course, the humans stupidly sign up as soon as they hear the word *immortality* and never bother to read the fine print. They end up getting conned when the coven turns them into brainless puppets with no free will, immortality, or soul.

Trusting the witches?

Who the fuck came up with that idea?

I take a deep breath to rein in my anger and immediately gag when the awful stink of blood and urine reaches my nose.

With the dagger clutched in my hand, I try to stand up but my legs refuse to hold my weight. Crawling to the bars, I fist them for support and clench my teeth before pulling myself up. I muffle my scream by biting down on my knuckles and squeeze my eyes shut when the world starts spinning.

Every bone in my body begs me to sit down before I pass out. The thought of resting my eyes flashes in my mind for a quick second before the wails outside break through my fatigue.

You can't give up, Nevaeh. Monkey needs you.

When I'm sure I won't plant myself face-first on the ground, I stretch my legs to regain some feeling even if it's just pure agony.

The only reason I'm not on the floor writhing in pain is due to the sudden silence. Screaming and crying are good; it means he's alive. It's the silence that chills my soul from the endless possibilities it leaves in its wake.

It takes a moment for my legs to regain footing, and I use the time to pace in my head and plan my next steps.

Slowly, I feel my Divine, the magic that runs in my veins stir after a decade of being forced to stay dormant. One by one, all my open wounds start closing up.

I choke on air at the sudden sharp pain of my ribs cracking in place. This time when I take a deep breath, my lungs don't scream in protest and I don't feel like a baby elephant is sitting on my chest.

Is my plan reckless and probably life-ending? *Yes.*

Do I have another brilliant plan? *No.*

To stop myself from overthinking my somewhat foolish plan, I strike the metal end of the dagger against the heavy iron bars creating a loud resounding sound throughout the dungeon.

No takebacks now.

Rushed footsteps paired with the mind-numbing stink of decaying flesh lets me know what's coming my way. The smell overwhelms my heightened senses, and I try my best to focus on getting out of this cell and ignoring the urge to throw up.

Not like I have anything in my stomach to throw up. I haven't been fed in *weeks* now.

The guard is about to rush past my cell when I use his distraction and his lack of a working brain to swiftly trap him in a chokehold through the bars. The moment my arms sink into his rotten flesh, I regret not stabbing him instead.

With time, a deviant's body degrades into fragile bones and decaying flesh that shreds like a snake. It's exactly as gag-worthy as it sounds.

The Deviant aggressively thrashes into my hold, and his touch burns the skin on my forearms because of the amount of dark magic that was used to create him.

He angles his spear to stab me from the side, and I evade just in time. Before this fool can alert the others with his antics, I squeeze my arms harder and watch his head fall to the ground and roll off with a splotch. *Yuck.*

Counting to five, I brace to see if the commotion attracts any unnecessary attention. When no one comes screaming bloody murder, I reach for the spear the Deviant abandoned and smash the heavy lock keeping me inside to pieces.

A quick glimpse inside the opposite cell reminds me why I need to abandon all hesitation and fear before stepping outside this nightmare. The broken and burnt bodies piled in a corner are a small example of what these monsters are capable of.

The scared and quiet ones are fun to play with, but no one wants to deal with a mouthy, sarcastic, and overall bitch. I figured out a long time ago that as long as they focus on beating the attitude out of me, their eyes won't stray to where my clothes are torn.

Using the walls as my crutch, I limp to the last cell and sigh in relief when I can hear soft whimpers again. I feel awful for being happy about the poor boy crying, but at least now I know he's still alive.

I would take him crying over being killed at the hands of these voodoo-doing barbarians any day.

'You hit first and hard, so they can't come after you again.'

The combat lesson from my childhood suddenly echoes in my head, and I freeze in place. I'm surprised I still remember his voice, even after all this time.

Papa.

After a decade of nothing but pain and misery, hope spreads in my chest that maybe, *just maybe*, I will get to see him again.

The possibility of seeing my papa again sends my Divine into overdrive. I feel my strength increasing with every dragging step, and the adrenaline rushing into my body helps me recount the combat lessons Papa drilled into me as a kid.

Stopping at the edge, I peek around the brick wall to glance inside the cell. When my eyes find the tiny figure bound to a chair he can barely fill in, a familiar rage fills my veins. The kind of rage I learned to keep dormant for most of my life, but today, I don't ignore the whispers of revenge. Today I'm embracing them.

For my little monkey.

A lump forms in my throat when my eyes get fixed on the open scar on his stomach that's bleeding heavily. His skin is pale, not from the loss of blood but from the raw fear of the warlock looming over him.

The rough plan I had in my head goes down the bloody drain. I'm no longer waiting for the perfect opportunity. My skin feels like and itchy from the need to skin that warlock alive.

Before the pathetic warlock can put his hand on the kid, my dagger cuts through the air and perfectly lands on the side of his neck. The cell goes eerily still as his body falls to the floor like a sack of wrinkly old potatoes.

Shouldn't have touched my kid.

Taking advantage of their shock, I storm into the cell and swiftly stab a Deviant right between his eyes with the spear. The last warlock who was enjoying watching my kid be tormented scurries back to avoid blood splashing on him.

The sound of my boy hiccupping and struggling to reach me snaps me out of my tunnel vision. Turning my head slightly to the left, I find him tugging on the chains which only makes them dig harder into his wrists.

Keeping my blood-dripping spear aimed at the last warlock, I meet my baby's eyes and shake my head once. Immediately, his movements halt, and the lack of crying helps me focus on the bastard in front of me once again.

"How dare you put your filthy hands on my kid?"

Poking his forehead with the spear, I apply the tiniest bit of pressure that has him shuddering in fear.

"I warned her, didn't I? I specifically said *not. him.*"

Despite the weapon aimed at his head, the warlock has the balls to hiss at *me.* "How did you get out?"

It shouldn't surprise him I broke free since I've done it before. Sure, only one of two prisoners escaped that time, but I still consider it a wild success.

The warlock's eyes frantically look around for help, and I see the exact moment he realizes he's on his own. Taking another step back, he helps me by cornering himself. This dungeon is drowning in black magic, making it impossible for inside voices to break free.

"We had a deal. You leave him alone, and I take his share of punishments," I wheeze.

It suddenly dawns on me that even when my Divine is healing me and doing its best to support me, my lack of a stellar diet in the past decade will be working against me today.

The warlock's shoulders stiffen, and I hear his heartbeat falter, but his pride won't let him beg for his life. Not like his begging would change my mind.

"That was before you started passing out every hour. The Queen asked us to train the kid. He is supposed to take your place." My blood freezes in terror at the casual way he mentions making the boy their next punching bag.

That's exactly what I wanted to prevent. My skin might be crawling with a decade's worth of scars, but I won't let them leave permanent reminders of this nightmare on my boy.

There are two types of magic bearers in our world. The first kind uses dark magic and pays for that power with their soul that chips away with every spell. And the second kind practices clean magic to spare their soul as their flesh takes the brunt of wielding such power.

Without a soul, the dark witches go straight to Purgatory when they die. However, the light witches still have a chance at finding eternal peace in *Azure*.

Purgatory: A place where rotten to the bones supernaturals are tossed to spend eternity in misery after death.

Azure: A version of Heaven created by the big bad Satan himself so his angelic brothers and supernatural creations had a place to spend eternity in peace after giving up immortality.

This warlock's mangled left ear tells me he is a light warlock, but that doesn't mean he'll be going anywhere near Azure in this life.

Grabbing him by his throat, I push the warlock against the moldy wall before asking the boy to look away. The kid doesn't object and turns his head just as my palm squeezes tighter, and I let my Divine come out to play.

The warlock's eyes widen in fear as the brown in mine vanishes, revealing a gold ring around my iris which reflects in his petrified eyes.

I've deprived my Divine of an audience for so long that it's no surprise the warlock hasn't seen my Divine make its presence known.

Sucking up every last bit of light and warmth from the dungeon, my thick gold essence circles me protectively. Dancing over my skin in wild patterns, the strings of gold search for a prey.

Without wasting another moment, I absorb the warlock's darkened soul and watch his skin melt beneath my palm. The foul smell of burnt flesh overtakes his wails growing louder as he tries to escape. Choking on his own blood, the warlock pleads with his eyes, but I wasn't born to be merciful... especially not to monsters like him.

Throwing my head back, I fill my lungs with every ounce of his Divine, leaving him empty before tearing his soul apart from his body.

The warlock falls to the ground with a thud when I finally loosen my hold. His face was now a deep shade of purple, and his body shrunken like he'd been dead for ages.

It's not my fault they forgot my mere touch can void them of their souls. What I can do is nothing short of barbaric, but what else would you expect from Dean's daughter, one of the Four Horsemen of the Apocalypse.

From the daughter of Death.

A hiccup breaks my trance, and I immediately fight to gain back control from my Divine. Albeit reluctantly, my essence fades so I can tend to who matters most.

Rushing to the boy, I crouch before him and hold his face between my hands. He doesn't flinch like he does with others just stares at me with those big blue eyes.

"Hey, monkey."

I search him for injuries, and except for a couple of scratches and handprints, the only concerning wound is on his stomach. The fast flow of blood is not helping ease his panic.

Quickly snapping the chains around his wrists, I wipe the tears falling down his pale cheeks and press a quick reassuring kiss on his forehead.

"Hey, don't worry kiddo, I've got you. I'll make it stop

hurting okay?" When I notice his shallow breaths, I know I don't have much time before he passes out from the pain.

"And then... and then we'll run away from this awful place. Somewhere very far away. What do you think, you want to leave with me tonight?" Fresh tears line his lashes as he nods up at me.

Cleaning the tickle of blood rolling down the side of his temple, I take an oath to never let anyone hurt my little monkey ever again.

When I go to remove my hands from his face, monkey jumps forward to grip my arm with both his hands and buries his face in the crook of my neck.

Okay. No problem. I just have to do everything with one hand now.

Covering his gash with my palm, I close my eyes and break the fragile hold I have over my Divine so it can surface again. My essence steadily flows from my palm to monkey's stomach, and it doesn't take long before I feel the large cut closing beneath my fingers.

Forcing my heavy eyes to blink rapidly, I try to get rid of the black spots dancing in my vision. I haven't had the strength to stay alive and use my powers simultaneously in a very long time, so I know it's time to skedaddle out of this nightmare before I start feeling the consequences.

Pride bubbles in my chest as watch as monkey's face regain some of his baby-pink blush. His body, which was covered in bruises before, is now free of them. Exactly how it should be.

But as the blood loss settles in, the boy starts trembling like a leaf and I quickly realize the hideous excuse for clothes we are wearing won't do anything to keep us warm outside this dungeon.

The little guy tiredly nuzzles his face in my neck, and I caress his matted hair while I try to figure out how I'm supposed to carry him *and* fight at the same time.

Searching the cell, I grimace when my eyes land on the bloody and dirty blanket in the corner.

Anything is better than nothing, I guess.

Using the blanket, I strap the kid to my chest, tying knot after knot and hoping it will be enough. This way, my little monkey will be warm, and my hands will be free to do whatever I want… *like pulling out someone's trachea.*

With the boy safe in my arms, the unyielding knot of anxiety in my stomach finally unravels.

Thank Fates, I woke up when I did. I don't want to imagine the damage these monsters could've inflicted on this innocent soul if I had stayed on the floor, lying in my own blood.

Standing behind the large wooden gates beyond which lies my freedom, I remind myself only the inside of the dungeon is soundproof, and I'll have to be quick and quiet from here on out.

It took me a minute to figure out how to fight with a toddler wrapped around my chest. That minute cost me my kneecap while taking out the four Deviant guards at the entrance.

My head reels with panic and adrenaline as I take off toward the thick forest surrounding the coven. I'm limping as fast as my broken knee would allow me when all of a sudden my Divine goes berserk.

The relentless bastard starts clawing at my insides in complete hysteria, trying to nudge me back in the direction of the dungeons.

So not happening asshole.

I get this odd feeling that the raw panic running through my veins is *foreign*—like it's not my own, but that can't be right. And even if I wanted to figure out why my Divine was pushing me so hard to turn back towards the coven instead of the border, the boy in my arms was my priority.

If this is my last night alive, I'll be damned if I die without making sure I deliver him into safe hands.

2. I'm still alive fuckers!

Nevaeh

I stumble through the thick, dark forest with the boy strapped to my chest. The logical part of my brain—*which is not that big*—is screaming at me to pick up the pace, but my body is on the verge of giving up.

The dry blades of grass act as little spikes beneath my bare feet. I keep limping forward, using the spear as my crutch, and it's taking everything in me not to let the bone sticking out of my knee stop my struggling steps.

The bloody footprints I'm leaving behind force me to keep pushing forward before the 'queen bitch' finds out her two favorite prisoners have escaped.

The bright yellow sun behind me packs up for the day, turning the sky a soft hue of orange and pink. If I wasn't literally on the verge of death, I would've stopped to appreciate the captivating beauty of this realm.

On second thought... they can have fucking diamonds in the sky, and I would still hate everything about this stupid realm and this stupid coven.

Like instant karma, I trip over a thick branch and wince when a sharp pain shoots up my left leg and travels to my head. My adrenaline is quickly fading, and the pain it had helped bury is now coming back with a vengeance.

I'm not sure I'll be able to get back up if I take a break, but if I don't, I'll definitely drop dead right here in this ugly forest. Finding a thick and strong tree trunk, I slowly sink to the ground to rest against it.

When monkey stirs from the change, I quickly cover his head with my hand so he can feel me near. Twice he has woken up with a start and only relaxed enough to go back to sleep after I rubbed his back or covered his head with my hand.

I hate seeing this sweet little boy so terrified all the time. I hate it even more that this has been a constant state for him. My blood boils as I wipe a smear of dried blood from behind his ear, and when he trembles in my lap, that fury only multiples.

If I survive this day, I'm going to rip this coven apart. *Piece by fucking piece.*

The icy breeze that follows the moon rising soothes my cuts, but it also makes it clear that we can't spend the night in the open. Not only would we freeze to death, but the guard dogs would find us too.

With a determined exhale, I stretch my left leg to push the bone back in, but the blinding pain that follows the slightest movement has me crying out in pain.

With silent tears rolling down my cheeks, I fall back against the sturdy tree trunk, breathing heavily. Feeling the energy slowly drain out of me and how my movements have become lethargic makes me painfully aware that I won't make it through the night.

Pushing closer to my chest, the boy sleepily nuzzles his head in my neck, and in my weak moment, I pray for a miracle.

I can't let this little boy go back to that shithole.

After *Harvey*, my best friend, escaped two years ago, I stopped fighting back. I didn't care if I died. But that quickly changed when my captors threw this little toddler into my cold, blood-soaked cell.

Through one-sided conversations—because the little guy refuses to talk—we bonded instantly. It took him less than two minutes to trust me enough to crawl into my lap and fall asleep on his *first* night.

That night, this little guy built up my heart before breaking it just as quickly. If it took him one gentle introduction from a stranger to unravel, then I didn't want to think about the treatment he was used to.

That was the first night I didn't beg Fates to let tomorrow

be my last day. Instead, I asked for strength to survive another. Not because I was overly fond of living any longer, but because my survival was now directly correlated to the survival of this 3-year-old.

'I'll get you out of here, monkey.'

It was a promise that started the shitshow I've been hosting this entire day. A promise that changed the course of my life. A promise that weighs more than my battered body can handle.

Taking in the addictive aroma of damp soil, I snicker at the irony. I'm the daughter of The Horseman of Death, yet I fight the death standing on my doorstep every night.

All this blood, the scars I can't get rid of, the trauma burned into my soul, and for what?

All because of a stupid fucking vision.

The top bitch of witches, *Queen Visha* of the crescent moon coven, is on top of the list of people I want to kill by *slowly* cutting their guts out and then feeding it to them.

At birth, she was bestowed a gift. A gift that became a curse for many.

Clairvoyance.

Ever since she was young, Visha could see glimpses of the future in her dreams, and for years, she watched the snippets and did nothing. But everything changed the night she saw a vision of her death followed by the destruction of her coven... by *my* hands.

That same night Visha killed her husband, the king, to gain full control of the coven.

A complete headcase, that woman.

According to her vision, my Divine reaching its full potential meant the end of her tyrant reign.

Enraged by my audacity to even dream about dethroning the most powerful witch in all realms, Visha hunted me down and came face to face with a 9-year-old girl.

A mentally stable person would've realized they were decades ahead of their vision and there was still time to fix their mistakes. But Visha has never been described as stable by anyone. *So she kidnapped me.*

Now I have an excellent reason to smash her face in and burn her precious coven to the ground.

Taking the Princess of Death from under her father's nose was daring; I'll give her that. Visha managed to trick her way into Papa's kingdom and snatched me... along with my best friend. An innocent fourteen-year-old bystander.

Imagine her surprise when Visha discovered that the boy was none other than *The Prince of War*. The only son of Horseman Adler and next in line for the title.

The four Horsemen of the apocalypse are mighty warriors of *The three sisters of fate* and the inevitable bringers of doom for humanity.

Conquer, War, Famine, and Death.

The four are known to be fearless, yet here I am, battling death and cursing another day when no one comes to my rescue. The mere thought makes me scoff.

It's been a whole ass decade, so if someone were coming, they would've by now. But dead people can't rescue you, can they?

One night Visha pranced into my cell, and my heart sank when I noticed the wicked glint in her eyes. I knew Visha enough to know her happiness always stemmed from someone's pain. And I was proved right when she revealed the reason behind her glee.

The crescent moon pack had just returned after destroying all four of the Horsemen kingdoms, and Visha was so overjoyed she could barely stand still. It was the last piece of her master plan to ruin me from within, and she had succeeded.

The thought of losing Papa, the people I grew up with, the people I was destined to take an oath to protect, was anguishing enough before Visha took one last swing at what was left of my soul.

During the attack, a man who she recognized as my *destined mate* figured out where I was being held captive, and Visha made sure he left the coven grounds in pieces for his attempt to free me.

Visha was kind enough to throw his arm in my lap so I could mourn the one I was supposed to spend my life with. Holding that bloodied severed arm, I cried myself to sleep that night. I cried for the fall of my kingdom, the pain I caused my papa and the life I could've had with my mate.

The following night, I helped my best friend escape. I had enough of watching my loved ones suffer because of my cursed destiny. And I wasn't going to allow Visha to destroy the last piece of my heart.

I huff when I can't seem to clean the dirt on my face, no matter how hard I wipe. The dirt might still budge, but I know the dried blood will linger like it's part of my skin.

Looking down, I find similar stains on the kid, and the rage that forever sits just below the surface of my skin itches for revenge. My heart aches to see his sunken cheeks. Just a couple of months and those monsters managed to dim his light.

It kills me how similar our stories are. Taken from our families and thrown into a cell for a destiny out of our control.

There were more of us at one point whose life's purpose was cruelly snatched awat before getting killed in the most gruesome ways. All because Visha won't stop abusing her power to destroy a future she disagrees with.

Furiously rubbing my eyes, I try to clear my glassy vision and find some hidden strength to pull myself up again. Out of nowhere, my head is reeling with tattered stories from my past as I limp toward the border, and this time, I don't block them out.

The familiarity of my father's voice in my head soothes my aching heart, and I'm grateful for the distraction of my jumbled memories.

I vaguely remember Papa telling me about *the three sisters of fate* glimpsing into the future for the first time since the universe was created. Nobody knows exactly what they saw, but something about a future led by immortals rattled them enough to change their ways by announcing a gift.

The gift of procreation.

News about this gift took Heaven by storm. Fates were suddenly offering everyone a chance to have a *soulmate* and a family, just like humans. A different life than what they were created for, i.e. being a soldier.

God was reluctant at first. It took him several centuries of watching his first children slowly get poisoned by unmatched power before he decided to sit back and let Fates take the rein.

Soon after that Heaven was torn into two pieces between those who chose immortality and eternal loyalty to Heaven and those who opted for the gift.

When Heaven announced those who stumble from their original destiny will have no right to Heaven or their creator anymore, Lucifer, the miscreant son, stood up to bear the burden of leadership and built an entirely new realm for his brothers.

Immediately after the split, the new king created several supernatural species like demons, vampires, and Dragons to bring quantity to *Hell.* The act was seen as retaliation which started a cold war between Heaven and Hell that has yet to end.

As time went by, the brutality between both realms steadily increased until a particularly brutal bloodshed released enough celestial energy in the universe that it almost destroyed the human realm.

Sensing the end of his precious humans, God freed the souls of the Four Horsemen of the Apocalypse to guide humans through the end of time. But before my ancestors could finish what they were summoned for, the sisters of fate intervened at the last minute and suspended the doomsday.

With the end of time postponed, the Horsemen were now trapped into existence *millenniums* before their services were needed. And since they didn't belong to either realm and refused to take a side, Horsemen decided to build a home hidden amongst the same humans they were destined to erase one day.

Slowly my ancestors became the only link between Heaven and Hell, working with both sides but answerable to neither.

However, in the last few decades, Horsemen found an ally in Hell after Papa met *Uncle Lucifer* and became fast friends.

If you count, there have been three significant wars between the two celestial realms. The first that drew a clear line between them. The second was when the original Lucifer found his mate. And a third that was instigated by the Horsemen.

That my dear father caused, to be exact.

Papa was seventeen and still learning the ropes of becoming the next Grim Reaper when he was invited to Heaven with Uncle Elijah—the second Lucifer to be crowned *King of Hell*—for an annual meeting with the Archangels.

What was supposed to be a professional meeting turned into a bloody brawl when the Archangel of Love taunted Papa about being born without a soulmate.

His exact words were, 'Thank Fates for not being cruel enough to punish a poor woman by pairing her with a Horsemen. The Grim Reaper, no less.'

The sudden revelation of his bleak future made Papa do something impulsive. Even Uncle Elijah offered the help of a 'Lucifer' and joined Papa in his quest instead of de-escalating things.

They *broke* into Heaven and *stole* a piece of Divine. Papa used that raw source of power along with his blood and essence to *create* a daughter. He thought if Fates weren't going to give him the future he wanted, then he would make his own fate.

So, he created his own family. He created *me*.

Guess what he named said daughter? *Nevaeh*. Heaven spelled backwards.

Tell me he wasn't aiming another dig at Heaven.

The Archangels were enraged. They believed since it was *Heaven's property* that created me, an unknown being with mysterious abilities on top of my Horsemen blood, it was only right that Heaven raised me to make sure I didn't turn *evil*.

Of course, Papa refused to give up his one-day-old baby girl *or* apologize, so Heaven retaliated. But when you have all of Hell backing you up combined with your chumminess with the literal devil, no one stands a chance.

Papa never found his mate in the nine years I was with him, but it never bothered him because he had me.

His daughter. His little troublemaker.

I was a unique form of supernatural who would one day be crowned *Horsewoman of Death*. But all of that was before I was thrown into a cell, never to be rescued again.

I curse my ancestors, who stupidly exchanged immortality for the ability to *procreate*. Only if those fuckers didn't want to get pregnant so bad, I wouldn't have been born—*or made*, to be precise—and stuck in that dusty ass cell for a decade.

Rustling and quickly approaching footsteps break me out of my pity party.

By the energy thrumming beneath my bare feet and causing a tingly feeling to spread through my body, I can feel how close I am to the force field that ensures no one gets in and out of this coven. But I don't have enough time or energy to fight off Deviants *and* break through it.

Limping faster, I pray to Fates to allow me one more day of this life. One more day to surrender the kid to someone I know and trust. One more day before they finally show me mercy and let me die.

3. Is that an Angel?

Nevaeh

I groan like a dying goat when I hear two more hurried footsteps approaching me.

I'm in the middle of slicing a Deviant in half, panting like I'm on my last breath with one arm secure around the kid. It's so not a good time for another dumpster fire.

Where's a fucking miracle when you need one?

I turn just in time to stop a Deviant from touching the toddler strapped to my chest and take the hit on my back. The said toddler is taking the nap of his life while my back continues to make space for fresh scars.

I know monkey is more than taking a nap, but I can't let myself dwell on that right now or I'll lose my edge.

It's fine. Monkey's fine. He's just a little unconscious.

Deviants are already energy-consuming with their rabid senses and little to no fighting style, but add my exhaustion, constant bleeding, and a dwindling Divine, and you've got the perfect recipe of 'how to enter Azure in five quick steps'.

And I'm going to Azure. No one can stop me. I refuse to be stuck in another nightmare after this one ends.

A girl needs a break dammit!

Surprisingly, instead of adding to my panic, the new footsteps have my Divine lighting up like a firecracker, aching to get closer. Maybe I'm losing what little is left of my sanity.

Suddenly, my spear slices through air and I'm stumbling forward from the force I was putting behind the attack. The Deviant before me drops to my feet with an arrow pierced through his head.

That was not me.

And now I have goo on my bare feet. *Ew.*

Two warriors covered in armor from head to toe sprint through the woods, arrows raining on their arrival. I warily take a step back into the shadows when the darkness surrounding the forest makes it impossible to see their faces.

Then I hear the sharp crack of a whip that vibrates the ground beneath me. Twin whips covered in spikes snake around two Deviants, digging into their flesh before it sends them flying away.

I wait for an arrow to come for my head next, but strangely, not a single attack is aimed at me. The two surprise arrivals are focused on the brainless puppets.

Is this a trick? Is Visha trying something different to punish me this time?

The warrior holding the twin whips and twirls them in a manner that conjures up a storm. *A fucking storm.* What begins as a small rush of wind quickly transforms into an angry black tornado with bright purple lightning wrapped around and inside it.

What. Is. Happening?!

I've been hit in the head countless times in the past so I usually blame everything weird I see on those head injuries. This would've been another '*hallucinating again because brain is useless*' moment if the goo sticking to my feet and blood dripping down my back wasn't uncomfortably real.

It becomes clear the strangers aren't on the coven's side judging by how the ground is tainted with deviant remains, but they can't be on mine either. No one is ever on my side.

Two giant tornadoes spinning in tight circles, fast enough to make me dizzy, sweep up the remaining Deviants before holding them against thick trees. And then the Deviants start barfing their black, gooey organs.

Wait... how... no... what?

There's no way I'm imagining Deviants coughing up pieces of decaying lungs and melting into boiled soup.

Side note: I think I'm going to be sick.

Whips? Arrows? And storms out of thin air. The ones with such powers aren't supposed to be strolling through coven grounds and killing Deviants.

Visha destroyed the Horsemen years ago, right?

More Deviants fall to the ground with arrows lodged in their necks before getting carried away by the wind.

The Horseman of Famine?

No, that can't be.

The arrows can be misleading. Anyone can have a bow and shoot with practiced precision. And the whips... they can be replicated too. For all I know, this is another one of Visha's mind games.

Oh, how I wish my Divine wasn't dwindling to uselessness so I could figure out *what* they are.

The two male warriors—*I'm guessing by their builds*— quickly finish off the remaining guards before they begin to frantically search the forest.

If they're looking for more Deviants should I tell them I already took care of the rest?

Taking advantage of their distraction, I silently drag my spear in front of me. It's a good thing they took care of the Devaints for me because it saved me enough energy to defend myself if they tried to ambush me.

"Nevaeh?"

My head snaps to the man carefully approaching me like you would a wild animal. *Good.* He should be scared shitless because if he tries to touch me or my kid, I will eat them alive.

I take another step back sensing his eyes on me, and my throbbing knee humbles me right away. I think he asks me a question, but the pain is temporarily blocking my hearing with a high-pitched ringing in my head.

With a mask of indifference, I cautiously lower myself to the ground without taking my eyes or spear off the two men. This feels an awful lot like submitting, and it bruises my ego more than my ribs. But then I think about face-planting in front of them. I would rather look meek than take that mortifying fall.

I hate that I don't look as terrifying as I want to, but for their sake, I hope they don't test me. Having more blood on my hands would hurt my gentle soul.

Ha. I would gladly carve them to pieces if they threatened me or my boy.

The man, who for some unknown reason knows my name, crouches at a safe distance as if to appear non-threatening, paying no attention to the weapon I have pointed at him.

Brave? *Yes.*

Stupid? *Also, yes.*

The moonlight plays a clever game of hide-and-seek, sneaking through the gaps between trees to bestow its soft hue on the face previously hidden by dark shadows.

When my eyes meet the most beautiful pair of dark emerald eyes I've ever seen, I'm almost certain I gasp out loud.

Mother. Fucking. Shitballs.

My eyes refuse to blink in fear of him disappearing into thin air and ending this beautiful daydream. My sudden shortness of breath should concern me, but staying alive isn't my biggest priority right now.

I can just *not* breathe for a few minutes, right?

Every bit of my pain and confusion is forgotten. I wasn't aware of how dangerously my body was shivering from the harsh cold until it came to a soothing halt from a single glance at this man.

Smooth ivory skin glowing in the moonlight has me in a trance, along with the way his loose chestnut curls sway in the wind. I tightly close my fist around the spear when my fingers itch to run along the sharp slope of his jaw.

A quiet ringing starts in my head when my eyes land on the curve of his perfectly sculpted plump lips, a shade of pink—

Snap out of it, Nevaeh! He could be the enemy.

As if I wouldn't let him stab me just to get him closer.

Why the fuck did I just think that?!

The way his hypnotic eyes reel me in and how my guard

crumbles with an innocent tilt of his head is unbelievably terrifying.

Finally, the unashamed staring between me and the perfectly sculpted *Angel of a man* is broken when his friend steps toward me from the corner of my eye.

Shifting my attention along with the direction of my spear, I point it at the man who broke my trance and fix my deadliest glare on him.

The warrior instantly raises his hands in the air indicating he isn't a threat. *For now.* "It's not polite to threaten people who just saved your ass, Princess." He says, clicking his tongue disapprovingly.

After sweeping the ground with his boots, he plops down to sit with his legs crossed. I'm about to ask how he's comfortable sitting like that with layers of solid armor on him, but refrain at the last second.

These people are doing something to my head.

When he dusts his shoulder, I notice his armor is overflowing with colorful stickers. His whole ensemble resembles a children's drawing book, and his smile is starting to feel borderline creepy. I admit the smiling idiot is cute, except for how he keeps gawking at me like I'm about to shoot rainbows out of my ass any minute.

The recurve bow on Angel's back is an ancient weapon I'm familiar with, but the whip the younger man has tossed on the ground—albeit similar—isn't what the Horseman of Famine wields. The markings on the weapon are different.

Having enough of them staring at me while my head spirals with unanswered questions, I ask, "Who are you two idiots, and what are you doing here?"

"Introduction sprinkled with insults? You're not very welcoming, Princess." The sticker guy huffs.

Raising my spear higher, I aim for his head. "How about I stab you as a welcome present, *princess*?"

"And that's my cue to shut up. Anxo, your turn."

The cartoon drags himself backward until *Anxo* is on the tip of my spear.

The prettier one, the one I'm going to continue calling Angel, mumbles something under his breath. With a determined nod to himself, he tries to come closer, but I'm not taking any chances.

"Come any closer, and they'll have to pick your pieces off the ground."

Angel's jaw visibly ticks at my warning. I wait for him to lash out, instead, he turns to his friend and they start whispering to each other. "Fates, she is frightening."

"Tell me about it. And Dean said his daughter was the sweetest girl ever." *Wait...*

"Well, that was obviously a lie."

'I killed your father. I enjoyed every second of it too. I held his beating heart in my hand and squeezed until it stopped.'

I shove *her* dreaded voice to the back of my head. I'm not stuck in her dungeon now, and I'll be dammed if I let her voice in my head control me any longer.

Lowering my spear as a sign of truce, I give them an opportunity to explain. "How do you know my father?"

"I'll explain everything, but it's not safe here. We need to leave. Now." Angel stops short in his approach when my Divine seeps out of me sensing my impatience.

A fog of dull gold circles me before it crawls to him. I expect my essence to be eager to attack, but it just floats around him dumbly, almost ruining my threat.

So now my Divine wants to act submissive?!

"Talk."

"Definitely his daughter." Angel man mutters in annoyance but once again calms down faster than anyone I've ever seen.

I've never met a man other than Papa and Harvey who didn't take their anger out on me. It's hard to believe Angel man might be any different.

I retract my struggling Divine before they can discover my strength is a bluff. I hate to admit it, but I need their help which means I have to play nice.

"Let's make a deal. If you can prove you are my father's allies, I promise not to kill you both."

I thought this will make them get to the fucking point, but their lack of regard for their own safety and their trust in me that I *won't* follow through is honestly astonishing.

The man, hidden behind Angel scoffs, "I'm not sure you are capable of anything like that right now."

"You want to try me, sticker boy?"

When my essence thickens feeling the sting of insult, and reaches for him faster, the manchild scurries back.

"I'm going to let it slide, but the next time you insult my stickers, I won't be as lenient." He points a finger at me. At *me*.

Fates, at this rate one of us will be dead before these idiots get to the point. I'm about to get up and leave, which will be painful as fuck when Angel raises his palm in front of my face.

I narrow my eyes at him. What does he want me to do with his open palm? I'm not a fucking palm reader, my man. Before I can open my mouth to rip into him, Angel turns his hand around, and my eyes immediately land on the white crystal on his index finger.

The ring.

Exactly like Papa's.

A moon-white crystal with strings of gold floating inside that resembles trapped rays of sunlight. The gold band at the base is shaped like veins crossing and climbing upon one another with delicate leaves following the curve of his finger.

Magnificent.

The ring with the marked weapon on his back, the one that's gifted to a Horseman on their coronation, tells me all I need to know. I had an inkling before, but now the truth is staring me right in the face.

My lack of response or reaction stumps Angel. It's clear he thinks I'm too dense to figure it out because he hastily removes the armor from his left shoulder to expose the markings engraved on his skin.

The markings of a Horsemen.

Despite being the firstborn or pure blood, the three sisters of Fate have occasionally denied an heir by not blessing them with these enchanted markings. They are equivalent to tattoos for humans, only we don't get to choose them.

It's said only a true Horseman receives the Fate's blessings and the strength to bear everything that comes with such power. And each pattern, writing, and symbol proves exactly who Angel was meant to be in bold, proud markings.

"Horseman of Conquer."

The moment my recognition registers, both jump in excitement before remembering we are still in enemy territory, so the celebration will have to wait.

So was all of it a lie? Did Visha lie about everything or just the attack? What else was she lying about? Is Papa alive? And my mate? Was that a lie, too? A Despicable scheme to break my soul?

The constant ache in my heart that reminded me of my part in ruining my kingdom is suddenly bearable. I don't know if Papa is okay or if my best friend is alive, but seeing my fellow Horsemen standing before me gives birth to a new hope.

"And I'm the *Prince of Famine* if it wasn't clear."

When the Prince bows his head, I mirror the action assuming it's a new custom, only for both men to erupt in snickers. *What weirdos.*

"It's good to finally meet you, Princess Nevaeh." Angel smiles at me softly.

It's strange to have someone smiling at me without malicious intent. And stranger to hear my name out loud. Harvey was the only one who called me by my name, and since his escape, I had to develop the habit of using my name when I talked to myself so wouldn't forget another important part of myself.

"Let's get moving before more of those things show up." Angel offers me a hand, but the action is so sudden and foreign that my instincts process it as a threat, and I flinch violently.

My eyes squeeze shut as I wait for the blow. Forcing a

breath, I hold still. Logic is screaming at me that this is not the same, but old habits die hard.

Come on, Nevaeh, don't act batshit crazy on your first meeting with important people.

Slowly peeling my eyes open, I find one hand clutching the kid in blind protection and the other in front of my face.

When I lift my head, I'm shocked to find Angel sitting right in front of me. The concern on his face makes me re-evaluate how hard I hit my head last night.

Is he worried about me?

I scoff at the silly thought. That's impossible. Why would he worry about me? He must've thought I was losing it and didn't want me to accidentally kill him or his friend.

With my sanity temporarily pieced back together, I casually nod at him like I didn't just flip my shit over him offering to help me stand up. Angel's eyes don't hide his unease, but he doesn't say anything.

This time, when he reaches for me, it's more tentative.

My conscience screams at me that it's a bad idea, but since I have a faulty brain, I ignore the suggestion and gingerly place my palm in his. The sudden rush of heat from the touch has me clutching his hand, not wanting to let go of the only source of warmth I've felt in years.

Is he too hot, or am I too cold?

Blowing a shaky breath, I let him lift me, but a sharp pain shooting through my leg made me fall back, erasing the little distance I managed to move.

Shit that hurt.

Biting the inside of my cheek, I steel myself to avoid highlighting the pain on my face, but I don't think I do a good job. Now Angel looks more worried. Even the other guy—*whose name I should've asked by now*—cautiously asks how he can help.

Angel shifts his gaze to the bone still sticking out of my knee before silently asking if I want to try again. I shake my head vigorously. I'll scream if he tries to move me now.

I can't walk, and we can't stay here forever. The only solution is to leave me. I don't care about me as long as I can convince them to take monkey with them.

I'm about to start begging Angel to take the kid and run when he surprises me by asking, "Can you pass the kid to Seiji, sweetheart? He can hold the boy while I help you. Is that okay?"

It takes me a minute to get over how he said *sweetheart.* Just like his eyes, his voice is gentle. Calming. If I wasn't on enemy ground and injured, I probably would've dozed off by his soothing presence.

Repeating the offer in my head I realize Angel's idea is much better than mine. Begrudgingly, I agree and let *Seiji* take monkey from my arms and bite my tongue to stop the onslaught of threats I have lined up.

Stop it, Nevaeh. He is trying to help. Be grateful they are not leaving you here to die.

"If he wakes up, hand him over to me immediately. He freaks out if anyone other than me comes near him." I warn Seiji.

"Noted."

For the first time since we met—*which was only ten minutes ago*—Seiji's face shows nothing but sincerity. The teasing smile he had plastered on until now is nowhere to be seen.

Angel waits until I'm sure the kid is safe before offering to help again. I'm dreading the next step because I almost passed out last time. I brace myself for the pain, but instead, I feel arms snake under my thighs and back, and suddenly I'm lifted off the ground.

What the—

Unannounced physical contact is a trigger for me, and I dread what comes next.

I wait for the panic to consume me, for my fight response to kick in, but all I feel is the sheer amount of heat radiating from this man. The comfort of his warmth and my lack of fear at our proximity stuns me into silence. I can't think of a single protest.

What kind of witchcraft is this?!

Angel's hold on me is strong, not enough to hurt me, but enough to keep me firmly in place. I'm so dumbfounded I don't even notice how my treacherous arms are looped around his neck.

I only grip him tighter when I peer down. Falling from his height would definitely leave a bruise.

How fucking tall is this guy?

"Relax Nevaeh, I promise I won't drop you. I'm sorry I startled you, but I couldn't stand to watch you hurt anymore. I had to do something."

His voice is so gentle. So damn comforting.

I don't trust it. I can't.

"The kid—"

"Still unconscious. Don't worry, I'll keep an eye on him for you."

Should I believe this Angel man? For all I know, he could be faking the niceness and waiting for the right opportunity to attack.

I can't drop my guard when I don't even know where he is taking me. What if I blackout, and he steals my little boy? What if he drops me back at the witch's doorstep? I would rather hammer nails into my eyes than go back.

In the end, my exhaustion wins over my anxiety.

My head drops on Angel's shoulder when it gets too heavy for me to hold up. I'll rest my eyes for a minute and then I will focus on the route we're walking, in case I have to escape him later.

Angel's chest vibrates as he says something to Seiji, and I burrow my face further into the crook of his neck. My need for warmth overrides my sense of shame.

"Sleepy?" The way my body goes from stiff as a board to limp in his arms must give Angel his answer.

"Take a nap, sweetheart. I'll be right here when you wake up."

I barely register the whisper. I know I should stay awake

because sleeping will only end in another episode, but right now, his arms are providing me a sense of safety I haven't felt in a long time.

Cocooned in Angel's arms, I let myself drift off.

This warmth will disappear tomorrow, and I'll be alone and cold again. So, for tonight, I will allow myself to indulge in the fantasy of having someone to rely on.

4. One look and I'm a caveman

Anxo

From the day I was crowned the Horseman of Conquer, I've carefully harnessed my reputation as the ruthless leader who never hesitates to punish anyone who dares to harm my people.

My unrestricted show of power means they fear me, and the blood I spill sends a clear message: *Horsemen aren't to be messed with.* It became my mission to have my enemies quaking at the mere thought of harming my loved ones.

Six years ago, the Horseman of Death forced my father out of his throne so I could take over. We both knew what was best for our people, and my father was not it.

I admit the pressure and responsibilities were heavy on the shoulders of a 17-year-old. But when the previous leaders were either too miserable with grief or too greedy for power, someone had to make sacrifices.

Instead of doing what most youngsters do at that age, I was spending all my time holed up in my office, making sure the kingdoms were running smoothly.

Each day, I had a new enemy to conquer, but I never allowed the pressure of my duties to stop me from searching for our missing Horsemen. In my heart, I knew Harvey and Nevaeh were still alive, and it killed me to watch people mourn them.

The day our future Death and War were taken, the entire supernatural world was thrown into chaos.

We had our fair share of enemies, but none that had ever dared to make a move against us. Then one day, out of nowhere, two young royals are snatched from their homes with no trace, clue, or proof of life.

Until last night.

One of the many spies I had spread around different realms came running to me. He barely allowed himself to catch his breath before telling me about the whispers he had heard about an imprisoned princess.

It took my Warriorhead an hour to pinpoint the exact location while I assembled my most capable warriors to attack at the first sign of light.

The crescent moon coven has always been a menace. Inventing problems, showing up places uninvited, and causing unnecessary disarray with intentions no one could put a finger on.

There were times I itched to warn the dark queen to stay within her limits. My Warriorhead was happy to deliver the message on my behalf, but searching for my fellow Horsemen and overseeing three large kingdoms was keeping me occupied beyond capacity.

The coven has always been high on our list of suspects. But when they keep relocating every couple of months with zero traces left behind, it's impossible to infiltrate them with spies or even cross their force field without starting an interspecies war.

But tonight at midnight, my troops didn't hesitate to break through the barrier because we finally had some solid intel. Within four hours we had assassinated every high-ranking warrior. Somehow, the Queen caught wind of our mission and had escaped long before our feet touched her coven grounds.

I had no time to waste on the witch because my priority was to find my Horsemen and get them home safely.

The moment I stepped inside the dungeon where they were being held, my heart nearly dropped to my feet. As far as I could see, the place was scattered with dead bodies. Some new, some old enough to have started decaying.

The Deviants sprawled on the ground were either burnt to a crisp or brutally slaughtered.

And I just knew it was *her.*

Nevaeh had managed to escape without our help, and Fates, our future Horsewoman of Death was *vicious.*

My Warriorhead *Hazel* and Bookkeeper *Grace* volunteered to cover the southern border while Seiji and I rushed to tear apart the surrounding forest in hopes that Nevaeh hadn't gone far.

On top of the lingering panic I hadn't been able to shake since last night, my Divine suddenly decided to act like an unyielding brat the minute I crossed over the coven's barrier.

As much as I wanted to take a moment to understand the flip in my mood, I was knee-deep in planning the attack and making sure no stone was left unturned.

Seiji and I were frantically searching through the forest when we stumbled upon a set of bloody footsteps. I'd been so focused on reaching the end of them that it never occurred to me how there was only one set of prints.

I thought the worst possible outcome of this attack would be going home with two dead bodies and facing a heartbroken father. But the broken body of his daughter clinging to a blood-soaked child, fighting her mightiest, wasn't something I had prepared for.

On the verge of death with her fading essence shielding her, there she stood. Balancing on bruised bare feet, Nevaeh drove her spear with such force and accuracy that it set my nerves on fire.

The dull gold in her eyes was spellbinding. I would've continued to stand there in awe of her ethereal beauty if Seiji hadn't crashed into my back, reminding me I was there to help, not gape.

I peer down at the frail girl in my arms who blacked out seconds after she wasn't responsible for her own weight.

My breath gets caught in my throat when my fingers accidentally graze another cut on her back. The bruises on her arms seem older, but the gashes on her back, forehead, and thighs are fresh and bleed every time she moves to hide from the sharp bite of cold air.

The thin material of her dress—*if you could even call it*

that—is soaked with blood, adding to her unease. Pulling the shivering girl closer, I pray Fates to look out for her until I can get us to safety.

Tracing every scar on her body, I tamp down the urgent urge to burn the world around us and hide her in my arms so the flames can't touch her.

I'm not surprised I already feel this protective of her. Nevaeh is a Horsemen, after all. But the surge of possessiveness building a home inside my chest is new.

Walking down the planned escape route, I push my Divine forward and create a barrier of fabricated reality around us. Casting the illusion, I hide our scents and sounds to completely veil our presence on the off chance someone tries to follow our trail.

Everything is normal inside the transparent hexagon bubble, but anyone passing by will see or hear nothing but wildlife.

"Oh, come on Anxo, yellow fits perfectly!" Seiji whines, destroying my train of thought.

With the kid in his arms, Seiji turns around and starts walking backward. Before I have to reprimand him for being careless, he turns back on his own to fall in step with me.

"No."

"Ugh, fine. What about purple?"

I have no idea why he insists on making us look like tooth fairies in colorful armor, but it's not happening.

Not in this lifetime.

"Seiji. I love you, brother. I really do. But now you're pushing your luck." I carefully sidestep a tall patch of grass to avoid jostling Nevaeh. "We are not painting our armors yellow or purple. Hazel already mocks us enough, I'm not giving the siren more material."

"But plain, dark armors are no fun." He stomps gently, destroying the whole purpose of stomping.

Seiji is silent for a long time. The uncharacteristically long pause makes me turn to find him lost in thought.

"Anxo? What do you think happened to Harvey?"

Man, I'm dreading that conversation. A single glance at Nevaeh and the boy tells me I'm not ready to find out what happened to Harvey. I can't even imagine anything worse than what these two have endured.

"I don't know, buddy. But we'll find out soon."

We're not far from where the girls are waiting for us when Nevaeh starts shivering in my arms. Her unease sets off a strange burning sensation in my chest that turns into a stabbing pain in my heart, and it keeps building with every step I take.

Trying to breathe through the pain, I force myself to keep walking, but when the world starts spinning off its axis, I have to stop.

I can't risk precious cargo.

Dropping my guard before I drop Nevaeh, I heave through the sudden rush of emotions. With every breath, every blink, every thought, I feel like I'm going to combust until suddenly everything goes numb. I try to push past the discomfort only to groan as a desperate longing fills me to the brim, almost knocking me off my feet.

My arms squeeze around Nevaeh without thought, and her proximity helps me breathe, but barely.

The instant Nevaeh sleepily nuzzles her face into my neck, I'm done for. As if her physical acceptance of me clicks something into place I feel her weak Divine eagerly trying to reach out.

Suddenly I'm a thousand times more aware of everywhere Nevaeh is touching me. How her soft, warm breath is fanning my neck or how the brush of her ice-cold nose against my skin makes me shiver.

I didn't let my eyes wander before since my Divine gave me no hints that Nevaeh was my mate—*now that I think about it, maybe it tried*—but glancing down at the sleeping beauty in my arms, I feel stupid for not appreciating this breathtaking view.

Despite the bruises, dirt, and blood shadowing her face, I'm mesmerized by her delicate features. Her button nose buries itself in my neck, and seeing her unconsciously seek my warmth and comfort is my downfall.

I've finally found her.

Seiji looks over his shoulder and backtracks. "Anxo? Hey, what's wrong? Do you hear something? Should I call the girls?" Turning in a circle, he starts searching for what made me freeze.

"*Mate.*"

Looking back at me with furrowed brows, Seiji huffs sympathetically. "*Oh.* Look, I know how much you want to meet her. You've been praying for her since you were like six. There's no way Fates haven't heard your *billion* pleas. Trust me, you'll find her soon. I have a feeling—"

"No, no, she—Nevaeh. Seiji... *she* is my mate."

My mate. My Nevaeh. My reason to keep going.

Seiji's jaw drops when I finally manage to find the words. His eyes keep bouncing between me and my girl in disbelief, making me pull my sweetheart closer to my chest.

Oh, drop it you caveman. He's not even into women!

"And how the fuck are you only figuring that out *now*? You've been holding her for like half an hour!"

"Her Divine wasn't strong enough to reach out before."

I don't know how I missed it before, but I realize this is the first time I'm sensing her essence. The little trickster tried to threaten us without a working Divine.

What a girl.

I know Nevaeh is strong, there's no question about it. I mean she practically saved herself and kicked some major ass doing so. And that's why I'm worried about what her reaction might be when she wakes up and finds out that she is now bound to someone for life. An hour after tasting a little bit of freedom.

If Nevaeh says she doesn't want me, I'll lose my mind and run away to the mountains.

Too dramatic? *Maybe.*

But I can't live in the same realm as my mate and not have her in my arms. That would absolutely wreck me.

"How do you think she'll react?"

"Don't worry, I'll pray for you." Seiji saunters away, leaving me to beg Fates not to tear her away from me.

I'm not letting her go. Never.

Following behind Seiji, I adjust my mate so I can rest my cheek on her head. I'm hoping the contact will help her Divine recognize me as its other half and heal her faster. I try and fail to keep myself from kissing her forehead gently.

Nevaeh's proximity is the only thing distracting me from the fury spreading inside me that demands I show those monsters what happens when they hurt my mate.

I make a silent promise the woman in my arms that I will never let anyone hurt her again. I promise to make this coven pay for every bruise on her delicate body.

They will pay for every scar I can see and the ones burned in her memory.

Crossing the coven's barrier, I'm not surprised to find Hazel covered in blood from head to toe, leaning against the car while Grace anxiously paces before her.

When her eyes land on the two unconscious bodies, Grace runs to Seiji. Her horrified eyes search the little boy, and she pulls on her waist-length cornbraids to keep her panic at bay. "Please tell me that's not his blood."

"I don't think so. Most of it is Nevaeh's." When her chin trembles, Grace turns to hide her face in my bicep.

I kiss the top of her head to offer some comfort. This girl always feels others' pain like her own.

"Where is Harvey?" Grace asks.

"Nowhere to be found. We can ask Nevaeh more about him after she's had some rest and a ton of stitches."

Hazel steps closer to scan the damage, and I can see on her face that she is taking inventory of every bruise so she can repay the ones who did this with interest.

"I'm going to skin that voodoo-loving bitch alive."

Straight to violence with this one.

Keeping in mind the fragility of our situation, I hurry everyone towards the car so we can take off. I'm in the middle of forming a plan of action when I hear Hazel and Seiji bickering lowly.

Sensing an upcoming fight, Grace gently takes the boy from Seiji and steps back from the explosive airheads.

No. Please Fates, I can't do this right now.

"Anxo, who gave him the keys? I'm not getting in that car if Seiji is driving."

"Then run home, bitch."

Hazel is clearly not in the mood to suffer through Seiji's driving, and I agree with her. There have been too many incidents with him running wild in the human realm to even consider letting him drive with Nevaeh and the little guy in the car.

My ears start ringing even before Hazel takes a deep breath to ready herself.

When words fail, Hazel starts *whistling*.

This is what I was hoping to avoid. Fates help me or I will lose my ever-going patience and kill them both.

"That doesn't work on me! I don't feel anything!" Seiji screams over the sound of Hazel's punishing tune.

"Yeah? Is that why you're covering your ears," Hazel retorts, which thankfully means no more whistling.

The crazy siren is going to burst my eardrum one day.

"Because you don't have any rhythm! You're so bad at being a siren, it makes my ears bleed." Swearing in Japanese, Seiji shakes his head, muttering about how Hazel very likely fried his brain.

You need a brain for it to be destroyed, Seiji.

Most days, I feel like a single parent to these morons. I spent too many days trying to break apart fights, dealing with their whining, tears, and angry teenager-like attitude to not be considered an honorary one.

It's like a rehearsed routine now. Seiji purposely gets on

Hazel's nerves until she snaps and runs after him with her daggers. Not long after, Grace comes to hide behind me because she knows there will be bloodshed.

"Do something, Anxo." On cue, Grace walks over to stand behind me, shielding herself and the kid the best she can.

I sigh tiredly and count to three to rein in my frustration. I need these kids to grow up like *now*.

"Stop. Both of you." Finally some quiet. "I'll drive. Give me a second to settle Nevaeh in the front—"

Seiji gasps, resting his hand over his heart dramatically as if someone told him his cooking tastes like shit.

"How. Could. You? I *never* expected this from you, Anxo. A pretty girl walks in, and you forget all about me? Oh, how the tables have turned on my poor soul."

I knew this was coming. Seiji is not good at sharing. He will give the world to someone he loves, but take away the last sip of water you need to survive if he hates you.

It's a strange balance.

Once my mate—*oh how I love saying that*—is secure in the passenger seat, I turn to a huffing and puffing Seiji.

Opening the door for him, I wait for Seiji to climb into the backseat. The idiot grumbled about how it was not fair of me to take away his driving privileges just because he *accidentally* hit one old lady before I shoved him inside the car.

I wish it was just one *old lady.*

Grace follows him with a relieved breath, sitting in the middle with the kid on her lap so Hazel and Seiji aren't tempted to start again.

Once we're on the road, it dawns on me that we can't return to the kingdom just yet. The amount of Divine we used back in the coven means there's a risk of witches tracing the portal we'll use to get home. Those portals are sacred to us. Even the thought of witches finding them makes me uneasy.

Both Nevaeh and the kid have some serious injuries that need to be tended to before they can make the trip back home. Not to forget we have no clue where Harvey is and what to do next regarding him.

Staying in the human realm is our next best option. The scent of humans mixed with other supernatural beings will ruin our trail for anyone to follow.

Parking at the hotel's entrance, I've just turned the engine off when Seiji asks, "How long are we staying? I'll need more clothes if it's longer than two days."

"You also need a new brain," Hazel mutters.

"And you need better comebacks. Just so you know, staying out of the water for so long is not helping your wrinkles either."

Before Hazel can tear him a new one, I cover his mouth and warn Hazel with my eyes.

I'm tempted to leave these two in this God-forsaken human realm and close all portals leading home.

"We're staying until these two have had some time to heal and we have figured out more about Harvey. There's no way we're leaving this realm without him."

After sorting out the details and ensuring everyone is on board with the new plan, I exit the car.

Hazel starts whistling after I have my mate back in my arms. But it's not low and pitchy like before. This tune is different from what she uses to torture us.

The power behind her tune intensifies, forcing every human within a mile radius to stand still with their backs to us as we enter the hotel lobby. She alters the tune once we climb the elevator to my penthouse. Her magic will make sure we don't leave witnesses of us carrying an unconscious girl and child into the building.

That would raise more than a few questions.

When the elevator doors shut, Hazel stops to take a massive gulp of air.

"I love it when you don't use your powers to make us deaf," Seiji taunts her. Again. I will never understand why this imbecile insists on poking the grumpy bear.

"Don't start with me right now or I'll make you run around

the block naked."

Seiji scoffs, his face glowing with arrogance. "And these humans will *thank you* for blessing their eyes with my beauty."

We gag in sync. I'm thankful for the doors opening before Seiji goes on about his privates.

The floor-to-ceiling windows in the living area reflect the lights twinkling from the hundreds of buildings in our view. The dark sky above reminds me how none of us have slept in two days.

Walking down the hallway, I stop near the stairs to wait for everyone to gather. "Grace, take the kid to the guest room and make sure he's comfortable. I'll link Khatri and ask him to send over two of our best healers."

"What about Nevaeh?"

"I'm taking her to my room."

I go to turn around when Hazel stops me, her eyes full of suspicion. "Why *your* room?"

"Be right back." I quickly escape her beady eyes and rush upstairs. I'm sure Nevaeh is tired of adjusting in my arms and wants a proper bed to rest on.

Opening the door to my darkened room, I pad over to my bed and carefully slide her into it, not minding the blood and mud stains.

Tucking her in, I decide to clean the grime on her face and the areas I can see without invading her privacy. I'm sure she doesn't want to sleep with dirt stains on her face. The last thought makes me freeze.

Anxo, you airhead.

Nevaeh has been living in such dreadful conditions for so long, and I don't even know the worst of it yet. I can't touch her when she's unconscious and vulnerable. It's probably better to wait until she's awake and can ask me to shoo away if she doesn't want me around.

Taking a moment to gather my rage and sadness before I cry, or break something, I leave the room. But not before silently covering Nevaeh with a soft blanket so she doesn't get cold.

Before going downstairs, I stop to check in on the little boy. After the condition I found him in, it's hard to stop myself from sitting at his door like a guard dog until his parents come to take over the protection duty.

Running down the stairs, I'm excited to tell my family about Nevaeh but stop abruptly when the three idiots are waiting for me, barely able to suppress their teasing smiles. When their teasing smirks turn into crude gestures, I turn on my feet to walk away, but Grace and Seiji stop me by flinging themselves on me.

Boy am I glad that Grace is such a tiny thing because Seiji alone is enough to break my back.

To my surprise and absolute horror, Seiji starts cheering loud enough to scare our neighbors while Grace is laughing with tears running down her face.

Hazel comes strolling behind them with a rare genuine smile on her face. She doesn't hug me like the others, but the twinkle in her eyes is enough to give away her excitement. "Congratulations on finally finding your mate, Horseman Alarie."

The way they are so eager to celebrate my happiness with me is why I call them family. Not the one I was born into, but the one I made. And I'll forever do my best to keep these smiles on their faces.

5. Brain = broke

Nevaeh

I 'm floating in an abyss of calm. It's a confusing place to be since I've never experienced bliss like this before.

Serenity is not something I'm used to between running from the monsters in my life and the ones that live in my. I'm always jumping from one nightmare to another.

This unfamiliar feeling of peace has me lowering my guard long enough to forget why I *need* to be afraid of the darkness.

'Silly girl. You really thought I'd let you go?'

The sound of my broken gasp startles me awake. Sheer terror grips me when I look around and don't recognize the darkness around me.

When my freezing hands suddenly brush over something silky, confusion trumps my budding panic. I scurry back making the extremely comfortable bed I'm sitting on bounce with my weight. The spine-chilling fear I woke up with was quickly replaced with surprise.

Where the fuck am I?

Clutching the silky material I hold on to it like it's the only thing keeping me from slipping back into the land of terror.

"You alright, sweetheart?"

The sudden deep voice of a man jolts me halfway to the ceiling.

Rubbing my eyes aggressively, I try to make out the figure hidden among the shadows in the corner. The rapid pace of my heartbeat slows down significantly when the man repeats his question in a softer tone.

Rising from his seat, the figure swiftly pulls back a set of curtains. Even when the bright light from the window blinds me for a second, I'm glad to have my vision back.

With his hands firmly tucked into the pockets of his dark pants, I watch the most bewitching man I've ever laid eyes on stride closer to me.

Am I dead? I have to be right or how else would you explain the presence of this beautiful Angel standing over me.

No, that doesn't make sense. I'm *not* going to Heaven.

I snicker at the absurd thought and the Angel tilts his head in confusion, effectively stopping my inner monologue. The frown on his perfectly sculpted face melts into amusement the longer I can't stop staring at him.

"Angel?" The word slips out without permission.

Wait, why does this seem familiar?

And why is he so pretty?

"Close enough, sweetheart. It's *Anxo*." His lips turn up in a smug smirk at my shameless gawking.

But I can't help it! His maroon sweater flawlessly hugging his broad shoulders is a cruel distraction.

Wait... did he just call me sweetheart?

Me?

Sweetheart?

Maybe we're both crazy.

I shake my head furiously, hoping to jumpstart my brain and try to rearrange the broken wires inside. A pinch of pain triggers something and suddenly last night's events hit me hard enough to knock me out of my sleepy daze.

Groaning, I drop my head in my hands when the pressure of my broken and mismatched memories makes my head throb. When my fingers graze a thick bandage on my forehead, I rip it out without thinking.

The Deviants. The coven. The *kid*—

THE KID!

Shit. Fuck! Shit. Shit. Fuckidy shit.

As if aware of my inner turmoil, the man I now remember as Anxo aka Angel, immediately rushes to my side. "Calm down, Nevaeh. The boy is fine. He hasn't woken up since last night, but the healers are helping him. He's fine, I swear."

I let Anxo's words sink in before tearing up this place looking for the kid like a crazy woman.

"Good. Now, can you take a deep breath?" I nod at his alluring voice and mimic his movements as he guides me to breathe properly. "That's good, sweetheart. Keep breathing for me."

Okay, what the fuck is happening to me, and why the hell am I obeying Angel man like a doe-eyed puppy?

Once my *subtle* panic fades, I open my eyes and find Anxo sitting close enough to brush my fingers over his cheekbone.

I immediately swat away the idiotic thought.

Fates, my head is so screwed.

Every time I blink, Angel finds a way to get closer. I want to ask him why he continues to erase the distance between us but for some reason, I don't.

It's not because I'm a little bit addicted to his scent, and the way my body hums at his proximity, and how the constant screeching inside my head stops, or—

I did not just think any of that! That was not me.

I think I'm a victim of witchcraft.

I shake my head to drop that line of thought and look around, hoping to see the man I've been dying to meet.

"Where's my papa?"

My question makes Anxo's eyes flash with uncertainty before he quickly masks it.

His calmness is suspicious to me.

I keep waiting for him to lash out, but how easily he distances himself from every aggressive and upsetting emotion is... *just suspicious.*

There has to be something wrong with him. No one can be *good* all the time.

"How about you clean up and eat something first."

"And then we'll talk?"

"Sure, sweetheart."

Ugh, why does he keep calling me that?!

I hate it. *Not.*

When he gives me a soft, dimpled smile, what's left of my brain dissolves into goo. This man is adamant on ruining my 'unbothered as fuck' facade.

I untangle myself from the feather-like comforter and slip out of the bed to compose myself. I carefully shift my weight on both feet to check if everything is back to its original condition.

When I turn to Angel, he's looking at me with a strange look in his eyes. His expression is so open and hopeful it tugs at something in my heart.

Shrugging off whatever was making him look so vulnerable, Angel offered me the set of clothes I didn't notice he was now holding and showed me his bathroom.

Stopping at the door, I turn back before I can lock myself in the bathroom and ask, "Why do you keep calling me that?"

"What?"

"Sweetheart. And the way you say it... *feels different.*"

Angel thinks my question is an invitation to stand mere inches from my face. Before I can understand what he's doing, his palm gently cup my cheek. The unexpected touch is scorching hot and starts a fire inside me that warms me to my toes.

But my head starts spinning when I *don't* flinch.

Not even for a split second do I feel the need to protect myself from him. My mind doesn't flash with every way a man of his stature can hurt me, and I don't even think about landing him flat on his ass.

Maybe I hit my head harder than I thought.

His palm feels incredibly soothing against the cold, rough skin of my cheek. My eyes flutter shut on their own accord, and I find myself leaning into his palm, unable to stop my reaction.

"I saw how fiercely you protected that kid last night. It gave me a glimpse into your heart. How pure it is. How *sweet.*" He stops to caress my cheek, a devilish smirk on his face. "And it makes you blush. It's my new favorite thing in the world." His whispered response was not what I was expecting.

His words, combined with his closeness makes my face flush with heart that slowly spreads to my neck.

Angel chuckles at my stunned expression. Before I can turn around to escape the tingly feeling in my stomach, a soft pressure on my forehead makes me freeze.

I swear I've felt this before.

Looking up, I see Angel's eyes pressed shut and his lips resting on my forehead. The soft touch lingers momentarily, and when Angel leans back, I have this strong urge to beg him to repeat it.

He should definitely do that again.

No! What is wrong with me?

When I can no longer stomach Angel's intense gaze that seems to be waiting for me to do or say something, I hurry back into the bathroom, shouting 'shower time' over my shoulder like a lunatic.

Why is this green-eyed stranger affecting me so much?

After banging my head on the closer door, I face away from it and freeze at the size of the bathroom.

So many buttons.

Stripping out of the rag, I start hitting every button on the panel until I find the one that pours hot water. It takes me fifteen minutes to figure out the shower settings and the products on the shelf, but it's undoubtedly the best shower of my life.

It takes a lot of hard scrubbing to remove the dirt and blood I was starting to think were a permanent part of me. Finishing up the relaxing shower, I thoroughly clean my teeth with a new brush and repeat the process since it's been too long.

But no amount of brushing helps me tackle the nest on my head. I rubbed my scalp free of a decade's worth of dirt, but now my eyes are floating with tears from tugging on my hair too hard. No matter what I do, I can't seem to reach the part where the comb slides from my scalp to the roots in one smooth move.

Well, I tried.

After putting on the new undergarments Angel gave me, I'm left staring at the top dumbly. I can't wear this.

The sleeves are short, and the T-shirt sticks to me like a second skin when I put it on. Most of my scars are hidden from view when I pull up the black sweatpants, but the ones on my arms have me reconsidering leaving the bathroom.

My scars are raised, jagged, and poorly healed.

No one is ever happy to see them.

I don't want my scars to be a topic of conversation today. I just want to pretend I'm somewhat normal for at least a day, but Angel will have questions if I go out like this.

Taking a deep, calming breath, I decide the best course of action is to ask Angel for a coverup. That will save us both from looking at the hideous reminders of my past.

My newfound nerves make me swallow thickly. I've never felt this nervous before. I normally spit in the face of my tormentor, fully aware of the consequences, and yet here I am, afraid to ask Anxo for a jacket.

Leaving the bathroom, I find Angel sitting on the edge of the bed, waiting for me. His eyes slowly take in the way I'm covering my shoulders and arms with the towel.

"Um, I... could I maybe borrow—just something? It doesn't have to be clean or anything." I stumble over my words for the first time in my life, suddenly afraid asking for more will make Angel react like *they* did.

How pathetic, Nevaeh.

When I finally gather enough courage to look up at his face instead of the alluring patterns on his arms, Angel is studying me with an intense look.

Maybe he's mad.

I would be too, if a stranger asked me for clothes, slept on my bed, and then kept asking for more things. I'm about to say I take my demands back when Angel erases the space between us in two long strides.

I don't think he understands the concept of personal space.

I don't think I mind.

Treacherous brain.

"Arms up," Angel whispers, and I submit without a thought. Another first for me.

I'm still lost in his deep emerald eyes when Angel starts guiding my arms through the softest material I've ever felt. I look down at the pale blue hoodie swallowing me whole. It completely engulfs me, and I *love* it.

Okay, riddle me this. *How* did he know I was asking for a jacket, huh?!

There is only one right answer.

Witchcraft.

The material is so soft against my scars. And the best part is that it smells exactly like Angel.

Side note: I want to be buried in Angel's hoodie when I die.

I'm greedily inhaling deep breaths of a scent that makes my Divine sing when Angel gently grips my chin to catch my attention. Suddenly, he is close enough for me to feel his warm breath on my face and his lips a mere breath away from mine.

"Nevaeh you can ask me anything your heart desires, and I swear on my life, I'll find a way to give it to you. I don't want to see an ounce of hesitation on your beautiful face next time, alright?" Anxo is so close some of his words allow him to brush his lips against mine ever so slightly.

I think I'm going to pass out.

I find myself nodding along without a protest, which I seem to be doing a lot around him.

Angel begrudgingly pulls away, and I have to stop myself from gripping his collar and pulling him back in.

Too engrossed in figuring out my reactions to him, I almost miss Angel saying it's time to meet the rest of the group.

For a quick moment, I wonder how bad it would be if I went back to the dungeon. Just the thought of meeting new people makes me groan. More people to judge, scan, and do threat analysis on makes my head hurt.

"Do I have to?"

"Yes, now stop pouting. I'm telling you, there's nothing to worry about, sweetheart. You'll love them." Angel winks over his shoulder. His hand holding mine is the only reason I don't trip and fall on my ass.

'No, they won't. No one likes weaklings.'

If they find out that the voice of my tormentor lives rent-free in my head, they'll realize just how many loose screws are up there.

I'm more worried about *them* not liking me, Angel.

"Come on, they're waiting."

I toss my head back and start complaining, but Anxo ignores my tantrum and keeps dragging me behind him.

"What kind of name is Anxo anyway? What does it mean?"

"Angel in Galician."

No fucking way. Is he messing with me?

"You're a *Horseman of the apocalypse,* and your parents named you *Angel*?"

I'm beyond confused, but then I remember my name is literally *Heaven* backward and shut up. Maybe his parents have beef with Heaven too.

"My caretaker did actually. My parents were too busy to sit down and name me. The old lady was a human who thought I was the spitting image of an angel. So when she started calling me Anxo, everyone just rolled with it."

The way he talks about his parents feels rehearsed. Like the topic is so draining he'd rather read it like a script and get over it.

I'm suddenly disappointed with people I've never met.

When did I turn into such an empath?

Angel stops when we reach a small kitchen and before I know it, I'm lifted off the ground and placed on the counter like I weigh nothing.

I'm allowing Angel a lot of physical contact for someone who usually acts like a rabid dog if anyone gets too close.

As soon as I'm alone, I'm getting to the bottom of whatever this man is doing to me. I can't go around not being skeptical of people anymore. That's how you end up dead.

Pulling out various packets from different drawers, Angel circles me with all kinds of snacks. "What do you feel like eating, sweetheart? I can whip up something quick. You must be starving."

Uh oh. I don't think I can eat. If I smell food, I'm not sure if I'll devour it or throw up.

"Maybe later?"

I can see Angel wants to push, but thankfully, he drops it when I ask for something to drink instead.

While Angel takes his sweet time to browse the contents of his refrigerator, I jump down from the counter to look around.

There's a shiny packet inside a cabinet that's practically calling out to me. I grab the handle with my left hand, and before I can figure out what I did wrong, the door is coming straight for my head. Squeezing my eyes shut, I prepare for the pain, only for something else to take the hit for me.

Hesitantly opening one eye, I find a palm covering most of my head, successfully saving me from an attack that was meant for me.

Clearing his throat, Anxo narrows his eyes and gives me the 'Are you serious?' look.

Shrugging with a sheepish smile, I raise both thumbs to show him I'm fully intact... *thanks to him.*

Angel shakes his head with a sigh, but I can see a smile begging to break free. I'm not happy that he's trying to hide his dimples from me, but then forget all about it when he hands me a bottle of juice and unexpectedly leans in to kiss my forehead.

Another kiss?!

I'm struggling to understand why I'm not bothered with the amount of physical boundaries I'm allowing Angel to stomp over.

I think the witches broke you, Nevaeh.

Grabbing my hand again like he can't get enough, Angel guides me through the maze of similar hallways while I sip on the surprisingly delicious juice.

Lost in the taste, I'm supposed to follow Angel, not the other way around. And I'm reminded of my mistake when he abruptly pulls me back into his firm chest by pulling on my hoodie.

I go to punch his arm for manhandling me, only to find myself face-to-face with a glass wall. A *very clean* glass wall that my blind as-a-bat ass was about to walk into.

Anxo silently takes the empty bottle from my hand and dumps it into a trash can nearby. I turn to thank him but stop when I see his shoulders shaking. Anxo finally turns to face me after a long pause, but like seeing me made the last of his control slip away, he bursts out laughing.

Huffing childishly, I turn to my right and start walking but stop when his laugh doubles in volume. If I wasn't so embarrassed, I'd be concerned about his bright red face and that he's not breathing right.

Don't get me wrong, if this was anyone else, I would've dislocated that perfect jaw a long time ago, but I can't seem to conjure a single harmful thought about Angel.

"Wrong... wrong way, sweetheart." Angel wheezes between his barely contained chuckles, clutching at his stomach.

I swear if he doesn't stop, I'm going to do something uncharacteristic... like cry.

'Do it. Show him weakness and see how quickly he turns his back on you.'

Seeing me pout and kick the carpet under my feet, Angel sobers up and engulfs me in a bear hug from behind. His arms wrap around my shoulders, his chest tightly pressed against my back, and his cheek resting on my head.

My body freezes in his tight hold. I wait for the wild thumping of my heart to trigger my fight response, my Divine to stir and demand chaos, for alarms to start ringing in my head and forcing me to do something drastic like poke Angel's eyeballs out, but nothing happens.

My heart keeps beating serenely as if this is normal. My

head is blank. No anxious thoughts make me overthink or form an elaborate plan to protect myself. Instead, a sense of peace fills me with his embrace.

My arms instinctively wrap around his, which are comfortably resting on my waist like this is not the first time he has hugged me.

He is hugging me.

What has this man done that my entire being, body, and soul, accepts him as my solace? Everything in me refuses to distance myself from his touch.

It's been a long time since anyone has touched me without the intention of hurting me, and I can't resist soaking in the gentle way Angel is holding me.

"I'm sorry, sweetheart, but you're a walking disaster." He snickers before kissing the side of my head. "I thought you had heightened senses and pure Divine power?"

"It's not my fault! The glass was too clean, and who even puts glass in place of a wall huh?"

My fingers trace the markings on Angel's wrists peeking from under the sleeves of his sweater.

After he's done laughing at me because I won't stop blaming the glass, Anxo leads me downstairs.

At the end of the stairs, he turns around and hesitates before asking, "Do you trust me?"

"No."

It's an automatic response.

I don't have to think about it because it's the truth. No matter how good Anxo is to me or how much I want to be in his presence, I can't trust him... *not yet anyway.*

And he shouldn't either.

Angel has no idea what they turned me into.

I'm not exactly proud of the blood that stains my entire being, but I learned to attack first and think later. If you think too long you become the prey with no way out.

"Wow. You didn't even have to think about it."

I search his eyes for signs of hurt, anger, or even

disappointment, but all I find is curiosity.

Ducking my chin, I hide my shame at not being good or normal enough for his friendship. Anxo has thousands of people counting on him, and I can't be selfish enough to think he will help me with the baggage I drag behind me everywhere.

Patting his back pocket, Angel surprises me by pulling out a bar of chocolate and waving it in front of my face. "What if I bribe you?"

I'm practically drooling just by looking at it. I haven't tasted anything remotely good in a decade.

Angel is silly asking for trust when I would've given my kidney for that bar.

I nod vigorously, "I'm willing to reconsider."

6. His collection of weirdos

Nevaeh

"Hazel!" Angel calls out.

The sudden high volume catches me off guard and I flinch without meaning to. My fists clench beside my thighs, turning white as I try to stop myself from reacting to my rabid instincts.

Taking a shuddering breath, I place a hand over my heart and wait for the pounding in my head to stop.

You're not in that nightmare anymore, Nevaeh. You're in a safe place. Anxo had the perfect opportunity to kill you in your sleep, but he didn't. I keep mumbling the words under my breath like a mantra until the tension in my shoulders disappears.

"I'm so sorry for startling you, sweetheart." Angel's voice breaks my frozen state, pulling me out of my head. He brings my hand—that I didn't even realize he was still holding—to his lips and kisses each knuckle as if apologizing to them on my behalf. "I'll be more careful next time."

"You don't have to," I try, but he doesn't budge.

Feeling the heat rising in my cheeks, I quickly avert my gaze from Anxo and turn away before the intensity in his eyes can trap me in a trance.

Anxo takes me to monkey's room first so I can check on the little guy myself. I was hoping to find him awake and eager to see me, but he was still unconscious.

The healer taking care of my kiddo explains it's a trauma response. He assures me there's no need to panic, and it's good that his body and mind are taking their time to heal and rest.

I'm reluctant to leave the kid vulnerable and defenseless

before Anxo tells me monkey's room is close to the living area, and I'll be able to hear if he wakes up and asks for me.

Anxo doesn't say anything when I pause at the door to observe the older man caring for monkey. The lack of alarm bells going off in my head when the healer gently applies a soothing balm on monkey's head helps me gather enough faith to leave him alone with my kid.

Walking down the hallway behind Anxo, I freeze at the sound of someone humming nearby. The soft tune is like an invisible force pulling me in its direction. Luckily, the door to the room is wide open... so I naturally stop to take a quick peek inside.

The room is cloaked in darkness except for the soft glow of a lamp sitting on the desk. A tall, lean woman hovering over the desk grabs a clean white napkin from the side and gently begins to clean a... *is that a bloody dagger?*

Resting a hand on Angel's shoulder, I rise on my toes to get a better look at the exquisite ancient daggers spread out on the desk. Like a magnet, my eyes are drawn to the one with a red handle carved with alluring patterns and a zigzag-edged blade.

A perfect combination of delicate and deadly.

Anxo clears his throat and the woman's head snaps toward us, her sharp onyx eyes narrowing on me.

I'm surprised to see nothing about her appearance matches her current activity. Her heart-shaped face, soft monolid eyes, and even softer features scream elegance and poise, but the dagger she is twisting in her fingers squashes that image— *more like stabs it.*

Judging by her stature, I can bet she's a warrior. The black full-sleeved high-neck top tucked into a pair of army green cargo pants highlights her curves and build.

How can a girl look so deadly yet equally alluring?

Cleaning her hands with a towel, she takes agonizingly slow steps to me, her boots clunking against the floor with every step. She squints at me, flipping her medium-length raven hair behind her shoulders.

Angel finally breaks the tense staring contest by introducing us. "Nevaeh, this is Hazel Seagrave, my Warriorhead."

Something about her name sparks my curiosity. Cautiously letting my Divine peek through, I wait for it to get familiar with her essence and tell me *what* she is.

Holy fuckidy fuck.

"You're a siren," I blurt out.

"Congratulations… your eyes work."

Oh, calm down woman with pretty daggers.

If I set aside her brazen response, it's clear my blatant ogling is making her uncomfortable.

Remember Nevaeh, you are a calm person. And calm people don't start shit with unknown Warriorheads.

"A siren Warriorhead for Conquer. It's Unexpected."

Raising her brows, Hazel retorts, "And a female Grim Reaper is not?"

"The *next* Reaper."

"Same thing."

I can tell Hazel enjoys giving people a hard time. *It's admirable.*

"Not really. But you're a little slow, aren't you, siren? Good thing your *cuteness* makes up for it."

Okay, maybe I'm not as calm as I think, but the steam coming out of Hazel's ears is *so* worth it.

The impassive mask the siren once wore dissolves into a sneer. But unfortunately, before the actual fun can begin, Angel interrupts our lovely interaction.

"All right, ladies. I think that's enough getting to know each other for now."

Angel starts backing out of the room, pulling me along with him. "Hazel, gather everyone in the living room."

"Oh, of course, your majesty. Do you have any other commands for this peasant?"

Oh, I really like her.

The siren follows her comment with a sarcastic bow, which

makes me snort out loud. Hazel smirk proudly at my reaction while Anxo looks confused at how quickly we called a truce.

"Hazel? My brave Warriorhead, would you be so kind as to do as I ask?" Angel requests rather than demanding like before. His words might be polite, but his eyes shoot a clear warning that Hazel is smart enough to catch.

Just as I turn to leave, I blow Hazel a kiss to irritate her one last time. She is quick to show me the finger, but I don't miss the twitch in her lips.

New life achievement: I made a siren smile.

"Uh, Anxo?" I ask, trying to match his pace as we enter the room surrounded by glass walls.

That can't be safe, right?

What if someone smashes into them without realizing it's glass and falls to their death?

And why are Angel's legs so damn long?

When he nods at me to hint he's listening, I look around to see if we are alone while trying to keep my excitement under wraps. "How the fuck did you convince a *siren* of all species to be your Warriorhead?"

I'm sure my shock is plastered on my face. My eyes hurt from how big I'm making them, but if it was anyone else in my place they would be equally dumbfounded too.

She's a siren for Fate's sake!

An extremely rare and powerful species that we know next to nothing about. And now I'm in her mighty presence. And her attitude is to die for.

Maybe I am in heaven after all.

"Do you always swear this much?" Angel asks, his head tilting sideways in genuine amusement.

"No, I'm being civil. This is me trying to make a good first impression."

My honesty is rewarded with Angel throwing his head back in a booming laugh. My heart swells at the fulfilling sound. Like I can *feel* his happiness in my heart.

"You are your father's daughter."

"Of course I am. Are you sure they let you have Conquer willingly because your intelligence makes me question your crown, big guy?"

Anxo chuckles and brushes off the insult like I never said anything in the first place. Now I'm officially starting to freak out because nothing I do or say makes him angry or even remotely flippant.

Getting comfortable on the small couch Angel chose for us, I wonder why we didn't take the much larger and empty one. When my thigh tingles from how his thigh is pressed against mine, I stop thinking altogether.

Something is terribly wrong with me if I don't care about people touching me anymore.

"Hazel is a runaway."

A runaway siren? That can't be right. Merfolk hates surface people and tends to stay in their cities deep underwater.

"Trust me, I was just as surprised. When I first saw her, Hazel was... lost. I offered her a safe place and here we are. I wish I could tell you more sweetheart, but her past is not my story to tell."

I know what running from your demons feels like but where Hazel had the strength to get out and rebuild her entire life, I lost all hope and faded away for years.

I can't shake the unwanted fury that comes with knowing someone wanted to harm the adorable woman who likes knives. I don't know Hazel well enough to care, but it doesn't stop my Divine from stirring uncomfortably.

The need to look out for our own is engraved into our bones so I understand the instant connection with Anxo and caring about him to some extent since we are both Horsemen descendants, but when did the moody siren get on that list?

"After I brought her home, she mostly kept to herself. Never really talked to anyone... just glared and growled. Until one day I saw Hazel sparring with a warrior double her size." Angel turns to me with a smirk that makes me think he is very proud of what Hazel did next.

"She was *fast*. The warrior never even touched her. Hazel won that fight without losing a drop of blood or sweat." Taking my hand in his, Angel looks into my eyes as if trying to justify what he did next. "I know it's not traditional to incorporate other species into our higher ranks, but Hazel has proved her loyalty more times than I can count. *She is my family*."

The fond smile on his lips is proof of his admiration. It's twice now that Angel has brightened up at the mention of his people.

I'm trying to figure out who the real Hazel is between what Angel just told me and what she allowed me to see when two people walk into the room behind the very siren with excitement radiating off of them.

A woman I have yet to meet offers me a small wave paired with a shy smile before ducking behind Hazel's frame.

So dainty and fragile.

"Nevaeh, you've already met Seiji Nakaya, our Prince of Famine." Angel points to the man I met yesterday.

Just like last night, Seiji still has a welcoming presence around him. The way he is so effortlessly comfortable with himself makes me instantly relax around him too.

"It was fun to watch you drool over my best friend's shoulder." *That never happened.* "I'm Seiji, like the sage witches use for their abracadabra, with an 'I'."

Judging by how he takes his time to make sure I know the proper pronunciation, I can tell Seiji doesn't take kindly to people mispronouncing his name.

"Oh, you look otherworldly in that hoodie. I think Anxo has something similar too, don't you, Anxo?"

"Behave," Angel warns, but Seiji blinks at him innocently.

"What? I can't compliment on how good she looks in your hoodie?"

They continue to bicker, while I admire Seiji's warm brown eyes which shine with such childlike innocence even with the things that come out of his mouth.

His dark locks are styled to perfection that compliments his tan beige skin.

Even with his large build, Seiji doesn't come off as threatening in the least. Mostly thanks to his boyish features and a mouth that lets everyone know he is a child stuffed inside a 6-foot man's body.

Seiji's East Asian features are similar to Hazel's, but not quite the same.

Now that I know him a little, his dressing style makes more sense. A royal blue boxy shirt with green leaves and red flowers printed on it, and a black undershirt that is visible since almost every button is open. I especially like the chain looped around the right pocket of his beige pants.

Everything about him is bright and colorful.

The woman I haven't had the pleasure of talking to nervously takes a seat on the couch opposite me. When no one pushes her to talk, I take the hint and follow the herd.

She thinks I don't notice the way her soft caramel eyes which look like she has fireflies trapped inside them, keep secretly glancing at me, but I do.

For someone who's roughly 5 '3, her braids seem heavier than her entire body weight. I want to ask if her braids hurt her scalp.

This is a lot of empathy for someone as unhinged as me.

She tugs on the sleeve of her loose pale pink sweater before rubbing her hands down her smooth bronze thighs and then playing with the hem of her black skirt.

Overall, this girl is sweating her weight in worry, and I think it's because of me.

Should I smile? Will that make her relax and not squirm like a chicken waiting to get its head cut off?

A timid voice gains my attention before I can conclude whether a smile is necessary.

"Hello, I'm Grace… uh, *Blackburn*."

Wait… That's *my* last name.

"Blackburn?" She looks down with a grimace when I look at her suspiciously. "Do I know you?"

And she's not talking. *Again.*

"Please don't tell me Papa found his mate, and I missed it— no, wait, that can't be right because then you should be like ten and not whatever age you are."

I wait for Grace to explain, but my questions render her speechless, so I have no choice but to continue forming irrational theories.

"Are you... are you his mate? Or—"

"For Lucifer's sake, here's an idea. Maybe if you stop rambling and give her a chance, she will talk." Hazel interrupts me.

I'm stumped hearing *Lucifer* from her mouth before I remember she's a siren. One of Lucifer's first creations. It's only reasonable she prays to him.

"You are one snappy siren."

The way Hazel's face remains blank should scare me, but I'm still in awe of her being here.

Thankfully, with time and a whole lot of awkward silence, Grace finally gives me some answers.

"Definitely not his mate. That's not..." When Grace turns to look at Anxo, he gives the jittery woman an encouraging nod. "I went on a camping trip and got lost. I was thirteen and an orphan living in a group home so when I saw a portal... I crossed it."

Personally, I don't agree with crossing portals when you don't know where they'll lead, but I do admire her courage.

Grace chuckles at my expression, her voice shaking. "It was a rare moment of bravery. When I crossed, Dean was waiting for me on the other end... like he somehow knew I would make that choice. He took one glance at me and then told me to follow him if I wanted to know who I really was."

Trying to figure out who or what these people are without my Divine is getting tedious now. I wish I could control my stubborn Divine better so I didn't have to wait for them to do the big reveal.

"Turns out, I'm a Bookkeeper."

No way.

How is Angel collecting all these rare mythics?

Bookkeeper: An individual gifted with the knowledge of literally everything in the universe. Every species. Every realm. From the supernatural history everyone knows to the one they keep hush-hush.

"There's *never* been a human Bookkeeper." I whisper in awe, staring at Grace as if she will disappear into thin air.

Now I understand why Seiji was looking at me with those eyes yesterday. Like him, I'm also waiting for Grace to do something *magical.*

"Before Dean, I thought I was crazy to know the things I did. He offered me the chance to be who I was always meant to be."

I know Papa has a thing for making sure power and potential are never wasted, but taking in an unknown human girl was maybe a tad bit drastic.

I'm glad he did, though. I don't want to imagine what could've happened if Grace stumbled upon the wrong people who wanted to abuse her gift.

I'm still in my head, mulling over all the details given to me when Seiji abruptly stands up and accidentally knocks over a vase in his hurry.

"Seiji watch out!" Anxo tries, but it's too late.

If it wasn't for Grace gasping, my attention would've stayed on the broken pieces of glass on the floor.

All my life, I've been immune to the sight of blood but a small trail of Grace's, and it feels like my soul is on fire. The need to get rid of the blood flowing down Grace's calf takes over my body until I can't see or hear anything but her heavy breathing and the way she is fisting the ends of her skirt in pain.

"Fuck Gracie, I'm so sorry. I was just going to make hot chocolate for everyone. I got a little too excited," Seiji sputters out.

"I-it's okay," Grace whimpers. *It's clearly not.*

Before I know what I'm doing, I'm crouching in front of

her and placing my palm over her leg. Within seconds, my Divine heals the small cut, and after sensing the opportunity, immediately tries to wiggle out of my control.

Squeezing my eyes shut, I try to rein in my essence but it's not enough. Only after Seiji grabs my hand to wipe the blood off it with a wet cloth my Divine finally settles down, once again allowing me full control of over own my mind and body.

First, my brain stopped working around Anxo, and now my Divine is *stealing* my body to heal Grace.

Fucking awesome.

I'm still on the floor when a hand touches my shoulder, and the rush of warmth snaps me out of my daze.

Standing with Angel's help, I'm still trying to wrap my head around why I revealed my biggest secret to people I don't even trust.

I thought the compulsive need to help was limited to Horsemen and their mates, but Grace is neither. Yet, the Bookkeeper's Divine feels oddly familiar.

Something is not quite right with this human.

"How did you do that?" Angel asks, walking me back to the couch. Grace's eyes which are still damp with tears follow me like she's trying to figure out what makes me tick. It's a little creepy.

"Do what?"

"Reapers aren't supposed to heal others, sweetheart."

"Yeah, but I didn't get the typical Reaper Divine," I answer absentmindedly.

My gold essence isn't the only difference between Papa and me. And just like healing, I have one more thing about my Divine that I keep to myself.

"Okay, miss 'I'm built different'." Seiji straightens with a scoff. "Now, who's willing to accept hot chocolate as my apology? Wait don't answer that, I don't care. I'm making it for everyone."

Seiji drops a kiss on Grace's cheek, mumbling another hushed apology before making his way to the kitchen but stops to ask over his shoulder, "Hey Nevaeh, do you like marshmallows in yours?"

Do I? I don't remember how hot chocolate tasted or how I liked it, so I'm not sure what the correct answer is here.

"I don't know princess. I was in a rat cell for a decade, concussed and dying for the most part. Whatever you make for me will be much better than what I'm used to."

Seiji's mouth falls open, but no words come out for a long while. "Poor soul doesn't remember hot chocolate," He finally choked out with his forefinger and thumb held dangerously close, "I'm this close to a breakdown."

When Seiji's eyes start to gloss over he turns to walk away. My head snaps to Angel in a panic. "Is he going to cry because I don't remember hot chocolate?"

"It's not your fault. Seiji is just a little sensitive." Grace assures me with a warm smile.

These people smile so easily. *It's weird.*

"I'll go check on the drama queen." Hazel runs after Seiji before anyone else can volunteer.

Honestly, I was expecting either Anxo or Grace to offer a shoulder to cry on, but watching Hazel turn an emotional Seiji into a pissed-off Seiji within seconds confirms my suspicion.

Hazel is just like her daggers. Sharp and life-threatening on one end and delicately detailed on the other.

7. So, my mate is not dead?

Nevaeh

U nfortunately, I still didn't remember the drink after Seiji made me one, but it was the best thing I'd ever tasted.

On my third cup, Angel suggests I slow down before I make myself sick from all the sugar.

To be honest I know I've been acting like a careless fool for the past two days. Not only am I staying in an unknown place with unknown people, but now I'm also drinking what they make me without a second thought.

It doesn't escape me that the instinct to protect myself is absent when I'm around them. Especially with Anxo. The familiarity of his Divine soothes the knots in my stomach allowing me to breathe freely.

"So, uh, there's something important I need to tell you." Angel hesitates, nervously shifting beside me until we are facing each other.

I'd noticed the four of them talking with their eyes and making faces at each other but stayed out of it. Maybe this group of four friends/family thinks I'm blind. I mean why else would they think I can't see their *secret* eye conversations? It's that, or they suck at being discreet.

Anxo looks cautious, acting as if what he is about to reveal will make me spiral. The nervous energy radiating from him slowly starts to seep into my skin, triggering my anxiety.

'I told you, they were dead.'

The voice I had shoved to the back of my mind wiggles to the front, forcing me to acknowledge it.

It's terrifying how every aspect of my life was once in *her* control. Her words were the only reality I knew.

The queen of all evil once told me how she took great pleasure in making sure everyone I loved was killed the day her coven attacked my kingdom. She drilled into me that I had no one looking for me anymore. That I was all alone in the world.

But now sitting in a room—*very high off the ground*— surrounded by Horsemen. By a family I thought didn't exist. The reality she made me believe is slowly starting to chip away, and all I can think is that I hope every word out of her mouth was just as false as her promise of never laying a hand on my monkey.

My head started spinning with all the stories she fed me over the years and I know I can't dance around this topic forever. I need to know what actually happened when Visha attacked my kingdom.

Taking a steadying breath, I ask, "Who's dead?"

Angel rears his head back like I struck him. Maybe he didn't expect me to know about the attack or how no one in my kingdom survived. I wait for him to prove Visha right and crush my hope, but Angel keeps staring at me with his eyebrows pinched tightly.

"No one is dead. Why would you even ask me that?"

I can't help the relieved sigh that escapes me. As my heart slowly crawls back from my throat, I notice the confused faces around me.

After shaking his head to collect himself Angel rounds back to the original conversation but it's nothing more than a mess of broken sentences.

"We are—uh, I'm your... well, you know how—"

"Oh God, this is painful to watch." Grace shakes her head disappointingly and bites back her teasing smile.

I'm about to tell her Horsemen can't take sides before I remember she is human.

The supernatural world might be divided in two about who they worship, but humans mostly lean towards God.

"Do you know about mates, Nevaeh?" Grace asks, seeing that our Horseman of Conquer is suddenly unable to form sentences.

"I know enough."

What I mean is, I know the highlights.

While many species under King Lucifer's rule gave up immortality for mates and procreation, some didn't want to rely on the matchmaking abilities of the Fates.

Mythical creatures like werewolves, dragons, and centaurs consider mate bonds *sacred*. Even the thought of rejecting the bond is seen as disrespecting Fates.

Whereas vampires, demons, witches, and fairies think of the bond as more of a *suggestion* than a lifelong oath. They choose the modern art of courting their mates before making permanent decisions.

Some species, like banshees, djinns, and gargoyles, denied the concept of mates entirely and only opted for the ability to procreate. They still openly express their distaste for anyone who values *babies* over *immortality*.

Horsemen fall into the category that respects Fate's chosen mates and wait for them their whole lives.

"So, you know who your mate is?" Seiji asks carefully but the question still makes my heart burn.

It's rare to lose your mate before you've even had the chance to meet them, so I don't know how to answer him without looking pitiful.

Usually, Fates are not this cruel, but I've come to accept I'm always an exception to their generosity.

I wish I got the chance to meet him even for a second before he was taken from me so cruelly because at least then I wouldn't be sitting here mourning someone I never knew.

After you find and accept your mate, your souls intertwine for life, so if one dies, the other follows not long after by sheer heartbreak. I hate that I didn't get the honor to take my last breath by his side. I hate that he was another thing Visha took from me.

Taking a shuddering breath, I reveal my truth even as my soul breaks at the words. "He uh... he died."

I expected them to be shocked, but I didn't think the news would be *this* surprising.

Grace looks like she's trying to count how many brain cells I lost in my time with the coven. Seiji and Hazel share a puzzled look before staring at Angel like he is a ghost. I startle when Angel suddenly stands up and begins to pace before me.

"No, he didn't." Angel grits out. The growl in his words was so unlike him.

"But he did."

"Woman... *I* would know if he did."

Does he know my mate? *Knew.*

My heart fills with immediate gratitude at the thought that maybe this is Fate's way of apologizing. Maybe seeing agony over losing my other half melted their stoic hearts enough to send me someone who could tell me more about him. More about what he looked like. Who he was.

I would be happy if all Anxo could give me was a name. I just don't want the only thing I know about my mate to be how he died trying to find me.

"You knew him? Will you tell me something about him? Anything will do." The desperation in my voice has Angel finally turning to look at me with pained eyes.

His expression makes my heart sink. Fuck, what if he feels bad because he didn't know my mate well enough to tell me any details.

So this is what it feels like to have someone stomp on your only hope.

And here I was, hoping to find things about my mate to last me a lifetime with his memories. I would've made do with just his name or his favorite color. Anything to ease this tight grip on my throat.

Angel looks heavenward and sighs long enough until he finds the right words. With a newfound determination, he stalks toward me before sitting on the floor at my feet.

Grasping both my hands in his, Angel looks at me with eyes shining with tears and breathes out, "Oh, sweetheart. *I am your mate.* Just like you are mine."

No. That can't be.

I try to snatch my hands out of his grip but Anxo doesn't let me. Even sitting in front of me he's blind to the damage his cruel joke is doing to me.

I'm cursed. I can't be lucky enough to have this... have him in my life... as *my mate.*

This has to be a joke.

'He is lying to you! You heard what Visha said. You sobbed into the arm that was torn out of its socket. Your mate is dead. They're all dead!'

Visha's voice echoes in my head, but it gets weaker the longer Angel rubs his thumb over my knuckles. He waits patiently as I struggle to accept or absorb what he is saying, trying to pick apart *her* truths from actual truths.

I think back to the day Visha threw that torn limb into my cell and told me all the gory details of how she took another part of my future in her hands and crushed it.

But there was no scent. That should've made me question her, but the weight of my mate's death on my shoulder, the guilt and agony over his death left no energy in me to question her.

She lied. Again.

Gazing into the pair of hypnotizing emerald eyes that had me spellbound since I first laid eyes on them, I try to imagine what this means for me. For us.

"She told me you were dead."

My eyes pinch shut briefly, and I have to bite my bottom lip when it starts to quiver. As I slowly run my fingers over his arms, I have to blink rapidly to keep the tears at bay.

Angel's warm hands squeeze mine and when I look at him, his glassy eyes reflect my pain. Lowering his head, Anxo places quick kisses on my knuckles, and the rush of electricity that follows is proof of our right to each other.

Rising on his knees, Angel's large palm covers most of my face as he brings our heads closer together. He tries to laugh but it comes out wobbly. "Not dead, sweetheart. I'm here. I'm right here."

The spark from his touch runs down my spine making me wrap my hand around his wrist to hold him there. Soaking in our proximity and the way my soul hums in content, I forget about the world around me.

'How pathetic of you to believe everything you hear. It was always easy to break you. Weak...'

The longer Anxo holds my face in his hands, the farther Visha's voice gets until it's a mere whisper I can mostly ignore. I need to find a way to get her out of my head for good if I want to stop her from ruining anything else in my life.

"Do you want more proof, sweetheart? I'm sure I can think of something to convince you."

The teasing glint in his eyes makes mine nearly pop out. Every cell in my body is suddenly on fire, begging for his touch.

I can't stop the subtle panic I feel over losing the small physical connection when Angel moves to stand. I feel as if someone stole the last breath from my lungs. My head finally stops spinning when Angel plops down beside me and drapes his arm over my shoulders, pulling me snug into his side.

His fingers brush my hair behind my ear before lazily running along the back of my neck. The feather-light touch is so hypnotic that I lean into his side and hold still hoping he won't stop.

Hazel clears her throat loudly, effectively breaking my touch-starved trance. "Now that you know your love life is not dead can we get back to business? We have some important questions that unfortunately only you can answer and I'm running out of patience."

Angel's warm breath fans my ear when he shifts closer while shooting Hazel a warning look, and I forget own my name, much less the million questions stashed in my head.

I don't notice I'm still dumbly staring at his side profile until Angel gives me a sly smirk before turning my chin with his thumb and index finger to where Hazel is looking at me exasperatedly.

At least now I know why my brain short-circuits at his touch.

Questions... right...

"I'll answer yours after you answer mine."

"Oh, of course, princess. We're happy to follow your lead." Hazel gives me the fakest smile I've ever seen and it's wide enough to be a bit manic. *Adorable.*

With an exaggerated eye roll, I dismiss Hazel's evergreen sarcasm.

"First things first, how are you both here together?" I point to Seiji and Angel, only to be met with confused faces forcing me to elaborate. "Horsemen usually stick to their side of the human realm."

Realization strikes Grace first and she dives in to explain. "After what happened with you and Harvey, the previous leaders thought it was safer to combine kingdoms. *The Tetrad kingdom* is—"

"...in a new realm. And we have five bitching castles protected by ancient magic." Seiji finishes eagerly.

"All four kingdoms together?" Angel smiles warmly at my excitement. "Harvey must love that! He always wanted to unite the kingdoms and even had it all planned out for when he took over. Oh, I've been meaning to ask, where is that dumbass, anyway? I thought—" I trail off seeing their sudden grim, crestfallen looks.

With brows pinched like he is trying to understand what I'm talking about, Angel observes me before he asks, "Sweetheart, why do you think Harvey is with us? We couldn't find him in the dungeon and he wasn't with you. All this time we've been waiting for *you* to tell us where he is."

I stop breathing when it finally dawns on me. I start to frantically look around the room as if Harvey would pop out any second and laugh at how easily he scared me, but when he doesn't, my heart falls to my feet, and it gets harder to take my next breath.

I can't lose him.

"He didn't come home?"

Despite his injuries, Harvey was strong enough to heal and find his way home. What if something happened to him after he crossed that barrier? What if I made a mistake letting him escape alone? But I didn't have another choice!

I don't realize I'm hyperventilating until Angel grabs my face and turns me to him, the spark of his touch snapping me out of all the horrible scenarios running through my mind.

"We'll find him."

His determination should soothe my worries, but it only reminds me of the time we *both* believed that. That someone would find us, someone would save us, someone would protect us, *but no one did.*

Now he is out there. *All alone.*

"How? Tell me how? It took my own people a *decade* to find me, and I escaped on my own! He could be dead. Oh Fates, what if he's dead—"

"He's not dead." Grace stops my downward spiral by thrusting a small box in my lap. When my shaky hands fail to open it, she does for me and reveals the red ruby ring similar to Angels' sitting inside proudly.

"The ring still shines."

With that, all my fear comes to a halt. I'm grateful Grace understood logic would help me see reason quicker than any promise could. Gripping the box in my lap, I nod to myself and repeat her words.

The ring still shines.

As long as the ring shines, its successor is alive and capable. The bright gleam proves he's alive.

Out of my reach, but alive.

A minute of silent support passes, and no one other than Angel tries to touch me, which I'm thankful for.

In the past decade, other than Harvey and my little boy, I hated anyone being close to me. Where Angel is a surprising exception, I don't want anyone to accidentally trigger me and get hurt.

I know I'll eventually have to work on my instinct that compels me to attack if someone touches me suddenly, but for now, I need to be extra cautious of my surroundings to minimize any unwanted damage to Angel's family.

"Nevaeh?" With a quick shake of my head, I hum to let Seiji know I'm listening. "How did he get out?"

"And why didn't you go with him?" Angel stops rubbing my back to squeeze my waist and bring me closer. I'm almost sitting on his lap at this point but it's still not enough to ease the storm in his head.

Hazel clicks her fingers, "What I want to know is how in the sweet hell did the coven manage to get past protected walls and take not one but *two* kids, without a single witness. How does that happen, mini reaper?"

Grace gives Hazel a stern look before assuring me that we don't have to do this now if I feel uncomfortable sharing those details. I think about taking her up on her offer since who wants to climb aboard my trauma train, but Papa liked saying the Horsemen are our fate family. And family trusts and supports each other.

I want to give them a chance. And I want to give myself a chance at all the good things in life. After living with my nightmares for years, I deserve to have what they have.

Friendship. Family. Loyalty.

Before I start, I warn them my story might have some plotholes since it happened years ago, and my memories of that time are either all gone or severely jumbled up.

A shit ton of head injuries will do that to you.

"Harvey and I have been friends since birth so we spend a lot of time together as kids. We were training by ourselves like we did on the weekends while Papa and Harvey's parents—"

"Hold up, you were training when you were *nine*?" Seiji asks, horrified.

"Well, my Divine has been wacky since I was born—"

The human Bookkeeper who's technically my sister now provides '*Made*', the accurate term for how I came into existence.

"Fine. *Made*. So, we were on the training grounds. That part of the kingdom was always cleared out for us because Harvey was a silent grump and didn't like anyone's company except mine. Then suddenly, Visha was there."

I shift closer to Angel, who doesn't shy away from kissing my head to offer some comfort.

"She gave Harvey an out. Asked him to leave since she was only interested in me, but the overprotective dumbass wouldn't let me go."

The two chances Visha gave Harvey to escape are the biggest regret of my life. I wish I could go back in time and tell my younger version to push him away as hard as I can instead of clinging to him in fear. He didn't deserve to go down with me.

"We fought them, or at least tried to, but we were just kids against more than a dozen dark witches. And just like that, we were in that dungeon, tied up and bloodied."

A bitter scoff escapes me before I can push it down. "We waited, you know. Held hope for a long time that someone was coming to save us, but then weeks turned into months, and months into years. Eventually, we had to stop deluding ourselves."

The hand on my back stiffens, and Angel's guilt and shame pour into his features. Taking his free hand, I intertwine our fingers to show that I don't blame him. I know first-hand how difficult it was to escape the coven, so I don't blame anyone.

But I can't help the bitterness in my tone from thinking about the days when our hope was beaten out of us. And now that I know they were still trying, even after a decade, the sting of betrayal fades inch by inch.

I can't even comprehend what it must've been like to be on the other side of this.

To have everything but not the people you love.

"I think it was around two or three years ago when Visha came into my cell, boasting about the attack she led on all four kingdoms and how her puppets killed everyone on sight... including my mate. Harvey believed her instantly, but he was too out of it at that point to think straight, so I asked for proof."

"That's when she gave you that arm," Seiji concludes.

I nod stiffly. I'm aware of how tightly I'm clutching Angel's arm, but I can't seem to ease my grip. I need his touch to distract me from the emotions bubbling up from these memories.

Tracing the patterns on his arm, I remind myself that everything Visha said that night was nothing but a thread from her web of lies.

"For years Visha kept killing off anyone that threatened her future but I never thought..." I swallow thickly to ease the tightness in my throat.

That was personal. Another mind game to break her favorite toys.

"The coven had a big celebration that night. The guards were stretched thin, and it was our first opportunity in years, so we took it. We almost made it to the force field when we got caught. *Again.* I was—he..."

I don't expect them to understand or support what I did next, but this conversation was bound to happen and there's no point in lying.

"I ran back. Back to the direction we escaped and straight towards the coven guards. Used every last ounce of my power to hold them back until Harvey crossed the protective shield before damaging the barrier enough to stop anyone else from crossing."

I steal a glance at Angel and immediately hate myself for his sorrow-filled eyes and the hurt I can see overwhelming him.

"I didn't have a mate. I didn't have a family to go back to— at least that's what Visha made me believe, but Harvey did. He still had a mate somewhere, waiting for him. He could start fresh. He was the obvious choice."

Angel ducks his head, and I can feel the weight of his heart breaking like it's my own.

Bumping his shoulder, I wait for him to look at me.

"He wasn't okay, Anxo. Harvey was basically dead at that point. Another week in that wretched place, and I would've lost another person I loved. I had the chance to pay him back for every time he chose me. I owed him at least that."

I hesitate to scoot closer, but to my utter relief, Angel wraps himself around me tightly and kisses my forehead three times.

Seiji shifts in his seat, rubbing the back of his neck with a grimace. "I think we all know why Harvey never made it home."

Grace throws her head back and groans, "The poor man doesn't know we shifted his home!"

Uh oh.

8. Tornado in the living room

Nevaeh

"How old are you?"

"23," Anxo answers while gently scratching my scalp as I lean into his side. He's like a heater with the amount of warmth his body radiates. *My personal heater.*

"Wow, you're old."

With a horrified gasp, Angel tries to stop the bone-relaxing head massage, but I quickly claim his hand back.

Grace volunteered to fill me in on the changes around the kingdom when she thought everyone could use a break from the heavy topics.

I was starting to feel a little strange suddenly getting so much information about these people yet not actually *knowing* any of them. That's when I decided to ask some basic questions to start with.

Turning to Seiji, I ask, "What about you princess?"

"*I don't know about you, but I'm feeling 22!*"

What a weird way to answer a simple question.

"And just so you know, I don't like that nickname." The overgrown teenager pokes his tongue when a loud snort is only my response.

I *love* giving people nicknames. They are usually based on major personality traits someone has, which helps me adjust how I interact with them.

Grace points to Seiji, mumbling 'Same' while staring at me like I'm her favorite new puzzle. Her curiosity is starting to get a tad bit creepy.

Hazel is already glaring at me when I turn to her. I have a feeling she thinks her bitter attitude will make me leave her be, but too bad for her, it's only making me like her more.

"26. One comment from you, and I'll find a way to bury your ass right where Anxo picked you up from." She bares her teeth at me. I think *Sharky* suits her better than Hazel.

Since supernaturals age significantly slower after their twenties, I'm not surprised we all look about the same age. Grace being the exception to that rule because she will continue to age like a normal human until she finds her mate. She might be a Bookkeeper but won't get any 'supernatural club' benefits without her mate.

Talking about mates...

"So... mates?" I ask them curiously—except Angel, of course.

Crossing her arms over her chest, Hazel grumbles about me asking too many questions for someone who just woke up from the dead.

She can be moody all she wants, but Angel has made it clear these people are family to him which means they are now my family too. Anxo has known these people for years, he shares memories and loyalties with each of them, so until I can form my own bonds, I have to make sure my mate doesn't feel forced to choose between us.

Seeing as Seiji and Hazel are both taking their sweet time to answer my simple question, Grace drops her head back with a groan.

"I'm human. I don't have one."

"That's stupid. You're also a Bookkeeper."

My sharp but casual rebuttal has Grace shrinking back. She continues to fidget with the hem of her skirt, and I'm shocked when I realize she genuinely believes that she doesn't have a mate.

Why hasn't anyone told this sweet naive girl that being a Bookkeeper means her mate will be someone very high up on the supernatural food chain?

I'm distracted by how deep Grace's irrational fear of not having a mate goes when Seiji claps to get my attention and leans forward for his turn. "Well, I'm not-so-patiently waiting for the day I meet mine."

Seiji goes on to explain how hard it is for him to be the most eligible bachelor in the kingdom. Especially now that Angel is off-market. I don't even realize when we go from talking about mates to why mixing cold milk in a dry cake mix will ruin it by forming lumps.

When Seiji explains how frosting is a multipurpose tool, Hazel smacks his face with a pillow, and calls him a 'disgusting pig'.

Relaxing in a bright, warm room with people I'm not planning to kill or run from is... new. Addicting.

As soon as the comfort starts making a home in my chest I shove the feeling deep down. Only fools fall for the first good thing offered to them.

But maybe I *should* fall for this. Willingly live with people who are nice to me. Who aren't out for my blood. It might be a nice change from what I'm used to.

Now that Hazel is the only one left, I wait for her to enlighten me on how she feels about the mate bond.

The stubborn siren ignores my burning gaze, but I don't give up until my persistence irritates her enough to talk. Scrunching her nose in annoyance, she twists her head in my direction and finally gives in.

"Don't have one."

Wow. Another idiot who thinks she doesn't have a mate.

The lie is as transparent as the wall I almost smashed my face in this morning. I don't understand what it is with women in this room not believing they have mates.

"She doesn't mean it." Anxo shushes Hazel.

"Uh, yes I do. I would've found them already otherwise. Let's face the facts, Anxo. I'm 26, and I'm never finding my mate. They're probably deep in the fucking ocean, happy with their *chosen mate* since I'm on stupid dry land and out of fucking reach." Her voice grows tighter the more she talks—or grumbles.

I make a mental list of things I've noticed about people who are supposed to be my fate family.

1. *Anxo is a touchy person.*
2. *Once Seiji starts talking, there's no stopping him.*
3. *Grace is not just quiet, she's timid.*
4. *Hazel hates having her emotions on display.*

The more I observe Hazel, the more I relate to her.

I see the way she keeps her daggers close. It's more than her love for the weapon. It's a telltale sign of someone expecting danger. She keeps glancing at the glass walls, listening for the chime of the elevator opening on each floor. I know she's doing all that because I'm doing it, too.

While Angel is quick to catch my twitchy fingers and paranoia, Hazel is much more subtle with her ticks.

It makes me wonder if this is permanent. Hazel shares my nerves and panic *three years* after living with the Horsemen and being a strong warrior. The constant fear doesn't leave— not entirely, at least.

I need a distraction from counting every guest that enters this building, and so does Hazel.

"Oh… now it makes sense. You're all grouchy because you want your mate." I coo in the baby voice I use with my little monkey sometimes. Judging by how Hazel is fuming, I'd say my noble plan to lift her mood is a success.

"If I knew a way to hurt you without hurting Anxo, I would've stabbed you hours ago." Even though Hazel tries to hide it, I don't miss the slight twitch of her lips.

She likes me. I know it.

"Sure, water fairy."

"Do *not* compare me to those emotional sissies."

"Isn't it a little weird how Nevaeh was *made* and not *born*? Like no one pushed her out of her *Va-jay-jay*." Grace squeaks, interrupting my fun interaction with Hazel.

"Ew, why are you calling it *va-jay-jay*, nerd?" Hazel scowls at Grace who shrugs sheepishly.

"Yeah, just say *coochie* like normal people." Seiji chimes in.

"That's not what normal people call it, fucktard! It's called a *vagina*." Hazel corrects Seiji, who refuses to repeat the word 'vagina' because it makes him feel queasy.

The debate on what the right term is for the female private part ends with Seiji running for his life with Hazel on his toes yelling how she is going to *'choke the stupidity out of him'* today.

When there are no signs of them slowing down, Angel tiredly trudges to the middle of the living room, and Seiji immediately runs to hide behind him, taking refuge from the deadly siren.

"*Drop it.* I don't want another kingdom to manage. I'm barely surviving three as it is." The stern order makes them both huff and reluctantly step away from each other.

I can't even pay attention to how *parental* that was of Anxo because what he just said is causing a streak of questions to line up in my head. "Three kingdoms?"

Suddenly, the room falls silent. Seiji and Hazel stop bickering and turn to me with wide, horrified eyes.

Fuck. I thought bad news time was over, but it seems like we're circling back to it. By the looks of uncertainty masking their features, I have a feeling they were hoping to avoid this for as long as possible.

Fear grips me when I turn to Angel and he looks like he would rather be anywhere else. Blowing a sharp breath that does little to ease my nerves, I stuff my hands under my thighs to hide how they've started to tremble.

Without breaking eye contact, Angel eats the distance between us in two giant steps and sits down on the floor before me. Tugging my hands from under me, Anxo grips them in his.

There's one only question on my mind and the reality of my worst fear coming to life forces me to speak past the lump in my throat. "Where's Papa?"

Angel's head snaps sideways to Grace, who mirrors his alarmed expression. Hazel covers her face, muttering 'oh shit' over and over again, and Seiji runs off to the kitchen.

I was starting to think he just wanted to hide from an uncomfortable conversation, but Seiji came back a minute later with a mug of hot chocolate to soften the blow.

I'm starting to hate how they give bad news. Idiots just stare at each other, talking with their eyes, and leave me out of the loop.

"He's dead, isn't he?"

It's not really a question. I already figured something was wrong if Papa didn't come for me yesterday. After the stories Visha has drilled into me, the only logical conclusion is that she killed him.

I was so naive to think everything she said was a lie because some weren't. My mate is alive. There was no attack on our kingdoms, and as much as I'm happy about that, I know she wasn't wrong about everything.

Maybe she did what she said. Maybe I did lose everything in that cell.

I'm busy imagining life as an orphan when they all exclaim in sync, making me jump in my seat. "No!"

So, there's bad news... but Papa is not dead?

"Okay, so why isn't he here then? Why did he send amateurs to help me rather than coming himself?"

Seiji gasps, "Uh, excuse me? These *amateurs* saved you yesterday."

"*I saved myself.*"

"But... B-but we're taking you home!"

"Wow. How mighty of you. It must take a lot of blood and tears to cross a fucking portal, huh?"

Sure, they helped me near the end, but I got myself out. *All on my own.* I deserve 80% of the credit.

"That's a lot of sarcasm for someone who lived in a dungeon for a decade. Who'd you learn it from, the rats in your cell?" Hazel snickers.

"Idiot. *I* was the rat in the cell." I snort very un-princess-like, and Hazel looks at me with a mix of stunned and impressed.

"Quiet!" Angel growls, and all our mouths snap shut.

Grace chastises Hazel for making light of my trauma, and her chin falls to her chest in guilt. I accidentally let a smile loose, watching Hazel get scolded like a child, and her remorse quickly turns into a snarl when she sees it.

Oops.

Pinching the bridge of his nose, Angel takes a deep breath. Without thinking, I let my fingers brush through his soft curls, mimicking the way he played with mine earlier. His shoulders sag, and Angel drops his head in my lap with a sigh of content.

After a quiet minute, Angel knows he can't stall any longer and looks over his shoulder to see if anyone else will volunteer, but the cowards avoid his gaze and look around the room like they're searching for something.

With his hand in mine, Anxo's eyes ask me for patience, and even though I don't have any when it comes to my family, I try not to get ahead of myself.

"Searching for his missing daughter day and night wasn't easy on him, Nevaeh. Every time a team returned without any information on you, he got more depressed and... just tired. He was losing himself, sweetheart."

With every word, Anxo silently begs me not to hold Papa's absence against him.

"Three years ago, Dean asked me if I'd be willing to take over for him for a while. He didn't dump anything on me, though. Before leaving, Dean sorted out his paperwork for a year in advance. And Grace spent so much time working with him that her insight helps me immensely."

Papa hasn't been home in *three* years?

If he did a year's worth of work and only wanted a break, what's taking him so long? What if he got tired of pausing his life for me and just wanted out?

What if he is never coming back?

"Dad will be back," Grace says confidently as if she read my mind. "He didn't want to leave, but he needed that break. Your disappearance was hard on him, Nevaeh. *He was fading away.*

I had to force him away when it got so bad that eating or sleeping was an occasional thing."

The images of him standing outside my old room, drowning in guilt and shame, start playing in my head.

His sadness, his anger, his remorse.

The thought of him neglecting his health and losing himself because of me makes my throat close up. That's one more thing Visha destroyed for me.

Turning to Grace, I wonder if she can help me find Papa. I don't realize I'm making her uncomfortable until her eyes sparkle with fresh tears.

"I'm so sorry. I won't call him dad if it bothers you. He said I could, but I didn't even think how that would make you feel—"

"What? No. Where did that even come from? I was wondering if your gifts can help me find him."

Grace slumps back with a hand over her heart, "Oh, thank God. You have a mean resting face, it almost gave me a heart attack."

When I don't encourage her nonsensical thoughts, Grace finally focuses on the part about her gift. "Sorry, but it doesn't really work like that. You can ask me anything about the supernatural world, and I'll have an answer, but that's about all I can do."

"She's like a dictionary and Google combined," Seiji adds. When I keep staring blankly, he pauses to explain what *Google* is.

Even when the kingdom of Death was in the human realm, I wasn't surrounded by human technology growing up. Papa used to say ignoring people and riding our horses was better than moving steel entrapments or answering plastic bricks.

For Papa, it's not *'what doesn't kill you that makes you stronger'*, but *'if you fail to kill me*, I'm going to kill *you'*.

"So your gift can't help us find our father dearest?"

The previously unshed tears now start falling freely down Grace's almond cheeks.

I turn to Angel, horrified by what I've done only to find him smiling like a fool. Seeing my distress, he whispers it's because I said *our father.*

"I still don't understand why you're crying, *Honeybunch.* Papa *adopted* you and *made* me. That makes us sisters. I'm sorry, but you're stuck with me now. And as you can see, I desperately need a mentally stable sibling in my life."

And now she is full-on sobbing with a broad smile showcasing all her teeth. My head is spinning with her range of emotions.

Maybe it's a human thing.

Angel assures me they are happy tears, and not because Grace is sad about our dynamic. Seiji rubs her back until she's only smiling... without the tears. I stare at Grace dumbfounded by how fast she can turn bright and sunny when she was weeping a literal second ago.

Finally sobering up, Grace shakes her head with a grimace at my earlier question.

"But is he okay? You know... *alive*?"

Hazel exasperatedly throws her hands in the air. "Why do you keep assuming everyone is dead?"

"Because almost everyone I knew in the last decade *is* dead. Not to forget I was *told* everyone was dead."

"Visha lied, golden glittery soul eater."

"No shit, shark in human meat suit."

"I don't like you," Hazel mutters with a straight face.

"Oh, But I *love* you," I say it sarcastically, but I have to admit I do feel protective of her on some level.

Papa always preached how important family is, and since Hazel is Anxo's family, she falls into the small list of people I consider family.

1. *Papa*
2. *My little monkey*
3. *Harvey the eternal dumbass*
4. *Angel*
5. *Grace, Hazel, and Seiji*

I thought the difficult part of this conversation was over, but then I remember Angel saying *three* kingdoms.

Feeling my questioning gaze, Angel scratches the back of his head nervously. I want this conversation to be done already, so I ask him to blurt it out.

"I took over *Conquer* and *War* at seventeen."

Rearing back, I look at him like he has grown three heads. Why the fuck was he crowned Conquer at *seventeen*, much less given *War*?

"Why *War*?"

I can come to terms with him taking over Conquer at just seventeen—which is a challenge itself—but why would Uncle Henry give him *War*?

"That's Harvey's bloodright."

I see the reflection of my eyes burning gold in Angel's as my Divine stirs wildly, sensing the possibility of going against my mate to protect my best friend.

Instead of looking offended at my unsaid accusation, Angel *smiles* at me. "It's still his, sweetheart. The title. The kingdom. The piles of paperwork and responsibilities are all his to inherit."

The way Angel genuinely hates paperwork isn't lost on me. It makes me happy to see how eager he is about Harvey taking over.

"Henry uh—he got sick. His health didn't allow him the stress of such responsibilities anymore, so he asked me to step in until Harvey returned."

I can tell Angel is holding something back, but I can't seem to ask for more. The way his eyes gloss over and warily study me, how tightly his hands are squeezing mine, terrifies me.

Angel waits to see if I want to know, but I shake my head. I need him to keep the rest to himself.

I can't ask more.

I can't deal with any more bad news.

Listening to Seiji talk about how things will change when

we go back to the kingdom helps me breathe better. It's a relief to see they genuinely want Harvey and me to go back home with them.

All our lives it's been the two of us against the world, but maybe now it doesn't have to be just us.

Anxo and Seiji share a mischievous look, and Grace suddenly starts laughing at Hazel's scowl.

Smirking like he's about to share a secret, Angel looks deep into my eyes before I hear his voice *inside* my head without his lips moving.

"What would you like for lunch, sweetheart?"

Wait a damn minute... "You can read minds?!"

Angel laughs loudly, and I'm stuck staring at the magnificent sight. "Nuh-uh, only tap in for a private conversation."

"Is that what you guys keep doing? I thought it was a shared creepy obsession with staring at each other."

Angel chuckles, brushing his thumb over my cheekbone. "I could cast illusions and create protective barriers before my coronation, but telepathy was a gift from the sisters of fate after they accepted me as the new Horseman of Conquer."

Horsemen bloodlines aren't born with all their gifts. The strength, extraordinary senses, and the presence of our Divine are given to us at birth, but Fates only award our final power once they choose us to lead.

"Since my final gift was intended to be used among Horsemen only, it took me some time to overcome that limitation. It's easier with you and Seiji with our bloodlines, but now I can link Grace and Hazel too."

It's ironic that I can't control the few Reaper powers I do have where my mate has surpassed all expectations.

I swear my heart stops when Angel's lips touch my hairline. After kissing my head, Angel casually leans back in his seat as if the simple gesture didn't just bring me to the brink of death.

Seiji clears his throat—unnecessarily loud, breaking my delicious eye contact with the green-eyed godlike man.

Horrible timing, princess.

"*That* is nothing. Let me show you something worth being impressed by."

Before I can tell Seiji I'm familiar with his gifts, I watch in awe as he rotates his forefinger in lazy circles. The wind around us follows his command, and an adorable little tornado starts to brew on top of his finger.

What I saw yesterday was a lot more violent, but now I can see the delicate side of his powers.

Releasing the little tornado off his finger, Seiji allows it to roam the room before he starts rotating his *entire palm*, manipulating the wind as he wishes. Just like that, the little tornado isn't so little anymore. It grows bigger, and darker, destroying the room in the process.

The thick windows shudder with force, and even the furniture starts shaking. Just as the tornado reaches its peak, Seiji adds bright purple lightning to the mix, turning the tornado into a dark storm.

This is exactly what I saw yesterday—minus the organ exploding and vomiting part.

When the storm begins to head in my direction, Seiji swiftly scatters it with a heavy gush of wind, and everything trapped in the tornado falls to the floor.

"You're responsible for cleaning this mess." Angel gives Seiji a pointed look. I can tell this isn't the first time Seiji has gone rogue trying to show off his power.

Turning to his Warriorhead, Angel says, "I think we're ready for lunch."

Taking the hint, Hazel takes a deep breath before whistling a soft, melodic tune. The sound is so soothing I want to close my eyes and curl into myself before falling into a deep peaceful sleep.

I soon find out the intent behind Hazel's tune when the elevator chimes and five waiters come rushing in with trays overflowing with food.

The staff completely ignores the jungle the living room

looks like and moves past it to place the trays on the kitchen counter before leaving almost robotically. As if they are in a trance—*Or being manipulated by a siren.*

I'm left gaping when Hazel finally stops whistling and winks at me. I don't even pay attention to her smug smirk because I'm so busy staring at her in awe.

"I think she's my favorite," I whisper.

"I made a *thunderstorm* and *she's* your favorite?!"

"I can't eat clouds, princess." I shrug, practically salivating from the delicious smell coming from the kitchen, while they burst out laughing.

9. Come meet my monkey

Nevaeh

I'm going to throw this stupid clock out the stupid window if it doesn't stop tick-ticking right fucking now!

Pressing my face into my pillow, I scream out in frustration. I've been lying on this cloud-like bed for the past five hours, and still no signs of sleep. I thought being in a safe environment would ease my mind enough to *finally* get some rest, but guess not.

Not being able to force my guard down is taking me back to my days in that cell. Even with all the comfort and warmth surrounding me, I can't stop feeling like the other shoe is about to drop.

At first, I was eager to have a room to myself. A place where my little monkey and I could relax and heal, but it's been four days and that boy still hasn't woken up from his sleep coma.

This room with its pale blue walls, a comfortable bed, and fluffy pillows had me excited in the beginning, but now I'm getting sick of the lingering silence. Most of my restlessness is my own fault since I haven't left this room for anything other than checking up on monkey.

The first night I locked myself in this room, I wasn't expecting a plate filled to the brim with food waiting for me in the morning.

Seiji stood by my door and watched me devour the plate within seconds. Only to throw up everything a minute later. Good food was a luxury my body rejected on my first day as a free woman.

Seiji came by a second time that same night, and I didn't understand what he wanted me to do with more food. I had already eaten once that day, and even if it didn't reach my stomach, I thought that was it.

When I made the mistake of asking what I did to deserve a second plate, Seiji stormed out and came back with Angel on his toes. They both stared at me for the longest time like I had kicked their puppies.

I ate half of what was offered the next morning and thankfully didn't throw up. Seeing that, Anxo asked Seiji to cut my meals in half and once a day because that was all I could stomach for the time being.

Seiji was worried and didn't even try to hide it. With a tight smile and tears lining his lashes he tried to convince me to at least have some fruit before Angel intervened.

Now thanks to my mate, everyone follows *my* pace with my rehabilitation into society.

Even when I refused to step out and socialize with anyone this past week, I still had food waiting for me every morning at eight without fail.

I've broken nine clocks since I got here so before I round up that number, I climb out of the warm bed and walk straight to my bathroom.

My own bathroom.

After a long burning hot shower, I look somewhat alive, but the purple bags under my eyes are proof of my less-than-stellar sleep schedule.

My closet—which is big enough for me to sleep in—now stores three pairs of new sweatpants and undergarments that Grace got for me and the two hoodies Anxo graciously lent me.

Picking a soft white hoodie and black sweatpants, I get changed. My lack of sleep has made the usual fog in my head thicker. It takes all my energy to stay upright instead of falling over from exhaustion.

I've tried to give in and take a nap twice now, but the nightmares from my past haunt me until I wake with a start, on the verge of a panic attack. I can't risk my Divine taking over in my sleep. That would be catastrophic for everyone in this building.

The sound of another door shutting breaks my train of thought as I close my door. I turn to see Angel coming out of his room, and when his eyes settle on me, there is a flash of surprise in them to find me out of my room—*voluntarily.*

Anxo leans against his door, strong arms crossed over his chest. Tilting my face to the left, I admire how the pale blue knitted sweater fits his broad shoulders.

"You look dead." He says with a straight face.

And here I thought he was the polite one.

"I feel it, too." Rolling my eyes, I take instinctive steps to him, wanting a taste of his addictive scent.

"Didn't get any sleep, sweetheart?" Anxo finally closes the gap between us. When his warm hand covers the side of my face, I immediately lean into it. My tired eyes fall shut on their own accord, and all I can muster is quiet *no.*

"Too busy daydreaming about me?"

Even with my eyes closed, I can *see* the playful grin on his unfairly gorgeous face. "Oh, bite me."

With one last step, I let my head fall on his chest, not being able to support its weight anymore. With one hand Angel pushes my hair behind my back to gently massage my neck while his other arm wraps around my waist to rub my back.

I go liquid in his arms. How is he so soft and cuddly with all these muscles?

"Tell me your safe spots first, I don't want to make you uncomfortable."

His quick, witty response makes me laugh sleepily. I'm already half asleep at this point. With my cheek pressed against his chest, I get lost in the rhythmic beat of his heart that soothes the dull ache in mine.

"You're so touchy. I'm not sure I like it," I mumble, burying myself further into his arms.

His chest vibrates, lulling me to sleep as he sways us side to side. "Mhm, the way your arms are squeezing the life out of me definitely proves that."

Angel's easy affection makes me blink rapidly to fight the tears threatening to fall. I have to fight the tightness in my throat as he continues to hold me so gently. I don't think I will ever get used to how he holds me like I'm the most precious thing in his world.

"You're so hot." I don't realize my error until Anxo snickers, the sound jolting me.

"I meant *warm*. That is definitely what I meant. Not that you're not hot, because you are. Trust me, I would know—" Just shut up, Nevaeh!

I wish the ground would swallow me up right this second. I'm ready for my demise Mother Nature, come and take me with you.

A soft kiss on my forehead stops me from begging any god that might be listening. Anxo pulls my face from the crook of his neck, and I have to face the embarrassment my tongue has brought on me.

Thankfully my mate doesn't mind that I'm a trainwreck more than half the time. With my face held in his hands, Angel kisses the tip of my nose, a barely concealed smirk on his lips before he starts to drag me away.

"Come on baby, let's get you fed."

Walking into the dining hall, I go straight to the glass wall and stick my face to it. "I love this fucking view."

"You swear like a sailor," Hazel mutters from where she is sitting on the counter with a pack of chips, sporting her usual 'don't mess with me, I'm scary' look.

"You whine like a child," I retort. Sluggishly walking to the giant table, I sit down with my chin resting on my folded arms.

I love the banter I have with this group. They don't bite their tongue when we bicker which means I don't have to either. I appreciate how they don't act like I'm something fragile that will break with the wind.

When I hear Seiji snort, I turn to find him stirring something on the stove while Anxo cuts different fruits into small pieces beside him.

"Did you not sleep? You look exhausted." Grace asks over the obnoxious sound of Hazel chewing.

"Not really. I had a nightmare—Hazel stop shaking the fucking chip bag so damn loud!"

Dusting her fingers, Hazel slips off the counter before walking over to where I'm sitting. "Aw, are you not feeling very *golden* this morning?"

Banging my fists on the table, I bear down at the siren with my deathliest glare. "Listen here, you fish on legs seascum, leave me the fuck alone before I wrap that unnecessary attitude of yours and shove it so far up your ass you're choking on it."

I don't realize I've slipped into my untapped rage until my essence is seeping out of me, circling me like it is gearing up for an attack.

Fuck. I can't believe that's all it took for me to lose my shit. This is why I need to sleep before my mind breaks, giving my Divine the perfect chance to go on a rampage.

The room is silent when I finally regain my composure. Everyone is staring at me with their mouths agape, tasks abandoned. Except for Hazel. That little devil has the smuggest smirk plastered on her face, showing off her sparkling white teeth.

She'll be toothless if she keeps instigating me.

Hazel likes to rile me up a little too much. But she won't be giggling the day my restraint finally snaps.

"My-my. Junior Reaper has teeth."

I'm going to kill her! I'm going to wring her little cupcake neck.

"You little shit—"

Pushing off my chair, I'm about to show Hazel just how hard I bite when the door to the dining room bursts open.

A young woman in grey overalls rushes in, her face pinched in irritation. A tiny figure runs out from behind her and before my knee can touch the floor, my little monkey is crashing into my arms.

My chest squeezes in worry when I feel him shaking in my

arms and the wet spot on my shoulder.

I never liked this nurse. She thinks I don't notice her stabbing me with her glare each time I turn my back to her, but I do.

If I find out she had something to do with my monkey being so scared, I'll make her pay by ripping off her limbs.

I stand up holding monkey securely to my chest. The little guy hides his face in my neck, rubbing his cheek against the soft material. Monkey doesn't stop shaking and I know I need to calm him down before he makes himself sick again.

I faintly hear Anxo thank the nurse before asking her to leave for the kingdom. She's quick to escape my glare, which only makes me more suspicious of her.

Turning back to me, Anxo's face is etched with concern for the little boy who's silently sobbing in my arms.

"Can you get him a glass of water, please?"

I'm waiting for Anxo to return when I hear Seiji quietly complaining about how I only ever say 'please' and 'sorry' to Anxo and not anyone else.

What a crybaby.

The kid has yet to release his firm grip on me, but at least his breathing isn't as choppy anymore. Walking over to the dining table I sit down with monkey on my lap as everyone crowds us wearing similar looks of concern.

Anxo rushes back with the glass of water, placing it before monkey then moving to sit next to me.

"You're okay, kiddo. You're safe, I promise. Here, drink some water." I try to pry the kids' soft arms off me, but his grip remains lethal. Monkey spares a quick glance at the people surrounding him and then at the glass of water.

Noticing his hesitance, Anxo carefully pushes the glass closer until monkey can grab it himself.

With the glass within reach, monkey turns to me as if asking for permission. His wide blue eyes filled with terror is like a stab to my heart. Visha did this. She made this sweet little boy so untrusting and suspicious.

"Don't worry, these people are nothing like that organ-harvesting witch. They're my friends." I assure him with a kiss on his head.

I said, friends. Are they my friends? We only met like a week ago. But they are *Horsemen*. A bond just as strong as if not more than our blood bonds.

Oh fates, focus Nevaeh!

Monkey hesitantly loosens his grip before turning in my lap to face the table. When he reaches for the glass, I don't expect it to be heavy for a toddler... but then it starts to slip from his tiny fingers. Thanks to Anxo's quick reflexes, he is able to place his forefinger at the bottom of the glass to keep it from falling.

Monkey takes a small cautious sip while eyeing the people surrounding him. Once his curiosity is sated, he gulps down the water in one giant breath and sighs deeply once the whole thing is finished.

Carefully placing the glass back, monkey turns back to wrap his arms around my waist. But instead of hiding his face, he keeps an eye on the room full of strangers.

"Do you want to meet my friends, kiddo?" Leaving behind some of his reluctance, monkey nods rather confidently. "So, this is Anxo, Grace, Hazel, and Seiji."

Everyone waves at monkey with bright smiles, which he shyly returns before his hand goes back to fisting my hoodie. I'm jealous Hazel didn't give me that warm smile when she first met me. *I'm love-deprived, too, woman!*

"He's so cute! Look at those big blue eyes. Aren't you a pretty little baby?" Grace coos and my monkey flushes an adorable bright pink.

"Aww, look how pink his cheeks are." Seiji's comment has monkey turning to hiding his face in my hoodie to cover his red cheeks.

"Come on, let's get our newest member something to eat, he must be starving." Standing from his chair, Anxo quickly kisses the top of my head before dragging Seiji back to the kitchen while Grace and Hazel set the table.

It didn't escape me how monkey eyed Angel when he kissed my head or how he breathed out when I didn't flinch from the sweet gesture.

I hope a safe environment surrounded by good people will help ease this little kid's fear. I don't want him panicking at every little touch like I do. His life should be better than mine. *Much, much better.*

Three days ago when I was lying in bed as everyone else slept peacefully it finally dawned on me that I was going to live with four people more evolved and mature than I am. So I made a rule for myself. To copy them.

When they eat, I try to. When they sleep, I lay down and pretend. I thought it would be easy. But that was before I knew they slept 8 hours a day and ate more for breakfast than I did in a whole day.

'And when they finally realize your true worth, you'll be thrown away like food scrapes on their plates.'

Oh joy, evil Queen Visha is back in my head.

I *really* hate this bitch.

Absolutely despise her.

Like I would love to chop her up and—*you get the gist.*

I'm about to say I'm not hungry and spare myself the embarrassment of using the wrong utensil when I realize I would have to help monkey eat anyway.

I don't even know what to give him. Not all of this can be safe for him to eat right? What if his stomach doesn't agree with this food like mine still doesn't?

Monkey sniffs like the little werewolf he is to see what appeals to him most before pointing at the large tray stacked with pancakes.

Turns out I don't have to worry about giving monkey the wrong thing because Anxo has it all under control. Fixing a plate of pancakes with liquid chocolate drizzled on top, he slides it in front of monkey.

I watch Anxo show him how to use the rubber fork—which I didn't even know was a thing. Monkey mimics the action perfectly while stealing suspicious glances at the man teaching him. But after his third bite, monkey forgets all about keeping an eye on Anxo and starts stuffing himself full of pancakes, happily humming with each bite.

I've never seen the kid so relaxed before. I thought staying in such close proximity for months meant I knew every little thing about this boy, but this was the time I was seeing him truly off guard. *And happy.*

Fighting the tightness in my throat, I wipe the chocolate smudge from the corner of his mouth and ask him to slow down and chew properly.

When I look up, Anxo is waiting on me with a fork carrying a small bite. I open my mouth to ask him what he's doing, but Angel seizes the opportunity to feed me.

The smile on Angel's lips widens when I moan at the chocolaty taste. Taking a bite himself, Angel ushers a bowl of fruit before me to eat between bites.

I don't know how he knew I was nervous about making a mistake with monkey, but I'm grateful for his creepy insight. I try to thank him for not making a big deal and handling it so subtly and sweetly, but words fail me throughout breakfast.

Anxo kisses my forehead when he sees how hard I'm trying to keep the stubborn tears from falling and I know I don't need to say the words for him to understand me.

Monkey suddenly tenses in my hold, and it becomes clear it's because of how close Anxo is to me. Grabbing Angel's hand, I place it next to where I'm holding monkey's, hoping to make him understand that I'm not afraid of Anxo touching me.

"So, the boy is…" Grace trails off.

"A werewolf," I confirm. "The witch had a vision about him and he was in my cell the next day."

"His Divine is strong for a kid," Anxo observes the boy, who is busy licking chocolate from his plate. I chuckle when monkey raises his sticky hands in front of my face, silently asking for help.

"Royal blood," Grace concludes, handing me a wet napkin.

"It shouldn't be difficult to find more about him. There aren't many royal bloodlines left."

Everyone nods in sync, but I'm left confused... mainly because of my rusty current affairs.

"What happened to *The Royal Six*?"

"Slaughtered for power," Anxo says with a sad grimace. "The supernatural world has been struggling for the past couple of years. There have been several uprisings, and the oppressed are fighting back just as hard."

I've heard stories of a time when werewolves were heavily criticized for their choice of lifestyle, and others only stepped in after it became too gruesome to ignore. It took centuries of negotiations and threats from Horsemen and vampire leaders to force them to stop their ancient practice of challenging an alpha for power.

The alpha challenge is still legal and accepted worldwide, but the terms have changed drastically.

Earlier, when a challenger defeated the current alpha, the victor alpha was free to do whatever he pleased with his new pack. More often than not the new alpha would kill any offspring of the old alpha before forcing the Luna to mate him and create a new line of a future generation.

To imagine this was just the tip of the iceberg is bone-chilling. Every time an alpha lost his title, the women of his pack paid the price heavily. Crimes like rape, forced markings, and watching their fated mates get killed before their eyes was once a norm.

Werewolves have come a long way since then, but there's still a lot that needs fixing.

"The Royal Six turned against one another. Their betrayal is now ruining their entire species." Grace added.

"A few more decades of killing their own, and they will be all gone." Hazel glances at monkey sideways, and suddenly, it clicks.

A vision is the reason my little boy was in that dungeon. Visha said whatever changes monkey is supposed to bring would change his world drastically. If that's his destiny, I just hope I will be able to help him fulfill what the Fates have trusted him with.

"Sweetheart, if you eat any slower, we can combine your breakfast with lunch."

I'm so lost in my head that I don't realize Angel has already finished his share and is waiting on me now. He chuckles when I open my mouth and show him I'm ready for my next bite.

Turning to others, Anxo says, "Let's call a council meeting. I need to update them on what we've been up to and let them know we'll be staying in the human realm a little longer than planned."

"Already done. They'll be here tomorrow afternoon."

"Your overenthusiasm to keep busy benefits me a lot, Gracie."

Grace slides a small piece of paper across the table to Angel. "I would gladly accept Dragon Mirah's latest book series as a thank-you present."

Angel shakes with a soft smile. "Of course you would."

10. Rick the dick

Nevaeh

I 'm shaking with nerves as I pass Anxo, who is holding the door open for me. Only when his firm hand settles on my lower back do I relax a little.

Ignoring the stolen glances and keeping a blank expression is hard when I'm the only new presence in the room. They might not recognize my face, but I'm reeking with my Divine even as I try to keep it under wraps.

The large, dark wooden table is occupied on one side by high-ranking warriors and elders of the kingdom, staring at me curiously. I'm about to sit between Angel and Seiji when the door to the conference room bursts open.

"Greetings, Horseman Alarie." A man rushes in, bowing to Anxo before striding toward the only empty chair left on his side of the table.

"Have a seat, Rick. We'll start in a minute."

Rick... sounds like dick. I hold back from snorting like a pig and remind myself to be professional.

Don't fuck up your first impression, Nevaeh.

"Prince Nakaya." Rick bows in Seiji's direction first then greets every other man in the room in a similar way, blatantly ignoring the female warriors in the process.

So, he is a dick, after all.

Rick's misogyny shines so bright that his once decent features now seem ugly. He is about 5'8 with tan olive skin and obsidian eyes. Shoulder-length hair pulled back into a neat bun.

Pity his personality pales in comparison.

While adjusting in his chair, Rick's gaze searches the room

until it lands on Grace. His cheery, happy-go-lucky mask is replaced with something darker in a flash.

Rick scans her thoroughly, as much as he can from above the table, and the disappointment in his eyes is evident even when his face stays nonchalant.

When his eyes meet mine, an unfamiliar face among familiar ones, Rick can't hide his shock. Or the way his eyes linger below my neck for longer than necessary.

I'm wearing Angel's hoodie, so I doubt he sees anything exciting, but men like him don't care what's on display as long as it's a woman.

"Oh, who's this pretty lady? I don't think I've had the pleasure of meeting you, miss-?"

"*Blackburn.*"

If the way my eyes flashed gold with the irritation didn't stun Rick, my name surely did.

Every head snaps to me with similar bewildered looks. I don't mind. I understand how strange it must be sitting with someone they assumed was dead for a decade.

One by one, Angel introduces me to the council of elders, Warriorheads, and elite warriors who all fumble their way through the introduction before he stops at a woman patiently waiting for her turn.

"It's a blessing to have you among us again, Princess Nevaeh. I'm head reaper, Vesta."

Okay, now the dark hooded cloak resting on her shoulders makes much more sense.

"Papa made you wear that?"

She chuckles, smoothing her hands down the sides of her robe. "As much as he loathes wearing one himself, he enjoys making fun of us in them more."

Of course, he does.

The Kingdom of Death is the only one among Horsemen actively involved with the human realm. The other three only pitch in when the fate sisters want them to, whether to strip land from life or cause enough conflicts to shake the world.

Papa might be *The Grim Reaper,* but even he can't be everywhere at once. There's a separate army of demons under him bestowed with the basic abilities of a reaper to help with his daily workload.

As long as a demon is willing, Papa doesn't hesitate to recruit them. He avoids being in the human realm like a fish avoids being out of water.

The last man I have yet to meet pales, but instead of shock, he looks like he might burst into tears of happiness as he stares at me expectedly.

Fuck.

His happiness will soon turn to dust when he finds out that while he is struggling to hold back tears of joy, I'm struggling to remember him. I knew a day would come when I would have to face someone from my past and look them in the eye when I say I don't remember who they are.

I hold my breath and scan my brain to try to remember him, but I come up blank.

A warm hand engulfs mine under the table. Turning to my mate, I shake my head subtly. Anxo's eyes fall shut in defeat, his grip on my hand tightening.

Within a moment, the crestfallen look on the warrior's face is replaced with understanding, and I don't have to guess why. Angel and I have a deal. If I tell him I don't remember something or someone, he will explain on my behalf, so I don't have to be responsible for crushing their hope.

I know it's selfish to put that on him, but I can't for the life of me, have people shedding tears because I don't remember who they are. The lack of empathy they will get in return will only hurt them more.

It's better to start over. And the way this particular warrior is holding himself back from smothering me tells me he's someone I won't mind starting over with.

My hesitant smile makes his whole demeanor light up, and it feels so good to see he doesn't feel betrayed by my broken mind.

"Nevaeh, this is Warriorhead Khatri, second in command to your father." Angel introduces him.

Khatri looks to be in his mid-thirties with a perfectly trimmed beard and dark eyes that soften considerably when he's looking at me.

That look. Seeing it feels like Deja Vu.

"It's good to have you back, Princess Nevaeh. My mate and I have been praying for your return for years." His deep South Asian accent is familiar but not enough for me to place him.

"Thank you. For everything." We both know I'm grateful for more than just watching over my kingdom. Khatri was there for Papa in his hard times, and his relief at my return tells me how much it must've hurt him to see Papa break in those times.

The mountain of guilt that permanently sits on my chest is gifted another heavy stone. Before that weight can make it hard for me to breathe, Angel laces our fingers together, bringing our joined hands to rest on his thigh. It's scary how easily this man can turn my misery into a faded memory.

Rick clears his throat, catching everyone's attention. "*The missing princess.* I'll be honest, no one thought we could salvage you after a decade."

Salvage me? What am I? A lost earring?

"Well, I am here, *warrior* Rick." He meets my emphasis on warrior and the blatant disregard of his title with a visible tick in his jaw.

Doesn't feel good to be treated like you don't matter, does it, asshole.

Whatever fire I start under his pants, Rick doesn't seem so concerned about reeling it back. He makes yet another attempt at concealing his disgusting words under the veil of politeness.

"If you don't mind me asking, Miss Blackburn, have you given any thought about your role in the kingdom? I know it's quite early, but I've heard there's an empty spot on the kitchen services." Rick directs his words to Angel even as the conversation is about *me.*

"If I were him, I'd tread very carefully," Seiji whispers to himself like he doesn't actually want to warn Rick. Hazel is watching Angel like a hawk, waiting for him to bash this idiot's face in.

Shame that's not Angel's style.

"My apology council members. Maybe it's too soon for her. After all, her scars are still fresh."

I tense when everyone's eyes follow Rick's to my knuckles where a single white scar disappears under the sleeve. I might hide my scars, but it's not because I'm ashamed of them. Rather, I don't want to subject others to what was done to me.

Angel's hand finds mine under the table, his fingers slipping under the sleeve of his hoodie until he is absentmindedly tracing the same scars Rick thinks I need to be ashamed of.

Keeping his frustration under control, Angel speaks firmly. "Nevaeh already has a path laid out by the Fates laid. She's our future *Horsewoman of Death*."

Guess who has a death wish: *Rick the dick.*

"I hope you're not serious, Horseman Alarie. She is a *woman*. There's no such thing as a female Grim Reaper. It's a commitment of a lifetime, sir." Rick looks around the room to gauge if he is gaining any supporters. "I think we should wait for Horseman Blackburn to find his fated mate and give the kingdom a *natural* male offspring worthy of such status."

Did he really just call me unnatural and unworthy in the same fucking sentence?

"Welcome to the 1850s bitches." Seiji mocks and leans back in his chair, waiting for Angel to drop his restraint.

As much as I love to fight my own battles, I'm enjoying someone else stand up for me for a change.

There are no Kings in the Horsemen kingdoms since after coronation, one becomes a Horseman of the apocalypse, and their partner, the Queen. The Queen is the one responsible for the welfare and prosperity of the kingdom. She's the one running things while the Horsemen focus on serving the sisters of fate.

There's never been a female Horseman so I'm not sure how things will work if I am chosen for the throne, but it's clear Rick doesn't like that possibility.

The look on Angel's face screams murder. If I didn't know with absolute certainty that he would never even think about hurting me, I would be worried.

Rage darkens his once bright green eyes. Anxo looks a flick of wind away from informing Ricks' family that he died from an unfortunate mouthing incident.

"Tell me, warrior Morgan," Angel doesn't look so angelic as the lid on his anger slips back an inch to address Rick. "Are you aware of the ratio between men and women in high-ranking positions in the supernatural world?"

"Uh, no sir." Rick stutters.

What a coward.

"7:3. Can you name the ten greatest leaders in our history?"

"No sir."

"*Six* of them are women." Angel stares directly at Rick while everyone waits to see where this is headed. "What do you think those stats prove, warrior?"

After a few minutes of Rick stumbling over his words and unable to produce a simple answer, the Head Reaper speaks up, "Women have a majority in *quality* leadership."

"Excellent observation, Vesta." The woman perks up at Anxo's compliment. "It also proves that despite men believing they rule the world, women are actually better at leading it. Imagine all the positive changes they could bring with a little more support and a little less narrow-mindedness."

Everyone is beaming at my mate with pride. I'm surprised he handled the situation so calmly without once raising his voice or throwing Rick off the roof.

I would've chosen the latter but to each their own.

"If you still have doubts regarding *my mate's* worth and capabilities, you're welcome to challenge her for a friendly duel."

Rick pales when Angel mentions us being mates. He

remains silent after that, lowering his head in sheer embarrassment while Angel starts the meeting without any more idiotic disruptions.

While the council members are shocked by Angel and me being mates, I'm having a hard time adjusting to different shocking news.

Grace and Rick are in a *relationship*.

Like boyfriend and girlfriend.

Like together-together.

Apparently, Rick's mate died when she was young, and since Grace didn't have one, he proposed a mutually beneficial relationship.

Let me go throw up before I have to continue.

I get that Grace is a little naïve, but I didn't think she was downright blind. I know Grace believes she doesn't have a mate because she is human, but surely Rick can't be the only available option in the entire kingdom.

For the past twenty-five minutes, I've been trying to understand how someone as sweet and bubbly as Grace chose someone that douchebag Rick. He has yet to show a *single* admirable trait about himself.

It's hard, but I get rid of my plans to get rid of Rick without anyone suspecting me to focus on the meeting.

With each new agenda, Anxo pauses to ask my opinion and each time, I have to contain my surprise and stop myself from acting like a blubbering fool. I didn't think Angel would need any of my ideas or suggestions, considering he is much more experienced at running a kingdom than I am.

"What do we have on the little werewolf?"

When no one dares to blink for a solid minute, warrior Vesta flips through some papers, bracing herself for the brief. "August Trevino. Son of Alpha Trevino."

August.

I finally know my boy's name.

Clutching my hand, Angel holds it over his heart as sharp intakes of breath echo around the room. Devastation and regret overtake every face in the room and it has my heart falling to my feet. I have a horrible feeling about what this means for my boy.

Gripping the edge of the table, Hazel asks the warrior to continue, but it's hard to focus on anything over Grace sniffing quietly and Seiji rapidly tapping his foot under the table.

This is going to be really bad, isn't it?

"The crescent moon destroyed the pack in an attack four months ago. The coven reduced the entire pack to ashes, Horsemen. We found the alpha, beta, and gamma families slaughtered, along with the rest of the pack. August Trevino seems to be the sole survivor. A future alpha if he ever wishes to rebuild his pack from the ground up."

Oh, Fates.

Holding my head in my hands I try to stop the flashes of my little boy running around his ruined pack, scared out of his mind as he tries to find someone to help him.

What if he watched his parents die? What if his time in that dungeon isn't his only nightmare? Did he forget it? Repress it? What if the invisible scars on his soul never fade and turn my sweet little boy bitter over time?

I can't let revenge swallow him whole. I can't have August growing up without a sense of justice and if it means setting every hand that touched him aflame, then I'll set the fire myself. His enemies are mine now and I don't hold grudges. I seek revenge until I'm the only one left.

I start to catalog everything that might harm my monkey's physical and mental health so I can destroy it all. The torture I create for myself only breaks when a warm mouth pressing soft kisses on my knuckles brings me back to reality. "He'll be okay, sweetheart. He has you... *us.*"

Anxo is right. As long as I'm alive I won't let anything happen to him. August is safe with me.

"*Micah.* What about him?" I ask Khatri in a daze.

If there's someone other than that wretched Queen I have a score to settle with; it's him. Not only did Micah actively take part in my torture, but I know he was the one who led the attack on August's pack.

I vividly remember the day he threw that little boy in my cell and never came back. The bastard got a promotion for the successful attack and his bravery.

"We're sorry, Princess Nevaeh, but he's still in the wind. I assure you we're doing our best to find him." I manage a small smile at Khatri. He looks determined enough, so I don't push.

"Just Nevaeh is fine."

"I'll keep that in mind, Princess."

Yeah, I don't think he got my point.

"Where are we with Prince Harvey?" Grace asks.

I've noticed Grace seems pretty invested in trying to find Harvey. I don't mind her enthusiasm, not one bit, but the hint of desperation in her eyes as she waits for an answer is… *odd.*

"Close. You know how hard it is to track down a Horseman that doesn't want to be found."

"The sooner the better. We just infiltrated the biggest coven and aided in setting free their precious prisoners." The way Angel says prisoners seems to burn his throat. "There's a war brewing, so expect retaliation. Increase security measures and proof the kingdom for surprise attacks. We can't afford a single mistake."

Angel lists a couple more things that need adjusting, and everyone diligently takes notes.

"Send word to our allies who aren't involved in civil wars for possible aid. Though I'm sure we won't need it. And Khatri? Find Harvey. Fast. I need to take my mate home, where it's safe."

Is the room getting hotter?

I can't stop stealing glances at Angel under my lashes as he commands the room. His voice is firm, along with his instructions, but his hand in mine remains gentle.

"Dismissed."

Yeah… it's not the room that's hot.

As soon as everyone leaves, it becomes clear how different

this group portrays themself in front of an audience. Seiji slumps back in his seat, his goofy nature returning while Hazel drops her feet on the table, crossing them at the ankles.

"I'm hungry." Patting his stomach, Angel searches me to see if today is the day I will ask for food on my own. I haven't yet, but talking about food and eating it without any consequence is helping me slowly build an appetite.

"Can we have Chinese? I liked that tangy chicken you gave me last time."

"I was thinking pizza, but whatever you want, sweetheart."

"It's so unfair how Anxo agrees with everything that comes out of Nevaeh's mouth. He is always saying no to me for everything," I hear Seiji whisper—*not so quietly*.

"It's sweet." Grace sighs dreamily.

For the past few days, Anxo has been trying to teach me how phones work. I understand about half of what he says but he doesn't mind repeating the same thing four times.

"Of course, you think so." Rick scoffs in disgust.

Grace dejectedly busies herself on her screen, completely missing all of us glaring at Rick the dick.

I don't understand why Grace deals with this tool when he blatantly disrespects her like this. I'm all for *fighting for your love against the world*, but Rick is not worth fighting for.

I'm tempted to knock his teeth out when Angel holds me back. Leaning closer, he murmurs, "We've tried. She needs to do it herself when she's ready."

Sensing my anger, Anxo waits until I assure him I will keep my opinions and fists to myself. *For now.*

Rick pushes off his chair and I watch his every move. There's something off about him and his friend who has been silent this entire meeting but keeps fidgeting and rubbing his sweaty palms on his pants.

When Grace's worried eyes look up to check if Rick has left, I feel this intense need to let him know the kind of unhinged people his girlfriend is related to. I want him to know what will happen the next time he tries to put my sister down.

Before Rick can leave with his buddy in tow, I motion for him to stop and bend down so I can bestow him a little parting advice.

Mason, the fidgety friend who is substantially smarter than Rick, tries to leave, but Rick being the egotistical asshole he is, doesn't mind bending to my will.

Without taking my eyes off Grace, who is purposely avoiding mine, I drop my voice to a whisper. "The next time you insult my sister, I'll cut your fingers off before aiming south, understood?"

I lean back when I don't hear Rick acknowledge me and enjoy how fast the color drains from his face. Giving him my signature deranged grin, I watch his friend drag Rick away before I make good on my word.

"I'm sorry about him," Grace whispers, almost too quiet to hear over the angry voices in my head.

Then leave him.

That's what I want to say, but as if Angel read my mind, he reassures her for me, knowing whatever comes out of my mouth will be wrong timing.

Seiji clicks his tongue to get my attention. "Don't worry about Rick, he can be a real dick sometimes... Oh, who am I kidding? He's a dick, period. Not even the perfectly circumcised and ravishing kind, but the slightly crooked and weird looking one, you know when it's a little—"

Thankfully, Hazel cuts off Seiji's extremely inappropriate rant on types of male genitals by pushing his chair with her foot and making him fall back.

I would've done it myself if I wasn't too busy choking on air. I'm sure my face is flushed red, mirroring Grace, who looks ready to slip under the table to hide.

"You'll get used to filtering his words in your head," Anxo adds sympathetically.

Will I, though?

11. Do you hear voices too?

Nevaeh

G etting my little sugar monster into the bathtub was hard but getting him out is even more challenging.

While I'm still learning to take care of a toddler, the said toddler keeps adding his toys to the list of things I'm responsible for.

Lately, monkey takes his new dinosaur stuffed toy everywhere with him. The toy is clutched in his stubby fingers whether in the bath, eating, or sleeping.

Angel noticed August's obsession with the toy and my struggle to dry the soaking mess every night so August could cuddle it, and bought three lookalikes of the same toy, solving the crisis.

Ever since monkey woke up from his temporary coma, he has refused to leave my side. His anxiety doesn't let him relax unless I'm in his sight, so sharing my room was the obvious solution.

August hated it when Deviants used to drag me out of our cell and away from him. He'd sit still in a corner and wait for me to be dumped back before letting himself cry to sleep, snuggling into me.

Tonight marks three weeks of our freedom from the coven and slowly but steadily I've started to rely more on the group for things like food or entertainment.

Not trusting them after everything they've done for me and my boy feels like I'm letting my past hinder my present, and I can't let that happen.

Today, August spent the whole day in Anxo's office coloring on papers I'm sure were important.

Did Angel ask for the papers back? *Nope.*

He simply printed more and let monkey draw all the ugly, colorful patterns he wanted to his heart's content. No wonder the little guy fell asleep ten minutes into the movie he begged me to watch with those large doe eyes.

Batting his eyelashes to make us dance to his tune has become August's superpower. That's how Anxo's office belongs to August now. Good thing he took pity on Angel and let him work there too.

Seiji was running in and out of the office with every possible snack he could think of. At the end of the day, my baby burped so loud I swear people on the floor below us heard him.

Surprisingly, August got comfortable with Seiji and Anxo before he did with the girls. Considering our past, I was guessing the opposite.

With Grace, I'm pretty sure my boy is too busy being tongue-tied to form a connection. But with Hazel, even if it seemed unlikely at first, a sweet friendship has blossomed between them. Hazel has gone above and beyond to make sure August doesn't just feel comfortable but *happy* around her.

Just the other day, I walked in on the siren trying to teach August the proper stance for throwing a dagger.

Fortunately for my poor heart, she was using a wooden dagger to teach him some tricks, but the boy is *three* for fucks sake.

Looking at August now, sleeping peacefully with the toy clutched to his chest, I'm eternally grateful to be alive and able to witness him live in a safe space and be a kid again.

Three weeks of us living here also means it's been three weeks of me surviving on less than six hours of sleep. Saying I'm exhausted would be not saying enough.

I'm trying to act more like my mate and his friends, but with each day, it only becomes more clear how fucked up I am compared to them.

I can't fall asleep no matter how much I need it. I can barely stomach food twice a day, and my humor makes them uncomfortable since it usually contains words like prisoner, blood, starving, and beatings.

Grace says dark humor is how I cope with my trauma and that I don't have to filter my thoughts because soon they'll get used to my quirks as I would to theirs.

If they can put up with Seiji and Hazel, then I should be fine. I swear Angel and Grace are the only sane ones in this group.

One thing I love most about living here is Grace and her connection to Papa. One day she knocked on my door and offered to show me all the secret videos she had taken of Papa over the years.

I swear I've never wanted to cry more. Seeing his face again after so long fixed something inside me that I thought was permanently broken.

In some, he was laughing—like a full-blown belly laugh. In others, he was walking around chastising people for bowing to him. Grace captured him mostly when he was in a good mood, but his happiness looked different now.

His chin wasn't raised high enough. I noticed the way he constantly avoided eye contact with people. His shoulders droop lower than I recall, and his smile doesn't make the corner of his eyes crinkle like it used to.

I couldn't stop the tears when he blew the candle on a small cupcake for his birthday and started tearing up in between laughing. It was like his facade slipped without his permission, and I didn't recognize that man at all.

Each video helped me get familiar with who he is now and made me hate myself for not remembering more of the happier version.

If Grace saw me secretly wiping my tears, she didn't comment on it. Locking her arm with mine, she distracted me with the story of when Papa told her touching a boy who was not your mate could give you a nasty infection.

Two years later, a 15-year-old Grace was terrified when Seiji hugged her. She spent *weeks* worried about getting infected before she confronted Papa. The man wasn't even sorry. Just sad his lie didn't hold for a couple more years.

I silently laugh to myself as I walk around the penthouse in the dead hours of the night. Since I can't fall asleep, this has become my nightly routine.

After a while, I return to my room to kill some time before sunrise. Planting myself on the couch nestled in the corner of my room I pick up the storybook Grace likes to read to August and flip through it.

Waking up screaming after a nightmare has not been an option ever since monkey decided to share my room.

At this point, I can feel the exhaustion seep into my bones. Maybe I should ask Anxo to keep a watch while I rest, so I won't accidentally kill everyone in my sleep.

'Are you trying to hide, little girl?'

A pressure on my throat startles me awake. My hands lift to get out of the tight grip before I remember the chokehold is invisible.

Not again.

The longer I take to break out of my daze the harder it gets to breathe and slowly the sound of my broken gasps fills the room.

Fuck, I can't wake August. If he thinks we're not safe here and sees me panicking like this, it will ruin all his progress.

I force my legs to move but they're shaking so violently I have to slide down to the floor so I can blindly crawl to the door. My whole body is paralyzed with fear as I drag it until my head bumps into the doorframe. With trembling fingers, I try to pry the door open, and it takes me two tries before I succeed.

As soon as the dim light from the hallway pours in, I crawl outside and softly shut the door behind me.

With silent tears running down my face and my heart beating in my head, I lean against the door. I waited to make sure I didn't wake anyone before I let myself break. Once I'm sure I'm not ruining anyone's night, I don't stop the tears but muffle my sobs behind my hands.

I know what bottling my panic can do to me, and if

trembling with sobs for a few hours will save me from completely losing it later, then I've learned to be okay with it.

I can still *feel* his sticky touch on me, his breath fanning my neck as he carved my thigh. The memory is so fresh in my head I can practically see it happening before me. The way his face twisted in shame when I refused his command in front of the Queen. The promise I saw in his eyes that later became my worst nightmare.

I don't know how long it takes my body to stop shaking, but now there's only a faint ringing in my head instead of the constant hammering.

When my broken wails fade and only a tightening in my chest remains, I use the doorframe to rise from the floor. The dark, quiet night helps me melt into the background without anyone having a front-row seat to my epic meltdown.

Back in the living room, I sit on the couch numbly for half an hour, as I try to hold on to my reality.

Stuffed between the cushions, I find the remote and start scrolling through rows of movies with no intention of actually watching anything.

Heavy footsteps break me out of my mindless scrolling and I turn to find Angel searching the room, rubbing his eye with his fist. He looks adorable if I ignore how he only has sweatpants on and his upper body is bare.

I've seen the markings on his arms before, but I didn't expect most of his chest and abdomen to be covered in unique patterns and writings.

Before I can figure out why he's up at this hour, Angel startles me by sitting on the couch before he lies down with his head on my lap, arms around my waist.

Angel sleepily nuzzles my stomach, and I tell myself this is not the time to hesitate. Burying my fingers in his soft curls, I comb through the mess.

"Why aren't you in bed, sweetheart?" His voice is muffled with his head pressed against me. I've been sitting here for an hour waiting for the numbness to fade, but not even a minute with my mate, and my muscles lose their tension.

"Couldn't sleep." I curse in my head when my voice breaks a little.

"Another nightmare?" His arms squeeze me tighter like he's trying to glue himself to me.

More like another dark memory.

Angel turns his head in my lap to face the TV. "What are we watching?"

He's staying?

"I don't know. I couldn't figure it out. Is Frozen good?" I hand him the remote when he waves for it.

"It's the best, baby." Angel shifts on his side so his back is pressed against the sofa. "Come here," He lifts his arm for me to slide in.

"You should sleep, Anxo."

I move closer anyway, unable to resist the offer. Pressing my back against his warm, naked chest, I let him pull me closer until I'm using his arm as my pillow.

"So should you."

My memories are still playing tricks on me, but now that I've had some time to settle down, I want to clarify one thing. I know I can't keep it to myself anymore... not after I've seen how vulnerable I can.

I need to trust someone to protect my kid when I can't.

"August. I can't—I *won't* leave him."

I'm not sure if Angel would want such a huge responsibility when he's so young himself, but August is mine now. He chose me on his first night in that dungeon, and that same night I swore to choose him over everything and everyone.

Just thinking about life without Anxo leaves a bad taste in my mouth, but my love and loyalty for that little boy trumps the possibility of a broken heart.

Angel intertwines our fingers beside my stomach and kisses the back of my head. "I knew it was a package deal from the day I saw you holding him in those woods. Anyone with eyes can see how attached you both are, and it's not just you, sweetheart. I adore that kid to no end. August needs stability, a family, and we can give that to him. I *want* to give that to him."

"You do? You want him to stay with us? Forever?"

"Of course I do. You are my whole world, sweetheart. Anything you want, I'll make it happen."

"I'm so glad you found us." His hold tightens when my voice cracks.

Taking the soft blanket hanging on the back of the sofa, Angel drapes it over us. His arms hold me hostage as his face nuzzles my neck, leaving reminders of his presence with sweet kisses.

In the safety of his arms and the gentle hum of our Divine singing, I fall asleep with a smile on my face. Not a single thought spared on what might come next.

I wake up hours later, and for the first time, it's not to the sound of my own screaming, my nails digging into my arms, or opening my eyes to find myself in an abandoned cell where the walls are soaked with my blood.

I wake up to him.

Sweet kisses peppering all over my face bring a sleepy smile to my lips. My eyes slowly flutter open to find Angel crouched on the floor before me, softly running a hand through my hair, coaxing me into waking up.

Sleep slowly leaves me when I see his soft chestnut curls neatly styled and still wet from his shower. Angel looks ready to start his morning in a fitted white dress shirt and black pants.

I miss the soft sweater look, but formal shirts on him are equally drool-worthy.

"Morning beautiful," he whispers, fingers playing with a strand of my hair. My eyes fall to his other hand lying idly beside my stomach, so I grab it with mine.

"Morning Angel."

I don't mind letting the endearment slip anymore. It never fails to bring my favorite dimpled smile to his lips so that's a bonus.

"Time to wake up, baby. I'm taking you out for a drive around the city, so go freshen up. And yes, I promise to buy you all the junk food you want."

With that, Anxo disappears to ask Seiji if he'll keep August busy for the day, not before kissing both my cheeks and savoring the blush his gesture brings.

I rush to my room, only getting lost three times. By the time I leave the bathroom, Angel is lying in the center of my bed, not caring about wrinkling his clothes.

"You take awfully long showers, sweetheart. I was—"

Anxo stops short when his eyes land on me... in nothing but a small towel covering the basics. For a second, it doesn't dawn on me. I'm clueless about his lack of words until I follow his gaze to the scars littering my arms and shoulders and cold dread washes over me.

Fuck. When did I become this careless? How did I forget about the scars consuming me whole like they've always been a part of me.

My hands start to shake next to my thighs, and I'm sure I look like I'm about to pass out. I want to turn around and lock myself in the bathroom, but I can't do that to myself. I'm not going to hide.

This is me.

My scars, flaws, and dark humor included.

This body has kept me upright long after my will to survive was broken. These scars are reminders of what I've been through and *survived.*

I won't let anyone—not even myself, piss on that.

When I finally let my eyes meet his, Angel beckons me closer with his arm outstretched. I let him guide me to sit on his thigh and wrap a hand around my waist to keep me steady.

Raising my chin with his index finger, Angel forces me to acknowledge the raw admiration and adoration he has for me.

He doesn't have to do anything but hold me like this, looking at me as if I'm the reason he is breathing, and every wall I've built around my heart falls over brick by brick.

"This is me." I'm proud of the conviction in my voice. I'm not going to let my past and insecurities lead my future. He deserves more than that. *We* deserve more than that.

"*Magnificent.* You are magnificent."

There's an aggressive determination in his voice like he is challenging me to think any differently. Like he would fight me and anyone else who dared say otherwise.

Leaning forward, Angel softly kisses the corner of my mouth—dangerously close to my lips, which leaves me wanting a little more.

Tucking a wet strand behind my ear, his eyes gaze at me so intensely that I feel stupid for thinking he of all people would ridicule me about my scars. All I've ever felt in his presence is safe and comfortable.

Anxo deserves every ounce of my trust, and I'm determined to give it to him.

"How?" When I don't understand, Angel rephrases. "We heal phenomenally well, sweetheart." *Oh.*

"Cutting open healing wounds is more painful than creating new ones. They started slicing over my old scars when I ran out of skin."

Angel is quiet as his fingers trace every scar they can reach on my thighs while he kisses the ones on my bare shoulder.

"Those bastards are going to die a painful death."

The promise in his voice *melts* me. For someone who hates inflicting more harm than necessary, Angel is willing to kill for me. *How romantic.*

"We could do it together! But you said you're taking me out for junk food. Let's do that first." I beam.

Angel chuckles, softly tracing my smile with his thumb. "Mhm… get dressed, and I'll take you."

"You're here to make sure I don't get lost again, aren't you?"

"What was that? I think Seiji is calling me. Go get ready,

baby." Anxo ushers me to my closet and hands me something before I can shut the door.

"Another one?" I feel like my heart is about to beat out of my chest when he hands me another one of his hoodies. I don't think he has any left in his wardrobe anymore.

"Last one, sweetheart. You've got to stop stealing from me."

"You gave me the first three of your own free will!"

"What about the other five?" He points to the shelf in my closet stacked with his hoodies. I not-so-discreetly close the door with my foot.

Time to accept my faults...

"August did that. He loves hugging me when I wear your clothes, so *he* took them from your closet and left them here. Strange kid, I tell you."

I quickly dodge past him and hide in the closet before Anxo can catch me. When I hear a thunderous laugh behind me, I open the door an inch to see his head thrown back and his hand clutching his stomach, looking as yummy as ever.

If being a moron means I get to be the reason behind his laugh, I'll be a moron for the rest of my life.

Dressing up in his comfy black hoodie, I pull on a pair of black shorts that disappear under the hoodie.

I have more than a few zagged marks on my thighs and calves from the wounds that healed poorly. Normally I would hide them, but I feel slightly more confident now that Angel has seen them and didn't even blink. Not one negative comment or expression.

It bothers me a tiny bit when people gawk at them, but in this penthouse, I'm around my mate and friends. And none of them have ever made me feel anything but welcome to be myself.

Maybe it's time to stop hiding this part of myself from them. I can't control what happened to me, but I *can* control how I let it affect my life moving on.

When I leave the closet, Anxo groans loudly, scanning me with a strange look in his eyes. I'm about to ask what's wrong when he makes a beeline for me and wraps me in his arms, dropping his head on my shoulder.

"Fates, are you trying to kill me? How am I supposed to share you with the world when you look like *this*?"

Mister Sunshine turned Grumpy Pants.

Angel is lucky I have such a strong Divine or this man would've broken my back by how he is leaning his weight on me.

"Okay, cuddly bear, I like you a lot, but I'm not missing fried food because you don't want to share me." I rub his back like he does to make him feel better and kiss his cheek twice.

Angel reluctantly lets me step back and lead him to wherever the fuck our dining room is supposed to be. But he doesn't stop grumbling until I ask if he wants to repeat how we cuddled last night since it helped me sleep better. He was suddenly very eager for the day to end.

It's good to know last night was important for him too, because after being in arms once, I don't think I can ever spend a night without him wrapped around me.

12. Kissing makes us official right?

Nevaeh

I never thought I would love driving around in a car this much. I've always been a horse girl, but aimlessly driving around a sparkling city with thundering clouds following us is captivating.

Rolling down the window, I relish how the cool air damp with tiny droplets of rain feels on my face.

With every corner we turn, Angel tells me a different story of Seiji causing havoc in the human realm. Or the time Hazel stabbed someone who Grace had to patch up—after profusely apologizing for her friend's wild behavior, of course.

I watch the sparkle in Angel's eyes or the way his goofy grin never leaves his lips as he tells me those stories. Angel clearly finds damage control amusing if none of these incidents made him even remotely angry.

I wonder if he has the same smile on his lips when he talks about me.

I'm busy carving Angel's essence into memory when he slows down at the drive-through of my favorite fast-food joint, and my heart soars at the gesture.

When Angel rattles off my order without asking, I bite my tongue before I do something stupid… like jump across the console and kiss him.

I think I just might.

I'm tearing open the heavy bag the moment it's dropped into my lap. The delicious smell of french fries floods the car.

I'm stumped when I see Angel has ordered at least two days' worth of snacks. I still have trouble eating large portions of meals, but almost everything I eat these days stays inside.

Angel calls it progress.

"Woah... sugar daddy?"

Angel throws his head back and his carefree laugh rattles the car. He barely manages to park the car between two white lines because of how hard he is laughing.

"Shut up, you fool." He chuckles, turning the car off. Thunder and wind flapping outside become more evident with the engine shut.

"Just Daddy, then?" I wiggle my eyebrows at my pretty Angel, and it earns me more of that husky laugh I love being responsible for.

Flicking my nose playfully, he says, "Keep it PG-13, sweetheart."

Sobering up, Angel turns to face me, giving me the perfect view of his face. I just want to squish his cheeks and eat him up.

Lately, I've been embracing what Seiji likes to call 'my inner whore', and it wants me to glue myself to Angel at all times.

Taking the bag from me, Anxo starts feeding both of us. I've gotten better with forks, spoons, and even chopsticks with Seiji's help, but Angel still insists on feeding me himself. Not that I mind being the center of his attention. *Or his world.*

Reaching into the small compartment before me, Angel pulls out a pack of sour candies, dropping them in my lap. Judging by his self-satisfied grin Angel knows he has successfully discovered my recent obsession.

"I think I'm going to ugly cry."

I'm genuinely holding back tears as I pout at him. Something as simple as a bag of sour candies and fries, and I'm close to tears. I blame Angel for being so good to me and overcompensating for all the years I had nothing by giving me everything now.

"That's impossible. You're never ugly." He leans forward to kiss my forehead.

"Even when I eat like nobody has fed me in years?" Fiddling with his fingers, I lean my head sideways on the seat.

"Especially not then."

Another kiss on the tip of my nose.

I'm definitely going to ugly cry now.

We settle in comfortable silence with him feeding me. I have a feeling Angel wants to ask me something but for some reason, he's hesitating.

"So, I have a question." Here we go. I wait for him to continue, but his nerves pick up again. "Promise me you won't get mad." Holding out his pinkie finger, Angel refuses to talk until I loop mine around his and make a promise.

"I can't get mad at you, Angel. I've tried."

"What—When?"

"That day when you took my sweatshirt."

"First of all, *my* sweatshirt. And second, I was washing it *for you.*"

"Tomato-potato."

"That's not how you use it." Shaking his head, he snickers, and I sit back and enjoy the heartwarming view that is him. *My mate.*

When we conclude that I genuinely can't stay mad at his adorable face, he finally blurts out. "Did you ever think Harvey was your mate?"

"Nope."

He blinks at my immediate response. "That sure?"

Swallowing my last piece of fry, I wipe the non-existent oil from my fingers with a tissue.

"Harvey was my best friend when I was two and will be when I'm 222. From the first day Papa told us about mates, we knew we weren't that for each other. And it was perfect this way. Having mates other than each other meant more people in our lonely 2-person circle."

"So, you wanted a mate right? You were waiting for me, too?"

I nod. "Ask Harvey when we find him. I was the girl waving around her papa's scythe that was twice my size to scare boys away because they weren't my mate."

"Keep talking and I'll marry you right here."

I snort loudly. Before Angel can say he's joking, heavy rain suddenly claps against the car's roof. I'm instantly captivated by it's ferocity.

This is the first time I've seen rain in a decade. Every time I watched it on screen in the last month, I longed to experience the feel of it on my skin.

Thinking about rain and movies, a thought strikes me.

"Hey!" My sudden enthusiasm jolts Angel from the unexpected attack on his ears.

"Sorry, Angel. But do you know how to dance—the slow dance thing they do on TV? You know when they hold each other and slowly sway. Sometimes they spin too, like—"

"I'm aware, sweetheart. I had to take classes when I was younger," he admits rather bashfully. I don't see what's there to be embarrassed about.

"That sounds amazing!"

"It was *torture,* baby. I was constantly teased about it. But no matter what I said my mother didn't let me quit."

Why wouldn't his mother let him quit? Who pushes their kid to do something they're not comfortable doing? I want to ask more about his blood family, but Angel has cunningly evaded that topic for weeks.

"What if I asked you to dance with me? You can say no. I don't want it to bring back bad memories." I want to dance with him in the rain. I love it when it happens in the movies, but I don't want to pressure him.

"I'd love to. What better time to show off my skills." I squeeze his fingers entangled in mine and wait to make sure he's doing this because *he* wants to and not because I asked.

I leap out of my seat when I don't find a hint of discomfort or uncertainty. I'm so excited to feel the rain on my skin that I quickly get out, and to my delight, I'm immediately drenched.

Angry black clouds with purple lightning shadow the sky above me. Our only source of light is the near-empty store behind us and the headlight of Angels' car.

Spinning in a circle, I spread my hands beside me. My trance breaks when two strong arms wrap around my waist and pull me against a wet chest. Glancing back at the breathtaking man behind me, I love the way his carefree smile breaks free, making him look younger and wilder.

The warm yellow light from the car lands on half of his face, giving him an angelic glow, with raindrops falling down his chin. *My Angel.*

"Lean on me, sweetheart." Turning around, Angel guides my arms around his neck and sways us until we are moving to his rhythm.

Taking a step back, Angel holds our twisted fingers above my head and spins me until I'm dizzy and laughing like a child before crushing me to his chest.

His fingers trace my arms and neck before spreading over my cheeks. Angel tilts my face closer to him, our noses brushing against each other, and his lips a thread away from mine. My breath hitches at our proximity, and my hold on his neck tightens.

"I really want to kiss you, sweetheart. May I?" He murmurs against my lips.

If I wasn't melting before, I sure am now.

His chest is pressed against mine as his thumb wipes the water droplets from my lower lip. His gentle touch is too much and not enough at the same time.

"Please do."

Everyone talks about feeling those fireworks that come with being with the right person and how two people who are made for each other feel electric in each other's presence... but when Angel's soft lips meet mine, all I feel is *calm.*

This is what—*who,* I've been craving my whole life.

Standing in an empty parking lot, drenched to the bone with lightning booming above us, all I feel is Angel's hands on my body and his soft lips moving against mine.

I feel at peace. All my prayers begging Fates for mercy are finally answered because they gave me Anxo.

My Angel. *My peace.*

Cupping my face, he pulls me closer to deepen the kiss, and I have to stretch on my toes to meet him. Curling my fingers in his wet hair, I gasp when Angel unexpectedly bites my lower lip.

My gasp allows him to slide his hot tongue into my mouth, teasing and tasting me feverishly. A rush of desire runs down my spine and I can't stop the moan that escapes me. Angel captures the sound before the world can hear it.

When Angel pulls back, I whine in protest. "More please."

His gruff chuckle is cut short when I grab his face and smash our lips together again. Fisting his hair, I tug him closer, his addictive taste making it impossible to stay away.

Angel traces the shape of my jaw with a feather-light touch that makes me shiver. When his palm wraps around my throat like a necklace and squeezes the sides, I lose the last thread of my control. Arching my back, I moan when his other hand finds my lower back to press me tighter against his chiseled abdomen.

I lean back to breathe, but Angel doesn't like the idea, and with an impatient groan, his head follows me, attacking my lips passionately.

Every stroke of his tongue, every nibble on my lips, every squeeze on my neck spreads another wave of desire from my head to my toes.

We stay like that for a long time, kissing like it's our last day and drowning in our newfound intimacy. I memorize every touch, every sound, every trace of his fingers, and where they linger the most.

Angel reluctantly moves away, but not before pecking my lips three more times. His forehead drops on mine as we pant heavily, trying to catch our breath. My heart is thumping in my head, and when I open my eyes, my heart skips a beat entirely seeing his eyes glow.

A ring of gold dances around his emerald orbs, resembling the sun, trying to peek around the ashy clouds to steal glances at the majestic rain. When I go to point it out, the glow dims until only his magnetic green remains.

This proves no matter how much I try to shove my Divine in a corner, it will always find a way to connect to Angel... its other half.

"I've wanted to do that for so long," Angel rasps softly, as if afraid to break the delicacy of the moment.

"I've been waiting, too."

Angel grins devilishly with those perfect rosy lips, brushing a strand of my hair back with the same hand that was wrapped around my throat a minute ago. The flickering thought has me turning bright red, but fortunately, I'm already red in the face.

"Come on, let's get you home before you catch a cold—and before you mention being a superior species and recovering faster, I don't want to see you sick at all."

How did he know I was going to play the Divine card?

Gently dragging me to the passenger side, Angel opens the door, but I don't get in. I don't want to get in the car and go back to how it was. I want more than what we had before. I don't want to move on from this. *From us.*

A kiss on my nose softens me. Angel grips my chin to make me look at him instead of his shoes.

"Nothing will change if you get in, baby. I promise to kiss you all day, every day, for the rest of my life." This time when Angel kisses me, he takes his sweet time to prove this doesn't end here.

Taking his warm face between my cold palms, I return his kiss with equal fervor and softness before letting him usher me into the car.

Our goofy smiles stay in place the entire ride back to the hotel, as we keep glancing at each other and giggling like teenagers. Angel doesn't move his hand from my thigh, and I lace our fingers together so he can't even if he tried to.

I used to think that after all I've lost, it's easier for me to start over and expect the worst, but after tonight, I know if I ever lose Angel... *I won't survive.*

13. My virgin eyes!

Nevaeh

I t's been two months since Angel kissed me in the pouring rain for the first time.

He didn't lie when he promised the kisses wouldn't stop. Anxo kisses me all the time now, whether in passing or throughout the nights we spend cuddling in his room or whenever he feels like it.

That night, we returned to the hotel looking like drenched rats and smiling like two lovesick idiots. The group caught one glance at our flaming red cheeks and intertwined hands, and it's safe to say we were teased relentlessly.

Seiji kept making kissing sounds every time he saw us together. Hazel made a short film about *safe sex*, only for me to run away within the first two minutes.

It was gruesome.

Thankfully, Seiji assured me the siren was only messing with me, and that's *not* how real sex works.

Some days, I really hate that tailless creature.

"I don't think we'll need backup." Angel thinks out loud, bringing me back to the present.

"Look at the *muscles* on this man!" Seiji shrieks like a fucking banshee. *Again.*

"But we'll have to be careful. We can't risk exposing that the Horsemen are in the human realm. Too many will think it's the perfect opportunity to corner us." Grace warns.

"The *tattoos!*"

"Can Khatri stay with August? I don't trust anyone—" Seiji cuts me off like he's been doing this entire time.

"Grey fucking eyes!"

"SHUT UP, SEIJI!" Everyone roars in sync, frustrated by his constant wailing.

"You don't understand! He looks like *that* and has *tattoos*, and OH MY FATES!!" Seiji continues to screech about how unfair life is.

I don't understand why he is going off the rails. Yes, my best friend is somewhat good-looking, but not enough to make a man completely lose his shit.

"It's the same *every. single. time* he finds someone attractive, and they're not gay or his mate. Suddenly it's the end of the fucking world." Hazel ignores Seiji's meltdown like an expert, tossing another grape in the air and catching it with her mouth.

"Oh, mama, I'm in love with a criminal..."

And now the princess is staring out the window and singing his heart out like he's in a breakup music video.

It's always way too dramatic with this guy.

Angel bangs his head on the table, grumbling that his friend needs to find his mate soon. Swatting the back of his head, I warn him to stop and rub the slightly red skin on his forehead.

"You guys are so cute," Grace sighs dreamily, shifting to rest her head on Hazel's shoulder, before realizing at the last second who she's sitting next to and backing off.

"It's disgusting, and I want you both to stop."

"Thank you for the kind words, Hazel." Angel grabs my hand before standing. "Time to get ready. It's a long drive, and I don't want to miss Harvey."

So we found Harvey...

Khatri barged in this morning with pictures of my best friend exiting an exclusive ghoul club an hour and a half away from the city. The Warriorhead is certain Harvey visits the club every two days at the same time to ask around for information on the coven.

In the last few weeks, the absence of information on Harvey had started to weigh heavy on my chest. I was slowly slipping from my present to darker times. To help me escape my head, the group made it their mission to keep me occupied with different activities. Angel stayed close by, constantly worried my anxiety would explode into something uncontrollable.

Their worry and concern initially made me uncomfortable and suspicious, but it didn't take them long to show me that this is what families do.

Stick around and lift each other.

In my two months living with them, they've managed to get under my skin. I don't know when, but they've become my safety net. And to think, there was a time I hesitated to call them friends.

"Another Horsemen... *jolly.*" Hazel squints at Harvey's picture as if trying to dig out his deepest, darkest secrets.

From what I've seen, Harvey has changed a lot... physically speaking. Now hc looks like a wall of muscles with those broad shoulders and biceps three times what they used to be.

The permanent bags under his eyes that I'm so used to seeing are nowhere to be found. He looks *healthy.*

Once the last detail is hashed out, Grace drags me away from Angel by my hand and orders Hazel to follow.

When the tiny Bookkeeper declares she will be dressing us up tonight, both Hazel and I exchange a wide-eyed look over her head. According to Grace, we don't know what dressing fancy means, and *she* is the only one who can save us from ourselves.

I don't understand what's wrong with me wearing my mate's hoodie. His scent keeps me from gutting people.

I've been patiently sitting on this chair for the last twenty minutes. I can't even feel my butt anymore. But every time I gather the strength to open my mouth, Grace shoots me a look that makes me quickly shut it back.

I don't think I'm supposed to piss off someone poking my face with sticks and brushes. Grace might look harmless, but she has the mean streak of a fiery black woman.

I didn't know someone as sweet could be so damn scary.

Ruffling through her closet, Grace pulls out three dress

bags and Hazel decides this is the hill she wants to die on by immediately protesting.

"If you put me in a dress, I'm not above stabbing you."

With hands on her hips, Grace asks, "Why are you against dresses again?"

"Where do I even start? Oh, I know—they're impractical. How the fuck am I supposed to kick someone without worrying about flashing my underwear?"

"Why do you think you'll have to kick someone?"

"Oh, Gracie." With a patient breath, Hazel changes tactics. "Okay... if you can find something other than a dress, I swear on Lucifer, I'll give it an honest shot."

When Grace starts cackling like a maniac, I know Hazel is not coming on top of this. By the evil glint in her eyes, I know my sister came prepared. Grace has Hazel right where she wants her.

The siren pales at the sight of a sophisticated black jumpsuit with a delicate golden chain around the middle.

Kicking and stomping, Hazel tries on the outfit. To check the fabric's flexibility she swiftly kicks down a poor vase that was proudly sitting on a high shelf. When the dress doesn't restrict her movement, Hazel reluctantly agrees to wear it.

The chain around the waist makes it easier for Hazel to hide a fancy dagger in plain sight which seals the deal.

Grace flutters her nonexistent wings when Hazel begrudgingly admits she won't mind having a similar outfit at hand for when she can't wear her trademark pantsuit with an armored corset.

I haven't seen any of them in their traditional clothes yet, but judging by how Grace keeps gushing over them, I can't wait for that day.

Trying her best to be gentle, Grace takes on the task of styling my hair. While brushing my stubborn waves she casually mentions cutting them and the out-of-the-blue statement catches me off guard. The aggressive *no* that leaves my mouth is pure instinct.

I feel Grace flinch behind me. When I'm sure she'll leave and never look back, Grace continues to brush my hair, effectively ignoring my freak-out.

"Breathe, Nevaeh. It was just a suggestion. I'm not cutting them now, just styling."

I apologize to Grace for startling her who brushes it off, not expecting an explanation. Unlike Hazel, who keeps annoyingly tapping her foot, waiting for me to start talking.

Sharky is too nosey for someone who doesn't even share her chips with me.

With my sister's fingers carefully running through my hair and Hazel sitting still beside me, it feels a little easier to let the words loose.

"Visha loved to use my hair against me. This is the first time I don't have random bald patches with how hard she used to pull on them. I'm so close to finally having an even length. I just... I don't want to lose this." My voice is timid in the end. I close my eyes and soak in how good it feels to say this out loud.

"No one is cutting it all, honey. I love your hair. I was thinking of a little trim, so it's healthier and has a nice shape."

That doesn't sound so bad. Not bad at all.

"So, I don't have to cut a lot?"

"Nothing more than a couple of inches." I finally agree because healthier and a better shape sounds so good.

Grace squeals, "We'll make a girls' day out of it. Face masks, spa, and wine."

"As long as there's wine, I'm in." Hazel chimes in.

Maybe drunk Hazel will be more willing to spill merfolk secrets. This woman loves torturing me with the lack of information, but I will get it out of her one day.

Hazel is next on the chair to get her hair and make-up done. Grace promises to keep it light and only adds a shiny power that makes Hazel look like a light bulb.

In a good way, of course.

I stand behind my sister the whole time, trying to remember the steps so I can practice them later.

Before starting on her makeup, Grace hands me a dress. I'm immediately doubtful seeing the way the material is scrunched up in a ball. When I don't move, Grace assures me it's supposed to look like that, and it will fit.

Escaping to the bathroom, I squeeze myself into a dress that quickly takes on the shape of my body. Looking at myself in the mirror, I instantly fall in love with how it looks.

The black bodycon dress has full sleeves and a somewhat deep V-neck with a Criss-cross cut on my abdomen, revealing a patch of my stomach. The dress hugs my body perfectly, a perfect mixture of sexy and classy.

The hem reaches mid-thigh, and it's a good thing the sheer stockings beneath stop my scars from stealing all the attention.

Stepping closer to the mirror, I admire how Grace used neutral shades to highlight my features and the shimmering glitter on my cheekbones and eyelids.

When she asked me to choose a lip color, I asked for the cherry lip balm because the matte texture of the lipstick felt too dry. My long hair falls over my shoulder in soft, defined curls. I can practically hear them cry in relief that, finally, someone is treating them nicely.

When I leave the bathroom, Hazel is sitting on the bed scrolling through her phone, and Grace has just put her hairbrush down. Grace squeals when she turns toward me, and Hazel forgets to close her mouth.

"You look so pretty!" Grace quickly wipes a tear before it ruins her perfectly done makeup.

"Your Angel is going to eat you alive tonight." Hazel wiggles her brows at me mischievously.

"Yeah? Let's talk about how good *you* look."

"Coming!" Before I can fluster her back, Hazel runs out the door. So, she can make a video about the weirdest sex to exist but can't take a compliment?

Focusing on Grace, I take in how good she looks in the champagne bodycon dress with tiny stones embellished all over it. The sweetheart neckline reveals her sharp collarbones and sleeves that flare around her arms.

"*Honeybunch*, you look like an ancient goddess."

Grace ducks her head, hiding her smile. The only reason her face isn't all red is because of her caramel skin tone. But the way she flusters can't be missed.

"Really? You don't think it's too short, or the neck is too low —"

"Hey," I grip her shoulders and wait for her to get out of her head. "Do you like how you look?" Grace answers with a shy nod. "That's the most important thing. As long as you feel comfortable and beautiful, don't overthink it, okay?"

I can only imagine the bullshit Rick must've fed her. It must be hard to shut his comments in her head, but I promise to squash her inner thoughts whenever I'm near.

Rick coming with us today isn't helping her nerves, either. Even when no one asked him, Rick insisted on coming for *security reasons*.

Security reasons, my ass. The bastard just wants to keep an eye on Grace.

Grace agreed before Anxo could shoo him away, and that was the end. I'm desperately waiting for the day she leaves Rick so I can settle the score with his pathetic ass.

"What about my hair? Should I leave it naturally? I've never done that before," Grace asks, fixing her naturally feisty hair pulled into a high ponytail, which puffs out with tight curls.

"It looks perfect. I love this look way more than when you try to tame them."

After a much-needed hype session, we leave her room to meet the rest of our wild group. I find Seiji in the kitchen helping August with his dinner, so I'll have one less thing to do before I put him to bed.

So thoughtful.

Seiji is a genius when it comes to fashion. Tonight, he stands in a sheer black shirt with solid black roses scattered on it. The sheer material of the shirt draws attention to his abs before you notice the leather pants it's loosely tucked into. For a finishing touch, he picked black boots to tie the outfit together.

"Look at you... you look so handsome, princess!" Turning at the sound of my voice, Seiji beams at the compliment.

I bend to kiss monkey's head while he stuffs himself full of spaghetti, ignoring the sauce on his collar. This boy feeds his clothes just as much as he feeds himself.

"Why thank you, pretty lady. You look quite fabulous yourself. I like you in your oversized mate clothes... but this? I *love*." Taking my hand, Seiji spins me once, and with a wink, he moves on to Grace.

Hazel pretends to gag when Grace and Seiji start to shower each other with compliments. Monkey laughs so hard at her silly antics, that he almost falls off his chair before I catch him.

I'm disappointed the man I was hoping to impress is nowhere in sight. Guess I'll have to wait a little longer to blow his mind.

Helping monkey off the chair, I lead him back to my room and put on a robe so I can scrub the spaghetti sauce off him and get him to bed. With a storybook in my hand, I don't even finish the second page before he doses off, cuddling his stuffed dinosaur.

Caressing his hair, I wait until August is soundly asleep before quietly leaving the room. For precaution, I leave the door slightly ajar so Khatri will be able to hear if something was wrong. August isn't prone to nightmares like I am but that doesn't mean I'm not worried his current state of calm is fragile.

Turning around, I freeze coming face to face with my mate. Leaning back against a wall with his arms crossed, Angel stares me down.

Motherfucking shitballs.

I quickly swipe under my chin to make sure I'm not drooling. Angel looks ravishing in a sleek black suit with silver sparkling vertical lines over it and a black dress shirt underneath.

The top three buttons are undone, giving me a perfect view of those hypnotizing markings on his chest. The way his shirt fits him, outlining those delicious muscles, should be criminal.

The jacket curls around his biceps and shoulders like sin. I have this strange urge to smooth my hands over the material of his pants to feel his well-defined thighs. Just the thought has me clenching my own thighs in desperate need of *something*.

I'm so busy admiring him that it takes me a minute to realize Angel is doing the same. His eyes roam over me, lips slightly parted like he is forcing himself to breathe. I want to squirm under his heated gaze, but my body loves the attention too much to move.

"I'm assuming you like it?" I ask, moving closer until I can loop my arms around his neck. I can't help but kiss his jaw. He looks irresistible tonight.

As my kiss startles him out of his daze, Angel immediately pulls me closer by gripping my hips. Eyes filled with longing trace every curve and dip in my body.

Suddenly I'm very aware of the material sticking to my skin. Or how I wouldn't mind if it accidentally slipped.

"You look *delicious*, sweetheart. Let me show you just how much I appreciate my gorgeous mate." Hovering over me, Angel smashes our lips together and I moan as soon as we touch.

The intensity of the kiss is unlike any before. Tonight, Angel isn't holding back from devouring me. He swiftly turns us around so I'm pressed between the wall and him. When his hips thrust against me, I feel his need for me in the form of a hard bulge poking my lower stomach.

Angel pulls away abruptly but before I can complain, his lips are attacking my neck. Alternating between soft kisses, passionate sucking, and desperate bites making my whimpers and moans louder with each touch.

"Oh... oh... *my virgin eyes*! Stop it, you horn dogs!" A sudden screech startles us enough to snap our heads in its direction.

I snicker when I see Seiji running away, screaming about how we ruined his innocence. Unfortunately, his interruption breaks the spell and we finally remember the world around us.

Huff irately, Angel drops his head on my shoulder. "I'll finish what I started, my sweet girl. Promise." Whispering into my neck, he lightly sucks at the skin there before grabbing my hand to walk us downstairs.

A short goodbye to Khatri turns into him assuring Angel and me that he can handle a sleeping toddler before he all but shoves us inside the elevator.

When we get to the parking lot, everyone is already settled into their car. Seiji, Grace, Hazel, and Rick are taking a separate car while Angel and I take one, so we'll have an extra vehicle in an emergency.

For the first half-hour on the road, I can't stop anxiously twisting and turning the rings of Angel's fingers. His paw of a hand slips under the hem of my dress, rubbing soft circles on my thigh where my stockings begin.

I can sense the silence is bothering Angel, but he doesn't push me to talk, even when my unease lingers in the air, choking us.

"You're awfully fond of my rings, sweetheart. Maybe I should buy you your own."

"No, I'll probably twist my fingers off and break them," I reply absently. Looking through the windshield, I count every white car I see to stay in the moment.

"But you have no problem twisting *mine*?"

"Nope."

It's not my fault his hands are always so warm and familiar. But tonight, even with my guardian angel beside me I can't stop the horrors of my past from replaying in my head.

Ever since we found Harvey, my mind has been playing cruel tricks on me, trying to convince me he wouldn't want anything to do with me after everything he went through *because of me*. What if I'm nothing but a living reminder of his horrible past?

"This is all your fault."

No.

"He is lying in a pool of his blood because of you—because you insist on being a weak little girl." She grabs my hair in a tight fist *and I taste blood in my mouth. "Always crying for daddy when you know he won't be coming. No one is coming, and it's all your fault."*

Please stop.

"D-don't listen to him, monkey. None... none of this is your fault."

Harvey is in so much pain. They hurt his back because he gave me his bread. Again. This is all my fault.

It was always my fault. Always.

"I'm sorry Harvey. I'm so s-sorry," I sob into her hold, but she doesn't let me go to him.

"Close your eyes, monkey," Harvey gasps just before the evil witch lashes his back again.

"Don't you dare look away little girl, or I'll do worse to you. You don't want me to call Micah, do you?"

I shiver in fear at his name. I don't want him to come.

I can't breathe.

"It's all right. We are all right." Harvey gasps out before falling asleep. *They always wait for him to fall asleep before punishing me.*

Please wake up Harvey.

"Now you're all alone, little girl. It's Micah's shift today, and he is furious."

Not him. Please, not him. plea—

"Nevaeh!" I jolt in my seat, flinching violently and bumping against something hard on my side.

Anxo quickly rolls down all the windows in the car before parking on the side of the road. Turning to give me his full attention, he starts taking deep breaths which I try to mimic the best I can.

Anxo. *Angel.*

You're not *there*, Nevaeh. You can't be there if Angel is with you.

"Hey, where'd you go, baby?" Giving me his open palm, Angel waits for me to make the first move. When I finally grip his hand, Angel tangles his fingers in my hair and presses our forehead together, grounding me again.

"I just... what—what if he hates me? What if he wants nothing to do with me? He went through so much because of me... he... he t-took for me a-and what I-if..."

Cutting off my stuttering mess Angel kisses me softly, and I grip his shoulders to hold on to my security. His lips softly caress mine, helping me relax the storm inside me with every peck.

"Nothing like that would happen, baby. If anything, Harvey would be relieved to see you out of that place."

"You think so?"

I hate that I sound so weak. I don't want Visha to win. I'm *not* weak.

"I know so. Now take a deep breath and turn that frown upside down. It doesn't belong on your beautiful face." Holding my face in his hands, Angel helps me clean my ruined mascara before kissing me softly.

To distract me from the chaos in my head, Angel asks me to list my favorite memories with Harvey. I'm so glad he was here to help me before I jumped off the edge into panic land like I always do.

For the rest of the ride, I recite every good memory I remember with my best friend, and our conversation becomes lighter, like my heart.

Before I know it, between Angel's soft touches and calming distractions, we reach our destination where others are already waiting.

When Angel climbs out, I follow suit. Only when I try to step out, hands on my shoulders push me back into my seat.

"Noooo, my beautiful idiot, I'm supposed to open doors for you." Shoving my legs back into the car, Angel shuts the door and counts to three before opening it again.

"Sweetheart." The weirdo offers me his palm with a cheeky

grin.

My weirdo.

Helping me climb out, Angel covers me behind his large frame so I can fix my dress that had ridden up. When I'm ready, I wrap my arms around his and hold it to my chest.

If anyone can help me not fall prey to my fear, it's him.

My Angel. My mate.

14. Follow the chaos

Nevaeh

I'm in a trance the moment we enter the dark club. Safely tucked between Angel's arms, my mate makes sure I'm out of reach from any slimy, grabby hands.

Angel doesn't even let someone brush past me, much less entertain the idea of a stranger touching me. He is acting like we are behind enemy lines and not in a club where the music is loud enough to make my ears bleed.

You're telling me people do this for fun?

I can't even attempt to enjoy the beats and the obnoxious music when it overwhelms my heightened senses in the worst possible manner. Filtering the surrounding sounds, I focus on the heartbeat of my mate and block out everything else.

Scanning the various supernatural creatures surrounding me, I understand why the gates are enchanted. The charmed gates are the only thing stopping humans from turning in this direction.

The warmth of my mate spreads through my back as he leans closer to gesture around the club.

"Any idea where to start?"

"With Harvey, always follow the chaos."

Commotion on the second floor overpowers the ear-splitting music and I drag Angel behind me, knowing the others will follow.

The crowd thins in half as we go up and the moment I come face-to-face with the ruckus, I don't have a single doubt in my mind who the orchestrator behind this is.

Two pixies are at each other's throats, and it's not a regular catfight. There is hair ripping, dress tearing, and drinks flopping on the floor. Their makeup is running down their faces, making them look like angry pandas.

Behind them, there's another bickering fest taking place between two demons, screaming what they *could* and *would* do if the other didn't stop talking.

The crowd is enjoying the show—oohing and awing with every witty insult. This looks like a poorly-written yet highly entertaining comedy show.

Looking around the room like a headless chicken, I desperately try to spot the director of this soap opera.

A mysterious shadow catches my attention. Invisible to the crowd, the stunning woman touches the shoulders of the two men in passing, and like magic, the men are on the floor beating the absolute crap out of each other.

My eyes follow the lean woman, and I tug my mate's hand so he can see the exact second she changes appearance from a beautifully shaped woman to a muscular man who passes the women snapping at each other.

Just a simple brush from him has the women losing control over their anger and jumping at each other's throats.

Angel snickers behind me, but my eyes stay fixed on the man stepping into a corner booth and dropping on the sofa in a dark leather jacket.

It's been two years, but the man who leans back with a drink in his hand is someone I can't forget. I've finally found the missing piece of my heart.

That's my best friend.

Harvey watches the chaos unfold with mischievous eyes and a confident smirk. The club is drowning in crimson, but I can spot him in a crowd of thousands with my eyes closed.

He runs his hand through his hair every ten seconds like an impulse and it makes me smile with nostalgia. Harvey had the same anxious tell when we were kids. I guess some things never change.

He's really here.

I can't believe I'm this close to him after spending two years not knowing if he was even alive.

Rubbing his hands on his thigh, Harvey shakes his head once before his eyes start scanning the floor, searching for something. The desperate way he's looking tells me his Divine has finally sensed my presence.

I wait for Harvey to look in my direction, but he snaps his eyes shut and starts muttering things under his breath. My heart drops as I watch him chastise himself for even entertaining the idea of me around.

Angel squeezes my shoulder in silent support, and I force a deep breath. Harvey would tease me for the rest of our lives if he saw me shed the first tear.

I start walking toward Harvey, my steps hurry the closer I get, but I freeze in my spot when Harvey lifts his head to glimpse to his left and his face comes to light.

His face.

I'm frozen with the realization that this is the first time in a lifetime that it's free of bruises. He looks *healthy*—more than healthy, because even sitting down, he resembles a small mountain.

When we were kids, Harvey never made any effort to style his hair, and now that his mom isn't around to scold him, his overgrown, messy hair makes sense.

Willing myself to move, I walk to stand before him with my arms crossed over my middle.

"Still causing chaos for your amusement?"

My shaky whisper is enough to break his trance. The second his eyes land on me, the glass slips from his hand and falls to the floor, breaking into a thousand pieces.

"Monkey?"

Harvey pales as if he's seeing a ghost. A real possibility for us, because we both thought death was our only way out of that dungeon.

His porcelain skin flushes as he continues to gape at me. Harvey blinks furiously and then looks away as if I would disappear the next time he looks my way.

When I don't turn into smoke after he slaps his cheek the second time, Harvey jumps to his feet and throws himself on me.

"*Monkey!*"

Burying his face in my hair, he exhales loudly, holding me like he's afraid I will disappear. I'm clutching him just as hard, trying my hardest not to let the way his shoulders are shaking tear my heart to pieces.

Holding each other close, we both sob into the hug. I can't believe I'm holding him, and I didn't even have to sneak into his cell for it.

When Harvey refuses to back away after seven solid minutes, my lungs start screaming for oxygen with how tight this giant is holding me.

"Can't breathe asshole," I choke out.

"Stop being a baby and let me crush you for a minute," His voice cracks and I give up on trying to get his paws off me. "I thought I lost you... I thought... I-I never thought I'd see you again. I'm so— I'm sorry Nevaeh. I'm so sorry, I should've done m-more..."

My stuttering mess of a best friend starts heaving with every word. I hate how he still carries guilt over *my* choice. It takes all my muscle strength to detach from his bear hug and cup his face in my hands.

I'm irritated I have to stand on my toes to be somewhat at eye level with him. Why is every man in my life so unnecessarily tall?

The light stubble on his cheeks grazes my palms as I force Harvey to look at me, wiping the tears that escape his familiar stormy grey eyes.

"Stop that. Stop blaming yourself for *my* choice. It wasn't your fault, okay? You had to leave. I would've blamed myself forever if they caught you again because of me. You saved yourself from that dreadful place, Harvey. *Never* apologize for that, you hear me?" Despite the tightness in my throat, I speak firmly. I can't let him live with this weight on his shoulders any longer.

"I swear on Fates, if I could—"

"You would've taken me with you in a heartbeat? *Of course,* I know that dumbass."

Leaning his forehead against mine, he chuckles freely, something old Harvey avoided in front of an audience. Wiping under my eyes softly, he takes me in as we both try not to sob in relief.

I have him back. I have my best friend back. I still can't believe we made it out.

"Still a smart mouth, I see." Harvey shakes his head in mock disappointment as if I didn't copy-paste my attitude from him and Papa.

Harvey was my role model growing up. He still is. Every curse word in my dictionary is Harvey's blessing. Papa helped too, but it was mostly Harvey.

Holding my hands, he backs up slightly and adores me with a rare loving smile. "Look at my monkey all grown up... *pretending* to be a lady."

"Better than your fake 'bad boy from Hell' look when everyone knows you're a complete softy at heart," I coo childishly, knowing he will hate it.

"Take that back." He glares, giving me his scariest look, which doesn't do shit for me.

I've been watching that face since he was six, and it only makes him look like a constipated pig.

I snort, but before I can retort with an incredible comeback, a throat clears behind me. I don't have to turn around to know it's Seiji.

Shoving our banter aside, Harvey takes a protective stance before me, falling into his overprotective papa bear routine. Ignoring his glare at *our* friends, I swat his back before the claws come out.

"Oh, back off Papa Bear, they're with me."

Standing between them, I ask Harvey to take a deep breath before his rage seeps out.

He scrutinizes the people behind me one by one. Taking extra long on Grace and not nearly enough on Rick.

Harvey was born with a crazy good bullshit radar. He can separate the good ones from the dickheads in a single interaction, and I know he's trying to figure out if they are worth our time.

The second his eyes land on Anxo's face and the shiny ring on his hand, Harvey takes a step back, eyes widening in shock.

I see the exact moment my best friend realizes he is surrounded by his *oath family*. Family that tried their best to find him. *To find us.*

"Prince of Famine, Horseman of Conquer, and how the fuck are you a Bookkeeper, my little human?" Harvey breathes out. "You are a Bookkeeper, right *darling*?" Grace nods shyly, and Harvey's gaze lingers longer on her than what's considered normal.

Interesting.

A subtle gesture from Grace and Harvey immediately conceals his excitement, but not before I see it.

I hate that it only took me a couple of months with Angel to know it's not my place to say anything. Even when all I want is to bang their heads together until they give in to what Fates have clearly decided for them.

They could both use a miracle made just for them.

I'm not surprised Harvey identified everyone so quickly. Our Divines have a way of knowing which mythical species holds what rank.

Angel steps towards a dumbfounded Harvey to welcome him into the family. "Call me Anxo. It's a pleasure to finally meet you, brother."

Clutching the hand offered to him, Harvey takes a shaky breath and looks sideways in search of me and I quickly go to stand beside him.

We did this all the time when we were young. Whenever one of us was nervous, the other would stand as close as possible to offer that extra boost of support.

It's so strange that I remember every detail about Harvey and our childhood together, yet simultaneously lost almost every other part of my life. It's like my subconscious refused to leave his memories behind, even when I lost everything else about myself.

Before Harvey could get sentimental about Angel calling him *brother,* Seiji pokes his nose into the heart-warming moment.

"Welcome to the twisted family, brother!"

In his excitement, Seiji throws himself at Harvey who malfunctions for a second before throwing his head back in laughter. When Seiji pokes Harvey's bicep and asks for his workout routine, Harvey steps back, shaking his head with unconcealed amusement.

Papa always said that Horsemen have a bond stronger than blood, and seeing the three men interact like they've known each other for years fixes another piece of my shattered heart.

Shaking me like he doesn't realize our size difference, Harvey fires off, "But how did you find them? And how did you get out? I've been trying to find a way into the bitch coven for over a year, but none of my efforts or contacts ever came close."

"Add that to the list of things we have to talk about because it's a *long* story. I would gladly tell you when we get home."

"*Home* home?" Harvey chokes out.

Patting his back, Angel answers, "Home, brother. *Our home.* The Tetrad kingdom has been awaiting your return for a very long time."

Harvey gulps loudly and shakes his head with an exhausted smile. I can't imagine how hard it must've been for him to get out of a dangerous situation, only to realize there was no way to get back home because it *literally shifted.*

Sensing the dark turn my thoughts have taken, Angel wraps his arm around my shoulder and kisses my head. I lean into him, basking in his familiar scent to calm down.

Looking up at Harvey again, I see that our causal display of affection has completely blown his head off. With his jaw hanging low, Harvey's confused gaze keeps bouncing between Angel and me clinging to each other.

I wait for him to cool off, but with each passing second, Harvey looks like he's about to go off the rails.

Such pity. The old man finally went cuckoo.

I decide it's my duty to antagonize him further and say, "The torture finally got to you, huh? I always knew you were fragile but I didn't expect you to lose your mind so soon."

"*I* am fragile? And you're what? The symbol of mental stability," Harvey scoffs, folding his big arms over his chest.

Is he eating the whole city's ration? How did he get so big and muscly?

"I'll let you know I'm sleeping *ten* hours a week and eating almost *two* meals every day. Beat that old man."

"I'm only five years older than you! And I'm eating *four* times a day."

What?!

I immediately turn to Angel, who is for some reason mortified as we discuss our achievements.

"You've got to start feeding me more. I can't lose to this asshole," I beg him, even when I know I can't possibly eat more, but I'm willing to try.

"*This asshole* is standing right here!" Harvey takes a deep breath to calm down before his Divine senses his frustration and starts to run amok.

Every time I comment on Harvey's age, something in him catches fire. It's so entertaining to watch him try to convince me twenty-five is not old. I know it's not, but irritating him like this is way too amusing to stop.

"It was *shock*, not old age, you little fucker. I was going to congratulate you on finding your mate, but now you're being mean, so fuck you."

"Fuck you too dumbass."

"You're so damn irritating. Come here." As soon as I'm within reach, I'm engulfed in another bear hug. "Do I need to get rid of him?" Harvey whispers, and by the restrained grumble I hear behind me, Anxo isn't too happy about it.

"No." I squeeze my arms around Harvey's neck. "I like him. A lot."

Not even a second later, my mate pulled me off my best friend and into his arms. Harvey is about to rip into Angel when Hazel walks over. Nodding at Angel once, she comes to stand by him.

I didn't even notice her leave. I bet she did a quick scan of the club to make sure trouble wasn't lurking around.

Harvey stares at her hard before slowly turning to me with wide eyes and asking lowly, as if everyone here doesn't have the same advanced hearing.

"A siren? *A Goddamn siren?!*"

Merfolk was one of our favorite conspiracy theory topics growing up. We know they stick to deep waters and don't like life on the ground, but other than that, their species is a mystery to the supernatural world.

Turning to me, beaming with excitement, Harvey reminisces. "Remember the theories Dean—"

"All lies." Hazel interrupts our fawning over her kind.

"What—*no!*" Harvey and I argue in sync.

There's no way Papa is wrong about his theories. All of them make sense.

Okay... *most* of them do.

"They're true! We know you can control water."

"Nope."

What?!

"You can only sing your manipulative songs in water."

Considering I saw her puppet-ting the hotel staff when we first met, I already know Hazel will stomp on another one of our theories.

"Couldn't be more wrong."

Turning to each other with similar disappointment, Harvey and I wonder how none of our guesses are correct. I don't want to imagine how Papa will react when I tell him we officially know nothing about Merfolk.

Harvey looks filled with hope as he gathers the courage to ask Hazel one last question, but not before I duck behind Anxo. *Safety first.*

"So, I'm guessing you don't turn blue after not touching water for 24 hours?"

"Who the fuck came up with that one?!"

If looks could kill, Harvey and I would be six feet under. Before Angel loses his mate and his Prince of War at the hands of his Warriorhead, he urges us to scramble away and take a seat.

Three love seats in a semicircle make a booth. Seiji and Hazel slide into the first one. Angel takes the seat next to them before helping me beside him. I'm about to say we are one place short when Harvey asks Grace—*ever so politely*—to take a seat and strategically times it so he's the one sliding in before Rick can.

My mouth drops open at how casually Harvey brushed off my sister's so-called boyfriend.

Scooting closer to Grace, Harvey shoots me a sly wink, and I know this dumbass is up to something. I've been his partner in crime for far too many years to not notice the signs. And if he wants me to play coy, I'm in.

Anything for Harvey.

With no place to sit, Rick chooses to stand behind Grace like a guard dog. I'm sure he can sense the tension between my best friend and sister.

I swear to Fates I'll kill him if he tries to ruin the first good thing Harvey has found.

Angel pulls me until my back is flush against his chest. Circling his arms around my waist, he kisses my head, making me abandon all thoughts of skinning Rick alive.

Lately, Angel needs constant physical contact, or he acts like he is dying. I can't even complain because I love the way my insides sing when he is near.

I'm falling so hard for this man that it terrifies me.

"So, they helped you break out?" Harvey asks.

Seiji answers before I can. "Yes, we did. We found her in the woods all bloody and about to die. She then *sobbed* and *thanked* us for our bravery."

Like always, the dramatic princess exaggerates.

"Oh, speaking of finding things." Harvey turns to Anxo, leaning forward to rest his elbows on his knees. Behind me, I feel Angel shift when Harvey directs his fury and irritation at him. "Who the fuck are you trying to keep out man? Fucking aliens? I've been running in circles trying to find a single portal for two years and never found shit. I'm the *Prince of War* for Fate's sake!"

Chuckling nervously, Angel scratches the back of his head. He sighs when, once again, no one steps in to save him from being the bringer of bad news.

With his eyes reflecting a world of unspoken apologies, Angel grimaces. "Sorry brother, but after what happened with you two... protecting the kingdom became a priority. I agree the previous leaders took it too far by changing realms, but—"

Suddenly Hazel throws her tablet on the table with a low growl, effectively saving Angel from getting his ass chewed on by the physical embodiment of war.

"Witches and their braindead puppets are here." That sentence is enough for us to spring to our feet. "A dozen by the east exit and more at the back gate. Looks like more covens have joined Visha," she adds, furiously tapping her fingers on the screen.

I was hoping I wouldn't have to ruin my dress with blood, but you can't fight destiny.

Grace contemplates before turning to my mate. "Anxo if they get in here, we can't be sure how many of these mellow partying creatures will turn on us given the opportunity."

"I agree," Hazel taps in. "Horsemen don't have a shortage of people who will happily rally forces with the witches. We need to wrap this in the bud outside and then get the fuck out of here."

That's one major risk of being in the human realm. The

abundance of mythics lingering in every corner means you never know who's waiting for the perfect moment to strike.

Angel sighs, throwing his head back. "Lately, it seems like we're gaining enemies by the day."

"My fault." Harvey and I take the blame in sync, which makes Angel shake his head with a smile and pull me into his side.

Clapping my hands together, I demand everyone's attention. "I have a plan."

"What are you proposing now, Lucifer spawn?" Seiji whines like he already knows what I'm thinking. I bet he is mainly pissy about ruining his outfit.

"He is my *godfather*, so technically, not his spawn. So here's the plan," I get ready to share when immature whispering stops me.

"Five hundred rubies it involves gore," Angel bets with Seiji, but Harvey clicks his tongue in disappointment.

At least my best friend has faith in me.

"Amateurs... it's *always* blood and guts with her."

I take it back. Harvey can go fuck himself.

Why they think I'm some psycho killer is beyond me. *I'm fucking adorable!*

Fine then, time for a new list.

1. *Papa*
2. *My little monkey*
3. *Angel*
4. *Grace, Hazel, and Seiji*
5. *Harvey (congrats on the demotion dumbass)*

Ignoring the men giggling and whispering like teenagers, I focus on the ladies who are more interested in getting things done.

"So, listen in... Angel, Hazel, and I will sort out the ones in the back while Rick and Seiji tackle the east exit." On nods of approval, I continue. "Grace and Harvey should stay inside and make sure no one follows us. In the meantime, maybe Grace can fill Harvey in on what he missed."

That's right. I've purposely put them together because I'm shipping.

Your friendly neighborhood cupid.

Hazel's forehead crinkles, but I subtly shake my head at her before she can protest. Taking the hint, murmurs of acceptance ring around me.

I get that Grace is in a relationship, and this is not exactly ethical, but Rick is an emotionally abusive asshole, and assholes don't get my morals.

I know Grace will probably want to maturely handle things with Rick before even considering anything with Harvey, but I hate the guy too much to feel bad for him.

Grace suddenly starts to choke on the water she was sipping. Harvey immediately reaches out to pat her back and we pretend not to notice the way Grace stops breathing entirely or how Harvey sucks a sharp breath.

My sister flusters and whispers a small thank you, but Harvey still looks deeply concerned.

Oh, relax Romeo.

"Are you sure you want me to stay? I'm not—"

"Do you want to switch places and get your hands dirty, Gracie?" With a disgusted face, Grace zips her lips shut and slumps back.

My gaze shifts to Harvey, and this man is ogling Grace with the most adorable puppy look I've seen.

Oh boy, he is *gone* gone.

The last time Harvey looked at something like that, it was his dad's sword. The tantrum he threw after he was told he couldn't have it, was *brutal.*

Naturally, Harvey stole the sword and hid it until his dad made a deal with the twelve-year-old that he could practice with it for two hours daily.

When Harvey wants something, he goes after it full throttle. And the way he is tripping over his feet for Grace; I know it's just a matter of time.

I'm already on team Harvey. Rick can choke on his dick for all I care.

With his hand on my back, Anxo stands and instructs Grace. "Don't leave this section unless absolutely necessary. Seiji, link me if anything looks even remotely suspicious." Seiji affirms by nodding once.

Usually, I'm excited to kick some ass, but this is the first time I'm facing my past since my escape. Just the idea of being surrounded by the nightmares I grew up with, terrifies me to my core.

The last two months with my newfound family have soothed some of the wounds the coven inflicted, but it doesn't change the fact that I still carry them on my skin every day.

I know I'm safe, and no matter how tonight ends, there's no scenario in which Anxo will let me go back to that dungeon, but having to keep confronting my past is starting to weigh on my sanity.

A past that hasn't stopped haunting my present.

15. My mate is a Greek god

Grace

I'm a little lightheaded as I press my lips together and will myself not to chew my bottom lip bloody.

I think I'm going to pass out.

If my trembling fingers toying with the hem of my dress don't scream 'I'm a nervous wreck', then my flushed face probably does. I don't think it's intentional, but Harvey oozes a certain confidence that makes it hard not to feel intimidated.

If it's not his presence, then I'm having a heart attack.

Not like Harvey's unashamed eyeing is helping my nerves at all. My stomach flips funnily when I peek at him—*my mate*— only to find his eyes already on me. *Oh God.*

Folding his leather jacket with more care than one would assume from such a large man, I watch him lay it on the seat next to him. Resting his elbows on his knees, Harvey waits for me to start the conversation.

And I was ready... until he started folding the sleeves of his dark shirt and I saw the tattoos covering his arms.

What in the modern Greek god— I mean my mate.

Red and black swirls start somewhere under his shirt and strategically follow down to his knuckles ending in the shape of a half-lotus.

Absolutely drool-worthy.

My eyes refuse to stray from the muscles in his arms. I have to catch the way my eyes follow his every move before I make my fascination too obvious. I don't want him to think I'm a freak for gaping like he's the first man I've ever laid eyes on.

But those eyes. God, I need to rein it in.

The second I saw the storm in Harvey's eyes, my whole

world turned upside down. That was also when Rick grabbed my arm to keep me from tripping over my own feet. At his touch, every bad decision I've ever made flashed before my eyes—including the man clutching my arm.

Rick's hand on me didn't go unnoticed by Harvey, and the agony in his eyes made me want to drop to my knees and beg for forgiveness. Guilt weighed on my heart when I asked Harvey to keep his distance, but it was the only fair option until I could talk to Rick.

I was shocked Harvey didn't immediately demand an explanation or made his frustration clear. Instead, he understood I needed a little time to embrace my new reality wholeheartedly. His acceptance only dug the knife of guilt deeper into my heart.

After surveying the exits to ensure all the party people were accounted for, Harvey takes his seat beside me and breathes out, "So the warrior—*Rick*, he's your boyfriend?"

I freeze at the question. I should've known he would want answers. I know no matter how I say it, it will only make him mad. What if he thinks I'm a whore for being with a different man and not waiting for my mate?

How do I make a man I just met believe that I genuinely didn't think someone was specifically made for me when Rick never trusts me, and I've been with him for two years.

"I'm so sorry, I didn't think—"

"No need for apologies, darling. I'm not interested in who came before me. But I need to know if you intend on rejecting the bond."

"No! I don't want that." Harvey's face softens from his stern expression, and I relax a little. "I genuinely thought I didn't have a mate because I'm human. Rick was sure I didn't." Harvey's lips turn down, and my heart burns seeing, so I quickly add, "But I always wanted one. I'm not rejecting the bond. *Never*. I'll talk to Rick. I'm sure he'll understand."

Will he, though?

The thought of telling Rick about Harvey makes my heart

rate pick up. My mind flashes back to the time he was so blinded by his anger that he didn't realize he was hurting me. This time, I'm giving him something to be mad about. I have a feeling he won't like this conversation.

As if he can see my fear starting to crack through my false calm exterior, Harvey grabs my hand and *smiles* at me. A warm smile that melts my insides and makes me curse every day of my life I lived without it.

I almost got electrocuted the first time his hand touched my back. It's a relief to know that won't happen every time we touch.

Nevaeh never mentioned anything about the spark being *literal*, and now I think it's because she was so out of it when they first met.

"Don't worry darling, I've waited years for my mate, I can wait for a few more hours... or days. But not forever." My face burns at the endearment. I'm starting to have a love-hate relationship with how Harvey makes me feel. With a nod, I agree to sort out my mess.

"Now tell me everything I've missed."

Clearing my throat, I try to pull my hand from his, but Harvey holds on tighter. The plea in his eyes is clear. He *needs* this. Stretching my hand, I let him entangle our fingers together.

"Let's start with the basics. So the previous leaders combined the kingdoms—Nevaeh told us it was your dream, so I bet you're excited."

The corner of his mouth tilt up. "Horseman of Conquer said the *Tetrad kingdom* was waiting for me. I'm assuming we rebranded?"

"Oh yes. We still have the four individual kingdoms, but now we present as one big dynasty among mythics. When they moved from the human realm—really sorry about the shift by the way—they built portals..."

I don't know how long we sit there talking to each other, but by the end, Harvey knows all the important facts about the kingdom.

The entire time, he sits patiently, listening to every word with genuine curiosity, waiting until I finish a topic to ask questions. He even asks how Hazel and I came into the picture.

Throughout our interaction, I can't help but think how refreshing it is to talk with Harvey. Where Harvey talks *with* me, Rick talks *at* me.

Rick would never let me go on for this long. He thinks my '*know it all*' behavior is annoying, and just because I'm a Bookkeeper doesn't mean I have to yap about everything constantly.

During our entire talk, I kept feeling horrible for not bringing up his parents, but that's a conversation Anxo didn't want me to touch. It feels like a betrayal to hide something this big from my mate, but I promised Anxo I'll let him handle this.

We agreed it was crucial to have Harvey in our corner before Nevaeh finds out what we're hiding. She will need her best friend more than any of us when that day comes.

"So, my little human, is there anything else I'm missing?"

If I were even a shade lighter, I'm sure my blush would've given away how his endearment creates a whole zoo inside my stomach. I can't keep my head on straight if he keeps talking to me this way.

I'm about to say *yes* because it's impossible to tell a decade's worth of information in such a short time when Rick stomps over to our table.

"Outside. Now." Rick sneers near my face and only backs up to let me stand.

I swallow thickly at the crazed look in Rick's eyes. I almost want to tell him I won't go anywhere when he's acting this way but decide against making a scene in front of everyone. *In front of Harvey.*

Glancing back, I'm stunned to find Harvey glaring at Rick with a murderous glint in his eyes. Noticing Rick's anger, Harvey stands to cover me but stops short when I subtly shake my head.

Harvey evades my eyes, but I can feel his disappointment pouring into the air. I've barely known my mate for an hour, and I've already managed to hurt him more times than I can apologize for.

As much as I would love some support, I think it's time I finally stand up for myself. Even when Rick doesn't deserve it, I want to part on civil terms. I've wanted to end things with him for months but never found the courage to... but the arrival of my mate has changed everything.

The front door of the club opens to an eerily quiet and empty parking lot. The second the door bangs shut behind us, Rick marches up to me seething in anger and snarls in my face.

"I don't even know where to start with you tonight. What do I say to my girlfriend for throwing herself at strangers like some cheap slut, wearing... wearing that tiny piece of cloth you call a dress! And what did I tell you about letting your hair down like that huh?"

Rick reserves his condescending tone and unfiltered fury for when we are alone. It's degrading and explicitly meant to humiliate me. I hate to admit it, but I've gotten used to it. No matter what I do, I'm always wrong in his eyes.

"There's nothing wrong with the dress Rick. I like it. And I feel more comfortable with my hair out of those tight braids." I keep my voice steady, praying it won't crack with fear. Rick expects me to roll over and take his verbal hits, but I can't look weak tonight.

"How many times have I told you this huh? It makes you look dirty and unkempt." I knew he would hate my hair. "And what about that man, huh?"

"*That man* is our Prince of War."

"So you're defending him now? It's his rank, isn't it? I knew you were planning to latch onto him like the power-hungry whore you are!"

Is this what he really thinks of me? Rick wasn't even an elite warrior when we started dating, so what power was I running after?

I can't keep quiet anymore. He already assumes the worst of me, but maybe if he knew who Harvey was to me, he would understand I'm not a whore for simply talking to my mate.

My mate. Just the thought of my bond gives me enough courage to blurt out the truth, even with Rick pacing before me, his hands pulling on his hair.

"Reject him."

My world stops spinning as soon as the words leave his mouth. I search his eyes, wishing Rick only said it out of anger and confusion, but all I see is a clear warning.

The idea of rejection reels me too far away from reason. My mind zones in on one thing, disregarding everything else. *I have to protect my bond.*

"I won't reject my mate."

"You do what I say!" Rick hisses and I will myself not to back down before I say what I want. Staying as calm as possible, I communicate my feelings to him for the first and last time.

"No. You get to ask me politely, but I will only do it *if* I feel comfortable. I'm supposed to be your partner, Rick, not your slave. Nevaeh was right. I can't keep making you happy by neglecting my own comfort and happiness."

"Of course, she's the one pulling your strings."

Rick kicks over the trash can behind him, mumbling something about 'counting her days' before stomping over to me and trapping me between him and a brick wall.

Don't panic Grace. He can't know how scared you are or he'll use that against you. I just want to leave him and this place. I'm tired of Rick treating me like a possession, something he can boast about among his peers and not someone he should love and cherish.

"This isn't about who said what, it's about how I feel and... and that is uncomfortable, ridiculed, and stepped on every time you talk to me. I-I keep fixing what you break, but you never stop breaking. And I'm t-tired of piecing myself back together. I'm sorry Rick, but it's over."

The words are barely out of my mouth when Rick roughly

backhands me. I stumble and my vision goes dark, giving him the chance to pin me with his arm under my chin.

Grabbing my cheeks, Rick squeezes harshly, forcing me to look up. There's no hiding my tears anymore, and I blink hard to make the stars in my vision disappear.

Everything happens so fast, I can barely keep up. I need to get out of here—or scream. I need to do something before Rick completely loses it. My head is spinning and the ringing in my ears is making it hard to understand what Rick is screaming in my face.

His eyes flash red, and I can see Rick is losing control of his demon. "—I'll make sure you pay for running your mouth. Once I'm done with you tonight Grace, you won't even *think* about disrespecting me again." His grip on my jaw is so painful I can't hold back from crying out.

"Please st-stop. Stop!"

"Not so brave now, huh, *darling*? I would shut up before you force me to punish you for disobedience too, you—" Rick's voice cut off when a fist lands on his cheek from the side. His grip on me falters as he stumbles back and lands on his behind.

Turning in the direction of the surprise attack, I'm stunned to find Harvey standing there, his furious gaze fixed on Rick—who already has a bruise forming on his cheek. Harvey stalks towards the man on the ground like a predator and I immediately cover my eyes when he starts pounding Rick's face into the ground.

Being as quiet as possible, I sink to the floor. Muffling my wails behind my hands, I bring my knees to my chest and curl into myself.

For a quick second, I pity Rick for being on the receiving end of Harvey's wrath. Part of me is glad Rick is being forced to feel what I did when he let his frustration win, but a bigger part of me just wants to go home and never see his face again.

For the next ten minutes, I don't dare open my eyes. All I hear is the sound of bone cracking, Rick's painful groans, and fist connecting to flesh.

When two hands grab my shoulders out of nowhere, a terrified scream rips from me. I try to crawl back so Rick can't touch me, but the wall behind me makes it impossible.

"It's just me, darling." A light brush on my cheek charged with electricity makes my eyes flutter open. I find Harvey crouched in front of me with concern and misery etched on his face and immediately relax.

"He won't bother you again, I promise." The dark edge in Harvey's promise soothes my fear. I try to look past him, but Harvey quickly pulls me on his lap making us both face the wall.

I don't stop to think before I wrap my arms around his muscled waist and hide my face in his chest. Feeling the cocoon of safety around me, I finally stop muffling my cries and let the tears flow.

I don't know how long we stay like that, Harvey comforting me, whispering sweet nothings in my ear, and gently rocking us side to side while I try detach myself from what happened.

When my cries reduce to small sniffs, I look up at my mate with a foggy vision. "Thank you for coming for me."

"You're welcome, darling." Holding my chin, Harvey kisses the corner of my mouth.

Harvey shifts me until I'm straddling him before standing up like I weigh nothing to him. Gripping the collar of his leather jacket, I hide my face in his neck and take deep breaths of my mate's addictive scent.

I stiffen when my fingers accidentally brush over a raised bump on the back of his neck. I immediately know what it is. I've seen enough of them on Nevaeh. Of course Harvey has his own share of poorly healed scars.

Suddenly, the tattoos covering his entire body carry a heavier weight. I've seen enough people with tattoos to know the difference between getting them because you like them or because you are trying to hide something.

It breaks my heart to consider the level of pain Harvey must've felt to hide his scars. Anything so his sufferings weren't on display each day, every day.

Tightening my hold, I press my nose in the crook of his neck. Unlike me, Harvey doesn't hide his eagerness to be closer. As we walk back into the club, Harvey holds my dress in place under my thighs, so I won't accidentally flash anyone.

Before I can steal a glance at Rick, who has been silent this entire time, Harvey spins us around so I'm facing the entrance.

"Is he..."

"Yes. Does that upset you?"

"No. But you didn't have to do that."

"Anyone who lays a hand on my mate deserves his fate." My stomach flips at the way Harvey promises of violence on my behalf.

"You'll have to walk backward, Harvey." I murmur into his neck, pecking a faded scar hiden beneath a rose thorn.

Just a little brush and suddenly I can't get enough of my lips on him. I've read the mate bond affect humans differently, the desire and need for our mate is tenfold for us. But I don't think Harvey minds judging by how he sighs with every small kiss on his neck.

"I'm a Horseman, *my saving Grace.* I think I can manage," he whispers, his warm breath causing goosebumps to spread on my skin. Patting my bum twice, Harvey gives it a firm squeeze.

Oh boy.

16. He wants me to be his what?!

Nevaeh

Before Hazel can throw open the back gate where brainless bimbos with horrible skin and a bunch of dumb warlocks are marching toward us, Angel blocks my path, looking uncharacteristically nervous.

"Do you trust me?"

Hazel silently backs away until she is out of sight. I'm sure she'll hiss about our lovey-dovey moment ruining her plans to gut some Deviants the first chance she gets.

The last time Angel asked me this, I didn't have to think before saying no, but now, the circumstances are different. I am different, and so is our bond.

He has given me things I didn't think were in my cards. A roof over my head, friends who have my back, and comfort I didn't know I was worth. So, there's only one correct answer. "I think I do."

Shrugging lamely, I force my eyes to track the patterns on the tile below me, not wanting to witness his disappointment, but all I get is silence.

When I hesitantly peak at Anxo, he has an excited smile he can barely suppress. Those dimples on display once again prove that I need to stop expecting the worst from people... from Anxo.

When Angel pushes the door open, he has more spring in his step than one should before facing Deviants.

Conjuring his bow out of thin air Angel stays a step ahead of Hazel and me and in the line of target.

I can't get over how envious I am about him magically summoning a weapon and not having to carry it on him at all times.

Because Seiji is not a Horseman yet, he has to disguise his whips as a jeweled belt looped over his waist, but anything is better than not having a signature weapon at all.

I can't wait to summon the scythe and raise hell one day.

I know Hazel and Grace also carry weapons on them. Grace because her Divine is no help in such situations, and Hazel because that deranged woman loves getting her hands dirty. Even when she can melt someone's brain with a whistle. *My kind of woman.*

I like getting in the face of my enemies, watching the light leave their eyes as I slowly strip them of their souls. It's strangely satisfying.

After creating a barrier in my head around my Divine, I let it come out to play. Using my essence in a limited capacity, I carve my path through the hoard of rabid Deviants by burning every soul I come in contact with to ashes. I just know their screeching wails will keep me up all night.

Deviants can't hold or conjure a weapon, but that doesn't make them harmless. Every touch from a cursed soul makes your insides shudder with dark magic.

When a melting hand lands on my shoulder, I thank the countless nights of torture that made my body used to this uncomfortable burn.

Grabbing the deviant by his throat, I squeeze until his head rolls off the decaying body. Watching my hands covered in melting flesh and goo, I regret not asking Hazel for a dagger.

A deviant drops to my feet with a deep gash on his neck, distracting me from fighting my share. I was worried their numbers would overpower us, but Anxo is dropping Deviants like flies.

He is fast and elegant. His movements are so effortless one would think he's taking a lazy stroll in a park.

A wicked laugh from behind me breaks my trance, reminding me I'm not here to cheer on Angel but rather to put some of my anger and frustration to end.

"Ah, there's my favorite prisoner!" The bigger tool steps forward with his mini tools, i.e., Deviants waiting for their master to say *go fetch*.

I should've known it was him.

This particular warlock loves a good villain monologue, and *of course* he wants one in the middle of us tearing apart his brainless soldiers.

The world believes Visha is the most powerful witch to ever exist and her coven the strongest, but I know how rotten her ranks are on the inside.

Other than a few dozen dark magic wielders, Visha heavily relies on Deviants and her elite warriors to walk through hell to keep her hands clean and image cleaner.

To entertain and maintain peace with other covens, Visha used to invite magic bearers from across the globe, offering them her prisoners as a form of stress relief. And *David* here was a frequent visitor to my side of the cells.

"Ugh, not you again!" Throwing my head back, I groan loudly.

"You really thought you could escape me, huh? Now you and your little friends will watch as I drag you back to where you belong."

This delusional motherfucker.

He continues to gloat about his strength and power, and I can't help but laugh at his wildly inaccurate assumptions. I legit ugly snort, and the sound resonates in the dead of night. On the other side of the empty lot, Anxo laughs in between stabbing a warrior with the pointy part of his bows.

David is five feet tall with a six-month pregnant-looking belly sticking out, and *I'm* supposed to be afraid of *him*. Now that I think about it, I think his anger might stem from the time I stabbed his cousin *down there*.

Good old days.

"Honestly, dickvid? You should—"

"It's David!" *Dickvid* exclaims furiously.

This guy should try yoga. I've heard it's good for anger

management.

"Yeah yeah, same thing... Hey, how's the wife anyway? Left you for that ugly face yet?"

I don't understand how they have women staying with them. I don't see one good thing, not externally and definitely not internally.

"You will never make it out of this alive! The dark queen *will* find you and drag you back. And when she does, your kind will..." Dickvid is red in the face, sneering at me as he continues his oh-so-evil monologue. And it's not just me, even his warriors look bored.

"Sorry dickvid, but I don't speak stupid. Didn't go to school... you know, with your people *kidnapping me* and whatnot?"

And *that* snaps his restraint. Roaring like a pig suffering from constipation, he charges at me along with his minions.

Flicking his wrists, David rains sharp thorns on me from the bushes behind him which I barely avoid by bending at the last second. Except the one that tears the sleeve of my pretty dress. Okay, now I'm *mad.*

Surrounded by Deviants and warlocks after months of safety is not as adventurous as I thought it would be. Being around them brings all kinds of tidbits from my past that I struggle to forget every night.

I feel a pinch in my chest when my Divine pushes against the blockade that keeps it in check. The danger around me has my Divine crawling to the front and demanding I release my leash over it.

Unlike the rest of the mythical population, I'm unlucky enough to have an overactive Divine with its own sense and demands. If my grip over my essence slips, it won't be Nevaeh defending herself anymore but my Divine aching for revenge.

I barely hold myself back when I have complete control over my Divine. I can't even imagine what would happen if I let my powers run wild when I'm not the one holding the reins.

I can't reach my potential without ripping myself apart, so

I do the one thing I can. I lock my Divine into the back of my mind and decide to depend on my skills.

In between crushing skulls with my bare hands and actively pushing my Divine back, I lose sight of the people I came with until Hazel shouts from behind me.

"Nevaeh, watch your six!"

My what?

A powerful kick to my back forces me to widen my stance to stop from stumbling to the ground face-first.

Before the warlock gets the opportunity, I turn on my feet and swiftly kick his stomach. Forcing him on his knees, I twist his neck, ending his miserable life for good.

"More coming from the south. Seiji is rounding everyone here, so stay on my three, sweetheart."

Why are they suddenly talking in numbers and time? I don't remember numbers and codes coming up in our planning sessions.

I'm going to regret spacing out in meetings, aren't I?

I've never been this disoriented in a fight before. The constant attacks are exhausting, coupled with the horrible stench clouding my brain. Not to forget the sudden change in strategy which is starting to make me dizzy.

"Stop screaming numbers at me. I'm not understanding shit, Angel!"

"They're directions baby, not numbers—you know what, we'll discuss that later," he shouts from my far left.

Did he forget I can hear him just fine without him screaming? The loud voices and constant screams are too much. I can't stand this for another second.

How is it possible that after a decade with these monsters, I somehow forgot the chaos and anxiety it brings me to be around them?

The first sign of safety and I get so wrapped up in the comfort that I can't access my fight response. I'm acting like a teenager learning the ropes of combat again.

Grabbing the warlock creeping up behind me by his neck, I

throw him to the ground and stomp on his skull repeatedly to release my anger until I hear bones crunching beneath me. I feel better for less than three seconds before a chilling pain in my spine blinds me, and I drop to my knees.

Abruptly grabbing the ankle of my attacker—a warlock too busy reciting spells and enjoying how he brought me to my knees—I pull with all my strength.

Falling backward, he hits his head on the concrete, effectively knocking himself out.

When a warlock sprints to me, I shake myself out of the deep-seated unease crawling up my bones and pull myself up just in time to dodge the kick.

Grabbing his ankle when it's right next to my face, I twist it at an unnatural angle. The warlock slumps forward in pain, his screech for help echoing in my ear. Cupping his head, I twist, and his body falls with a thud among the dozens lying around me.

"There's too many!" Hazel roars from somewhere, but her voice sounds muffled to my ears. My hands haven't stopped pulling out decaying hearts and crushing skulls, but I'm losing myself. "I have a plan. Just be ready!"

I think Anxo says something, probably another useless command I don't understand. Even if my head wasn't fogged with my Divine's need for blind rage that demands me to soak in enemies blood, I wouldn't have understood anything.

I'm beyond pissed at this point. My rage is not limited to my past and fighting the feeling of helplessness that's eating at me from being around my tormentors but at my friends too. Because we *ever* discussed any of this.

Anxo asked me to follow his lead, and *I tried*. I tried my best, but my efforts have been utterly useless, not to forget severely damaging to my body.

The unclear instructions are pushing me off balance. I've never taken this much damage in a fight before. I'm bleeding from multiple places, there are fucking thorns sticking out from my arms and thighs, and because I've healed over them, now they're tearing me from the inside with every movement.

I'm frustrated and angry, but most of all, I'm disappointed in myself. I thought I was finally settling in with the group, but tonight has been a harsh reality check.

My spine crawls with disgust, feeling eyes on me. The rush of panic consuming me screams at me to turn around and hide. The familiarity of this gaze makes my skin itch, and I clench my trembling fists to hide my fear.

Frantically searching the dark trees surrounding me, I desperately wait for my Divine to settle down so I can convince myself it's nothing more than a hallucination. That I don't see *her* mangled face peaking from behind a tree hidden behind shadows.

Eyeing me.

Calling for me.

Swallowing with my heart in my throat, I flinch back. But before I can do anything, I'm pushed back by a thundering blast.

Anxo's invisible shield circling us eats up the roar of the explosion, but the strong vibrations make me lose my footing and twist my ankle, trying to stay up.

I shift my upper half just in time to save my face from the aggressive blow of fire, but it catches on to the side of my dress. Anxiously patting down the fire with trembling hands, I forget about the thorn the size of a lemon sticking out of my shoulder and hiss when a hand suddenly grips me over it.

Anxo drops his grip and steps back like I burned him. His hands hover over me, searching for a safe place to touch, eyes tracing over every bleeding spot and cut.

Abandoning my fear, I peek at where Visha was hiding—or where I *imagined* her because no matter how hard I squint, there's no trace of her ever being there.

"You didn't duck?! Why didn't you duck? You could've seriously injured yourself, Nevaeh."

Anxo cups my face with one hand while the other moves all over me. He looks genuinely concerned, but I don't trust myself not to release my frustration on him.

Turning away from him, I take in the Deviants burned to ash and see if I hallucinated anything else. But Anxo doesn't stop pestering me.

"Nevaeh, answer me. Hazel gave the signal so why didn't you—" I commend him for not raising his voice even in frustration, but his worried rambling finally makes me snap.

"WHAT SIGNAL?" I didn't mean to scream—I really didn't, but my anger and fear in the past hour took over.

My voice shakes when I try to speak, and it's a good thing because I don't want to hate myself even more by raising my voice at Anxo when he actively tries not to do that with me around.

"How? How was I supposed to know the signal? You said *nothing* about a fucking signal. *Never.* I didn't understand a-any of your signals or the stupid numbers or... or gestures... I... *fuck this shit.*"

I try to hide how tonight has hurt in more ways than one, but it's hard when his eyes reflect his fear. The fear that I'm too reckless... that I don't care enough about myself to keep my limbs intact.

I admit I can be careless sometimes, but he should know better than anyone that I won't risk myself like that when I have August to think about and a brand new lease on life.

"You can think I'm reckless and impulsive all you want... but this," I gesture to where I had to put out of the flames on my shoulder. "—was not my fault. I didn't fuck up tonight, *you* did."

Turning on my feet, I limp as fast as I can to walk away without sparing Anxo another glance.

I don't care if he's disappointed or thinks I did a piss-poor job at keeping up with him and his perfect training. I just want to leave before something convinces me I didn't imagine my worst nightmare eyeing me tonight.

Click

My Divine claws at my insides urgently, snapping my head

at the faint sound. Skimming through the tall trees, I chase the sound when a tiny movement at the top of a tree catches my eye. A shadow. When a shiny weapon glistens under the moonlight, I quickly realize the click I heard was from a gun.

A human weapon.

I follow the aim to *Hazel*, who is too engrossed in a heated discussion with Anxo to notice the weapon pointed right at her. Ignoring the sharp pain radiating from my ankle, I run to the siren and cover her before yanking the dagger strapped to her waist.

Putting every remaining ounce of my strength behind my throw, I aim at the shadow above us. It's silent until a bang echoes right after the dagger leaves my hand. I'm worried I missed my mark when a heavy thud makes me sigh in relief.

Breaking out of their shock, Anxo and Hazel turn to where the sniper fell with a stab wound decorating the center of his forehead.

And here I thought I missed my mark.

The man's dark eyes stare at me—or behind me, to be exact, before his body withers and melts into liquid right before my eyes. *Fucking liquid.*

I've been away from the supernatural world for far too long if that's considered normal now.

"Find me a medical kit. *Now!*" Anxo growls, bringing my attention back from the man—*who is now a puddle of water*—to Hazel who's running into the building just as Seiji bursts through the doors.

A pressure against my shoulder makes me whimper and I see blood seeping out of a wound I didn't know I had. *Great.* One more wound is exactly what I needed tonight.

When did I get shot, though? I know the gun was fired, but I didn't even feel it. I stumbled back because of the power behind my throw—*or maybe it was the bullet.*

I'm guessing the sniper was aiming for Hazel's heart since the bullet is embedded in my left shoulder right below my collarbone from our height difference.

Seiji stands behind me so I can lean on him. Angel takes my hand in his, eyes shining with unspoken apologies. I don't have it in me to let go, so I squeeze as much as I can with my shoulder throbbing in pain.

Hazel returns quickly and opens the box filled with all kinds of medical stuff. I hastily grab the scalpel and cut a line over the bullet wound. Dropping it back into the box, I ask a flabbergasted Hazel for a pair of tweezers.

I hold my bottom lip between my teeth before digging the tweezers through the cut and clamping on the bullet. Under ten seconds I've pulled the piece of metal out.

It might seem strange, but I've been treating my own injuries since I was nine. Our bodies heal fast and it hurts like hell when wounds can't close because something is blocking the path.

It's impossible to make out the bullet in the dark and over all the blood around it, so there was no way Hazel could've pulled it out here. I refuse to continue this torture until we get back to the hotel.

Since I'm already on it, I quickly pull out two thorns from my left thigh and one from my shoulder.

The tremble in my fingers gets stronger every second, and everything about tonight is slowly catching up to me. Seeing Dickvid, facing the Deviants, ultimately failing as a team member... and *maybe* seeing Visha again.

"Let me," with a tone so gentle I would think I'm hallucinating again, Hazel takes over cleaning the blood and bandaging me.

At the sound of someone heaving I turn to my left and find Seiji bend over a bush and throwing up his lunch.

Maybe I shouldn't have done that in front of him.

I didn't even realize when Anxo took Seiji's place. Softly kissing my head, he holds me close while Hazel works as fast as she can so I can finally sit down.

Once she's done, I move away from Angel even when everything in me screams to hold on to him and quietly limp to a nearby wall. Sitting on the ground, I wipe the blood from my hands on my dress, but it's no use since the dress is soaked in red, too.

Just like old days.

Shifting to get more comfortable on the cold hard ground, I freeze when arms wrap around my hips and pull me against a firm chest. My body is so familiar with his touch, his scent, even his breathing patterns that there's no way to mistake who it is.

Angel shifts me until my back is flush against his chest, and my head resting over his heart. The steady rhythm helps me relax, and I finally lose the tension in my shoulders. It's terrifying how a single touch from him can make me feel safe in a place littered with my worst nightmares.

"I'm so sorry, sweetheart." Anxo places one of his angelic kisses on the side of my head before burying his head in the crook of my neck, making me melt into him. "I agree with you. It was awfully ignorant of me to forget what I know came from years of training. You just mesh with us so effortlessly that for a moment I forgot you're still new to everything."

A small smile grace my lips. *Effortlessly.*

"I'm so sorry for overwhelming you like that. I hate how much you're hurting because of my oversight."

I want to say it's not all on him, but Angel doesn't give me a chance. "Maybe we can have a few training sessions together. That way you can learn our methods and we can learn yours. What do you think, sweetheart?" I'm nodding my head before he is even finished.

"And... I would appreciate it if you could avoid getting shot next time. You almost gave me a heart attack, and I'm too young to die."

I want to laugh, but I can sense he is genuinely worried. I don't want to make a joke and brush it off like I usually do.

Gripping my chin, Anxo turns my head to him. "I owe you everything for what you did for Hazel, but don't you dare sacrifice yourself like that ever again." His fear shines so brightly in his eyes that I hate being the reason behind it.

"It wasn't that big of a deal."

"Shut up and stop underestimating yourself. You were *magnificent*. The way you move? So elegant baby. I had to keep reminding myself we were in the middle of something and I couldn't just run to you. And I'm stealing some of your moves... especially the one where you broke his ankle and then twisted his neck. *Epic sweetheart.*"

I'm blushing like a fool, but Anxo keeps complimenting me. I'm just glad I didn't fuck up like I thought I did.

"Do you want to be my boyfriend?"

Oh no. Oh no. *Oh fuck no.*

Why the fuck did that come out of my mouth? This is not the place or the time to ask this, Nevaeh!

Yes, I've been dying to ask him for days, but now that I've blurted it out like an amateur, I have no option but to brace for impact.

"No."

Stupid Nevaeh! You just had to go and build fantasies about things that are only happening inside your head.

"Oh, um... okay. That's okay. It wasn't like I wanted that or anything. I couldn't care less. Pfft."

I try to look away but Anxo cups my face, the sincerity in his eyes locking me in a daze.

"Nevaeh Blackburn, I don't want to be your boyfriend. That word is temporary and represents too little of what I want for us. I want *forever* with you."

I think I've stopped breathing. Anxo has no regard for my poor heart and continues to kill me with his sweet words.

"I want to be your home, your every kiss, your forever. I want to be there when you finally free yourself from your past. Beside you when that same past keeps you up at night. I want to be there for all of it. I want my mornings to start beside you and my nights to end inside you. I have waited my whole life for you, and I'm not settling for anything less than permanent."

For the first time, I don't want to hide behind my mask. I don't want to hide how much his words mean to me. I want to allow myself the chance to have this person break into my heart and make himself home.

Tears cascade down my face. Anxo doesn't ask me to stop, only wipes them softly and kisses my forehead.

"I don't want a little something with you, Nevaeh. I want *everything* with you. *You* are my everything. In a world where even being soulmates is not enough, I'll have to keep adding more titles to keep you forever. And I'll start by making you *my wife.*"

I'm so lost in this bubbly feeling and his sparkling eyes staring into my soul with that heart-warming smile that it takes me a second to process his words.

"What—no. I don't think that's where you start." I stare at him dumbfounded, but he cups my face so I can't focus on anything but him.

"That's exactly where we start in my world."

He's not fooling anybody. I've watched movies. *Tons of them.* I know that's not where you start.

"I'm not sure I like the ways of your world then." I have to bite the inside of my cheek to hide my amusement at his antics.

"You'll love it soon enough, wifey."

"Not your wife, Angel." I can't help but giggle like a schoolgirl at his persistence. My stomach flutters every time he sounds so sure about our future together.

"Yes, you are. You just don't know it yet."

This goof! I laugh even harder. The healing wound on my shoulder stretches and stings, but I can't stop. Anxo turns me around to face him, trapping me in his arms again.

"How—" Angel cuts me off with his lips, kissing me fiercely.

"Hush, women. Stop questioning our life plan." He shushes my very logical protest before breaking his act and laughing with me.

Sitting here wrapped in my mate's arms, I wonder how I got this lucky.

17. You can't hide everything

Anxo

Carrying my mate like this reminds me of the first night we met.

Who would've thought that one day her being in my arms wouldn't be out of obligation but because of my desire to be around her all the time.

Snuggling into my chest with a bright smile, Nevaeh animatedly talks with Seiji about the *chemistry* between Harvey and Grace.

Tuning them out, I peek at Hazel and search for signs of distress. She might be walking beside me, but her mind is still on the sniper. The way he disintegrated into liquid made it pretty clear who was behind the attack.

Despite my constant reassurance that The Tetrad kingdom will fight tooth and nail on her behalf, Hazel insists on hiding behind the shadows as long as possible.

At one point I thought it was fear holding her back, but with time, I realized she actually detests the idea of confrontation with that man... even if it's for revenge.

But I've ensured Hazel knows my entire kingdom and cavalry will be at her disposal if she ever says the word.

"A month. Grace likes to take things tortoise slow."

"I say a week."

Seiji turns to Nevaeh with a ridiculous expression. He's willing to bet everything that Grace and Harvey would take things slow, but Nevaeh is practically buzzing with excitement.

"I know Harvey. That man has been begging for his mate for *years*. He won't let some douche get in the way."

I watch my mate try to convince Seiji to back out of the bet before she embarrasses him, and the depth of how hopelessly taken I am by this woman settles in.

It's easy to lose sense of self in her eyes. The darkness inside them is a mere shade and never the reflection of her soul. Those eyes could capture entire galaxies if she wanted, and *of course*, I fell into her trap. I'm a simple man, after all. A man hopelessly devoted to his mate and willing to surrender his last breath to her.

In the distance, I recognize our newest family member leaning against my car. A limp body in his arms catches my attention, making me walk faster.

Dread washes over me when Grace's tear-stricken face comes to light. Before I can ask what happened, Harvey shushes me, nodding at Grace. Her makeup is scrubbed off, and she is fast asleep bundled up in Harvey's leather jacket.

The crease between her brows makes the pit in my stomach grow deeper. My mind starts reeling with every awful possibility, and I'm immediately cursing myself for leaving her alone.

Stepping closer, I look for signs that will tell me she is at least unharmed and ease my tension, but my eyes squeeze shut when angry red fingerprints on her cheek glare back at me despite the dim streetlight.

Bringing Nevaeh closer, I subconsciously tighten my grip on her. She's the only thing keeping me from turning around and hunting the person responsible for this.

"Who?" The growl comes from deep inside my chest, and I have to swallow my rage when Nevaeh flinches in my hold. I know I should look away, but I can't tear my gaze from the light purple bruise on Grace's cheek mocking me to do something reckless.

Taking a deep breath, I press my forehead to my mate's and apologize for startling her. She brushes me off with a quick kiss to my jaw, but I need to do better. *Be better.*

I promised myself the first time I saw her flinch that I would never raise my voice at her or do anything to make her feel scared around me. I have to calm down before I accidentally break that promise.

"I'll explain everything, but first, let's get out of here."

I tamp down the urge to argue when I see others wanting to do the same. Grace needs rest and I need an explanation, so begrudgingly I make everyone get in the car.

The sooner we are on the road, the sooner Harvey will open his mouth and I'll be able to punish whoever dared come after my family.

Harvey tries to remove Grace from his arms, but she holds tight in her sleep. He has no choice but to get in with Grace on his lap. Even a blind man can see how happy the giant nutcase is about Grace sticking to him like that.

It's taking all of me not to bark at him to keep his hands to himself and maintain a respectable distance, but I can't do that when it's clear as day they are mates.

Harvey will still hear my full 'if you hurt her, I'll kill you' speech.

It took me a year to control the urge to squeeze Rick's neck every time I saw his face. But the delicate way Harvey cradles Grace, makes me think I won't have to ask my mate to help me cover up his death as 'an unfortunate accident'.

I back out of the parking lot with Nevaeh sitting beside me, anxiously twisting the rings on my hand that's resting on her thigh. Twenty minutes into our drive, Harvey finally recalls the night's events.

To be brutally honest, I completely forgot about Rick until Harvey brought him up.

Hearing what he did, I wanted to turn the car around and find that loser. I'll take my sweet time picking out every nerve in his body with my fingers. Instead of living that fantasy, I dig my fingers in my mate's thigh to keep myself grounded.

To say I'm livid is an understatement, but when Harvey assures me there aren't any bones left for me to break, I can't lie and say I'm not relieved. I arranged for someone to clean up the mess we left behind at the club and take care of Rick's body.

Nevaeh almost rips my head off when I ask a warrior to take care of Rick's funeral, but after I explain it's either them or we wait until we get home and host a proper funeral, she calms down rather quickly.

I'm worried about Grace, though. I don't want what she endured today, especially from someone she thought loved her, to crush her delicate heart.

What happened was horrible, and the only bright side is that Rick is now permanently out of her life and can't keep hurting her.

In the past, I had to bite my tongue when Rick treated her poorly because Grace kept *begging* me to leave it alone and that she could handle it. I'm so proud she finally stood up to him and that Harvey beat the shit out of that beetlebrain the moment he stepped out of line.

I'm especially glad about that.

Seiji doesn't mind filling Harvey in on how our night went. I don't think Harvey appreciated the details about him throwing up after watching Nevaeh pull thorns and bullets out of her.

My sweetheart turns in her seat, carefully taking Grace's hand so she can heal the bruise on her cheek. My stomach burns, seeing how easy it is for Harvey and my mate to communicate without words. He didn't have to say anything —just whispered her name, and she knew exactly what he wanted.

It's not jealousy, but rather from the ache in my soul that demands her to be wholly mine. I can't wait for the day our hearts and minds link the way our souls are, so no part of me would ever long for her like this.

But I'm a patient man if nothing else. My mate was deprived of making choices for years, and I'm not about to be yet another thing in her life she has no choice but to accept.

In our relationship, I follow her lead. Whatever pace she sets, that's what I'm following. She can ask me for as much or as little, and I'll give it to her.

When the purple bruise fades I hear Harvey sigh in relief and sit back with Grace snuggling into him. I don't want to get in the middle, but I'm pretty sure Seiji is going to lose his bet.

It's around four in the morning when we reach the hotel. Quickly running to the passenger seat, I'm ready to carry my sweetheart, but my independent mate wants to walk. It's good that we heal fast enough that she's not limping anymore, but it's bad for my lonely arms.

Since it's Harvey's first time here, I show him around a little. When I ask Harvey if he has the same directional disability as my mate, Nevaeh gives me a look that makes it clear she didn't appreciate my joke.

And now I'm afraid I'll be denied kisses tonight.

Instead of splitting into two groups everyone climbs in the elevator at once, sticking to each other as if the machine only works once.

The commotion makes Grace stir, and before she is even aware of what planet she is on, she is bombarded with hugs. The knot in my chest eases a bit when she leans against Harvey and talks about how he helped lift her spirit after everything went down.

Not to anyone's surprise, our little Miss Goody-two-shoes wants to put everything behind her and start over. She doesn't want to make space in her precious heart for any hate and resentment for Rick.

Sometimes, I hate how good she is. I don't like people taking advantage of my family just because they refuse to stoop to their level.

A tiny body tackles my legs as soon as the elevator opens and I'm surprised to find August out of bed at this hour. Raising his arms, he asks me to pick him up, and I don't dare deny the little man.

I guess my clinginess is rubbing off on my son.

Picking up my boy, I walk out, clearing the path for everyone to do the same. I have him for less than a minute before his eyes find the one he actually wants.

Any other kid would thrash in my arms or wiggle until I put them down so they could chase after my sweetheart, but August still has trouble asking for what he wants without overthinking about the consequences.

Kissing his head, I pass him to my mate, who is equally desperate to hold him.

August might enjoy me loving on him, but he needs Nevaeh to fall asleep—or for basically everything else. Resting his head over my mate's shoulder, August fists the neckline of her dress, ready to shut us out and go back to sleep.

Khatri comes out and passes bottles of water to everyone as we lazy around the living area. Apparently, August was out of bed as soon as we parked and waited by the elevator for us. He might be getting better, but it's not hard to see how important being around people he considers safe is for him.

Telling me he will be back in a short moment, Khatri escapes to a private balcony, no doubt to assist in cleaning up the mess we made tonight.

Nevaeh walks behind my seat to pick up the soft blanket on the back of it. Separating the dried blood on her from the kid, she bundles up our little guy. Patting his back and humming, she coaxes him to sleep.

As long as those two have each other, they don't need anyone else. Every day I spend with them, it becomes clear that August is and always will be my mate's priority, and I wouldn't have it any other way. He deserves every bit of love she showers him with.

"Nevaeh?" A broken whisper shatters the peace.

I didn't even notice Harvey stopped at the elevator.

The unmistakable terror in his eyes makes me push off the couch, but Harvey is not looking at me. His eyes are stuck on August, and the sheer horror on his face is unsettling.

Nevaeh, on the other hand, has gone quiet. *Too quiet.* Whatever she sees on Harvey's face reminds her of something she doesn't want to recall.

Before she can say anything, Harvey chokes out. "Is he... I-is he yours?"

Every second Nevaeh fails to answer him, Harvey becomes more agitated. He can't even look at August without his face crumbling in agony.

I'm not too fond of whatever silent conversation they are having with their eyes. I want to know what's gotten Harvey so mad and my mate petrified unlike I've ever seen her.

Gaining some composure, Nevaeh stutters, "Not in that sense. I mean, he's mine, but also not quite. I—we—in the dungeon. I mean, he..."

"Monkey!"

And just like that, August is not sleepy anymore. Tightening his arms around Nevaeh, he faces Harvey head-on. That boy is fearless when it comes to my mate. Harvey doesn't want to piss off the little werewolf by being loud with her.

As much as I want to take him away because I don't like the direction this is taking, the way Harvey just lost his cool means separating August from my sweetheart is not an option anymore.

The tension floating in the room starts to make him anxious, and I can't have August feeling unsafe around us. Channeling my Divine, I link my boy to assure him.

"It's okay, monkey. Nevaeh is okay. I'm right here. Nothing will happen to you or her. Relax, kiddo."

August blinks at me before laying his head back and getting comfortable, leaving me to handle this.

Everyone thinks August doesn't talk, and *technically*, that is true, but once he got comfortable with me, I created a link between us so he could reach out without actually speaking.

He's still shy and primarily communicates with single words, but it's still progress. I'm just waiting for the day he finally speaks his first words to Nevaeh.

"Promise Papa?"

Like every other time August has called me that, I struggle to keep my composure.

He recently started referring to Nevaeh and me as 'Mama and Papa'. The first time he said it, I thought it was an innocent mistake. The second time, I thought maybe he was confused and probably missing his parents.

I went to ask Khatri for advice since he's the only one I trust to talk about something so personal. Plus he has kids, so he's supposed to know how they work.

It took me some time to accept that August wasn't just missing his parents, he was *replacing* them with us. He was feeling the same love and safety he did with them, and for a small kid, the two people who care for you like we've been doing simply means we are *Mama* and *Papa*.

I didn't know whether to cry because he thought it was normal to have a new set of parents just like that or to cry in relief that he understands we're permanent... that we're not going anywhere.

"Promise, kiddo."

Now that I know August is essentially going to zone out until he wants to involve himself in the conversation again, I tune back into whatever the two best friends are trying to keep under wraps.

"You're not making any sense, Nevaeh. Did that happen again? Because I swear on Fates if anyone dared touch—" Nevaeh stops him from giving out more details, but one glance at her pale face, and I start to piece it all together.

Again?

My blood freezes under my skin when I consider the possibility that someone *touched* my mate. Touched her *without* her consent, touched her when she was weak and vulnerable. The more I think about it, the angrier I get with myself for not being there for her... for not seeing it sooner.

"No! nothing like that. *Anxo*. Nothing like that happened. I promise it happened once, and Harvey was there—" She can barely get the words out, watching me shake my head as my mind tortures me with the worst-case scenarios. "Angel, nothing happened, I swear." Her voice is tight, and the way she looks at me, I can see how badly she wants me to let this go.

Seeing her desperation, I take deep breaths to calm myself and sit down before beckoning her closer. As soon as her eyes fall on my open arms, she rushes over, settling sideways on my lap with monkey snuggled in hers.

Burying my face in her neck, I wrap my arms around both of them. This is the only way I can contain my rage and convince myself that she is safe and protected. Kissing her neck, I rub August's back soothingly.

With her fingers running through my hair, Nevaeh lays her cheek on my head. "Please. No more disturbing thoughts about something that never happened."

Rubbing his face tiredly, Harvey waits for his best friend to explain before he even thinks about taking a seat. My instincts say if Harvey hears what he fears most, I will have to chase after him as he runs out to hunt down Visha himself.

I'm not saying I won't help, only that I don't do things halfway and never without a solid plan.

My head is still nuzzled in my sweetheart's neck. I don't even care about the dried blood anymore, I just want to hold my mate and plan the perfect witch hunt of all time with her.

Sighing, my mate leans sideways into my chest, and I tighten my arms around my little family.

"It was another vision," Nevaeh tells Harvey how she met August and how they got out before vaguely adding details about his family.

August is now wide awake, so we use big words and codes to tell the complete story. We aren't ready to have that talk with August yet. It would be years before we sit him down and talk about his biological parents and his pack, but for now, there's no way we're putting the weight of that knowledge on his tiny shoulders.

"That b—" Grace blocks the curse with her palm over Harvey's mouth, nodding toward August.

The kid sees my mate and half his family swear in every sentence. I don't think stopping Harvey is going to accomplish much.

Shifting the topic to lighter things, Nevaeh introduces Harvey to the kid he couldn't look in the eye before.

"Monkey, that's my best friend, Harvey. He's a Horseman too, just like me." I feel him nod his head on her shoulder, dropping the protective glare Hazel taught him to master, and shyly waves.

The big guy practically melts from the gesture. Good to know the big bad Horseman with tattoos and a leather jacket isn't immune to my toddler's charm.

My boy shyly offers his little hand, looking to Grace for approval, who's already beaming that August remembered what she taught him about polite gestures.

Harvey grasps the hand rather gently, as if afraid to accidentally crush it. "Funny, a monkey introducing another monkey."

"Don't make me stab you." My mate glares at Harvey, who waves his hand, dismissing her threat completely.

"She absolutely would, you know," Seiji warns, but like Nevaeh is immune to Harvey's threats, he seems immune to hers.

"Oh, I'm used to it. Nevaeh started threatening to choke people and cussing like a pirate when she was barely five. I don't doubt she will go through with it, but if you know anything about monkey, you know she would *never* hurt someone she cares about."

Scoffing under her breath, my mate is intent on not letting Harvey see how much his words mean to her by grumbling 'Sappy asshole' under her breath.

"Why do you keep calling her monkey? I thought little August was our one and only monkey here."

Before Harvey can answer Grace, Nevaeh practically growls, "Don't. You. Dare."

Harvey ignores her completely. *Again.* I think I'm starting to love their connection and banter. Even when she had all of us, Nevaeh needed something or someone good from her childhood to remind her that not everything had changed in her life.

"Ever seen a monkey in action?" Everyone nods, but I keep my head buried in her neck, kissing her, breathing her scent to relax.

"Well, she was exactly like those mischievous little beasts. She ran after every shiny thing and then watched the chaos unfold when she stole something important and hid it. The entire kingdom would go wild trying to find it. Let's not forget her red chipmunk cheeks—"

A door to our far left bangs shut, and Khatri strides in to update me. Harvey shoots up from his seat, and in three long strides, both men engulf each other. I don't think I've ever seen Khatri laugh this loud for as long as I've known him.

The reunion between teary-eyed men who reminisce about days before the light was stolen from our kingdom gives me a little peek into how everyone back home will react to having their missing Horsemen back home.

Nevaeh goes stiff in my arms. I just know it's because she feels worse now that Harvey remembers Khatri and their past, but she can barely thread two memories together without blanking on the details.

"Nothing to fret about, sweetheart. We can always make new memories." Whispering so only she can hear me, I bring her back to the present.

Turning to me with a sad smile, she whispers, "Black magic."

I can't help but chuckle at my silly mate. I don't know how it started, but every time I comfort her about something without her verbally telling me, she says the same thing. But it's not black magic or witchcraft, but my boundless devotion to her. Could also be how I can't keep my eyes off her.

Everyone is starting to show the effects of our long night, but there's one thing left to do before this day ends.

"We need to talk."

"About?" Strangely, Harvey stares at me expectantly.

I nod in assurance at Grace, who is chewing her bottom lip so hard I'm afraid she will draw blood.

Turning towards my mate, who is fighting sleep, I ask her to freshen up while I have a quick chat with Harvey. Nevaeh doesn't hesitate before kissing my cheek and taking off to her room.

My mate is a walking contradiction. The same woman who is so stubborn and loudmouth in the most adorable ways is also so trusting and depending with me. I feel proud to be someone she doesn't have to doubt or question to know if I have her best interest in mind.

"Come on," I lead us to the elevator and then to the roof. If I have this conversation on our floor, Nevaeh will hear it, and I can't risk telling her just yet. I have to wait until she is in a better head space before I dump this on her.

Harvey, the daredevil, climbs the railing to sit down on the edge of the roof, so I have to follow.

We're silent as I try to figure out where to start, but there's no good way to say this. "Harvey..."

"If you're going to tell me about my parents, I already know."

My head snaps in his direction in shock.

I hate the way he blankly stares at the city lights with that faraway look in his eyes. He is trying to act as if his whole world isn't falling apart, but it is, and I don't want him to hide that from me.

"Visha told me. I didn't believe her at first, but then I *felt* it. The shift in my Divine. The surge of power that didn't belong to me. I so badly wanted it to be another thing she was using to manipulate me, but I could feel she wasn't lying. Not this time."

I don't know what to say or how to start apologizing for everything he has lost, but when he turns to me with a sad smile, I don't have to say any words for him to know.

"I've had *years* to come to terms with it, brother." With a weak chuckle, Harvey shakes his head, running his hand through his messy hair. "Not going to lie, I had a little hope... just a bit, that maybe by some miracle when I got home, they will be waiting for me. It was nothing more than wishful thinking after all."

"I'm sorry, Harvey. I wish things were different." My hand rests on his back. I do my best not to flinch as I rub his back and feel the raised skin I know came from years of abuse.

"I don't. I decided to stick by Nevaeh, and if given the chance I will do it all over again. She's always been a part of my family. And I like to think they were proud of that decision."

"They were." The surety in my voice makes his eyes gleam with hope. "Your dad never stopped talking about how brave his son was. He was proud you didn't leave Nevaeh when she needed you the most."

His head falls forward, barely holding on when he asks tiredly, "What the fuck happened man?"

I take large gulps of oxygen to stall, but it's not fair. Harvey has every right to know what happened in his absence, even when it guts me to say it.

"Stella fell sick after you were taken. The grief was too much for her and unfortunately, our Divine can't heal a broken heart. The pain slowly ate her whole. She was gone within a year."

That's when the first tear falls, but I push forward. "Henry held on as long as he could. I found out too late that he was only waiting for me to take over before he gave in to his heartache. Not even a day after he handed me War, he followed after his mate."

I don't hide the wobble in my voice, and Harvey doesn't hide his tears anymore. We stay like that for a while, letting our hurt wash pver us before we have to pack it all up and move on.

Inhaling sharply, he rubs under his eyes, laughing bitterly. "Fantastic, so I'm an orphan now."

I couldn't help it. I smack the back of his head just like I do whenever Seiji says something stupid. "Never say that again." Harvey is so shocked I hit him, he can't do anything but blink at me. "You have a family, and you will always have one. Every single person waiting for us downstairs is your family. Blood or not."

Nodding slowly, Harvey let my words sink in before his shoulders sagged as if a weight had finally dropped from them. Not knowing what happened except that he lost the people most important to him must've felt awful. And to think Visha used that information to break him some more.

"You know I'm not too fond of kids, but that little werewolf is one cute as fuck toddler."

"Right?!" I agree a little too enthusiastically, which makes him laugh.

"I'm going to ask Grace for one as soon as we finish the talking, sharing, and 'getting to know one another' part."

I'm shocked he's ready to move that fast. Maybe Nevaeh was onto something when she said Harvey would be wrapped around Grace in less than a week.

"Fates, you don't waste any time, do you?"

"They snatched a lot of time from me, brother. I don't want to wait to do the things I thought I would never get to in this life." When he says it like that, I understand where he's coming from.

I can see how differently Nevaeh and Harvey deal with their past. Where Harvey wants to grab life by the balls and never look back, Nevaeh can't stop glancing back, worrying about making the same mistakes and ruining her future.

Having Harvey around would be good for her. For selfish reasons, I want Harvey to stay close so she has more people in her corner than me.

"That kid will be lucky to have both of you as parents. With your genes combined, you'll make some adorable babies." Harvey is practically swaying, smiling like a lovesick idiot. Nevaeh was right, Harvey is a giant teddy bear on the inside.

"Imagine a little one with her curly hair and my eyes. That kid would rule the world."

"I see your ego is exactly as big as your head."

"Hey, *you* don't get to call me a giant alright." Shoving my shoulder, his demeanor changes to the man I met a few hours ago. "You're good to her, right? Because I would gladly bury you in my future backyard if not."

"Hey, I would never. I can't even think of a scenario in which I would purposely hurt my mate. I will do anything to keep her safe and happy. It will take her some time to believe she deserves those things though."

I sigh tiredly and try to fix the mess my hair looks after Nevaeh plays with it. "Sometimes I worry she thinks she's too damaged to be pieced back together."

"She is."

The certainty in his voice startles me. I don't understand why they both believe they aren't worthy, but I bet it has something to do with that witch. It will take time and a truckload of love for these two to believe we aren't leaving or hurting them. *Ever.*

"Just don't give up on her."

"Never," I promise before climbing down and dusting my pants, which once held the perfectly ironed look. *Pity.*

"Let's go back before they come up looking for us. This place is kind of a private spot for me."

Everyone has retired to their rooms when we return except Grace, who is waiting on Harvey. The smile on her face as Harvey walks into the room almost blinds me.

Smirking, I walk past the couple that's too busy drowning in each other's eyes to notice me leave.

Seiji is going to lose the bet and this mind.

18. What rhymes with love?

Nevaeh

I never would've taken that bullet for Hazel if I knew this would happen.

Just after Angel disappeared to have his secret talk with Harvey, Hazel barged into my room. She let me take a shower in my room before forcing me to rest in Anxo's room. She even had Grace to put my little boy to bed, who was more than happy to take over bedtime duties.

I wasn't enjoying this generous version of Hazel, and unfortunately, my freedom meant promising her that I would leave the sniper incident alone and wouldn't pester her or Angel for more details.

But when the siren fluffed my pillow, I had to stop her.

After drowning me in blankets up to my chin, she reluctantly left me alone—more like ran out when my eyes flashed gold.

Even my Divine thought she was being weird.

Sharky has some serious issues owing people. A couple of snacks and a reluctant smile would've sufficed, instead, the siren chose to steal my baby on a night I needed his help to stay sane.

His presence would've helped me keep the tsunami in my head bottled up until there weren't so many eyes following my every move.

Don't get me wrong, as surprised as I am to be on the receiving end of Hazel's rare affection, I don't have it in me to not act like a ticking time bomb tonight.

The mere thought of accidentally falling asleep and seeing that dungeon again has my anxiety shooting to the roof.

Staying in a safe place among people I trust made it easy to convince myself that I was not haunted by my past anymore. But a single confrontation was enough to remind me that I'm not invincible. My past might be behind me, but I still carry the parts they broke.

Facing a small part of my past has triggered the part of my brain that doesn't understand how to separate my memories from my present. My fears from my reality. The blood I lost from the blood I drew.

But I can't knock on that door tonight. Opening the smallest window to my past could crumble my sanity—which I'm barely holding on to as it is.

The tremor in my fingers grows as the flashes start taking over my vision. I focus on breathing and shoving down the bile of nightmare crawling up my throat. You've been holding on perfectly fine the entire day, Nevaeh. Don't let yourself slip now.

'Think you can hide from me?'

My breathing picks up at her voice echoing in my head. Why can't she leave me alone?

It's been two months, Nevaeh, why can't you be *normal* like everyone else? Why do you still have to keep yourself from spiraling every single night?

When Anxo knocks on the door before entering, I shove my hands under the covers, clutching the material tightly.

"You feel any better, sweetheart?" His worry breaks through my panic, and I'm glad it did before Visha dragged me deeper into her tricks.

"I'm fine." I clear my throat when my voice shakes. I'm not sure how to act put together when my insides are being clawed with terror.

"No, you're not, you're shivering. I'll go grab another blanket for you."

Angel moves to leave, but I stop him quickly. "No! I mean... I'm good. No more blankets needed." I nod urgently to prove I'm okay but Anxo keeps looking at me strangely, noticing my odd behavior.

"You don't look so good, baby. Wait here, I'll make you something warm and light. How do you feel about soup?"

He can't leave. I have to stop him, but my voice is stuck in my throat. An invisible hand made of my fear of being alone in this room chokes me, paralyzing my muscles until I'm useless against my own brain attacking me.

'You're all alone now, little girl. No one's coming to help.'

Shut up. Shut up. Shut up!

"I know it's not your usual time to eat but humor me tonight. I'll be right back—" Anxo turns his back to me, ready to leave.

"No! You d-don't have to... have to go... s-stay plea-please." I'm struggling to take my next breath.

There's no more hiding the fear in my voice or the way my throat is closing up. I don't want him to see me like this, but I can't help the shiver of panic running through me at the thought of being left alone.

Alone with my thoughts and *her*.

"Nevaeh? What's wrong, sweetheart? You've gone pale." Anxo rushes to my side immediately.

His hand reaches to touch my face, but I flinch without meaning, and Angel staggers back. The more he steps back so I don't panic, the more I hyperventilate. If this keeps up, my Divine will take over, and I'll seriously hurt everyone around me.

There was a reason my chains remained untouched for a decade.

I can't do that again. The blood, the hearts I ripped out... I'm not doing that again. Not for them to laugh at my face as I beg them to stop.

I can see Anxo's lips moving, but the ringing in my head is louder than his voice, making it difficult to focus on anything but the constant throbbing. My breathing is tattered, and I'm heaving, trying to fill my lungs, but it's not working.

When I don't respond, Angel grips his hair desperately,

trying not to reach out for me again.

"Nevaeh!" The way he growls my name successfully snaps me out of my head long enough to catch his eyes.

Scratching my throat, I look up at Anxo, and the tears I've been trying to hold hostage finally escape, filling the room with my broken wails.

Nausea crawls up to my throat as I squeeze my lips to stop the bile. Curling into a ball, I press a hand over my ear and push my face against the mattress to block out the noise in my head.

Angel paces the length of his bed, waiting for me to let him approach, but I can't talk... so I do the one thing I can. Anxo never fails to read me. He can always figure out what I want by just looking at me, and I'm hoping his witchcraft will help me now. Looking up, my eyes search his, and within a second, he's next to me.

Swiftly picking up my curled frame, he cradles me on his lap. I cry out because every part of my body feels like a truck ran over me.

Angel guides the back of my head to bury in his neck, and that's when I break. Circling my hands around his waist, I let the broken sobs escape me. My wails are loud enough to soak our walls with my pain. Crying on his shoulder, my body trembles, but I clutch onto him with my life.

The scariest part is I'm aware there is nothing to fear anymore. No matter who's chasing me, I have people to watch my back now. But who's going to tell the 9-year-old in me that I don't have to hide in a corner anymore? All that little girl knows is to hide and make no sound, no matter how hard the hits are, hoping they'll stop.

I've grown up muffling my screams until one day, the only place my cries felt safe was inside my head.

With my mate's arms around me and the buzz of his Divine creating a bubble around us, I know I can be as loud as I want without fearing the next hit will be harder.

Angel covers me with his thick duvet, thinking my shivers are from the cold, and slips a hand under my shirt to rub my bare back in soothing circles.

I can barely regulate my breathing, but I don't stop begging him not to leave me between my broken cries. Angel keeps kissing me, reminding me he is right here and to breathe before I pass out.

I soak in the feeling of his kisses on my head, his comforting words in my ear, and his fingers in my hair, replacing my memories with this moment. The way Angel clears his throat and his voice wobbles tells me I'm scaring him.

As he sways us, Anxo keeps talking to me, hoping something will bring me out of my head.

"Nevaeh, I need to know what triggered this."

"Please don't leave," I croak out a desperate plea.

"Shhh, I'm never leaving, baby. Come on, focus on my heartbeat. Take a deep breath for me, yeah?" I mimic him taking deep breaths when his chest moves with my head resting over his heart. "That's it. Keep breathing for me, sweetheart. You're doing so good."

I know my effort is not perfect, but his encouraging whispers and how he holds my face against his heart help drain the panic from me slowly.

Nuzzling my face in his neck, I tense when Angel tries to pry me off of him. He shushes me by gently swaying us side to side. Taking my hands in his, he guides them around the band of his sweatpants before leaning back.

It's less than five seconds, but that's enough for my tears to return and panic to grip my throat.

In one swift motion, Anxo pulls off his forest green hoodie and pulls it over my head before letting me erase the wretched gap between us.

Wiping the fresh tears with his palm that covers half my face, he lets me rub my face against his bare chest like a cat. I calm down considerably faster with his scent surrounding me and being able to touch his his skin.

We stay like that for what seems like hours before my eyes feel too heavy to remain open.

"You'll be here when I wake up, right?" I'm not ready to let him go, and I don't want to fall asleep only to wake up disoriented without him.

"I'll always be here."

Anxo slides down the bed with me still on top of him and his arms around my waist. His fingers playing with my hair lull me closer to sleep, and I completely relax on top of him, not caring about him bearing my weight.

He smells irresistible, and I have this insistent urge to bite his neck, but I settle for a kiss instead, which makes him hold me tighter and squish me to him.

I want to be squished like this forever.

"Got to sleep, sweetheart. I've got you." His chin rests on my head, and his hand softly rubs my back under his hoodie.

In my sleepy haze, I let my deepest fear slip. "Will you hide me if they come back?"

"I'll burn them to the ground for you."

The conviction in his voice is my anxiety breaker. I know as long as I have him by my side, I'll be okay.

"My Angel." I kiss his neck before letting myself get dragged deeper into the darkness without fear of what might be hiding behind it.

Before I completely fall asleep, I hear him softly murmur something that sounds a lot like love and kiss the tip of my nose, but I don't remember the words when I wake up.

19. Adding names to my shit list

Nevaeh

I watch Angel stride toward me, and before I know it I'm thrown over his shoulder in one smooth move.

With my stomach pressed against his back, I shiver when he kisses my hip and starts walking like I'm not dangling from his shoulder like a rag doll.

Swatting his bum, I ask, "Uh, what do you think you're doing?"

"Taking you on a date."

"And making all my blood rush to my brain is part of it?" Angel snickers but doesn't put me down until we're on the roof.

When he turns to a hidden corner, I see a set of stairs someone could easily pass by without noticing. I expect Anxo to put me down, but he continues on the stairs to a smaller roof.

Once my feet are on solid ground and the world stops spinning, it's impossible to tear my eyes from the sky above me. I'm not particularly fond of humans, their realm, or their existence in general, but I can't say the same for their sky. The night sky above me is littered with thousands of twinkling stars and half a moon peeking from behind an odd-shaped cloud.

That one looks like a man with a horn.

When Angel clears his throat, I shift my attention to my very own miracle instead of the one above me, and my jaw goes slack.

A comfy mattress lies on the roof with a fluffy blanket thrown at the end. My favorite snacks are neatly arranged in a corner with a mini cooler, which I'm sure is filled with all the sugary drinks I love—the ones Angel thinks are unhealthy. Dozens of flickering candles create a perfect square around the mattress. I step closer and the invisible dome of protection ripples to let me through.

"Why?"

Angel looks at me ridiculously as if the question is the stupidest thing he's ever heard. "You like stargazing. I thought this would make a perfect second date." He shrugs shyly and pulls back the comforter before asking me to get in. "Come here, sweetheart."

The way he beckons me with that irresistible curve of his lips, it's hard not to obey. Leaving my slippers behind, I carefully slide in next to him, making sure not to knock over any candles accidentally. Angel immediately pulls me to his side.

I told Anxo about my love for starry nights *once. In passing.* And this man didn't just remember that tidbit but used it to do something so cute for me. I don't know what I did to deserve him, but I won't let that deter me from having him.

Nuzzling my face in his neck, I bite playfully so he knows I need my fill of kisses and attention. Our affection has only increased with time. Before, Anxo always had to be around me, but now he has to touch me at all times, or he throws a fit.

I love the way he craves me.

With my head on his shoulder, I look up at my second favorite view after my mate. I've always been comfortable with darkness, whether it's around or within me. The dark sky above reminds me not to look at my own darkness as something that weighs me down, but what makes my stars shine that much brighter.

Angel clears his throat, stealing my attention again. The way he swallows tightly lets me know tonight is for more than just gazing at the stars.

I watch the fog around his mouth float by when he breathes out, "I admit I have an ulterior motive for this date. There are a few things I want you to know before we go home."

"What's wrong?"

When I do a poor job hiding my worry, Angel quickly reassures me. "Hey, no need to let that brain go haywire. I just thought some things about my life are best if you hear from me rather than in hushed whispers around the kingdom. I've got a few stories to tell, and they are not all fun."

"I don't care if they're good or bad. When it comes to you, I want it all." Nodding my head against him, I snuggle closer and prepare for whatever he throws at me.

His hesitance hits me at once. I feel so juvenile to think my struggles with sharing my past were only affecting me. From the day we met, Anxo has been hyper-focused on helping me heal, and I never once bothered to ask if *he* was okay, too. I have to be a better mate than that.

I can't ask him to soothe my wounds and nurture my broken soul and not do the same for him.

Sighing heavily, Anxo grips my fingers on his stomach and holds me as if he's gathering strength from my presence and lays it all out in the open.

"Growing up in Conquer was... it wasn't the kind of environment I would want August to grow up in. Life was pretty much awful before the kingdoms merged. My parents..."

The force behind his last words tells me I won't like my future in-laws much after tonight. "They aren't the greatest at parenting. I was never enough... always a disappointment. Now that I'm older, I recognize the signs of emotional abuse and manipulation."

He stops to search my face. "Sometimes it got physical. Don't worry, it was an occasional thing. They didn't have much time for reprimanding anyway. And then I had my growth spurt quite early compared to other kids my age, so it didn't work for them longer."

Rage unlike I've ever felt before settles in my chest. I'm explosive when I'm angry, but the anger simmering just below the surface is new to me and much wilder.

Squeezing his fingers, I count the beat of his heart to settle down. I'm harboring this rage on purpose because his parents aren't here for me to tear them apart, but I refuse to let this go.

I have a long list of people I want bound and bleeding in my torture cell, and his parents just made the list. I don't give a fuck who they are.

Anyone who touches my mate deserves everything my fucked up head comes up with.

"Take me home, Anxo. *Right now*." Before I can leave the warm mattress, he pulls me back against him, and I feel his shoulders shake.

Laughing like everything is good and dandy, my mate stops me. "Relax, my avenging goddess. There's no need to rip out any heads. It doesn't matter anymore."

"It matters to me! They *hit* you, Anxo. They put their hands on *my mate*. I'll rip those arms out—" Warm lips crashing over mine stop my murder rant.

Burying my fingers in his hair, I kiss him harder, hoping to lose some of my fury in his touch. Angel kisses me until I melt into him, and my muscles relax before pulling away with a goofy smile that I want to lick away.

This man loves it when I get protective over him, and I don't know which one of us is crazier. I don't think he understands how much I'm itching to get my hands on his folks.

"Want to hear about the time I ran away from home?"

He did what?!

"Oh yeah…. and I was just sixteen. My Divine wasn't as strong then, so blending with the crowd and disappearing was easy. I was jumping from one realm to another with only one thought in mind. That I didn't want to go back to that house."

I don't understand the faraway smile on his face when I'm barely keeping myself from tearing up. Playing with my fingers on his stomach, he keeps gazing at the dome over us. Unlike when he told me about his parents, he seemed more relaxed and open.

Chuckling to himself, Angel reminisces. "No matter how

much I regretted leaving behind my responsibilities, I would've kept running had Dean not found me."

Moving to lay on him, I rest my chin on my knuckles and momentarily lose my train of thought when Angel's fingers softly brush my cheek.

"He wasn't happy I hid the abuse from everyone or that I let those 'good-for-nothing bastards', as he called them, drive me away from home. Dean absolutely hated my mother, and now he had a very good reason to do something about it. When I told him I wasn't going back to them, Dean looked *so* offended that I thought he was taking me back to my parents."

His laugh warms my stomach, and I watch his breath hitch when I kiss his chest, right where his heart is.

"You already know what happened next."

"Uh no, I don't. I wasn't there, remember? So elaborate, please."

"Smartass." I squeal when he tickles my stomach. "I stayed with Dean after that, and not even a month later, he got my father to announce that he was stepping down. Father told the council I was ready, that he had taught me more than enough."

I snort, "I doubt that."

"And you're right. I was the one running everything behind the curtains since I was eleven while my father did Fates know what with all his free time."

"Your father didn't fight Papa at all?"

"He didn't want the stress or responsibility anyway. My parents wanted to travel the realms and be free of things holding them back—Including me. It worked out perfectly for them."

Staging a whisper, I ask, "You sure you don't want me to *accidentally* kill them?"

Snickering under his breath, he ignores my offer.

"That year, I took over Conquer and decided I wanted a life free of their constant taunts, so I moved into our Horsemen castle."

Tucking a loose strand behind my ear, Angel's forehead

creases as he thinks about something hard. "You know, now that I think about it, I have a theory that your dad threatened my father to back down. He didn't want the responsibility, but I don't see him giving up his title just because I refused to help him out anymore."

"Good. Remind me to thank Papa for that. You deserve the title and the respect."

Holding my waist, he sits up so I'm straddling him with my thighs on either side of his hips. I don't realize I'm still staring at him with my head on his shoulder until he ducks to place a chaste kiss on my lips, and I blink out of my daze.

Angel certainly knows how to face his challenges and mold them into something that makes him happy. His ability to always see the brighter side is admirable.

I could never—but I love that about him.

Cupping his warm cheek in my cold palm, I try to free myself from the trance his glistening green eyes always bind me in. "You are enough for me." I recount what his parents made him believe, hoping I can make him see how wrong they were. "They have no idea what they're missing out on."

Kissing his pout twice, I lean back to look him in the eyes when I say, "You are more than enough, Angel. You're so good to me and our little boy that it makes me want to be better, to do anything that will make you even half as happy as you make us."

His hands dip under my sweatshirt, and I hate how his hands are still warm when I'm freezing, even with his warmth surrounding me.

"I'm so glad you found me that night. I never thought anyone would want this damaged version of me, but you? You didn't even blink before embracing all that I am."

Holding my face, he brings us closer. "Don't you dare talk about yourself like that. You're not damaged, Nevaeh. Far from it. You're the strongest woman I know. *A survivor.*" With a soft kiss on my lips, Angel seals my adoration for him. "I'm so darn proud to be your mate. So proud of *everything* you are."

Blinking rapidly, I hide my face in his neck until the lump in my throat gets easier.

The silence reminds how easily Angel can make me feel safe around him. How he always catches my triggers before they can explode and makes sure I don't have to face anything on my own.

I never thought I could do this, but the care Angel has shown me with the slow burn of his warmth spreading in my chest gives me enough courage to make up my mind. I want to tell him my truth. I want him to know my scars.

"Can I tell you what happened?"

Angel stiffens against me. "You don't have to sweetheart. I know how much you want to bury it and never look back. Don't open your scars for me, sweetheart. I don't need to see them to love them."

Resting my cheek on his shoulder, I feel the wall around my heart crumble to dust.

I want him to know. I don't want him to wonder why I can't sleep through the night, why my balance is worse than terrible on my best days, or why he has to fuss over me not eating enough all the time.

"I want you to know why I am the way I am. It hurts to explain in pieces or to leave you guessing. For selfish reasons, I want it off my chest so I never have to repeat it. This way even if no one else does, *you'll always understand.*"

Angel is considerate enough that he will prefer being clueless for his whole life than hurting me by making me repeat the worst times of my life.

Seeing my hesitation, Angel turns me around so I'm sitting between his thighs with my back against his chest. His arms hold me protectively as he nudges my head with his. "Look up, sweetheart. Watch the stars you love and let it all out. Don't worry about anything else. *Lean on me, baby.*"

The mess in my head calms down at his assurance, and I do what he said. I lean on him.

"Do you promise not to run away after I tell you

everything?"

I'm joking. *Only a little bit.*

"You can push me off this roof, and I'll still find a way to come back to you."

Just like that, he makes me forget why I was worrying in the first place. This is Angel. My mate. I can always trust him to stick by me.

Clearing my throat, I prepare to recite my horror story. Angel tightens his arms around me as if asking if I'm ready to rehash those memories. To ease his worries, I kiss his jaw and nuzzle my cheek against his heart to steal some courage from him.

You're not there anymore Nevaeh.

They can't take you back.

I hold my Angel's arms around my waist and start spilling. "I was kept alone in the beginning. Complete isolation. They didn't let me see Harvey for *months* and stuck me in a small concrete room with no windows. Fed me maybe once a week."

For the first time in my life, I willingly replay the memories, selecting the ones I want to share so I can sum it up without going into too many details.

"When we were kids, we were shoved around and struck occasionally but that was it. They mainly used us as the Visha's little helpers. We cleaned her chambers, served food—things like that. As we grew up, they moved to tougher methods... l-like physical punishments, keeping us awake for days and starving us to see who would snap first. The one time I lost control... it was so bad Angel. A bloodbath. I don't even remember most of it."

With every word out of my mouth, Anxo gets quieter. He is holding me as if afraid I will break if he doesn't.

Angel is the only one who will ever get this piece of me. I've never bared my soul like this to anyone and never will. Now he'll know where my darkness comes from.

"They forced me to watch as they skinned other prisoners alive or burned them until there was nothing left. Visha thought if I knew what she could do, it would make me more compliant. *It didn't*. But she loved my disobedience. It gave her a reason to show the power she held over me. Each scar on my body was a warning, a reminder that I was only alive because of her mercy."

I stop after that because I might throw up if I give out more details. I wait to see if Angel wants to ask something, but when he doesn't make a sound, I take a relieved breath—concluding my stay at the *Royale Coven Plaza*.

When hot tears drop on my neck, I lean back into my Angel and hold him to me. Cupping the side of his face, I trace my fingers in his hair and just let him *feel*.

I sit with him as he lets it all out. I let his pain consume him because bottling it up won't help him. I had to school my emotions and expressions for a decade in fear of making things worse for myself, so I know how exhausting it can be to keep your composure at all times.

It's quiet for a minute. Angel stays wrapped around me, placing kisses on my neck and squeezing me to death. The neck of my—*his* sweatshirt is soaked with his silent tears, and my chest burns, knowing I'm the reason behind them.

"On the bright side, I survived. My life is so much better now that I have you. You're always following me around like a guardian angel, making sure I'm safe and *happy*."

Anxo finally lifts his head from my neck to turn me around in his lap. Those bewitching green eyes are puffy and red, lips pursed in an adorable pout.

His protective hold doesn't give me much space to move—not that I want to. Burying my fingers in his hair, I kiss his forehead, grateful when he relaxes against me.

Seeing the reaction from just one little kiss, I start peppering kisses all over his pretty face. Angel sniffs before snuggling closer.

"Feel better?" I lean back as far as he will allow me to cup his face.

The other day, I mentioned to Hazel how Angel is always

warm and cuddly—like my personal heater and she said maybe it's me who's always cold and creepy—like a psychotic killer.

Yeah… that girl doesn't do romance.

"Only a little. Maybe more kisses would help," he says cheekily before pressing our lips together.

Anxo leads the kiss, and before I know it, we are a mess of needy kisses and grabby hands. Angel slowly lowers his hands to my ass before giving my cheeks a firm squeeze, which earns a breathy moan from me.

Woah.

I think I should accept Seiji's offer of sex education. I don't want to be clueless and ruin our *sexy time* together.

When I feel Angel softly nudge into my mind, I don't hesitate to let him in. A tingle spread down my spine when he starts building a mental connection with me. There's a small pressure in my head as the metaphorical knot tightens, strengthening the link between us.

I'm amazed by the rush of warm feelings spreading in my chest and how right it feels.

We keep making out right there on the rooftop. And judging by the bright smile on his face or the way his hands won't stop caressing me, I'd say Angel feels much better now.

Oh, the lengths I would go for that smile.

20. My rules are not your rules

Nevaeh

"Aren't you a vision for sour eyes." Angel runs up the stairs to where I'm standing and kisses me softly.

I Look down at my outfit—yet another pastel purple pullover I stole from Angel and jeans that Grace gave me.

"Yeah? I like it too. It's someone's mother's jeans, but I'm not sure whose." I shrug, rubbing my hands on my thighs over the rough yet smooth material.

"What?" Seiji looks around to see if anyone knows what I'm talking about.

"Grace said these are 'mom jeans.' I just don't know *whose* mom gave them to me."

Behind Angel's shoulder, I look for Grace so she can confirm it. Sitting beside her mate on the dining table, I find Grace with her cheeks between her palms, pressing hard enough that I can see her knuckles turning white.

Then suddenly, the room is loud. Obnoxiously loud. Every corner of the penthouse is filled with roaring laughter that I'm sure humans from the other side of town can hear.

I have a family full of weirdos.

After wiping a tear from his right eye, Anxo holds my face in his gigantic hands and smashes our lips together before I can ask what is happening.

"You are adorable, sweetheart." The words come out wobbly since Angel hasn't stopped laughing quite yet.

I had a feeling these people were weirder than average, but now I know how much.

I am surrounded by idiots.

"I don't have time to fix every brain in this room, so I'm

letting this go." I reach for the suitcase I had abandoned, but before I can, Angel takes it from me, lifting it with ease. *Show off.*

I'm willing to ignore their stupidity because I'm jumping off the walls, excited about finally going home today.

Now that Harvey is here and we've gathered all we can about August's biological family, there's no need to stick around humans.

After the night at the club, we took a few days to recuperate before the talks about leaving began. I used that time to talk to Harvey about what happened after he escaped. We are still coming to terms with the memories and hardships of a time that will forever stay with us.

It's not easy to accept we'll always be the two people who look for the exits as soon as they enter a room, but at least we are not alone anymore.

The last week was filled with one emotional breakdown after another for me. Surrounded by *my people* has soothed the little girl inside me who was afraid of dying alone with no one to remember her. The banter, silly fights and constant care from my newfound family have soothed my inner child.

I don't remember the last time that kid felt so safe and cherished.

The night after the club wasn't the only time I allowed myself to let it all go. Now when I break, I don't have to fear about piecing myself back together because Angel is there with me. Holding me. Caring for me.

With my mate by my side, that voice in my head taunting me to keep looking over my shoulder feels so far away.

A sudden thought strikes me when I take in the bags huddled around the elevator. "Wait, how are we going home?"

"Same question," Harvey says with a mouthful and dives right back into his breakfast.

He is eating from *two* different plates.

This man eats like no one fed him for a decade.

Oh, wait.

Seiji pushes some bags around to make space for all *four* of his bags. How long did he think he was staying here? "I'm not staying in this realm a day longer, that's for sure. The pollution alone is a deal breaker. If humans keep this up, I don't think we'll need to step in. They are very capable of killing themselves on their own."

"The cars are ready." Hazel strolls into the living room, tapping her phone at lightning speed.

"Again? I thought we could finally ride our horses," I complain.

Seiji turns to me exasperatedly. "We can't just ride our horses—that *fly* mind you, among humans! Honestly, woman, have you forgotten the rules?"

By rules, I'm guessing he's referring to the guidelines our elders left for us.

What they don't know is that Papa thought he could do better than those elders and gave me his version of rules to follow.

By the grimace on Grace's face coupled with her sympathetic smile, I know Papa fed her the same rules.

Rule number one: Don't let anyone fuck with you. Always hit first and hard so they never get another chance.

Rule number two: Don't go showing off your mumbo jumbo to humans because I won't be cleaning up your mess. You know how annoying those little shits are, and I don't like dealing with humans unless I absolutely fucking have to.

Rule number three: Mates are the most precious gifts in life. When you find yours, love them unconditionally. Give them all your love and devotion.

Rule number four: Family is everything. Consider Horsemen your second family. You protect them with everything you've got.

"It's not the best idea to risk an attack with August traveling with us. Not to forget you and Harvey don't have your rings or weapons on you. We don't want *Mr. Big Bad Grim Reaper* to kill us for getting his daughter killed or kidnapped again." Hazel comments.

"Actually... Nevaeh doesn't need a ring or weapon." Everyone stops what they are doing and turns to Grace curiously.

Thanks for the unwanted spotlight, Honeybunch.

"We don't either, but they boost our powers significantly." Angel agrees it's not worth the risk with Visha's coven waiting for us to make one wrong, careless move.

Grace nods, but I can see she has more to say. "Yes, but Nevaeh is also the purest form of Divine in the flesh. Her powers are already on par with a crowned Horsemen without a ring or weapon. She doesn't exactly need them to—*pardon my language*—kick some serious butt."

For every other supernatural being their Divine is their primary source of power. But with Horsemen, our weapons and rings blessed by Fates magnify those powers drastically.

Even without the extra boost, the Horsemen are a death wish to challenge. The magic our rings and weapons contain, when combined with our Divine, makes it impossible for anyone to stand before us.

Ask Heaven. They paid a huge price by underestimating my kind when they went after Papa for creating me.

We aren't known as the physical manifestation of the apocalypse for nothing.

Harvey leans back in his chair smugly. No doubt, waiting for them to realize 'what I'm capable of' is entirely different from 'what I can actually do'. And what I can do is stuff my Divine as far back as possible because I've got zero control over it.

Anxo's forehead creases when he asks, "How's your Divine treating you these days, sweetheart?"

"Good," I answer through clenched teeth, maintaining a bright smile.

"Hmn." Folding his arms over his chest, Angel leans against a wall. "Let's meet your essence then."

I'm stunned for a moment at the firm order. Angel always gives me a wide birth over things I'm uncomfortable with, but it seems I've finally run out of luck because he isn't budging on this.

His eyes soften when I bite the inside of my cheek, hard enough to draw blood and hesitate. "Hey, I only want to see what you're dealing with. I need to know how to help with your—what do you call it? Oh yeah, your *wacky Divine*. I'm right here, sweetheart. I will step in the moment something goes wrong."

At least he's aware this will be a mess.

The day August and I broke free from the coven is the only time my Divine decided to let me take the lead. And I'm pretty sure it was only because I wasn't stopping it from wreaking havoc. But if Angel is so sure he wants to be a part of my mess then who as I to stop him.

Scratching the back of my head, I give up and let my Divine peek through. The room darkens with my Divine's presence as my essence seeps out, surrounding me with a thick gold fog. But before anyone can blink, the fog dissipates.

Angel encourages me to try again, so I do. I take a deep breath and this time push my Divine out more forcefully. I certainly wasn't expecting a pushback strong enough to make me stumble.

Every lamp, ceiling light, even the TV running in the distance shatters when my Divine reaches out to aggressively seek every ounce of light it can. Only to fail at containing that energy inside me.

We're never on the same page.

Thank Fates, I don't have to differentiate between the living and the dead too. I'm messed up enough without having to guide souls. What if I accidentally scare off a freshly passed soul into running away?

That would be bad for business.

Angel smiles at my pout and pulls me in for a hug. I don't know if I should hate or love the way I'm starting to depend on Angel for my peace, but the acceptance he gives me is addicting.

I've witnessed people freak out countless times when they see my essence and how out of control it is, but this man doesn't even blink.

Sheepishly smiling, I look up to the passive faces that scream 'We knew you weren't fine'. "Maybe we should take the cars."

Everyone laughs at my sullen expression, but Angel reminds me it's perfectly fine to take my time. He promises to help me practice control before mentioning Diamond, and I instantly forget my disappointment.

Yes, I named my papa's pale horse of Death, *Diamond.*

Whoever has a problem with it can fight *me.*

"Are you sure you're not forgetting something?" Angel asks Seiji once he double-checks the luggage in the second car that will be following behind us.

"Of course, I'm not. I'm *very* responsible."

Snickering at our dramatic Prince of Famine, Angel clears his throat louder than necessary and taps the wheel with his fingers.

"Where's your phone?"

"I'm... getting a new one... yes." *Liar.*

"And you packed your whips, right? Because I think I saw a familiar belt when I..."

Seiji leaps out of the car, screaming he'll be right back. August giggles when Seiji almost trips over his legs, trying to run back inside the hotel. Smiling warmly at my little boy, Grace pats his head from the seat behind him, next to a sleeping Harvey cuddled into her side.

Suck on that, Seiji!

He owes me so many brownies.

21. Turns out we are super rich

Nevaeh

I can't take my eyes off the magnificent pale pink sky scattered with twinkling stars and multiple planetary bodies as soon as I step through the portal.

On Earth, only the sun and moon are visible with their size, but here, I can count several planets looking like a burning moon or an icy sun, splashing the sky with different colors.

Begrudgingly, I look down at the enormous gate before me. If I didn't believe in the strength of supernatural beings, I would be worried for the ones operating this monstrosity regularly. "Why is this so big?"

"That's what she said!" In point three seconds, Angel hits Seiji on his head.

"It's so the bigger vehicles can easily pass through the portal. You don't exactly need cars to go around the kingdom, but it helps to have your own vehicle when we go to different realms." Angel explains, signally to whoever is behind the gate.

"And I bought a plane!" Seiji cheers.

Anxo looks like he's regretting the decision to spend his entire day with us, not to mention the rest of his life.

"There was no convincing him otherwise."

But why? We have our winged horses for that.

As if Anxo senses my confusion, he ducks his head in defeat. "He did the puppy eyes. I was tired. The next day, a plane was delivered."

The way my monkey's eyes brighten, I just know he's storing that little information for later use.

The roar of the gates opening steals my attention again, and Seiji was right when he said I will be in awe the moment I walk through these gates because my jaw falls open in par with them.

The entire realm is a large island floating in the air with water falling down its edges and disappearing into thin air. But that's not what makes my breath falter. It's the four magnificent castles strategically built on four corners of the island with personal waterfalls in their backyards.

Sturdy bridges connect every castle's third level around the entire Island. The architecture is fascinating The perfect blend of modern and traditional.

"An enchanted dome goes around the entire kingdom. It's capable of withholding even the strongest spells." Grace walks by me with August in her arms, pointing at different things and beaming with excitement.

"Think you can guess which castle belongs to which Horseman, sweetheart?" Angel brushes past me into the *empty* kingdom.

It was decided the first time Harvey and I toured the kingdom, it should be without an overwhelming crowd. Everyone was asked to make themselves scarce for a few hours, but that didn't stop the residents from welcoming us. The sidewalks are decorated with rare flowers, fireflies circling them and welcoming us at every turn.

It's a relief to know they are happy with our return.

Frankly, it's not hard to guess which castle belonged to whom since each was built to cater to the taste and power of that Horseman.

On my far right is one that gleams and captures my attention without even trying. I gasp when I step closer and see how precious jewels are embedded into *gold* bricks that glisten under the sky. The bricks have delicate, intricate designs carved into them from the stairs to the top.

The back of my head touches my shoulder when I crane my neck to see the top. This building screams power and wealth. Every window, door, and arc is carved out of gold.

"Conquer." I don't have to guess since the outside of the

castle is a dead giveaway.

Smiling tightly, Angel leads me away with his hand on the small of my back. His discomfort seeps into me, and it's clear how uncomfortable he is around here.

My heart hollows when I notice how much his past still affects his present. The way he can't bear to stand outside what is supposed to be his house and the sadness exuding him makes me itch to storm inside and break a few bones. *They ruined home for him.*

Anxo's shoulders lose their tension the farther we get from Conquer. He excitedly shows me his favorite spots and where his most trusted warriors and favorite people live. He tells me about the old female elf who visits him every month to deliver the most delicious pasta casserole he has ever tasted.

The story boosts his morale to right where it was before we passed the castle built on his pain.

We briefly stop in front of a building split into two parts. The smaller section is a school for kids and the bigger one is where the kids train twice a week.

A couple of years ago, Khatri proposed to the council that every kid should receive some form of basic training regardless of whether they want to join the ranks in the future. He explained that for selfish reasons, he wanted his daughters to be able to defend themselves should the reason arise.

I don't expect anything less from a man who closely witnessed the aftermath of Grim Reaper's daughter's abduction from her own house.

Next, we stop in front of a layered castle. The area cuts down significantly with each floor, creating a giant triangle structure.

Unlike Conquer, this castle is forged with solid black bricks, with every floor railing embellished with dark ruby jewels. The design of the building resembles a warrior fort. It's not hard to guess that this masterpiece of battle strategy is *War.*

"Each floor has a weapon specialization. The top level gives archers a complete 360-degree view. See how every floor after the top starts expanding? it's a labyrinth. Horsemen families are supposed to stay there in case of an attack since it's practically impossible to reach the top."

It's clever how the stairs attached to the side of the mighty castle are purposely uneven to make the intruders trip and give our soldiers time to retaliate.

"How long did it take to build all of this?" I'm in awe of everything, and I'm sure my face mirrors Harvey's shock.

Angel answers, "We had a large number of centaurs and dragons volunteers, so not that long."

Ex-fucking-cuse me?

"Did you just say *centaurs* and *dragons?* What happened to good old demons that lived in our kingdoms?"

Grace has to step in when Angel is busy trying not to laugh at my flabbergasted face. "They still do. Once a separate realm for Horsemen was announced, we received a lot of transfer requests from several species. Most of them got accepted."

"Tell me we have banshees here."

"Sorry, sweetheart, they—"

"—are total bitches. I've never met a more entitled species —other than Heaven-bound Archangels, of course." Seiji interrupts with a disgusted face.

Nooooo. The one species I want to interact with is not here. And to think I'll have to wait for a decent one to come along is *torture.*

Amused by my disappointment, Angel pecks my lips until my pout disappears before turning back to Harvey, who hasn't stopped asking questions in the last hour.

My mate has the patience of a saint, but I'm about to deck my best friend. It's crystal clear Harvey is nervous about letting his people down, but I don't get why he thinks overcompensating by diving into work immediately is the correct answer.

Grace finally pulls him away when she sees how her mate is starting to fret too much for someone who's been in the kingdom for less than an hour.

I'm admiring a jewelry store with the door embellished with different shades of sapphires when Grace tells me that the shop is owned by a family of dragons who moved here after losing their home in a vicious mountain fire.

Who better to run a business with precious stones than dragons? Dragons have the unique ability to pick out the most precious jewels, and hoarding doesn't do them any good these days. Opening a jewelry store is a great idea.

Jogging over, Seiji pulls me into his side by throwing his arm over my shoulders. "Oh, you're going to love Famine. I sketched the design myself, so expect to be dazzled."

"I thought we were letting her guess."

"I'm giving a tour Anxo. Stop being so needy."

I snicker at Angel's pout, who demands Grace to 'give him his baby back' because he misses the little monkey. August is happy as ever, loving not having to exert himself by doing something as menial as walking.

My boy takes full advantage of being the only toddler around and stays off the ground almost all day, every day.

Seiji walks me to his castle, talking about his creativity and hard work, which Angel discredits as 'nothing but a bunch of big fat lies' in a hushed whisper.

"See the giant lotus-shaped roof? *My idea.* I wanted something unique... something that would fit my style, you know?"

"You knew your style when you were *eleven*?"

"Again Anxo? Stop stealing my limelight, brother."

Leaning closer, Angel whispers in my ear, "You know he is lying, right?"

"Look," I turn Angel to see how Harvey is completely roped up in Seiji's lie. The Prince of Famine is sneaky when he wants to be. He has Harvey so wrapped up in trying to prove Seiji wrong that he has forgotten all about his earlier panic.

Shaking his head with a fond smile, Angel shares a secret wink with the mischievous Prince.

I turn to the castle and admire how the gates are arched

pointedly with the roof tilted 70 degrees to make the pattern more visible. I love the use of tinted glass in shades of green and blue.

I was starting to think glass walls were poor thinking from a safety point of view until Hazel whistled her sharpest tune, and the structure remained unaffected.

We pass the only construction business in the kingdom run by centaurs next. Only it looks more like an evil lair. A mini black castle—which I'm guessing was an intentional choice. One would think twice before crossing them or their business.

I recognize the patterns on the dark bricks from the Conquer castle, and I have no doubt they helped make this realm the dreamland it is today.

Hazel clears her throat loudly. When she doesn't stop fake coughing, I turn to check on her and realize she is only doing it to grab my attention. She could've just called my name instead of trying to act subtle.

"Fun fact: the dungeons were built below surface level, so if a prisoner escapes, they will free fall until they reach the other end of the protective dome and get scorched to ashes."

I watch her closely to check if she genuinely thinks prisoners escaping only to get burned to a crisp is fun or if she's messing with me. Her straight face tells me she actually finds it interesting.

"That's not what you call a fun fact, Hazel," Grace softly corrects her.

"Oh? Just a fact, then."

I love this woman and the way her brain works.

"Nevaeh, you remember what Dad always says about death?" Grace suddenly asks.

"There's no hiding from it?" She nods with an eager smile and points behind me. When I follow her finger, my steps falter and slowly come to a stop. It's *magnificent.*

I was expecting it to be jaw-dropping like others, but I didn't expect *this.*

The castle is a rectangular structure that reaches the clouds.

The clear glass panel in the middle gives the impression that it's filled with glistening water, and it takes me a minute to realize it's not water... but *thousands of souls* trapped and floating inside the glass.

"Those souls power our realm. The king of Hell and Dean designed it so that every soul that belongs to Hell passes through here first, so as long as a Grim Reaper is alive and working, this realm will never fall apart." I hear Angel explain, but my eyes are stuck on the trance-inducing view before me.

The use of gold, black, red, and forest green jewels to hold the glass panel at the corners perfectly represents how each Horseman equally contributes to the survival of this realm.

Nudging me, Grace asks, "You want to go in?"

I do. I really do, but it doesn't feel right. Not until I can walk inside and Papa will greet me instead of haunting silence. Grace understands that and pushes everyone to keep on exploring.

August is fast asleep on Anxo's shoulder, clutching the dark sweater's neck in his tiny fist. Angel keeps rubbing his back, quietly answering Harvey's millionth question.

"Ready to go home, sweetheart?" Taking my hand in his, Angel brings it to his lips to kiss my knuckles before leading me towards the center of our kingdom.

I let my eyes wander to the approaching castle. If I thought I liked the individual castles, man do I love this even more. The design is minimalist and relatively modern, which lures attention to the realistic horse sculptures.

On each of the four pillars is a magnificent horse standing with its feet in the air, the castle resting on their back. The four horses of the apocalypse, a blood-red horse with black wings, a solid black horse with pale green wings, a spotless white horse with gold wings, and lastly, my Diamond, a pale horse with crystal wings dipped in red and orange at the bottom.

This symbolizes our respect for their centuries-old loyalty to our bloodline. These horses are our partners in crime, not to mention immortal, so they've seen more than we've lived.

"The Horsemen castle was originally built to act as an office, but it has more than sufficient rooms. I've made sure to maintain a home-like environment."

My heart aches when I understand why Angel never called Conquer or Death our home because *this is.*

"You already know it was your dad's idea that I stay here until I wanted to return to Conquer, but this just became home after so many years."

Seiji interrupts, "Well, *Anxo* wanted a place to live. I just wanted to get away from my amazing yet over-loving mother."

Grace chuckles and helps Hazel open the heavy door so we can step in. I swear if I open and close these damn gates twice a day, there won't be any need for exercise.

I'm shocked when Angel guides me inside. The interior is modern, similar to the hotel we stayed at, but with the royal touches of richness. When I look closer at the walls, I know they're not ordinary.

The floors are polished diamonds. *Diamonds.*

I get that we are somewhat rich, but a diamond floor has to be too much, right?

"It has everything you could want from private rooms to training and gym area. I even got a movie theater built in recently."

Angel walks over to a couch and picks up a blanket to put it over August. The boy pokes his head out of Angel's neck to look around occasionally, but Angel likes to carry him around just as much as August likes the ride.

"Come on, sweetheart. I have one more thing to show you and Harvey before we can retire to bed."

I follow him without a peep because I'm looking forward to lying down after all the walking and getting shocked at every turn.

Hazel strides ahead and throws open the doors to a room. I look to my left curiously, only to find a large *empty* room. Yes, it has jewels and a pretty shiny crystal roof, but I've seen enough of that already.

A smack to the back of my head makes me turn to glare at Harvey. Shaking his head with a sigh, he grabs my cheeks before turning my face to my right. Oh… *oh.*

It's a throne room. *Our* throne room.

On an elevated stage that I assume is enchanted since nothing holds it up are stairs that lead to four exquisite thrones placed in a straight line.

The thrones are the same color as our rings with horse sculptures proudly standing behind them.

One thought enters my mind, and I blurt it out without filtering it. "These chairs look like they would poke your ass with all those jewels."

Seiji laughs *loudly.* Angel covers August's ears so he won't get startled while trying to keep his own shaking to a minimum.

When Grace yawns audibly, Seiji teases her about having a few rough, sleepless nights. Grace turns into Harvey to bury her face in his chest.

Clearing his throat Anxo interrupts Seiji's fun. "Grace, I believe you can show Harvey his room."

"Or *your* room." Seiji wiggles his eyebrows, but Harvey shuts his teasing with one look.

After wishing everyone good night, we exit the room, and I volunteer to close the door behind me. I was right. I have to push them twice a day, and I won't need any more exercise.

"August? Kiddo, you sure you want a separate room?" August nods sleepily, but I know he's confident about his decision. He even brought it up with Angel himself.

I was a little worried about leaving him alone in a new environment, but Angel settled my worries by showing me August's room, that turns out was opposite to *ours.* Now I'll be able to hear if monkey calls for me, and the little guy won't be subjected to my nightmares anymore.

A win-win, I guess.

22. I'm so fucking mature

Nevaeh

After a quick shower and change of clothes, I went to tuck in my little monkey for the night.

When I hear the door squeak, I look away from a sleeping August just as Angel walks in. He gave me twenty minutes to lull monkey to sleep before he came to collect me. *I love his clinginess.*

Striding to the bed, Angel abruptly picks me up and throws me over his shoulder. I have to bite the side of my cheek to stop myself from accidentally squealing in surprise because my little werewolf has better hearing than most kids his age.

Quietly shutting the door behind him, Anxo walks to our room with me hanging off his broad shoulder.

"Would you stop stealing my hoodies, sweetheart? I just bought this one."

"Nope."

As if he was expecting my answer, a sharp sting on my bottom makes me gasp loudly.

Did he just? He did not... Did he just *spank me*?

Carefully lowering me back on steady ground once we reach his room, Angel disappears into his closet, leaving me unsure of how to feel about what just happened.

Question for Seiji: should it feel as good as it did, or am I too far gone to save my humanity?

Returning a minute later Angel settles himself on the edge of his bed, making space between his legs before asking me to sit—on the floor.

"If this is a sex position, you have to wait another week because Seiji hasn't covered that part yet." Also, I'm not sure about this position. It doesn't feel comfortable enough for *sexy time.*

Once I've made myself comfortable on the floor, I bend my neck backward to look up at Angel upside down and find him staring at me, frozen, with his mouth wide open. "What?!"

I cringe when Angel starts choking on air.

"Yeah, he is teaching me about intimate stuff so I don't look like a complete idiot when we do *things*—you know." I'm a little embarrassed saying this out loud but Seiji says clear communication is very important in the bedroom.

I'm caught off guard when he gently removes the rubber band from my hair and frees the messy bun before he starts to comb my hair.

"We are not doing anything intimate anytime soon. We both need more time to be completely at ease with each other before *that* happens. And tell me why Seiji is teaching you all that instead of your mate?"

Brushing my hair takes longer than it should because my lazy ass didn't want to tackle the waves tonight.

"The love interest isn't supposed to do that, Angel. The best friend helps with these things. I've watched movies. *Lots of them.* And sometimes the guy teases the girl for being a 20-year-old virgin loser." I mumble, a little ashamed to admit it, but I've learned no secrets and good communication means a healthy relationship.

I'm so fucking mature.

"I would never make fun of you, sweetheart. *Ever.* And I don't mind you asking Seiji. But you know that you can come to me, right?"

"Yes."

"Good." He gently kisses the top of my head, and I *melt.*

"So, if this is not sexy time, what are you doing with my hair?" Angel chuckles, pressing another kiss on the side of my head.

Sometimes, I think he laughs it off and kisses me instead of saying, 'Nevaeh, you're an idiot'.

"Braiding. I know you usually leave your hair down because you're not sure what else to do with them. Now they won't get in your face while you sleep."

A lump forms in my throat until it's hard to swallow. I throw my head back, and Angel swiftly ducks to kiss my pout. I love how he knows exactly what I need before I know it myself.

Gentle smoothing down my waves which now fall just below my chest, Angel is careful not to tug as he braids.

I remember when Visha used to cut random pieces of my hair. When they used my hair as a tool to control me, pulling on it to demand submission or running their filthy hands through it. I breathe out to ignore how I still recoil in disgust when I think about it.

As much as I try to live here with them, every little thing threatens to pull me back into that familiar, chilling darkness. I dread the day I will have to face Visha again. Day and night, I'm persistently torturing myself by thinking of ways she can make my baby suffer... like she made *me* suffer.

I feel trapped in my own head and the torture is never-ending. I'm physically safe, but my head is too tangled up to let myself *just breathe.*

"Where do you go, Nevaeh?" Angel's soft voice brings me out of my head, and I startle when suddenly he's sitting right in front of me.

"Huh?"

I didn't go anywhere. He was holding my hair the entire time, so how could I?

"You're physically here, but I've seen that dazed look enough times to know when you slip away. You sit there and observe everything with those dreadful eyes like you're waiting for the other shoe to drop."

He scoots closer to grasp my cold hands between his warm ones. "I hate it when you get so lost in your head that it hinders our time together. I hate how your mind tries to convince you this won't last forever or that you don't deserve this because *you do.*"

I close my eyes and feel the tears roll down my cheeks when Angel kisses my head.

"I want you to be *here* and not miss out on little moments. I'm willing to be the best version of myself for you baby, to be someone you can always rely on. I promise to stay by your side for however long I have in this world if you promise to hold on to me... *to us*. Let me be your tether to our world."

I can't hold back anymore. Smashing our lips together, I take him by surprise. With his arms around my waist, Anxo ushers me to straddle him.

Every time one pulls back to breathe, the other follows until we are kissing again. I never knew holding someone could become my addiction, but looking at Angel now, I know I will fight battles every day of my life to keep holding him like this.

"You make me feel safe," I whisper, our foreheads pressed together, both of us panting like we ran a marathon. Angel picks me up and falls back on the bed with me on top of him. I adjust myself until I find the perfect spot on top of him.

"I'm sorry you got a mate that's so much work. I promise to be better for you."

"For me, you're already perfect."

Warm sunlight peeking through the curtains and soft snores act as my alarm. I try to wiggle under the heavy man lying on top of me, basically squishing me to death, but it's no use.

Softly running a finger along his cheek, I engrave this serene feeling into my memory.

Angel's head is nuzzled into my chest, his arms tightly around my waist. Sometime in the night, my fingers found their home in his curls, gripping like I was afraid he would move.

Anxo stirs, pulling me closer and burying his face in my neck, leaving sloppy kisses there. I feel his lips turn up when I shift back to move even closer to him.

Damn him and his warm kisses.

"Morning, beautiful."

Hearing Angel's husky sleepy voice my soul leaves my body and floats straight to azure. I shiver like a teenage girl touching a guy for the first time.

I mean, it's true...

"Morning Angel."

He all but purrs when I scratch his scalp and kisses my throat before biting softly. I gasp at the sudden change, which makes him chuckle before rolling off me. My lungs finally stopped screaming when I took a massive gulp of air I was severely lacking.

He really was trying to squish me to death, wasn't he?

"Freshen up, sweetheart. We have tons of people dying to meet the missing Horsemen." With a quick kiss on my nose, he lifts himself off the bed.

The wretched day for introductions is finally here. Today I get to meet people who are important to my mate. I'm not really worried about that part but his parents? I'm not sure if I can hold back from killing them on sight.

You're not a barely sane prisoner anymore Nevaeh. You're a *princess. Act like it!*

After a thorough scrub down, I left the bathroom in the soft silk coverup Angel asked me to wear until he brought my dress from Grace.

My jaw drops when my mate walks in with a dress bag and lays it on the bed. If I knew Angel looked this good dressed as The Horseman of Conquer, I would've dragged his ass back home a long time ago.

Western human clothes are widely adopted among Horsemen since we lived among them for so long, but since this is my first impression, Seiji suggested dressing more traditionally. I'm mentally patting my back for agreeing.

Angel is wearing a lavender jacket adorned with sparkling gold strings that fall to his waistline. The embellished designs on his sleeves give the illusion that the patterns are dancing over his arms.

A sheer white shirt is tucked neatly into his trousers—trousers with similar designs threaded near the pockets. The shirt does little to hide the intricate Horsemen markings on Angel's chest and abdomen. It's my favorite part about the outfit.

I'm still tongue-tied when Angel strides to my side and picks me off the ground before walking to the dressing table. This man has arms carved with muscles, a strength that's my haven.

"Let's get you all dolled up first, and then we'll tackle the dress. Grace made sure it was catered to your style and comfort, so I'm not too worried about you wanting to kill her when you see it."

Carefully lowering me on the seat, Anxo opens the makeup bag before telling me to do what I like, not what I think others would expect. I barely pay attention to what he's saying when he starts combing and curling my hair into loose waves—*just how I like*.

I stare at him with lips parted.

How is he so perfect? And looks like *that*?

I don't realize I'm tearing up until Angel turns off the curling rod and crouches in front of me, not giving a fuck about wrinkling his clothes.

I love his attention.

"What's wrong, baby?" He wipes a tear that lands on my cheek with his thumb. The softness in his eyes is going to be the death of me one day.

"It's too good. Everything you do, everything you are…" He blinks rapidly when I start blabbering. "You're so good to me that this feels like a dream. *You* feel like a dream. It doesn't that you don't even look real! So fucking handsome—"

My rambling cuts off when he suddenly captures my lips, but it doesn't last long because Angel can't stop smiling into our kiss.

Leaning back, I see his smug face—*and that smirk.*

Somebody kill me now before his smile does. I groan and hide my face in his neck. "I can't even look at you without wanting to kiss you again."

Angel starts chuckling but it comes to an abrupt stop when I give into the urge and bite his neck and suck, loving how he tastes.

He groans needily but pulls back, "I need to focus on getting you out of here before I don't let you leave at all."

I'm not sure what it is about feeling his rough breaths against my neck that damn near compels me to yell, *'Sure, let's do it!'*

Containing himself better than I can, Angel goes back to curling my hair while I try the makeup tricks I learned from Grace.

"Sweetheart?"

"Yes, Angel?"

"Khatri found something that suggests Micah is hiding in the forgotten realm."

I remain calm despite how my body locks up. That man is not worthy of my fear. *Not anymore.*

I'm not worried about Visha. I'm familiar with her tricks, but Micah was always more vicious. I need him out of the picture and away from Visha. Without his strategies, Visha isn't clever enough to wage a war against the Tetrad kingdom.

"And why are you telling me this before the council meeting?"

Angel applies serum to the ends by brushing his fingers through my hair. "You get anxious when we plan something on short notice, so I'm giving you enough time to overthink and calm down by then."

"I don't know if it's creepy or endearing that you know me so well."

I giggle when he brushes my perfectly curled hair aside to kiss my neck. Great, I'm a giggler now. Having a loving mate is bad for my badass reputation.

But I love his kisses.

"Well, we'll be married soon, so it makes sense for me to know everything about my beautiful bride-to-be." Angel teases, resting his chin on my shoulder.

I love how he makes me feel all giddy inside.

"You look like my queen, sweetheart. Good enough to eat." He follows the compliment by biting my neck before sucking softly to soothe the sting.

Like he can't stop himself, Angel kisses my cheek once more before bringing the dress over. It takes us some time to understand how to get me into the dress, but together, we figure out it's not exactly a dress.

Oh wow. It's clear Grace kept my comfort zone and preferences in mind while designing this.

The one-piece lavender jumpsuit is made of silk with beautiful gold hand embroidery covering its entirety. The designs are similar to the ones on Angel's jacket, and I don't think it's a coincidence.

I love how we both are wearing the same color.

Before I can second guess the deep V-neck, Angel helps me put on a long cape and fastens it between my collarbones.

The cape gently drapes over my shoulders and arms. I'm so excited to see it trail behind me as I walk. It doesn't just cover the deep neck but also conceals the scars littering my arms. *It's perfect.*

"We can ditch the cape if you want."

"Not yet."

No more arguments, no trying to convince me to think it over. Angel simply helps me wrap my arms around his neck and tells me to take all the time I need.

Always so good to me.

Combing the back of his head with my fingers, I kiss his cheeks, nose, and eyes and watch him all but sway from the soft attention.

"Thank you for everything, Angel. I appreciate everything you do for me."

I love you.

That's what I actually want to say. That's what I've been dying to say ever since it hit me the warmth I feel in my chest every time he smiles is not because of the mate bond but because of how much I love being the reason behind his happiness.

Is there an appropriate amount of time to wait before telling someone you love them? But we are also soulmates and have loved the idea of each other for years. I'm just sure I would bury myself six feet under if he said, 'Thanks, but no thanks'.

"It's my privilege to care for you, sweetheart."

I wish I had more alone time with my mate to come to a conclusion, but then Seiji yells for us at the top of his lungs that it's time to leave. We are supposed to meet his parents first in the Famine castle, so his excitement is justified... his whining is not.

I reluctantly step away from Angel and lead us downstairs. Naturally, we get lost two times before Angel shows me the *actual* way out of this labyrinth.

Halting by the main gates, I take everyone in, and damn if they don't look so fucking good.

Seiji is wearing a tea green suit with no undershirt. The brass-colored belt over his waist is *beautiful*... like veins climbing around his waist and up to his shoulder.

Grace is dressed in a flowy gown in a soft shade of arctic blue with puffy princess sleeves and slim straps on her shoulders. Her bare shoulders do nothing to hide the dark red, almost purple hickey just below her collarbone.

I bet Grace tried to cover it, but Harvey wanted everyone to know she found her mate.

Beside my Honeybunch is my best friend in an all-black suit. Harvey hates flashy things and has a weird hatred for colors, but I'm grateful he at least doesn't mind the black stones to spice up the outfit.

After Angel told me about Harvey not wanting to wait too long, I told him that even Grace was already infatuated with my idiot best friend. It won't be long before they take the next step.

Hazel is a pleasant surprise because hot damn if she doesn't look flaming hot. Now I understand and completely support the hype around her armored corsets.

She stands tall in a forest green pantsuit with a pastel green corset top made like armor. The shiny material of her corset has gold patterns carved into it, giving it an otherworldly shine.

"Now that we all look our best, let's get going before Maa comes here and drags me home by my ear." Seiji scoops up little August, who is adorned in his velvet suit.

I can tell August likes the soft material seeing he can't stop running his hands down his arms. Since everyone was going to be in glamorous clothes, Grace designed something for my little monkey that was fancy yet comfortable.

Seiji insists on holding August, complaining about Angel always hogging the little guy. August on the other hand, has zero issues as long as no one makes him walk.

If these people think I'm lazy, my son outranks me.

I drone out of the conversation when people around us suddenly start murmuring—*not so quietly*—about the missing Horsemen returning home. I smile tightly when they start *bowing* as I pass them. Their tears of joy making me impossibly uncomfortable.

"Can you tell them to stop doing that?" I whisper to Angel.

"Stop what?"

"Bowing. It's so fucking awkward. What am I supposed to do? Bow back? Smile? Not react at all, but that would be rude right—" A ring of chuckles follows my request, and I realize I'm not ranting to just my mate.

"You're just like your father." Anxo shakes his head with a soft smile, and thankfully, the bowing stops.

Everyone resorts to waving instead, which is much better. If they thought I was going to be a typical *Princess*, they better get used to the disappointed.

23. Delusional mothers

Nevaeh

The first thing I notice when I enter the elegant dining room is the enormous table that can fit like fifty people at once. The second is the mouth-watering scent wrapping me in a warm hug.

Whatever Seiji's parents asked their cooks to prepare is making my stomach growl ferociously.

Walking further into the room, I'm surprised to find two people playfully shoving each other as they cook. I don't even have to guess who they are. The resemblance between the older man and Seiji is uncanny.

I've heard that they are in their mid-fifties in human years, but neither looks a day over thirty-five. I wonder if they asked Fates to give them their immortality back in exchange for Seiji —*a real possibility.*

When the couple senses our presence, they abandon their tasks and rush over with bright smiles. Harvey is ahead of me with Grace on his arm, so he's the first one showered with hugs and compliments about how handsome he grew up to be.

That will definitely go to his head.

"They would be so proud of you." Seiji's mother chokes out.

I think her emotions made Harvey uncomfortable because after their *very long* hug, he cleared his throat and excused himself with Grace behind him.

I'm confused why a simple statement like that would affect him so much. I know he misses his parents, but the dumbass is acting like he didn't go see them last night after our tour.

The older couple greets August with the same love, then it's Hazel's turn. Their interaction has no touching whatsoever... a simple nod with warm smiles.

Then it's my turn, and I know I can't keep hiding behind Anxo anymore. Their two steps forward have me taking two instinctive steps back, and it immediately stops their approach. To their credit, my reluctance doesn't falter their teary smiles in the least.

I turn to Angel, silently asking if I should leave the safety of his arms. He doesn't hesitate before kissing the crown of my head and whispering he is right behind me before lightly nudging me forward.

"Nevaeh, this is my maa Yua Nakaya, the Queen of Famine." Seiji introduces us from behind the woman, August still in his arms—carefully observing the unfamiliar environment.

The woman holds her hands out and waits for me to initiate contact. When I do, she grips them firmly, mumbling in her mother tongue.

"Dean is going to sob like a baby when he sees you all grown up, Watashi no taisetsuna ko."

She moves in for a hug. I stiffen at first but soon melt into her warm, motherly embrace. The familiarity of her gesture reminds me of Harvey's mum.

I can't wait to see Stella again.

"And that's Horsemen Famine aka my dad, Akihiko Nakaya."

I notice the numerous markings covering Seiji's father on his arms and neck that are on display since he's wearing a deep brown suit with sheer sleeves. I've noticed how Horsemen are always proud to show off their markings. Papa used to fold his sleeves just so the markings were visible.

"Oh, how long I've waited for this moment." Seiji's father's voice falters near the end, but he maintains the heart-melting smile that forces me to let my guard down and give him a small but honest one in return.

The kind-looking man steps closer, arms wide open. "Can I get a hug too? I've been waiting to meet *little Death* for so long."

What a cute nickname!

"Chikusho, you're not calling her that!"

"Hush Yua, it's my turn now. Don't leave your favorite old man hanging, little death."

I don't get why Horseman of Famine is calling himself old. Since when do people in their Divine late thirties call themselves old?

Taking a deep breath, I slowly step forward and fall into his arms. The second his arms enclose me in a delicate and protective hug, the tight restraint I've had on my emotions nearly shatters.

I really need to stop crying every time someone hugs me.

Ever since I started encountering people from my past, even if my brain can't comprehend their importance, my Divine never misses a familiar presence. The warmth that spreads in my chest is my Divine acknowledging and accepting someone I remember being safe around.

The first time Angel hugged me, I felt a similar rush of feeling that overwhelmed me, but I've grown a little more accustomed to physical contact since then.

"I don't think you can call yourself my favorite old man when you're the only old person I know."

"Yeah... you're his daughter, alright. I pray you're more mature, or I will have to retire sooner than I'd like *little Death*."

My shoulders shake when I laugh into his chest. I gradually move back, fearing I will start crying if I stay too long. Thankfully, he gives me an understanding nod and doesn't mind the distance I've created once more.

"How do you like home, *little Death*?"

"Didn't I tell you to stop calling the sweet child that?" His wife swiftly smacks the back of his head.

Now I see where the smacking culture comes from.

"It's perfect though! It will help everyone once Dean is back and they start working together. *Death* and *Little Death*."

Alright, I need to add my new favorite people to the list.

1. Papa

2. *My little monkey*
3. *Pretty-pretty Angel*
4. *Grace, Harvey, Hazel, and Seiji*
5. *The Nakaya folks*

I was forced to upgrade Harvey because he is my sister's mate and I have to respect her mate. *Ew.*

And maybe because I love the guy a little bit.

"How about you retire now and take me on a trip? Or give me that second baby you promised."

"Nope. No sex talk on the dining table, guys." Seiji objects, rounding the table to take a seat beside his mother.

"Watashi no akachan," she coos at her son. "My baby boy is so shy and quiet sometimes."

The water I was drinking goes down the wrong pipe and I start choking. Angel hides his face behind me, stifling his laugh as he pretends to pat my back. Everyone is barely keeping it together, and Seiji looks at his mother with such fondness as he shakes his head.

"Forgive my lovely wife. She's a little delusional when it comes to her son."

Eventually, the conversation flows in a different direction, and we forget about Seiji being so *shy* and *quiet.*

Angel and Papa Nakaya talk about security, politics, and things leaders with responsibilities on their shoulders discuss.

I grip Angel's hand under the table when Uncle Akihiko mentions waiting for Seiji to find his mate and spend some quality years together so he can finally retire.

Compared to humans, supernaturals age twice as slowly once they reach their twenties and live around three centuries if they're lucky and healthy. So normally the horsemen wait until their successors have experienced life, found a mate, and built a family before shouldering them with such a big responsibility.

I hate how unfair life has been for my Angel. It's so unfair that he had to take over when he was just seventeen. Decades before he was ready or wanting.

With his hand in mine, I promise to never be like his parents. I will never let him bear the weight of our world alone.

He will always have me.

After lunch, we leave the Famine castle with dozens of Tupperware boxes filled with food and promises to keep visiting. Nakaya folks even ask us to drop off August whenever we need some *alone time* because they adored having my little monkey around.

It's safe to say they won over monkey's heart quite easily. All that boy needs is good food and some pampering, *and boom*, he will follow you to the edge of a cliff.

Others collectively decide to walk around the kingdom after the feast, strategically leaving Angel and me alone to meet the previous Horseman of Conquer and Queen. Anxo agrees that it's best he deals with his parents himself and spare others the mindfuck.

It was quite apparent by the way Seiji made a sour face and Hazel literally walked off to escape the meeting that they didn't want to come along anyway.

An icy feeling engulfs me the moment I step into The Conquer castle. Nothing about this place is welcoming, even if it's made of gold. Standing in the center of the grand hall below a giant chandelier, I gape at the place.

The castle looks like it was stolen from one of the ancient Gods. With high ceilings made of glass, vintage paintings hung on the walls.

If I lived here, I would keep forgetting which door led where and don't even get started on the names.

But *of course*, Angel doesn't have that problem. Holding my hand firmly yet gently, he greets everyone on our way. And the craziest thing? He knows *everybody*.

Even a blind person could see how much these people look up to him, and I feel pride bubbling inside my chest with every interaction.

Walking down an empty hallway, Anxo attempts to drop

my hand, but I hiss at him before tightening my grip. "Don't do that! I'll get lost in the first fifteen seconds of you leaving my side."

I'm drop-dead serious. I've never been good with directions... it's a curse.

Angel looks amused and gives my hand a reassuring squeeze. "I'm sure you'll learn your way around in no time." Pressing a button, we wait for the elevator to arrive. They have an *elevator* in a *castle*. Talk about filthy rich.

"No, I won't. I'm telling you this now, if I'm ever late for something; I'm lost. Don't think of any other reason. I'm not late, I'm not keeping you waiting; I'm lost and you need to come to find me. I'm directionally challenged, Angel."

He throws his head back, laughing like I just told him a hysterical joke, and not about my very serious struggle.

If I wasn't so obsessed with his beautiful face, he would have a lovely purple bruise on his jaw for making fun of my genuine problem.

He's lucky he's so pretty.

Anxo leads me into an office made of gold and jewels, just like the entire castle, and pulls out a chair for me at a table in the corner of the room instead of the main desk.

Honestly? I don't like all this yellow. Angel tells me it's all his parents' designs, so I don't like it at all now.

"I will hit you, Anxo," I warn him when he still doesn't stop snickering, but my warning only makes him laugh harder. Leaning into me, Angel buries his face in my neck, and I feel the vibration of his laugh spread throughout my body.

As much as I want to act pissed, I can't help smiling proudly. I made him laugh like a dying hyena. *Me!*

Currently, we are waiting for Angel's parents, who paused their vacation to meet me for a few hours before leaving again. *Assholes.*

I just hope I don't kill them. Anxo was clear earlier that he doesn't want to clean up blood from this office. Also, killing the previous leaders without an altercation is considered treason.

I just have to wait for them to slip up, and then I'll have the perfect excuse to dig their graves. In the meantime, I can practice being a future leader.

Calm and composed. I should use my sharp tongue instead of the sharp weapon I actually want to use.

I don't know much, but from what I've seen so far, Angel could use a lot more help so he didn't have to work himself to the bone. They're vacationing while their only child is burdened with so much. It makes me feel a lot more hateful toward them than I already do.

The sound of the door opening ruins my Angel's happy mood. In a flash, his whole demeanor shifts, watching the couple walk into the office hand in hand.

I know for a fact that Seiji's parents are older than Angel's, but by the looks of it, all the *vacationing* has them aging twice as fast. The woman is already showing faint wrinkles that would make anyone assume she was easily in her late forties.

The older man has a similar build to my Angel—if you ignore the lack of muscles and confidence in his walk. He and his mate both have prominent signs indicating that their aging has not been affected much despite them being supernatural.

I can't wait to gossip about this with Seiji.

Someone looks like they pissed off the All-knowing Fates.

"Nevaeh, this is my mother, Kiara Alarie, and my father, Luke Alarie." Anxo's voice is stiff, like his posture.

I'm afraid his act might break if I hold his hand too tight. Angel curtly replies to the small talk they initiate after they *bow* to him.

Ugh, kiss-asses.

Angel and I take the small couch when the older couple sits on separate chairs opposite us. The meeting has barely started, and I want to go back to my room and never see them again.

This is so fucking awkward.

As if Angel's womb provider can hear my thoughts, she turns to me with a look that screams false pity, and I dread her next words before she even opens her mouth.

"I remember how Grim's heart shattered the day you were taken. The misery of Fates not giving him a mate was cruel enough, but then he let his only *offspring* get kidnapped?" She tsks, "I hope you both can find some semblance of peace if he returns."

Let her get kidnapped? Is this woman on drugs?

And why is she talking like we are from medieval times? She could've said, 'Your father was fucking wrecked and disappeared to find some inner peace' just as quickly.

"It's so exciting to have you back with us. Maybe your presence would help the kingdom. The way things are running now is lousy at best." she scoffs and continues like she isn't badmouthing my mate in front of me.

I can't stop myself from interrupting, "Why don't you lend a helping hand, then?"

Angel squeezes my hand that's on his thigh, maybe to ask me to shut up or help me calm down, but something—no, *everything* about her tone is testing me.

I'm surprised how comfortable she is openly criticizing Angel and his work with her snide remarks as if no one has ever told her to shut the fuck up before.

She doesn't know me if she thinks I will sit back and let her insult my mate's hard work.

Kiara weakly chuckles and puts down the teacup she filled for just herself. *Inherently selfish.* "We're old, child. We've worked for years and deserve this time off. And anyway, Anxo has to learn someday. We have given him everything he needs, he just has to learn to do better."

Oh, now she's *really* testing me.

"By everything, you mean the insecurities or the bruises you gave him growing up?"

My response stuns both Angel and his parents. I've heard him talk about how the beating stopped as he grew older, but they never apologized for it. Hell, they act as if it never happened in the first place.

But it did... and I'll be damned if I let them slide scratch less. Especially after being shameless enough to continue to demean him, even after all the respect he has shown these undeserving assholes.

I glance at Angel to check if I am crossing a line by confronting them and if he wants me to step back. My sweet Angel is essentially ignoring everything and holding my hand as if his life depends on it, his fingers tracing the lines on my palm.

Watching him so distant and indifferent in their presence sets me off. My vision blurs and all I see is a kid who was constantly told he wasn't good enough.

The way he shut down as soon as they started talking about him shows me how deeply their words cut him even now.

By keeping a lid on his emotions and not paying attention, Anxo is trying to protect what little patience and love he has left for them, but it pains me to see him so quiet. No hint of the smile I love so much.

How long is he going to let them walk all over him just because they gave birth to him? Angel might not be ready to put them in their place yet, but I will no longer let them take him for granted.

They want someone to target?

They should try me.

Plastering a phony, sweet smile, I turn to the 'parents', and try to keep this conversation verbal before I act on the urge to suck their rotten souls out of them.

"And aren't Seiji's parents older than you? Yet they're both still working. Waiting actually, until *Seiji* thinks he is ready for such responsibility." I squeeze Angel's hand in apology for bringing it up.

"My papa lost his only family and still worked for a decade until he *physically couldn't*. If you so firmly believe that the kingdoms are doing poorly, why are you vacationing instead of helping?"

They say nothing.

Of course, they don't because what excuse could they spit

out now?

When I feel my mate's burning gaze, I turn to find him blankly staring at me. With a warm smile, I say the words to him, instead of the two making my Divine bloodthirsty.

"Anxo is doing his absolute best, and it's more than enough. And now that he has his mate, the Princess of Death by his side, I hope your concerns will fade with time." *Just like you will.*

After an uncomfortably long pause where they stare at my face, stunned and struggling to form words, *Luke* says, "Of course. We have immense faith in you both."

The sperm donor's face is red, full of shame because he realizes I know every little detail of his disgusting acts.

"Hope you have a wonderful vacation. Maybe you'll start visiting less and less with time."

With that hint, I see anger lighting up in Kiara's eyes at the insinuation. Get up, woman. Give me one reason, to show you I am indeed my father's daughter.

When she keeps her lips pursed, I stand and tug on Angel's hand. "It was nice meeting you both, but we are on a tight schedule."

I'm still fuming as we walk away from that dreadful office. The further we walk from his parents, the lighter I feel.

The elevator door chimes shut, and in a blink, Angel traps me between his arms and kisses the anger right out of me. With a small kiss on the corner of my mouth, he steps away with his beautiful smile back on.

"I'm *definitely* marrying you soon."

Shaking my head at him fondly, I peck his lips one more time. As we leave Conquer, Angel looks like an invisible weight has disappeared from his shoulders and stands a little taller.

Well, taller than he already is.

We find the others outside the castle waiting for us, and even when I can see how tired they are we have one last stop before heading home for the night.

But imagine my surprise when Harvey starts leading Grace

and the others back to the Horsemen palace.

"Hey, where are you going?"

Harvey hesitates, looking over my shoulder at his mate before saying, "Back home. I thought you could use some space."

Something is off about his behavior, and when Harvey wraps me in a tight hug, telling me how much he loves me, my heart falls to my feet.

With every molecule in my body, I hope my rational conclusion is just my brain mocking and trying to break me. But I wish I didn't know any better. I wish I didn't have to enter the castle of War with Angel tentatively following behind me. I wish I could turn in for the night and forget about this until morning.

A shrine glares back at me. They've set it right in the middle of the hall so people could pay their respects as soon as they walked in, but I don't want to pay my respects because it's not true. It can't be.

No no no no no.

My feet drag me to the framed pictures to make sure I'm not dreaming. I have to be wrong. I have to be.

Stella and Henry Adler.

Loving parents, fierce leaders.

I didn't come to see a shrine built for Harvey's parents. I came here to hug my uncle and aunt. To smell Uncle Henry's famous burgers, not the candles and flowers decorated around his picture. I didn't come here to be weighed down by a stillness their house has never experienced but to dance with them as they sang that crazy jungle song Aunt Stella made to tease me once Harvey started calling me monkey.

They left, and now they're not coming back.

I killed them, didn't I? This happened *because of me*. Their son suffered *because of me*. Papa is not here *because of me*. They must've cried, begged, and searched tirelessly for their son *because of me*.

I don't remember asking, but Angel hesitates before telling

me what happened, and that's when I completely broke. "I'm so sorry. *I'm so sorry.* It's all my fault. It's all my fault." I repeat the words in a tired loop. That's the only thought in my head, the only words I can utter.

My knees buckle, and before I can hit the ground, Angel scoops me into his arms and lowers us to the floor, so I'm sitting on his lap instead of the cold, hard floor.

I can apologize for eternity, and it still wouldn't be enough. My words become indescribable, but I keep apologizing for ruining their life.

My body trembles with sobs, and I know I deserve it. I deserve this pain in my heart. I deserve the punishments I got in that dungeon. Maybe that's why Visha wanted to kill me. Because I ruin everything. I'm the cause of everyone's pain around me.

"It's not your fault, sweetheart."

"Of course it is! He was protecting me. *Me.* If I had done *something*—"

"You were nine, baby. It wasn't your fault."

I hide my face in his chest to hide from the shame of what I've done. "But their deaths are on me. They died heartbroken for their son. Harvey wasted a decade of his life in that fucking dungeon beaten to death because of me! Because he made the mistake of looking out for me. I ruined their family, Angel. *I killed them both.*"

"Don't you dare talk like that." Cupping my face, he forces me to look at him instead of the shrine. "You are the victim here, not the culprit. They snatched you from everything you knew too, and Harvey willingly risked his life for you. Don't reduce his love for you by calling it a mistake. Any debt you think you owed him got paid the day you risked your own life to set him free. He is home, back to where he belongs because of you."

"But he never got to say goodbye," I croak.

Angel holds me tighter because there's nothing he can say to that. Even if I believe I wasn't at fault, it still doesn't change the fact that I'm the reason Harvey returned to find his world ripped to shreds.

"Does he know?"

"He knew way before I told him."

"Why didn't you tell me before?"

"I didn't know how to." Kissing my head, he tucks me against him protectively. "You were already drowning in so much guilt about Harvey and your dad, all while looking after August and helping him get better. I didn't know how to tell you without you burdening yourself with this misplaced guilt."

With his thumb and forefinger, Angel turns my face to look into his eyes. "Trust me on this sweetheart. Believe me when I say this wasn't your fault."

I clutch his shirt between my fingers. "What if he hates me for being the reason he came back to no family?"

"He doesn't hate you, baby... and he has a family. Harvey has two brothers, a mate, a clone, and an amazing best friend."

"Monkey," I remind him.

"Of course, add an adorable nephew in the mix, and there's no way he is ever alone."

"He doesn't hate me?"

"No way."

"Promise?"

"I promise." Angel easily lifts me off the ground in his arms, leaving behind a place full of guilt and hurt. "Come on, let's go home before they think you got kidnapped again."

I gasp, "I didn't know you could make dark jokes."

"Anything to see you smile."

24. The siren I love to hate

Nevaeh

"Shake the can before you open it. It'll make the flavors mix nicely."

I should've known better than to trust Hazel.

When has Sharky ever given someone *advice?*

So why am I surprised that the moment I open the can —after shaking it profusely to get better flavor, the drink splashes *everywhere.*

From my hoodie to the kitchen counter, even the ceiling is dripping with soda. A loud ring of laughter drowns my horrified gasp, and I turn around to see August doubled over in hysterics next to the woman I should've killed a long time ago.

Dumping the can in the trash I take off towards them, intending to watch the siren's souls reach purgatory. Before I can get my hands on either of the tricksters' Hazel makes a run for it with August on her tail.

"You're a dead woman walking!"

Rushed footsteps echo the hallway followed by Angel barging into the kitchen, panting heavily like he ran two floors to get here—*which he did.* I'm not at all surprised he got here so quickly when I shrieked like a woman on fire. This man is so tuned into everything I do that I expected him to be here *before* I even shook the can.

With frantic eyes, Anxo scans me from my wet hair to the pool of sticky liquid I'm standing in.

"I heard you scream."

"That evil siren told me to shake the fucking can!"

Angel shakes his head disappointingly, "Oh, sweetheart. I thought you knew better than to trust Hazel acting nice."

Grabbing a rag, he runs it under the tap before wringing it. Tangling his fingers in my hair, Anxo tilts my face up to clean the mess, and I relax as the sticky feeling goes away. My shoulders slump when he peels off the soaking hoodie and throws it in the trash.

RIP my favorite blue hoodie.

Washing my arms in the sink, I think of a plan to get back at Hazel. Preferably when she least expects it.

"Done. Now, turn that frown upside down or I'll kiss you silly to do it myself."

The intensity of his gaze burns in my stomach. Like he feels the same need running through me, Anxo pulls me against him, and I get lost in the searing kiss he offers.

We would've stayed in our own world of sweet kisses if Seiji hadn't popped out of thin air, threatening to throw up all over the kitchen if we didn't stop immediately.

How do I never notice him sneaking up on us?

Angel reluctantly steps back to glare at Seiji, who hides his mischievous smirk by taking another bite from his apple.

Angel doesn't even attempt to chastise Seiji, instead tucks his face in the crook of my neck and slumps against me. His exhaustion has finally stripped the last of his energy. Angel has been dog-tired this past week as he guides Harvey through the process of handing over War to the rightful heir.

There was supposed to be a grand event for Harvey's coronation, but those plans got derailed when my sister and best friend announced they were hoping to get *married* on the same day to avoid another event.

That's also when shit hit the fans.

Before Harvey could finish telling us the reason to combine both events, Seiji was out of his chair, screaming and ordering anyone in hearing range to stop lazing around and start planning the grand wedding.

"*Three weeks!* Only you lovesick fools would think I can pull off a grand wedding and a once-in-a-generation coronation in just twenty-one days—Daisy let Elma know I need those cake samples *yesterday!*"

Elf bakery: A place where smaller-than-average beings with sharp, pointy ears work their magic and make the most delicious desserts in the realm.

Just kidding. Elves are not little. But they do have pointy ears and sharp features, and no one in the supernatural world can beat their desserts. Elf bakery is the best in the kingdom, hence why Seiji demanded we get all the wedding desserts from there, including the cake.

I didn't understand why it came as a surprise to Seiji when I was expecting the couple to be married and off to honeymoon a day after we stepped into the kingdom. Harvey and Grace waited a whole month before announcing their wedding.

That's like a year in Harvey's world.

It was chaos to sum it up. Grace told Seiji that he could have total dictatorship over her day except for one condition that damn near gave him a heart attack. The request was to keep everything *simple* and *minimal*. Nothing too extravagant.

Boy, if Seiji didn't nearly faint at that.

He wanted to go overboard and cover the entire kingdom with floating lamps, flowers, and dragons in the sky. But for Grace's sake, he agreed to tone it down to the best of his capability while still giving her a wedding the entire supernatural world would be jealous of.

I hear monkey tiptoeing back into the kitchen before I see him. Innocently hugging my legs, the little werewolf acts like he didn't side with the evil water fairy earlier.

Those two have become thick as thieves in the past month. August has started letting people he trusts into his personal space and understands why Hazel doesn't allow the same from anyone. Not once has he tried or accidentally stood too close to her in case it made her uncomfortable.

I hate that August understands what it's like to want to protect your body, but it helps to see how much Hazel lets her guard down around him.

When I act like I don't have a little boy with his cheek

pressed to my thigh and continue my conversation with Seiji, August huffs loudly, stretching his arms to signal he wants me to pick him up.

Those big blue eyes are my weakness, and I can't stay mad at my little monkey when he pouts like that. Picking him in my arms, I smother his face with kisses, which makes him giggle wildly.

From the corner of my eye, I see Sharky trying to sneak out, using August's cuteness as a distraction.

"Don't make me run after you because you won't like what happens to your dark soul afterward."

"I wasn't running. I was—I was going for a walk."

When I hum suspiciously, her eyes narrow on me, waiting for the attack that won't come.

I'm not going to do anything. Watching her sweat and anxiously wait for my next move is punishment enough.

With a loud smooch on August's cheek, Anxo takes him from me. "You ready for bedtime, little man?"

August shakes his head but yawns in the next second. Angel chuckles and starts swaying slightly, knowing that would put the boy right to sleep.

Leaving me alone to tuck our son in bed, Anxo lets Seiji drag me into an argument about the best centerpiece that Hazel *obviously* disapproves of.

It's been a month since the night I came back to the Horsemen castle after visiting the Adler's shrine.

That night, Angel carried me home. I was so devastated that I could barely manage to stand up. On the way back home, I couldn't stop thinking how I'd ever face Harvey again. But there he was, standing by the front gates, waiting for me.

The moment he saw me, Harvey pulled me into a tight hug and we both cried for life that was cruelly snatched from us.

We spent hours on the living room floor talking about everything and nothing that night. By the time morning rolled around Harvey had drilled into my head how none of it was my fault. He made me promise to stop blaming myself for every bad thing and start working on moving on and growing from our disastrous past.

I'm not a hundred percent better, and there's a lot I need to work on, but now I remind myself that I was a kid too—*a victim* just like everyone else.

The mantra has helped me gradually overcome the guilt I've been carrying for years. I have a long way to go, but I won't stop now.

One day, I'll be better.

"Are you even listening?" Seiji complains.

"Oh I'm listening, I'm just not interested in how you think purple suits you better than indigo." Hazel doesn't even bother looking up from scrubbing her perfectly clean dagger.

"You're just jealous of how handsome I am." Shaking his head, Seiji feigns disappointment. "It's a myth that there can only be *one* pretty person in a group. I'm willing to share the title with you... even when I deserve it more."

Hazel starts cackling like a mad woman at that.

"Handsome, my ass. You're so ugly, you scare the shit back into people!" Her uncontrolled howling forces me to join her. I'm sure our hysterics can be heard in every corner of the kingdom.

"Screw you bitch. Now, I'm not sharing my title with you at all."

Slipping off my chair, I sprint out of the kitchen before I'm trapped between two crazies.

When I heard Seiji yelp, I knew I escaped just in time.

We have way too many wackos in our group.

25. My saving grace

Harvey

Since before the sun came up, I've been running around the kingdom like a headless chicken to ensure everything is perfect. It's a special day for Grace, and I refuse to let anything or anyone mess it up.

My mood tanks when I remember I can't see my mate until we are standing at the altar. Grace didn't spend last night with me due to some stupid custom... and I slept like shit without her. Maybe that's the reason why I'm biting people's heads off this morning.

splash

As I pass the kitchen the sound of something dropping makes me stop dead in my tracks. My feet slide on the shiny stairs and I almost slip and ruin my face before I steady myself.

Please Fates, let it be something completely unrelated to the wedding. Flashes of an Asian man-child hovering around the kitchen come to mind. The amount of dessert stocked in that kitchen and its easy access to Seiji makes me run faster.

Standing on the threshold, I feel it in my bones that the moment I throw this door open, it would be my tipping point.

Taking a second to fill my lungs to the brim, I link Anxo and the others to meet me in the kitchen if they don't want me to kill their Prince of Famine. Someone will have to clean up the blood I'll be spilling.

The wedding cake.

My wedding cake... is on the floor.

Seiji fucking *Nakaya.*

Blinded with rage, I'm ready to pounce but freeze when August peaks out from behind Seiji's legs.

Damn it. One glance at the toddler with his big blue eyes and mouth covered in cake and the need to reprimand someone flies right out the window.

Why does he have to be so fucking cute?

Anxo rushes in with the others, and fortunately, no one is dressed up, so at least I won't feel bad about ruining their clothes with Seiji's blood.

The moment Anxo's eyes land on the cake—the same cake my darling was so excited about, he cautiously nudges Grace into my arms, knowing I'm seconds away from murdering our future Famine.

It will be fine. I've heard Akihiko and Yua are thinking about having another baby. There's no way the next one will be as bad as Seiji, so I'll be doing the whole kingdom a favor anyway.

"I didn't do it, you guys!"

It's a stupid thing to say when both culprits have cake-dipped spoons clutched in their hands and chocolate smudged around their mouths.

Facing my blank stare, Seiji sighs in defeat. "Okay, I might have something to do with it. But we just wanted a little taste, and it fell all on its own. I swear on Fates... ask August."

The little doe-eyed werewolf nods vigorously, hiding the spoon behind him. I see so much of Nevaeh in this kid that it's truly terrifying to think what our future holds with the two of them.

My Divine inches closer to the surface. When I feel my control slipping, I turn to my mate. "I want to kill him."

"It's okay, baby."

"No, it's not. Now, there's no cake. I wanted this day to be perfect for you and look what happened."

Cupping my face in her dainty palms, she brings my face down to her. "It's still perfect. I'm meeting you at the altar, and that's the most important thing."

Like her, I try to focus on the good, but my eyes keep drifting back to the ruined cake. I can't relax until I figure out how to find a new cake in the next hour.

Grace lightly pushes my chest before walking over to the fridge. Not being in my arms is a horrible idea if she expects me to behave.

My head is reeling with scenarios of how upset my mate will be when our wedding reception tanks that I don't focus on what she's doing. Out of everything, I never expected her to pull out a two-tier cake and carefully place it on the counter's far end so there was no chance of it *accidentally falling* again.

Smiling cheerfully, she gestures to the cake. "I knew you would overstress yourself if something went wrong today, so I arranged two of all the important things."

This woman is my miracle. Once again, she proves my fears are nothing compared to her determination to stand by me.

My saving grace.

Pulling her closer, I capture her sweet lips in a searing kiss. "Do you know how enamored I am with you?"

"Mhm, you tell me at least twice a day."

I peck her lips again. "Not nearly enough. I'm going to double it."

"So…"

If Seiji thinks I won't make him pay for almost giving me a heart attack on my wedding day and ruining this for Grace, the man is delusional.

"Yes, you can eat that cake, but only the part not touching the floor, and get a plate for God's sake." Before Grace even finishes her sentence, both kids dive into the top part of the cake.

My bride smiles at the idiots before wrapping a napkin around the front of August's suit so he wouldn't ruin his cute little maroon velvet suit.

I'm going to fill her up with a baby as soon as we're alone tonight.

After Nevaeh asks Khatri to keep an eye on her little boy and the big idiot, Anxo drags me out to get ready before the guests arrive. The girls quickly steal my mate, so I have no choice but to follow him.

Placing my suit next to me, Anxo runs out to get ready, telling me to do the same. Instead of doing what I should be doing, I sit on my bed thinking of everything that could go wrong and spiraling down a rabbit hole.

What if I act like an idiot and Grace figures out my good looks are just on the outside and on the inside, I'm nothing but a pile of garbage?

Wait—I think she knows that already.

Why else would she say yes when I proposed if she didn't want me or had doubts about us?

Anxo returns wearing a black suit with golden embroidery and finds me sitting like a statue, still in my sweats and sweating about ruining this special day.

Instead of hurrying or pushing me to talk, he sits beside me quietly and waits until I'm ready to stop spiraling and voice my fears.

I know he can tell I'm shitting myself because, let's be honest, *Anxo always knows*.

Ever since we met, Anxo hovers over me like an older brother would when actually *I'm* the older one. He has made sure I'm more than prepared, whether it's my duties as a Horseman or my relationship with the light of my life.

"What if I'm not good enough for her? What if I'm holding her back from being genuinely happy? What if being with me makes her an even bigger target for my enemies, and I fail to protect her? There are so many ways I can fuck up Anxo." I bury my head in my hands when the room starts spinning.

I think I'm going to be sick.

"What if you don't?" I scoff when the man finally says something, and it's not even good advice. The one day I need this asshole to give me a big speech to boost my confidence, he's giving me the stupidest advice.

What if I don't fuck up? *What a load of bullshit.*

"What if you make her smile every day and keep trying your best so that smile never dims? What if you protect her from the world while protecting your relationship from the doubts threatening to destroy your bond? What if you *don't* fuck up?"

Huh.

Why am I only focusing on what I could do wrong when I have so much more to offer? I've craved someone to love all my life, and now that I have the perfect woman to share my life with, why am I only fixating on ruining it? I would rather hurt myself than hurt my little human.

My eyes stay glued to Anxo and sting when I let myself imagine his version of my life.

"I want to give her everything her heart wants."

Chuckling like I said something funny, he nudges my shoulder. "It's a good thing you're marrying her then because the only thing her heart wants is *you.*"

I rest my head on his shoulder when his arm pulls me closer for a side hug. With a shaky chuckle, I breathe out and compose myself.

Nevaeh might be onto something. *I am a dumbass.* Why else am I sitting here and sulking when my mate is waiting for me to show up at the altar?

Abruptly Seiji barges in, screaming at the top of his lungs, "What the fuck are you doing? It's too late to change your bride, Harvey! Nevaeh will skin you alive if you steal Anxo from her. Grace is your *only* option. Go. Change." He yanks me up before chucking my suit at me.

"Where's my flower and ring boy?"

August flies into the room holding a small basket of Grace's favorite flowers and pats the small pockets of his suit to show where the rings are. The determination on his face doesn't surprise me. He is the most dedicated to this wedding after Grace and me.

August had an opinion about *everything.*

The cake, the flowers, the dress my mate chose. He all but threw a tantrum to stop me from getting the plain black suit I wanted because it wasn't *unique* enough.

It was a long process, but we finally agreed on one

which despite being all black, had strings of ruby-red stones embroidered on the sleeves.

When I saw the little werewolf and Seiji high-five in 'secret', I knew my torture was pre-planned. I never really had a choice.

Standing on the stage waiting for my bride is both exhilarating and nerve-wracking. Seiji's dad, who is officiating the ceremony, gives me the 'before I do' talk to ease my nerves, which helps immensely.

Seiji decorated the entire Castle of War for this day. I can't name half the flowers he used to decorate the back garden facing the waterfall. The rushing body of water surely helps create a more magical atmosphere.

In front of me, the chairs divided into two sections are filled, and the guests are equally eager for my bride to walk in.

An unfamiliar soft melody starts playing, and I glance to my right to see two centaurs playing harps to announce the first duo walking the long path.

A thick forest-green suit adorns Seiji. The lower part of the jacket is pinned with numerous gold accessories. I don't think this man has ever had a bad outfit day.

Beside him is my close friend, or as people call her— *my soul twin.*

Hazel is a vision in a teal silk jumpsuit that flares around her calves. The shimmering material has a delicate silver chain on her waist, which I bet holds at least two of her daggers.

Giving me a rare warm smile, Hazel takes her place beside me as one of my *Groomswomen*, while Seiji takes a stand on Grace's side as one of the *Bridesmen*.

Don't get me started on the titles. It was a long, excruciating debate before everyone settled on these.

Next, my best friend and her mate walk down the aisle hand in hand, making everyone stare at the stunning couple with green monsters over their shoulders. I don't remember a single day where these two haven't matched or coordinated outfits.

Nevaeh strides to me in a black jumpsuit with sparkling

gold stitching from her neck to the waist and a sheer black cape draped around her shoulders. When my eyes catch the poorly healed scars on her arms, just like every eye here, I clear my throat to get rid of the tightening sensation.

When Grace designed these attires, I suggested adding sleeves, but she shook her head with a smile and said this way, Nevaeh would be able to flaunt her strength when she felt ready. And until then, the cape would hide her scars while also making her look *chic*—as Grace called it.

Taking in the sheer black cape, I'm stunned at the realization that *today* is the day she has decided not to care about the judging eyes.

She's not bound by her scars anymore.

Once Anxo helps his mate onto the stage, he kisses her head before running back to the start of the aisle, making everyone laugh at his rush. My best friend takes her designated spot next to me, and I bend to kiss her cheek.

Nevaeh grabs my hand and squeezes, knowing I'm a moment away from breaking.

I remember how hard it was for Grace to finally admit that her dad wouldn't be walking her down the aisle. I think the fear of walking down this path alone made things worse.

Anxo solved that dilemma effortlessly by asking Grace if she wanted him to match his suit with her dress so they looked *aesthetic* walking down the aisle together.

That man is always on top of things. His ability to stay ten steps ahead of everything and everyone is sometimes so fucking creepy.

Grace was over the moon by the gesture, and it took us twenty minutes to stop her tears. Thoughts about how I *really* soothed my mate fly out the window when the most adorable mini werewolf walks down the aisle in slow, careful steps.

August refuses to take the next step until he's sure there are enough petals for Grace to walk on as she follows behind him.

I'm definitely begging Grace to give me my own August.

My eyes search for my solace, and the second they find my

jittery mate walking down the aisle with Anxo supporting her, it's like the world around me stops existing.

The large, flowy ball gown drags behind her. Even when the fabric is bulky, I can see how incredibly light it is, and I don't have to worry about Grace feeling weighed down by it.

Nevaeh gave me so much shit for being 'a softy' when I kept asking if what my mate was wearing was comfortable. Once I got my answer, I let it slip to Hazel how Nevaeh has become oddly fond of chilled soda, and she did the rest.

Tit for tat monkey.

Seeing my beautiful bride, I understand why August was adamant about this suit. Grace is adorned in the exact shade of red as the rubies embroidered in my suit.

The thin off-shoulder straps fall to her smooth honey-brown shoulders, and I internally curse myself for not leaving a trail of love bites along her slender neck.

She's marrying you, dumb fucker. The world already knows she's yours.

"How are you feeling now?" Seiji's dad pats my shoulder from behind.

"Like I'm the luckiest man alive." I barely hide my voice breaking, but when Grace smiles at me with those warm caramel eyes, a tear falls on my cheek anyway. She shakes her head with a soft smile, and I keep staring at her like a lovesick fool.

This is the first time I've seen Grace in a dark color. She usually prefers cool pastels, but after tonight, I'll try to convince her to let me see her in red more often.

The second she is close enough, I step in to help her onto the stage and ignore Anxo standing beside her, giving me the side eye. The feel of her soft hand in mine finally helps ease the tight knot in my stomach.

"Dearly beloved, we have come together in the presence of The sisters of Fate to witness and bless the joining of this man and this woman in their soul linking for eternity. The bond..."

Lost in her eyes and beautiful smile that gets brighter as the ceremony proceeds, I completely zone out of what's happening around me. I could've missed the whole fucking thing if my eyes didn't stop drinking her in, but when she tugs on my hands and chuckles, I turn my focus back on the ceremony.

"I take it you have your own vows?"

We both nod, and Horseman Nakaya asks Grace to go first. I can't help the flash of panic at that.

What if she says all the perfect things, and when it's my turn, I spew some nonsense instead of what took me weeks to prepare? My rapid thoughts come to a halt at her soft voice.

"Harvey Adler, you've held my heart in the palm of your hand since the first day we met. A part of my heart clicked in place as if it always knew I was supposed to find you, even when I didn't let myself believe it. You captured my soul the first time we talked and you didn't dare blink in fear you might miss something." I duck bashfully.

And here I thought I was being cool about it.

"You became my whole life from the first time we touched, and my heart found its home the moment my eyes met your stormy ones. I promise to be by your side, *storm comes sun.* To keep your worries locked away and to pour all my sunshine into your life."

I carefully wipe the tear from her cheek, sure not to ruin her perfectly applied makeup.

Before my doubts hinder our moment, Grace brings my knuckles to her lips for a kiss—knuckles that are covered in tattoos that hide my deepest scars. I promise myself that one day, I will have the same faith in myself that she has in me.

With a shuddering breath, I try to put my heart into my words. "Grace Blackburn. *My mate.*" The ache in my heart simmers down at her encouraging smile. "I've put on a brave face in front of the world most of my life. Showing no weakness, keeping everyone at arm's length so they don't find out how broken I am."

Grace shakes her head, and I can practically hear her telling me not to let my mind bully me.

"But with you, I feel like I have a place... a place to hide from everything and just be. A place to let my mask fall. A place where I can sort my disoriented thoughts with no judgment. I can hide in your arms without worrying about someone stabbing my back because *I know* you'll always look out for me. Save me... even from myself."

With all my sincerity, I vow to her. "I promise to be the person who helps you grow, hold you up when you feel beaten down, to love you with every broken piece of my being."

"*Ah fuck.*"

Snapping my head to the voice, I watch Hazel turn to hide her face and grumble about 'our sappy vows messing with her head'. The guests snicker before awing in sync when August runs to her with a handkerchief held out.

This kid has single-handedly given everyone baby fever.

Clearing his throat, Horseman Nakaya steals our attention again. "Grace Blackburn, will you have this man to be your husband? To live with him in the covenant of marriage? Will you love him, comfort him, honor and keep him in sickness and in health? And, forsaking all others, be faithful unto him as long as you both shall live?"

"I will."

"Harvey Adler, will you have this woman to be your wife? To live with her in the covenant of marriage? Will you love her, comfort her, honor and keep her in sickness and in health? And forsaking all others, be faithful unto her as long as you both shall live?"

"I will."

Scanning the audience Akihiko warns, "If anyone attending has an objection to this union, meet me after the ceremony, and I will *personally* take care of you."

A roar of laughter echoes above the sound of the waterfall. I'm thankful for these moments of humor, otherwise, one or both of us would've sobbed through the entire ceremony.

"Let's see the rings!"

August comes running with a bright smile and two boxes

clutched in his hands. Grace bends to kiss his chubby cheeks, which August assists by standing on his tiptoes so she doesn't have to bend too far.

After his final task is complete, August beams with joy and runs to his dad, who picks him up and kisses his head for a job well done.

Horsemen Famine guides Grace to repeat the words while sliding the ring on my finger. "I give you this ring as a symbol of my love, and with all that I am and all that I have, I honor you in the name of the All-knowing Fates and our Divine spirit," I repeat the words before slipping the ring on her finger and kissing her hand.

"With the power invested in me by Fates, I announce them husband and wife. You may kiss the bride... *and he has already started.*"

Our guests cheer when I don't wait to grab my bride by her waist and smash our lips together. Holding her soft cheeks, I kiss her until we are breathless, and Seiji is begging us not to act like horndogs in front of the entire supernatural world.

With a bright smile on her face that I feel myself mirroring, Grace and I make our way to the ballroom hand in hand for our reception/coronation.

Unlike the garden outside, which had a fairy tale theme, Seiji didn't restrict himself when it came to the reception/coronation. The massive ballroom sparkles with flowers, lights, and *fire*. I'm sure he had fun with this darker aesthetic.

My only concern is if Grace likes it, but when I watch her mouth drop open, I have to remind myself that we still have another ceremony before I can have her all to myself. I want to run my fingers through the tight curls flowing down her back. Slowly take out all the glimmering clips before—*Okay, the bedroom will have to wait.*

Soon enough, the ballroom is filled with supernatural allies who wish my wife and me a long happy life together before mingling around, filling themselves with the special brew our earth fairies came up with.

I'm disappointed that the King of Hell, couldn't make it because of a 'Heaven emergency', but the shiny enchanted sword he sent with a letter promising a visit soon, almost makes up for it.

Once everyone has a drink in hand and is twirling around to a soft melody, Anxo decides it's the best time for the second big announcement.

"I know everyone is anxiously anticipating the second big event of the day—I can hear you all complaining, you know." Chuckles follow his words. "So, without waiting another moment, let's get to it. Harvey, join me on the stage, brother."

Turning to my mate, who already knows I'm thinking about bolting, she kisses me fiercely and whispers a few things I definitely mind sharing. Grace knows exactly how to make my nerves run along like little bitches.

I walk to the stage with renewed confidence, thinking about the promise I'm going to collect later tonight.

"Are you able and willing to take the blood oath?"

"I am."

Satisfied with my answer, Anxo picks up the ceremonial dagger, which is polished to perfection. From the corner of my eye, I see Hazel practically salivating over the weapon and cover my laugh with my hand.

A crystal bowl sits on the center of the table as Anxo and I stand on opposite sides with our side profiles facing the audience.

The only question lingering in the air and sticking to my doubts is if the Fates see me worthy. Because if they don't, this would be so fucking embarrassing. I haven't been around for long, but that doesn't mean anyone is more worthy of being the next War than I am.

Anxo gestures for my hand, and I prepare for when he will slash my palm open. To my surprise, he only nicks my index finger before guiding it directly on top of the War family ring proudly sitting in the center of the bowl.

A single drop of blood falls from my finger and directly

on top of the ring, and before my eyes, the ring absorbs it completely.

The ruby smoke inside the crystal ring comes to life, glimmering like a fiery blast of unstoppable fire. The scarlet entirely takes over the white crystal of the ring.

Anxo wipes the dagger with a neatly placed napkin and asks for my hand again. Carefully—trying his best not to dig any deeper than necessary, Anxo cuts a line on the index finger of my right hand before turning my palm and doing the same. The cut looks like a blood ring on my finger.

I don't remember it happening this way. This part of the process was much bloodier for the generation before us. A few murmuring voices complain about the process lacking the usual brutality, and it solidifies my thoughts that this is yet another thing Anxo changed for the better.

At first, I didn't understand why everyone had a habit of following Anxo so mindlessly, but over time, I've noticed why. The man doesn't have a single malicious bone in his body as long as you don't hurt the people he protects.

Anxo backs up before asking me to slide the ring on, knowing he'd get the shock of his life if anyone other than the destined successor touched it right now.

Here's goes everything...

Once I nestle the ring on my finger without getting electrified, *thank Fates*, Anxo finally demands my oath.

"Harvey Adler, son of Henry and Stella Adler, now mate to Grace Adler, do you solemnly swear to remain loyal to the Tetrad kingdom and govern all beings justly? To be a faithful soldier to the sisters of Fate and act as a shield against any harm to your fellow Horsemen?"

"I do."

Which was a little loose around my finger, the ring warms up until the crisscross veins holding the crystal move to fit me snuggly. The ruby gleams brightly as if agreeing with my oath. The crystal returns to its usual shine with red smoke floating inside... accepting me as its next owner.

The pain that came next was not something I could prepare for. I stumble from the sudden gut-wrenching ache, but Anxo is immediately on my side, bracing my shoulders. He keeps me upright instead of letting me fall in front of the world, withering in pain.

When I look up, the pride on his face is unmistakable as his eyes trace my neck and arms. The pain slowly subsides to a gentle tingle, and I straighten up with newfound strength.

It's done. *The Fates have marked me.*

Every single tattoo on my body has burned off, and instead, the ancient markings of my destiny cover my skin. Red delicate swirls and cursive writings tell a different story than my tattoos.

Though the scripts are in Latin and only a few alive know how to read them, I know what every word and shape on my body represents. This is my pain, suffering, strength, and history, making way for my destiny.

"It's my absolute honor to introduce Harvey Alder, The Horseman of WAR!"

Loud cheers fill the room, and the glass ceiling above us lights up with countless firecrackers going off at once.

For the next hour, I greet people and accept thousands of good luck and whatnot. I'm ready to take Grace to bed, knowing she is tired and sleepy, but the way her eyes linger on the dance floor longingly, I figure one last dance can't hurt.

"Dance with me, *my Queen?*"

"With pleasure, my Horseman."

On the dance floor, I snicker when I turn to find Nevaeh standing on Anxo's shoes because she can't dance for shit.

The other day, Anxo cleared his entire schedule when Nevaeh told him she was nervous about the formal dance routine.

Their day ended with Nevaeh almost bursting into tears from her lack of dance skills when the idea struck him. Now Nevaeh is standing on Anxo's expensive shoes as he moves them around in limited moves. He doesn't complain though.

And why would he, given their intimate position.

Grace is wrapped around me as I sway us to a soft melody, smiling at each other and stealing kisses.

The sound of my best friend laughing freely after a decade of nothing but pain and tears hits me somewhere deep within.

This is it... we got out.

We are finally home.

26. The circle of idiots

Nevaeh

I t's been eight days since the newlyweds refused to leave their room.

The last I saw them, Harvey was twirling a giddy Grace before he picked her up bridal style and all but ran out of the ballroom. The ridiculously horny and loved-up couple locked themselves in their room that night and haven't come out since.

Diamond huffs out of boredom, making my head bounce where it's resting on his stomach. Technically, Diamond is Papa's horse, but he lets me bother him because he loves me so much.

When I first came to see Diamond, the horse kept his distance. It hurt to know he forgot the only little girl who was allowed to touch his grumpy butt.

On day three, I had enough of him acting like I was a stranger. So I took the risk of him headbutting me and reached out to touch him.

With trepidation, the horse sniffed my hand once, and immediately wanted me to be his best friend when he finally recognized my scent. The horse refused to stop nuzzling into my hands for more pets. The desperate need for touch squeezed my heart.

It was clear how much Diamond had without the only two people capable of touching him.

Usually, when people see Diamond, they either run away screaming or stand there with pale faces about to pass out. It's not the poor animal's fault the Fates chose him to be Death's immortal horse.

Since every horse was made to reflect its rider, Diamond has skin paler than a ghost, and scorching fire erupts from his legs, tail, and wings. The fire makes it impossible for anyone who doesn't have Blackburn blood or isn't mated to the Grim Reaper to stand near him without burning to a crisp.

When I was little, it used to bother me so much that Diamond was the only horse who wasn't pampered like others because no one could touch him without getting hurt. After Diamond knew I was family, I spent days hovering over him and grooming his beyond-dirty skin and hair because the task had been impossible without Papa.

As much as I was missing him, I hated Papa for leaving Diamond alone like this. I get that he wasn't fine, but that doesn't make up for abandoning his horse. I think both Diamond and I will be holding a grudge for a while.

I remember the angry tears dripping down my chin when I scrubbed him for the first time. The poor animal hadn't been cleaned or showered with love in almost three years.

My grumpy horse huffs again, signaling me to get off his stomach. He likes to show that he only tolerates my clingy ass and constant blabbering, but I know Diamond loves my company. He just thinks he's too cool to admit it.

Diamond is still a little huffy puffy with me, and I think it's because he's mad about me leaving for such a long time.

It's not like I wanted to buddy.

"The filthy couple is finally here." I hear Seiji exclaim from the training grounds and sigh tiredly, even though the day has just begun.

Dusting myself, I pat Diamond once more. He likes to pretend I ruin his alone time, but I don't miss the little whine whenever I leave him for the day.

When the Deviants attacked us in the human realm, and we failed miserably to fight as a team—*mostly because of me*—it became clear we needed to fix our team dynamic. It's been a grueling week of perfecting our individual skills since the entire gang isn't present yet.

While we work our asses off, sweating and bathing in dirt, Harvey thinks the only exercise he and his wife needs can be achieved in bed.

A dozen dirty jokes later, Grace hides her face in her mate's chest while Harvey seriously contemplates strangling me and Seiji to death. Thankfully, I have Angel on my side, who diverts Harvey's pent-up aggression to the combat field before his mate is murdered.

Just like that, it was time to sweat like pigs. *For them.*

Stuffing my face with a handful of spicy Cheetos, I watch Harvey jot down notes between pummeling the poor dummies to the ground with his fists.

One would think a whole week with his mate would leave the guy with nothing but happy vibes, but *no.*

Harvey is pissed he had to leave his room *at all.*

I trace the rough pages of the ancient-looking book in my hand. The consistent overuse screams of its importance. The spine quivers each time I turn a page, so I have to be extra careful before I ruin my mate's precious work.

Anxo's book of battle strategies is filled with illustrations and tricks I've never heard of before. This is a significant insight into how sharp my mate is when it comes to planning and strategizing. I have yet to see him unorganized or careless, even about minor things.

While everyone swims in their sweat and hard work, I sit under a tree with Anxo's notes because I refuse to waste my energy on things I have already known since I started training at four years old.

Some thought Papa was being hard on me because I was the future Grim Reaper, but I knew it was to help me control my overbearing Divine before *it* controlled *me.*

I was fighting men thrice my size and defeating them before I was eight years old, and that gives me credit to sit on my ass and eat my snacks in peace.

It takes us under twenty minutes to realize we are nothing but a bunch of fuckups tied together in a group who—*for some insane reason*—have weapons of mass destruction at our disposal.

Looking at us now, anyone would assume the three sisters were high when they made this decision.

I'm amazed that despite being a unit at the core, we can't work together because all of us are so used to fighting individually.

The air around us starts to heat up, and it's more because of Harvey than the sun blaring down on us. He is pouring out his frustration in the air, causing the already tired and irritated group to start fidgeting with the urgent need to snap.

Anxo is tense. I watch him swallow loudly to bury his irritation. Seiji hasn't stopped whining that his whips won't work how he wants them to.

I mean how can they when he won't let them do what they are made for? *To cause havoc.*

Harvey is solely interested in breaking as many combat accessories as possible, which pisses off Hazel to no end since she spends a significant amount of her time overseeing and maintaining these fields.

And Grace, my poor Honeybunch, is tired of being the only voice of reason.

I won't lie; this is starting to resemble a sitcom. I'm actually torn between interfering or quickly running inside to grab popcorn.

When Harvey misses an attack that could've been his winning strike, Hazel blows out a quick tune that paralyzes him before swiftly dodging behind him and kicking his back. The large man falls to the ground with a loud thud, cutting off the last thread of his rage he was holding on to. "Oh, for fuck's sake!"

"Aww, don't be mad, big guy. I'm sure it's hard to move around with all those muscles."

"I. Will. Kill. You."

"Yeah? Bring it on fucktard."

When the two start stalking in each other's direction, I

jump up and run to stand between them. Before I can tell them off, another round of argument starts behind me.

"Nevaeh, can you tell Anxo off? He keeps hitting my head. I think all my brain cells are scattered on the ground at this point."

"That would be true if you had any brain cells." *Oh my.*

"I will give you a stroke on purpose," Seiji's eyes darken as he glares at Anxo, and a dark thundering cloud forms over his head. If this continues, Seiji will accidentally electrocute someone.

"You can't even walk in a straight line on purpose."

Damn Angel bites when he's stressed.

Turning to Harvey with a pointed look, I ask him to drop it. Harvey looks guilty for a second before throwing his head back and groaning. Taking a few deep breaths, he pulled back the anger and frustration he had released in the air so he didn't have to bear it all himself. *Dumbass.*

"It's not like you're any better," Grace points a finger at Angel. "You act like you're immortal. You're distracted watching everyone's backs, but your own. I have hit you *nine* times now. You would've been hurt or worse that many times if this was real."

Before Grace is even finished, everyone seems much calmer. Turning to Harvey, who is muttering to himself, they realize he is the one escalating their emotions and bombard him with a few not-so-polite curses.

He groans, slumping to the ground and taking his mate down with him. "This isn't working."

I watch them abandon their weapons, plant their asses on the ground, and talk about leaving already. I guess I'll have to be the one to keep my head on straight with all of them acting like fussy children.

Sitting before them, I carefully put the book aside when Angel immediately crawls over to where I'm sitting and leans against me, bringing my arms to wrap around his chest. He grabs his book and holds it to his chest, so I'll have to hug him if I want to reach for it.

Suddenly, my cheeks feel hot under the burning sun, and I have to tamp down the urge to squirm.

He keeps touching me like I'm his lifeline. I love it.

Forcing my heart to relax, I face the people in front of me. "I have a list of what you're all doing wrong."

Snatching the book Harvey was writing in, I scanned his notes. It takes a minute to make a list of ways we can fix our coordination issues. I tear the parts that are rubbish and fold the ones that make sense while they watch.

"I want to say fuck off *so bad*, but that's a long ass list, and I'm intrigued," Hazel comments over my shoulder before coming over to sit down with the rest.

"Seiji strikes first and hard." The idiot blows me a kiss like I won't point out his mistake next. "But you need to stop hesitating and questioning yourself at every turn."

Harvey snickers at Seiji's expense, and that's my hint to pop his ego balloon next. "This dumbass gets way too involved with his victims. You don't focus on your surroundings enough—or at all, to prevent any surprise attacks."

"I just make sure they don't get up again," he grumbles, leaning against Grace, who shushes him, knowing I'm right and it will end badly if he keeps it up.

Leaving your back exposed in a battle is nothing short of a death sentence.

"Honeybunch, you're incredible at foreseeing attacks unlike your mate, but hand-to-hand combat is just not your thing. Don't worry, though; I have a plan for that." Grace takes my observation with stride, unlike her stupid mate.

"And Angel—"

My heart takes off, beating wildly when he drags my palm over his heart.

I've been on edge ever since Angel came closer, but now, I can feel it affects him, too. His heart thumps under my palm as if he ran a marathon, and the realization helps me relax.

"You're good with close combat and far-sighted attacks

but... you're not focused enough. Like Grace said, keeping tabs on everyone puts your safety at risk."

Angel pouts so adorably that I forget how to breathe. Tracing his cheek with my finger, I forget where I was until Hazel nags me, "Hey soul eater, can you blush after my turn?"

I avert my eyes from hypnotic green ones to the impatient siren. *Did she just call me a soul eater again?*

"Yes... Right. You're perfect, sharky. I've never witnessed such clean and precise combat skills, and I don't think anyone here can hold your hand when it comes to this." Her smug smile disappears when I continue, "But you have a death wish."

"Uh... no, I do not."

Looking around, her confidence falters when everyone agrees. Cursing under her breath, she motions for me to continue.

"You dive in headfirst, no matter how overpowered or outnumbered you are. You're good, *incredible* even, but you're not a cat with nine lives."

Seeing her contemplating my words, Angel tugs on my braid, "What about you? Do you have any flaws, or are they only for us lesser beings?"

With one hand holding my notes and another brushing through his hair, I shrug. "I take on too much. I don't get to channel my rage nearly enough, so when I get the opportunity, I'm cutting through people without a plan. I'm emotionally compromised most of the time, which makes me vulnerable... and a liability."

Seiji sighs, "We need a proper plan."

Harvey steals the words right out of my mouth. "What about block on block?"

That's exactly what I wrote as our best solution. I send him a knowing look, which makes him chuckle, probably recalling those days.

Block on block was something Papa taught us as kids whenever we couldn't perfect an attack. Like the colorful blocks kids play with, you strategize one block upon another to create a strong tower. Harvey and I were the blocks, so where one lacked, the other helped to increase our combined efficiency and strength.

Throwing my notes at him to look over, I work on the pairings. "Angel and Grace should be our eyes. A higher vantage point will be perfect with their weapon of choice. This way, they can have each other's back *and* ours."

Angel sits up straight, turning to me with his eyebrows reaching his hairline. The proud gleam in his eyes starts a fluttering in my chest.

"Seiji and Harvey would work best together. Seiji could be the initial attack that Harvey finishes off. This way, Harvey won't be vulnerable to surprise attacks, and Seiji can plow ahead without his conscience taunting him... saving them both time and despair."

I don't understand why Seiji is surprised. This idiot is my family; so of course, I understand what goes on in his twisted, guilt-conscious brain.

For a Horsemen of the apocalypse, Seiji is timid about taking lives. While Anxo is the same, he doesn't let that stop him from getting his hands dirty if it means protecting his people. I need to talk to Angel about it. If anyone can relate and help Seiji, it's him.

"That leaves us."

Nodding at Hazel, I explain my reason. "We both love inviting trouble and don't mind a challenge. If we constantly have someone to look out for, we won't have the luxury to linger around our opponents. There won't be any teasing or baiting. All our focus will be on doing our part and not giving into the temptation of doing more."

"That's..." Hazel starts, or at least tries to.

"*Brilliant.*"

"I'm too impressed to search for a better word, so what he said." Seiji points to Angel, who doesn't even bother hiding his pride.

"Why have we never sparred before?" Hazel asks me

incredulously.

"Because I'm better than you, and I know everything. Also, I don't enjoy sweating unnecessarily."

Seiji leans into Angel and whispers, even though we can all hear him just fine. "It's so creepy how she keeps repeating his words."

"Right? It freaks me out all the time."

I hand Hazel the new techniques when she gestures for them and say, "We'll have so much fun together. You'll gather the dummies with your captivating tunes, I'll steal their Divine and then we can take turns—" I trail off when I realize everyone has gone quiet.

Then comes chaos.

"You'll steal their what?!" Hazel shrieks.

"I knew you were hiding something about your Divine!" Grace accuses.

"I told her to just come out and tell you guys the truth, but you know Nevaeh, always so stubborn and secretive," Harvey lies straight through his teeth.

He'll pay for this later.

Damn it. I totally forgot about this. At first, I was waiting until I could trust them better but as more days passed it completely slipped my mind.

"Sweetheart?" Angel links me, standing across from me with his lips pressed tight. *"You forgot, didn't you?"*

When I nod my head like a guilty person, Angel starts howling in laughter.

I'm starting to get turned around by all of them talking over each other.

"Don't just stand there, help your one and only mate!"

Angel barely composes himself to pull me behind him and says, "Relax guys, Nevaeh wasn't intentionally hiding it... my beautiful idiot just forgot."

Hazel is quick to scowl at me, "Sometimes I'm genuinely worried about you. Does your brain even work at this point?"

"Trust me sharky, you don't want to know what goes on up

here," I tap my head.

I spend the next ten minutes telling them about my unique talent, answering their questions, and apologizing for forgetting to mention it before.

Once chit-chat time is over, we decide to put my idea to test. Harvey and Seiji go against Angel and Grace, and though both teams have very different approaches to a fight, it's fascinating to watch them tackle against a different attack style and try to come out on top.

Hazel breaks my attention by blocking my view of the fight. "Want to tell me why we are practicing without our powers? We have them for a reason, you know."

I watch Harvey abandon his sword with a dopey smile when Grace's sharp crossbow cuts through it like butter.

"It's not a special combat tactic if that's what you're wondering." I wait for Hazel to lose interest now that it's not combat-related, but she keeps staring.

Sighing, I answer honestly, "It's for selfish reasons. The coven stripped me of my powers every single day for a decade, and the only reason I survived is because they didn't want me dead... yet."

From the corner of my eye, I watch Hazel's eyes set ablaze with anger. I've noticed how the topic of my time with the witches affects her differently than others. It's terrifying to think she might relate to it on some level.

"I waited for my Divine to save me, or *anyone* really, but in the end, what saved me was my training." I shake my head to get rid of the flashes from my past. "I'm not saying you would ever have to experience that or be without your Divine, but if that day ever came, I want all of us to make it out alive."

I see the reason settle within her. A strange spark of emotion flashes through her eyes before she backs off. I thought she was done with the conversation and walking away before she turned to ask 'If I'm blind and if not, then why am I not following her'.

That's Hazel Seagrave. Kindest woman in all of Tetrad

kingdom.

I quickly signal Anxo about where I'll be before taking off after her.

Hazel avoids eye contact as she plants herself under a thick tree that gives us more than enough shade from the sun. I've never seen Hazel look so unsure and weary. I don't make a sound in case I spook her.

"You took a bullet for me."

"Yeah... I was there."

"If you're going to be a smartass about it, I'm leaving." She springs up, but before she can stomp away, I stop her.

"Woah woah. Okay, sorry, look." I zip my lips together with an imaginary chain and make a show of throwing away the key.

Hazel presses her lips together before she accidentally gives away her amusement and sits down again.

I've known Hazel was hiding a massive, life-altering fuck up ever since I first saw her cleaning those daggers in the kitchen. Anyone with eyes can see her paranoia after spending ten minutes with her.

But I'll tell you what happens when you keep bottling and shoving things down so you don't have to deal with them in the present. First, the cracks show up. This is the perfect time to empty your bottle of horrible stuff rather than concealing the fractures because the cracks *will* grow deeper until, finally, the bottle shatters.

By then, it's always too late. You were so busy hiding from your fears that you didn't prepare to face them.

With Hazel, I can see her cracks and the way she actively tries to hide them. I really hope those fears won't swallow her whole when she finally decides to face them.

Hazel uses the silence between us to spill her guts.

"I was sold to the king of the Eldoris kingdom when I was three years old. His other slaves groomed me to be his chosen mate and their future queen. *Tiberius...* kept his distance until I was fourteen, but then he wanted more. *I didn't.* But nobody cared about what a glorified slave wanted."

To distract herself, Hazel pulls out a dagger from her boot and starts drawing shapes on the dirt. For the first time since we've met, Hazel intentionally lowers her guard.

Hazel is not afraid to tell me about her past, but the way she avoids my eyes makes me think she might be afraid of my reaction to that past.

I don't understand how she still doesn't know that even the devil would blush if he heard the gruesome acts I'm willing to commit for her.

"The night before our mating ceremony, I killed his brother and ran away. After that, I jumped around different realms, hiding for twelve years until I stumbled upon Anxo, who— *bless his mushy heart*—thought aiding a stranger hide from the mermen king was a good deed instead of the total clusterfuck it actually is."

I'm gaping at her in shock, but Hazel continues drawing patterns in the dirt to appear nonchalant. She would've fooled me if not for the barely visible tremble in her fingers screaming in the silence.

I rub over my heart when a weight suddenly leaves me breathless. Living with these people, I'm starting to think I have heart problems.

"He's *never* touching you again." I feel my words settle in my soul. The way my Divine stirs, I know this is not just a promise but an oath.

Pursing her lips, Hazel stares blankly at the sky above us and nods. She doesn't believe it.

I know that look. I've seen that look too many times to know she's *waiting*. Waiting because she is confident that that rat bastard is coming for her. Maybe not today, next week, or even next month, but he's coming.

"Hey, say you believe it. I'm not letting that deranged octopus king touch you again." Shaking her head with a snicker, Hazel tries to dismiss my insistence, but I can't let it go.

I don't care who that man is, but he will face the Horsemen and our entire army if he tries to come near her again.

"You want me to drag him by his tail to you because I will. I'll even set my Divine loose on him. Asshole won't know what hit him because no one knows what my wacky Divine might do next. I can even bring you his balls on a silver platter. You know what? That's exactly what I'll do. *First*. Men hate losing their precious parts. And then we can—"

The sound of her carefree laughter stops me from planning his death out loud… but I'm storing my good ideas for later.

"I'm fine without the revenge plans, you psycho."

"But you know I will do it for you, right?"

"Oh, I know. My favorite thing about you is how many lines you're willing to cross for us. That dungeon made you *dark*. Weird too, but I can tolerate weird."

I snort, "*You* tolerate *me*. I'll let you know people are *dying* to be in my Divine presence."

27. Bromance and pixie weed

Anxo

Nevaeh and I started sleeping in the same bed the night after her first panic attack, and ever since, I've made her day always starts with me spoiling her rotten with my love.

I quickly discovered Nevaeh sleeps a lot better with me around, so every morning, long after my internal clock has woken me up, I stay in bed wrapped up in my mate so she can get some well deserved rest.

It usually takes me about half an hour to get my sleeping beauty up and about every day, so color me surprise when I wake up this morning and not only is my mate missing from my side but she dared to leave without giving me my morning kisses.

Waking up with my nose buried in her neck with her sweet scent drowning me is a treat in itself, but when she stirs in her sleep and I get to be the first one to witness that lazy smile spread on her lips, it makes my entire day.

After a quick shower to calm my nerves, I walk straight to the kitchen where I can feel my mate. My steps halt when I hear Nevaeh's laugh and instantly all my blood rushes south. There's no way to hide my raging boner now.

This is why I need to have my fill of my mate every morning. I'm like a teenager salivating over his girlfriend these days.

Stopping at the threshold, I'm struck with the gorgeous view of my sweetheart leaning against the counter, looking drop-dead gorgeous in that small, flowy dress. My fingers twitch impatiently, wanting a reason to run over her curves and imprint my existence on her hips.

Ever since Nevaeh started wearing these mouthwatering

dresses inside the castle, it's been a bittersweet experience. As much as I love to feast on her curves and daydream about her creamy thighs hovering over my head, there are only so many blue balls and cold showers a man can take.

Fates have mercy on me.

Before my other head starts making decisions for me, I get rid of that image... image of my mate in our room, no clothes between us, *under me—*

Without my permission, my legs take me to her. I lose control over my desire as soon as her delicious scent hits my nose. Once I'm behind her, I push my sweetheart's wild curls out of the way to kiss the faint scars on her neck, relishing the way her heart skips at my touch.

Ignoring the girls teasing and cooing over us, I drag Nevaeh's sweet ass out of the kitchen. Finding a secluded area, I sit on a chair with my legs spread wide so Nevaeh can sit on my lap, her shoulder pressed against my chest.

The teasing smirk on her lips widen, feeling my hard-on under her ass, and I damn near spank that perfect ass for teasing me when I feel so deprived of her taste.

Biting her bottom lip, Nevaeh playfully shuffles on my lap like I can't see how much she enjoys the effect her presence has on me. I have to grip her hips to still her when the little minx starts grinding over my bulge before I drop my restraints and take her right here.

My free hand slips under her dress to caress the soft skin of her thigh, and that does nothing to erase the image of them around my waist. Around my neck. Covered in red marks I made with my lips.

Looking into her not-so-innocent doe eyes, I need to calm down before my balls explode.

Holding the back of her neck, I bring those sweet lips to mine. "You are irresistible."

"I believe you because I'm sitting on the evidence." My sweetheart giggles and I swear it's my favorite sound in the world.

"I don't want to go to work today. Maybe we can stay in our room." I kiss her nose. "In our bed." Her bare shoulder. "Or in the shower." I kiss the slender slope of her neck until she's humming in pleasure.

"But it's spa day."

"I can give you a massage. A thorough one." Kissing her neck, I use my grip on her hips to pull her directly over my bulge so she can feel me where she needs me the most. "I can help loosen you up. Make you shiver."

Her head falls back on my shoulder, and she loses herself in our movements. I take full advantage of her daze to mark every inch of her skin I can reach with my lips.

"*Or* I could keep my promise with the girls and make it up to you tonight."

I can't help but whine and nuzzle her neck, taking in her sweet scent to control myself. "But that's so far away."

"What if I tell you Grace is taking me to get my birth control mark today, and I was hoping we could have a little *sexy time* tonight?"

The image makes my already tortured balls squeeze painfully. When my mate looks like she's enjoying my torment a little too much, I bite her neck which makes her shriek and try to squirm away from me.

"You're killing me, sweetheart."

I'm glad Grace thought of birth control.

While I would love nothing more to fast forward our relationship to a place where I can be as close to Nevaeh as possible, I don't want that at the expense of my mate's well-being.

Adding another kid to the equation is not the right move for our little family. For one, August deserves our undivided attention for at least a couple more years. And two, Nevaeh and I are in no place to handle the responsibility and stress that comes with a newborn.

Hazel interrupts us to my immense displeasure. "Shoo away, Conquer. I can see you're trying to ruin our day."

"I'm doing no such thing."

"Liar!" All three women call me out in sync.

Tickling my mate for not taking my side, I don't stop until she is breathless and laughing so hard it fills every crack in my heart. I don't think I'll ever find the right words to tell her how much *I love her*.

Getting up from the chair after kissing her one more time, I turn to leave, but the sight of her smiling like a fool makes me turn around and stand behind her chair.

Ten more minutes won't hurt.

There was a time I would've smacked myself for even thinking about not going to work, but all my work ethic has vanished since my mate came along.

Now, I find reasons to spend my days with her.

"Will you look at this lovesick fool? Go away, Anxo. You have to work for both of us today." Hazel reminds me of the pile of paperwork waiting for me.

Wrapping my hand around Nevaeh's throat, I tilt her head back. "I'll be back soon. Do you need me to bring anything for you, baby?" I give her a soft peck.

"Nope. Just be back soon, please." When she pouts ever so adorably, I can't resist the urge to kiss it away until she blushes and smiles again.

My beautiful sweetheart.

"Don't make me throw up my breakfast." Hazel throws a chip at me, and that's my ultimate signal to get lost before she throws something sharper.

Groaning, I leave for my office when what I actually want is a day alone with my sweetheart. Preferably in our bed.

I bitch and moan about the amount of work I have to do for half an hour sitting in my office before I actually start working. I miss having Grace and Hazel work alongside me. At least they made sure I didn't purposely choke myself on paperwork.

It's a good thing my parents left again for another *vacation*. They came by a week ago, and the whole time, I was constantly worried about dragging Nevaeh off of their mangled corpses after she finally killed them.

I've noticed their presence sparks something darker in Nevaeh and she hovers over me like she's waiting for them to strike.

I learned quickly how protective my mate can be of the people she loves, but she has no reason to stress about my parents. They haven't looked in my direction for *years,* much less planned to hurt me.

Because I have the worst luck possible, my peace lasts about an hour before my office door bangs against the wall. Seiji, aka my childhood headache, leisurely walks in followed by his muscleman Harvey.

"There's a reason you have your own office."

"He does, too." Harvey points to Seiji.

"He's the leech of my life. I hoped at least you would let me work in peace."

"But I *love* your company, brother."

I scoff, "More like the advice that keeps Grace from figuring out you're an idiot."

"Hey!" Harvey protests. "She already knows I'm an idiot. Your advice just helps me show it less often." Mumbling to himself, he folds his arms over his chest, and I see why Hazel enjoys teasing him so much. The guy is packed with muscles like my son is with sugar.

"I'm here to announce a guy's day out. We've been training our asses off for weeks. At the very least, we've earned a break. And if the girls can have a day to themselves, I want one too." Seiji drops into the seat next to Harvey.

"Let me guess, they refused to let you come along."

Harvey covers his snicker with a cough when Seiji glares at him.

Obviously, they grumble when I list the number of things I have on my agenda today. When Seiji starts ruffling through my office, I give in before he messes with my filing system.

"All right, what's the plan?"

Harvey bends over my desk to shut my file while his partner

in crime works on closing my office before dragging me out the door in a blink.

"Party in my backyard!" *Oh boy*.

Seiji tells me we're eating at his favorite diner before we go to the cliffside behind the Famine castle. That place is off-limits to the rest of the world, unlike other waterfalls in the kingdom. Seiji doesn't allow anyone near his sanctuary.

I'm surprised to see a celebration already taking place when we reach the diner for lunch. I don't argue when Seiji proposes we join the festivities.

Class five of adorable little earth fairies completed their plantation class with remarkable success; hence, the diner is filled with fairies ranging from age eight to ten, including the owner's little girl.

Needless to say, we pig out on the food like it's our last meal, celebrating our future food providers.

Thanks to the preceding leaders allowing other supernatural species to live in the kingdom, we haven't had to look elsewhere for food because of the earth fairies, construction is handled beautifully by the centaurs, and banks are in the care of leprechauns. Not to forget the delicious dessert treats curtsy of elves.

When the idea was initially proposed, unsurprisingly, my father opposed saying we were mudding our bloodlines by inviting other creatures. He detests the idea of our inter-species mating. Thankfully, Seiji's dad has continued to be the loudest voice in the room when it comes to equality among species.

After we stuff ourselves to the brim, Seiji warns me to buckle up for an adventure. His adventures are fun no doubt, but they always come with a sprinkle of risk.

Thankfully, Seiji doesn't suggest we dive down with the car like last time. For the longest time, Grace was worried Seiji was suicidal before we eventually concluded he was just a reckless knucklehead.

Slamming the car door behind him, Seiji retrieves an

enormous picnic basket from his trunk and dumps it on a blanket near the edge. So, he wants an innocent picnic by the Cliffside. That's completely safe. Nothing to panic about, Anxo.

Opening the basket, he reveals dozens of snacks, ranging from sugary to spicy, like we didn't just eat two days' worth of food an hour ago.

Fishing out a packet from the basket, Seiji hollers, "Special leaf!"

Narrowing my eyes on the fool, I ask him if he paid the full price this time. The last time he took this stuff from Pixies he failed to mention he didn't have what they wanted in return.

Let's just say I had to fix his mess before the pixies decided to build tiny bombs in their backyards and rained them over the Tetrad kingdom.

Ignoring the food before I throw up, I accept the puff pass. It's been a long time since I've had the chance to escape the stress of our reality, so I'm glad for this break.

"You know cannibalism can solve both the hunger *and* overpopulation problem among humans."

"Oh wow. You would make a fantastic Famine on doomsday."

If Harvey is agreeing with Seiji, that means these fools are *high*. Looking at my friends on the verge of incoherence, I realize the amount of trust I have in them to sit on the edge of a cliff and *not* jump.

The three of us smoke and banter about Fates knows what until Seiji stands up on trembling legs and starts undressing.

"Dude! Not a bathroom. What are you doing?" I cover both mine and Harvey's eyes when he strips his pants, leaving him in just his boxers.

I think I jinxed myself.

"We're diving!" Seiji whoops, throwing his clothes in my face before running back to create a little distance for his run-up.

The world spins as I stand to stop him. "You'll die, you fool! And if you die, who will feed us?" I try to reason with a half-naked, crazed Seiji.

"Really, Anxo? That's all I'm worth to you? My finger-licking recipes?"

"No, that's just the surface reason, man. You're my best friend and—"

"Anxo. My brother. I love you, but I'm jumping." He grips my shoulders, attempting to shake me, but we're both too stoned to use our muscles in the way we want.

Who expected pixies to come up with something this strong? *Not me.*

"Me too!" I hear another voice and turn to find Harvey almost naked like the other high peabrain. *Oh, my eyes!*

Am I the only one with working brain cells?

I quickly let go of Seiji and run towards Harvey who is seconds away from jumping, and barely catch him before he can.

I'm way too high to be babysitting these morons.

"Anxo, it's okay to be afraid. We all have our fears." Seiji comes up to hug me from behind and pats my head, telling me, 'It's okay to be a scared little puppy'.

Maybe I should let him jump.

"I'm not scared, you airhead. If I die, Nevaeh will kill me. I promised her I wouldn't let you rope me into something life-threatening—which in hindsight, would have helped if I remembered it twenty minutes ago." I drone on, slowly dragging them away from the cliff.

My sweetheart.

The thought of Nevaeh spreads through me like wildfire, and I know it won't settle until I feel her soothing touch. The brown-eyed beauty has me wrapped around her pinky. Nevaeh is why I'm *living* instead of going through the motions of life.

The love of my life.

My sweetheart, the rarest of sites, the most seductive view. She's like a comet that comes around once in a lifetime, and I'll be damned if I don't sit back and watch her shine.

"What I'm hearing is you're pussy whipped, and I'll take

your throne when you die." Seiji stumbles around.

"What throne?"

I never agreed to that right?

"Harvey, tell him we need to jump, and it's fun. Anxo, stop being a grandpa!" Seiji whines, leaning his head on Harvey's shoulder and whispering about his oh-so-strong muscles.

What's going on again?

"Sorry buddy, I think Dad is right. Grace would be upset if I got hurt." Harvey supports me.

Finally, someone with a working brain!

"Whipped bitches. Announce your defeat, King Anxo!" Seiji cries, picking a soda can from the ground and pretending it's a sword. "Charge ahead!"

I'm suddenly attacked with breadsticks and soda bottles being used as weapons. I barely dodge them while doing my best not to get hit, but it's not easy when the ground keeps moving.

Harvey, on the other hand, can't stop laughing and rolling in the dirt.

After an hour of running around and eating the rest of the snacks, we our way back to the Horsemen castle. I make sure each of us look as sober and presentable as possible before I go look for Nevaeh.

I can't wait to end this day with my mate in my arms.

28. Are you sure you love me?

Nevaeh

Pulling Angel's hoodie over my head and his boxer briefs over my legs, I leave the closet dressed top to bottom in my mate's clothes and fall face-first into our bed.

With a long sigh, I groan into the mattress. My mood keeps getting worse the longer I'm away from Angel.

It's the first time since we met that Angel and I aren't in touching range, and I have discovered it's my least favorite thing in the world.

Lost in my head, I don't hear the door open until the person I've been craving the whole day walks in. I spring up with a wide, giddy smile when I finally get a glimpse of him. My excitement is equally reciprocated because Angel hurries across the room before jumping on top of me like a silly man.

"Hello to you too," I giggle and hold him close.

Before I can blink, Angel flips us until I'm straddling his lap. Face to face, I adore the way his lips curve into a gooey smile.

"Your hair looks amazing."

I didn't expect him to notice because of how little I let Grace trim. "Really?"

"Hmn, I'm glad you didn't cut much. I love your hair."

Our lips brush against each other, but every time I try to get more than a simple brush, Angel moves away. Why is this beautiful creature teasing me when he knows how much I've been craving him all day?

"I missed you like crazy today."

I whine when his teasing doesn't stop, "Then let me kiss you!" Grabbing his face, I smash our lips together.

Finally, the familiar spark of his touch washes over me.

Angel smiles into our kiss before biting my lower lip, eliciting a soft moan from me.

With his hand behind my head, Angel pushes his tongue inside my mouth to taste my desperation, but before things can get heated, he pulls back, leaving me a mess of wanting more.

"I love you," He murmurs against my lips.

Angel drops his forehead to mine, he is gripping my hips as if he's afraid I'll pull away after the confession. The same confession I've been hiding for *months* because no matter how I looked at it, I couldn't believe someone like *him* could love someone like *me*.

I wasn't even built properly to be considered broken.

For a long time, I was taught to feel worthless. It was drilled into my head that I wasn't worthy of love, especially from someone like my Angel.

My pity train derails when he starts rambling, "Finally. It feels so good to say it out loud," Angel breathes out. "I've been dying to say it for so long, baby. My love for you is imprinted on my bones, and I'm sick of hiding it."

I'm dumbfounded. Completely lost for words. I'm trying to figure out if this is all a dream when Angel starts leaving small butterfly kisses all over my face.

"Horrible decision, Angel. *I'm crazy.*" That's what leaves my mouth when I can finally move my lips.

My answer doesn't affect the way he keeps looking at me. A look I can finally put a name to. *Love.*

The love I've seen a thousand times in his eyes and actions, only to brush it off as comfort or safety. I can't believe I never let myself dwell on it before. I could've avoided so much self-doubt thinking I was the only one falling.

"Shut up idiot," Angel chuckles, not allowing my inner thoughts to hinder our moment.

"You love me? like *love-love*. Are you sure?" My voice lowers with every word as doubts start seeping in.

If I offer him a way out, will he take it? Will he say it was just a joke and that he didn't mean it?

My question doesn't anger him. Angel is as calm as ever and continues to pepper my face with sweet kisses.

"Am I sure? Sweetheart every time you're near me, my heart jumpstarts like it has come back to life. Every single touch from you, even the slightest brush of our hands, linger on me for days. It's not just love... I'm devoted to you, mesmerized beyond sanity."

I'm trying my best to control my emotions, but with every word that leaves his mouth, I feel myself falling deeper than I already have.

"I love you doesn't even begin to cover what I feel for you. You make my world feel so much lighter, so much brighter. I love you, Nevaeh, with every inch of my being. I'm sorry if I'm not making much sense, but I didn't have time to practice, so this is all just coming out, and... *now you're crying.*"

I didn't realize I was until Angel wiped my cheek, still looking at me with those world-melting eyes that hold so much understanding.

"I... uh... we..."

"Take your time, sweetheart." He brushes my hair out of my face, wiping the few lingering tears. "I know if you said you loved me out of the blue like this, I would be stuck on words, too. I want to say you don't have to say it back, but honestly? I don't think my heart will survive that... but don't say it now because I said that—"

I cut him off by kissing the daylight out of him. The thought of Angel doubting my love for him is enough to snap me out of my doubts and embrace his love without my self-created reservations.

I don't let him pull away, wanting to savor this moment a little longer just in case I wake up tomorrow and find out it was all a dream.

"I love you, Angel," I say before pulling him for another soft kiss.

Angel tenses up, but before I can start panicking that I

heard it all wrong and he didn't mean it, he mirrors my doubts. "You do?"

"Of course I do. Anxo, you accept me... *all of me*. Even the crazy parts. You love me without hesitation. Take care of me more than I've ever been cared for. Not to forget how fiercely you protect me from dangerous table corners—" I shriek when Angel pinches my waist before tickling me until I'm a giggling fool.

Holding his face, I confess, "Falling in love with you was easy. Inevitable. And let's be honest, those gorgeous emerald eyes have held my heart captive since the night you saved me. Why do you think I call you my Angel, huh?"

I'm pinned under my mate before I can blink. With my hands held hostage over my head, Angel straddles my hips.

The kiss starts soft, both of us teasing each other, expressing our feelings through it, but the moment he bites my lip, the kiss isn't as innocent anymore.

Tracing my bottom lip with his tongue, Angel asks for permission, and I happily oblige, opening for him to slide his tongue inside my mouth. I moan from the sensation of our warm tongues tasting each other.

I whimper when Angel pulls away, but it turns into a breathy moan when his lips find my neck. Feather-light kisses press against my jaw and travel down to my collarbone. Soon the soft kisses turn into harsher sucking and biting; every bite is followed by his tongue soothing the sensitive skin.

I become a mess of loud moans and whimpers beneath Angel. Fingers burying into his curls, I bring his lips back to mine, wanting to taste him again.

Angel tugs the base of my hoodie, asking permission to pull it off, and I'm glad because the temperature in the room has suddenly hiked up. Swiftly removing my hoodie, his mouth is on my neck again, creeping to my collarbone and down to the top of my covered breasts.

"Can I take this off, sweetheart? I want to know how your tits feel in my hands." Too stunned by his words, I only manage a nod. "Words, sweetheart." Pressing a kiss to my lips, he waits with a stern expression, funnily enough expecting words when I can barely breathe.

I whisper a small yes, and my bra is off in the next second, tossed somewhere in the room.

Angel has branded my soul with his love in a way that I don't even think twice about my scars being on display. The way he looks at me... it's easy to convince myself that my past doesn't make me who I am.

Angel lets out a pained groan, which forces me to snap my gaze from his lips to his eyes, but his remains fixed on my chest. The look on his face is pure lust, and I can see it overpowering him the more he stares.

His hands caress every inch of my flesh he can reach and his eyes follow their path hungrily. Softly tracing every scar on my body with warm kisses, I gasp when Angel suddenly takes my nipple into his hot mouth, sucking like his life depends on it.

My eyes roll back and I fist his hair to keep him in place. Angel kneads my breasts, playing with their weight before squeezing them in his hands. I moan his name louder with every lap of his tongue over my nipple.

I think I'm about to pass out.

Releasing me with a pop, he switches to the other one to give it the same attention while using his hand to tweak and twist the nipple that feels abandoned.

A hand on my stomach keeps me from squirming when he bites my nipple, warning me to stay still. I thought it couldn't get any better, but Angel proved me wrong by sliding his hand down until he reached my upper thigh.

His lips find mine again, and I breathe into it when his hand strokes higher, dangerously close to where it throbs. Hiding his face in my neck, his hand stops moving to where I'm impatiently waiting for him to touch.

I squeeze my thighs together trapping his hand between them to rub away the feeling when he cups me down there. I'm embarrassingly wet, and the boxer briefs I'm wearing are now damp since it's the only thing covering me.

"Can I touch you, sweetheart?" Angel's raspy voice doesn't help my lusty daze, and I realize I'm not above begging if he doesn't touch me soon.

I'm about to agree happily, but my words get stuck in my throat when his fingers start rubbing me over the material, and only a breathy whine comes out.

"You're drenched, baby. Tell me you want me to touch your dripping pussy. I promise to make you feel good, but you need to ask, my sweet girl." Angel rubs small circles on my clothed clit. I didn't know he was cruel enough to expect an answer while doing *that*.

I nod vigorously and squeak a small yes, but when he slows the movement, I know it's not enough this time. "Please touch me Angel... p-please..." I plead, looking straight into his eyes.

A tear of frustration rolls down my cheek, and I forget everything when he licks it away. Grabbing his face eagerly, I lose myself in our kiss as Angel removes the last layer of clothing on me while remaining fully clothed. *How unfair.*

His mouth muffles my surprised gasp when I feel his fingers massage my slit, getting to know my edges and studying my reactions to see what I like.

"Still okay, baby?" Angel murmurs, our lips never separating for more than a second, and I hum into his mouth. When I pull his hair harder than intended, the majestic groan that follows makes me want to do it again.

Angel moves his fingers side to side, rubbing my clit when he sees how my hips buck from the motion. His strokes get more confident with every flick, driving me to the edge of my release. The sensation is overwhelming, but I never want it to stop.

Angel trails kisses on my jaw to my nipples, sucking on them while his thumb rubs my clit. "I'm going to put a finger in, sweetheart."

He waits a second to see if I want to stop, but at this point, I'll take whatever he's willing to give. I'm drunk on this feeling.

The only thought in my head is of him and how good he makes me feel.

Angel coats his finger in my wetness before slowly sliding it in. There's no pain, and his finger slides right in.

"So soft and warm," he whispers, sliding his finger in and out steadily.

I'm in a daze. This feels too good to be real. I gasp when his thumb finds my clit again, and the sparks that follow make me lightheaded. Angel completely pulls his finger out before sliding in two this time. It feels strange at first, but soon I'm almost screaming from how his fingers are brushing against parts of me that make stringing a coherent sentence difficult.

"Such a good girl. Taking my fingers so well. So warm and wet, baby." Angel groans when my walls clench on his fingers pumping into me. With every push, I feel myself tightening around his fingers.

"More."

I don't know what comes over me, but apparently, my body wants more than what Angel is already giving.

"Is my sweet girl greedy for more? How can I ever say no to my sweetheart." His husky voice dripping in lust is the best form of torture. Angel starts thrusting his fingers faster and going deeper, making my eyes roll back.

I cover my mouth to stop myself from screaming out, but suddenly, my high comes crashing down as Angel stops. His fingers are deep inside me, pressing against something that makes me lift my hips to feel more, but Angel stops me with his hand on my stomach.

"You deprive me of your moans, and I'll deprive you of an orgasm. Understood?" His deep voice sends shivers straight to where his fingers are buried. I nod heartily to make him move, but his rule of verbal answers comes in the way once again.

"Yes! Yes... please m-move," I cry desperately, and thankfully, he thrusts his fingers harder, making my sanity slip with every touch. "Oh, Angel!" I scream when he grabs a pillow and wedges it under my hips.

"I can feel how close you are, sweetheart. Don't fight it. *Let go*." When Angel bites my nipple, I'm screaming as something warm takes over my entire body with a vengeance at his rough command.

I cum on his fingers, screaming his name over and over like a broken chant. My legs shake uncontrollably, and my arms fall limp beside my head.

With my eyes squeezed shut and my mouth parted, I try to breathe in the oxygen our *activities* deprived me of. After fighting the black spots covering my vision, I find Angel hovering over me with a cheeky grin.

"Hey." He grins before kissing my lips ever so softly.

I think he melted my brain.

"Hey," my voice cracks. I feel the corner of my eyes leak when I smile, and Angel wipes them lovingly before kissing my cheeks and forehead.

"You look so beautiful when you cum."

I hide my face in his chest and swat his bicep when his shoulders start shaking with silent laughter.

My eyes feel heavy, and I'm already halfway asleep, but when Angel makes a move to leave, my eyes snap open. Holding his arms to my chest, I look for signs of what I've done wrong.

Sensing my inner turmoil and seeing the fear on my face, Angel scoots closer to kiss me so fiercely I forget all my worries. Picking me up bridal style with the sheets covering me, he walks us to the bathroom before carefully setting me on the counter.

"Pee and freshen up, sweetheart. I'll get you some clothes, okay?" Before leaving Angel checks on me again and I hesitantly nod. Pausing, he starts kissing all over my face and tickling me until I'm laughing and pushing his face away.

I'm not oblivious. I understand everything about the intimate moment we just shared. Seiji taught me pretty much everything about this part of adult life, but I can't stop myself from worrying. I want a little more assurance after that, even when I don't want to dump my insecurities on Angel.

I pee before taking a quick shower. On the counter, a beige silk wrap and a fresh pair of underwear is waiting for me. After drying myself, I wrap the night dress around me that reaches mid-thigh, with sleeves that flare on my elbows.

Stepping out of the bathroom, I find Angel sitting on the bed with his back against the headboard. His warm eyes find mine, and when he opens his arms for me, I walk into them without wasting a second, climbing on the bed to sit on his lap.

Angel hugs me to his chest, and I bury my face in his neck, inhaling his sweet scent and relaxing against him.

"You feeling okay, baby? Does anything hurt?" He asks, softly rubbing my back and pulling me closer.

"I'm good. We are good, right?"

I can't help but ask. I won't be able to shut the storm in my head until he confirms we are still good and that he won't leave.

"Of course, we're good sweetheart. *I love you.* There is no one in this universe who wants you in their life as desperately as I do, and I'll be damned if I let you slip away because of your silly doubts."

I love how he can destroy the walls of torture I create around myself within seconds with his touch.

"I love you, Angel."

"I love you more, sweetheart."

Not possible, but I'll let it slide.

I hold Angel tighter when he slides down on the bed with me still on top of him and pulls the warm comforter over us. We always go to bed with me on top of him, trapped in his arms, but I always wake up underneath my giant Angel—still trapped in his arms. My favorite place in the world.

"So now that you've said *I love you...* when are we getting married?"

"Angel!"

29. I'm not pushing out six kids!

Nevaeh

The room darkens when I suck in every last bit of energy and light around me, making the stillness in the room creepier. Strings of thick gold smoke circle me like a predator.

Flexing my fingers when the tingles get stronger, I tighten the control over my Divine. After months of practice and patience, I'm finally at a point where I'm one with my Divine and not fighting against it.

My Divine now respects my limits... as long as I understand its need to wreak havoc once in a while.

With my mate and son in the room, there's only one thing my Divine craves, and today is the day I give in.

For months, I've avoided my Divine's need to familiarize itself with my family and their essence because I was afraid of losing control.

But now I don't fear the show of over-enthusiasm. Now I know even when my Divine craves chaos, it will never hurt my family.

My fingers twitch beside my thighs as I inhale shakily before I let my Divine loose. In a blink, the smoke leaves my side and floats over to the two, creating a barrier around them.

Looking over to my monkey, I watch him hop around the room and giggle wildly as the fog follows him. I completely let loose when my essence takes the form of a small monkey to stop August from running into the center table.

Unlike the rest of the supernatural population, my Divine pushes the boundaries of my flesh like no one has ever seen. Where Divine is supposed to be a simple source of power for others, mine has its own will, and that same stubborn drive clashes with me until one of us gives in.

Until now, my little monkey was the only one to witness both versions of my Divine. The side that likes to cause chaos and the other that likes to entertain a little boy with animals made of smoke.

It's nothing compared to what I can do now, but on the nights I had some strength to amuse him, I used to push my weak Divine to create a flock of birds from gold smoke that circled over my boy. Those were the nights August went to sleep with a smile on his lips instead of dry tears on his cheeks.

I always thought the reason I could use my Divine without losing control was because of how weak we both were. But maybe my essence has always been in my corner. I just couldn't see it yet.

Reigning in my Divine, I watch the mist crawl back to me and disappear completely. August walks through the fog monkey, watches it go up in smoke, and falls to his knees, laughing freely with tears in his eyes.

When Angel opens his arms for me with an excited grin, I don't hesitate before running to him. I know he will never say it, but I've seen him worry every time I failed to control my essence.

Where a normal person would be worried for themself with the way my Divine slips from my fingers, all my mate said was, 'I can take it, sweetheart, just don't hurt yourself'.

What he doesn't know is that all my life, my Divine has been the one in control. When I was younger, there was no way for me to be in charge of such power, and after Visha took me, I didn't have enough control of my limbs, let alone my Divine.

But with his help, constant encouragement, and support, for the first time in my life, *I* am in control. The amount of power radiating from me today is nothing I've ever felt. This is the first time I feel like I belong with the Horsemen.

Angel gives me a loud smooch on my cheek and tells me how proud he is of me with August in his arms, who mimics Angel and kisses me too. Before Angel leaves for the council meeting, he warns me not to be late—*again*—but I brush him off because I'm never late; the elders and Warriorheads just like to be early.

Quickly doing my morning routine, I try my hardest not to think about last night and all the ways I lost sleep.

I've only recently discovered how amazing sleep is, yet I have no problem losing some if I get to have my Angel's mouth or fingers between my thighs, making my entire body shiver with pleasure.

I grab up the energy bar and the bottle of juice Angel has left for me on the bedside table as a quick morning snack before I start looking for the conference room. I've been living here for three months and still can't get around without help.

Whose idea was it to make the conference room soundproof anyway? I can't even follow their voices like a blind bat.

I peek into a room, thinking it will be another dead end, and come face to face with four angry faces snapping in my direction. I can only describe it as an 'I'm going to bury you in my backyard' look.

I laugh nervously when their expressions don't change. Conjuring up my innocent facade, I smile extra sweetly. "Sorry guys, I got a little lost." I apologize, taking a seat beside Angel.

Running my hand on the rich circular wooden table, I avoid the eyes on me by looking outside the glass dome at the northern side of our kingdom. For some strange reason, the sky outside is looming with dark clouds haunting the horizon. It's not enough to rain, but the cool wind is chiller than what this realm is used to.

"For forty minutes?" Seiji questions with his mouth filled to the brim with chips.

"On the same floor?" Grace is utterly perplexed too. I'm sure she's losing brain cells trying to figure out where I knocked off mine. *In a dungeon, Honeybunch.*

"I'm directionally challenged, okay." Hiding my face with my hair, I look anywhere but at their baffled expressions.

"You're *never* on time." Hazel remarks in her usual, 'I'm not interested in your shit, but it's fun to watch' tone.

"Of course I am."

I have no idea why I'm defending myself.

I know they are right. *They* know they are right.

Still doesn't mean I have to admit it.

"We have to wait nearly thirty minutes for you at every meeting. We got here thirty minutes *after* you should've been here, and you know what? You're *still* late." Harvey ruins my defense with a smug smile, his eyes doing nothing to hide his mirth.

"I might have a slight issue with time management too, but it's not completely my fault." I turn to Angel with a pout, praying to Fates for a helping hand.

"Of course, sweetheart. Silly of us to blame you for such outrageous crimes." I know he's mocking me, but the way his face brightens and his dimples make an appearance, I completely forget what everyone is babbling about.

I love the warmth that cocoons me every time he smiles at me... or because of me.

When I ask Angel about the round table, he doesn't comment on my blatant attempt at deflecting and simply explains it's to establish that everyone is equal and that we don't value one voice over another.

When a small team of elite warriors and elders join us shortly, Angel eases into planning. The matter at hand is our visit to *The Forgotten Realm,* where Visha's right-hand warlock, Micah, is hiding.

Angel didn't want any security issues while we were gone in case of an attack, so he decided to change patrol patterns near the portals just to be safe. He's not too worried because Papa Nakaya, our Horsemen Famine would be here, and he is more than capable of handling things.

After preparations are made and necessary precautions are set, the council scatters out. A few remain to chat, but soon, only our group and Khatri are left behind.

Scrolling through his phone, Angel shows the guys pictures of August playing with blocks, who all fawn over how cute he looks surrounded by wobbly structures.

"I want a kid," Harvey announces abruptly. I almost laugh when I see him all but begging Grace with his eyes.

"I want kid-*s*," Angel adds casually, watching his screen but subtly glancing over to make sure I heard him.

"Don't be greedy, Anxo, you already have one. Nevaeh, your next baby is mine. Promise me your biological firstborn because I'm your best friend."

What the fuck do I even say to that?

Turns out, I don't have to say anything because Angel refuses to entertain the idea, yelling about how he needs *all* of our babies for his big family dream.

How many kids is he dreaming about?

"Don't be selfish, Anxo. I want little demons too!"

"How about you find your mate and ask *him* for little demons instead of stealing *my babies*."

Is my mate really fighting over babies that don't exist?

"We have baby-hungry men in this group." Grace shakes her head, trying to smother her smile.

I know she's more than happy to oblige with Harvey's request, but she's holding back on letting him know just yet. I know Harvey says he doesn't like kids much, but I see the way he looks at Angel and my monkey. That man is dying to be a father.

"And half of them are still children themselves," Hazel snickers. The only person of the male species who is spared from her disdain for the gender is August.

No matter how much Hazel tries to keep her emotions under wraps, her icy exterior thaws when August looks up at her with his big blue eyes.

Pushing his chair back roughly, Seiji stomps to Hazel. "You give me one more side look, and I'm tornadoing your ass to Azure!"

"Away from you? Let me go pack a bag."

I chuckle at the start of yet another bickering fest. My attention shifts to Khatri when he stands from his chair with a smile, ready to leave. "Anything you need from me before I leave Princess Nevaeh?"

"How many times have I told you not to call me Horsewoman or Princess? Just say Nevaeh? *Nuh-vay-ya*."

When I don't back down, Khatri turns to Angel, who completely avoids his stare, making it clear he won't be of any help.

Sighing in defeat, Khatri says, "Your father already makes me call him by his name. Why do you insist on being just as stubborn, young lady?"

"Cause I'm his daughter, duh."

Suddenly Khatri's eyes soften with the same adoring look I've seen on Papa Nakaya many times.

Maybe that's a dad look. I hope one day Papa will look at me the same way too.

"Okay, Pri—*Nevaeh*."

"That's what I'm talking about."

Before he can disappear, I stop Khatri for a long-awaited chat. I don't know anything about the demon who has been the right-hand man for my father all these years, and it's high time I changed that.

We start by talking about his training days. Khatri laughs at how it took him months to believe Papa chose him as his second in command instead of the man with bloodright to the position.

Since Khatri comes from a family of dungeon guards, Papa picking him solely based on his exceptional skills was a proud moment for his entire family.

Angel and I exchange amused looks when I ask about his mate, and Khatri turns into a lovesick puppy with heart-eyes. He talks about his mate for fifteen minutes straight, about how she is a werewolf, likes sweet over spicy, tomato soup over vegetable before realizing he might've gone a bit overboard.

Not that I stopped him. Seeing a man so dedicated to his

mate and family is awfully endearing.

"What about kids?"

"Lucifer blessed me with two wonderful daughters. Unlike me, they take after their mother with her beauty, but their battle skills are all me."

"They sound wonderful. Have I met them before?"

"I'm not sure Pri—*Nevaeh*. My older one is only fifteen, but she does weekend warrior training, so it's possible."

South Asian demon girl with epic combat skills? Who *doesn't* know her?

"Wait—is she the one with blue hair who carries that insanely cool sword like it's an extension of her?"

"That's the one. That's my Skye."

"No way, *I love her!* You will never believe what she did the first time we met. Obviously, she didn't recognize me so when I asked for a combat partner, none of the seasoned warriors came forward due to fear, but that girl? She didn't just step up; she made me work for that win."

I can't believe I didn't guess she was Khatri's daughter. Of course, that level of competence comes from a warrior like Khatri. That girl is my favorite teenager in the entire realm.

I would kill for that sassy little lady.

"Her fire is what I most love and fear about her," Khatri says fondly before falling into deep thought. Turning to me, he looks like he's trying to solve a puzzle. With a final determined nod to himself, he says, "You know she could use a trainer. I could ask someone else, but—"

"I'll do it!"

Hazel volunteers before I can jump at the chance.

What a warrior-stealing bitch!

"Sit your finned ass back down before I drown you in the same ocean you crawled out of."

Smirking, Hazel backs away with her hands raised. "Lucifer, you're testy today. Fine. Have her. But Khatri? Just so you know, I'll always be here to teach Skye the *right ways* when golden reaper here screws up."

I swear to Fates I will kill her one of these days.

Khatri laughs, watching us fight over who gets to train his super-skilled offspring.

Folding my arms, I regain my cool. "Sorry, you had to see that. The siren is out of control on good days and more than a little manic on her worst. Forget about her. Tell me about your other daughter. How old is she?"

Khatri softly smiles at the mention of his little girl, "Well, my Aurora is six with the soul of an old lady. She's already reading books on supernatural history when she should be doing whatever kids her age do."

He palms the back of his neck, and his worry for his little one is quite evident. "I can't really blame her for keeping to herself though. We don't have many werewolf children in the kingdom, so there's no one to keep her company."

Interesting.

It's not uncommon for two different kinds of supernaturals to find mates in each other, and since her mom is a werewolf, Aurora taking after her is no surprise.

Even for adult werewolves, it's a struggle not to be a part of a pack. Having her mate and family must help Khatri's wife, but it won't help the little girl. Being a rouge at such a young age is not good for her fragile mind.

"Maybe she needs a friend. Someone like my August who can teach her the wonders of eating cake with his hands and watching a mouse make a cat's life hell on TV."

Khatri blinks rapidly at my suggestion and agrees in a blink. Not only is the playdate good for both kids to come out of their shells, but having alpha blood means that even if August doesn't have his wolf yet, he can help Aurora not feel so alone anymore.

I'm sure August will like her. He doesn't mix well with the hyper kids his age because of how skittish he feels around them, but maybe a calm little girl with a reading addiction could complement his subpar social skills.

Maybe he will finally make friends who aren't twenty years

older than him.

After an afternoon with Khatri, Angel and I leave the conference room to discuss the playdate with August.

Talking about kids...

"Oh before I forget. We're not having a whole village of kids."

"What—*Why*?" Angel stops dead in the hallway.

If anyone saw him right now, they would think I just told him his puppy died. Angel looks genuinely heartbroken.

"What do you mean why? I'm not pushing out that many kids!"

I thought that would be argument enough, but guess not. Angel keeps looking at me like I'm breaking every dream he's ever had. I can see that this is truly heartbreaking for him, and if it was anything other than pushing multiple watermelons out of me, I would've given in.

"Okay... let's compromise. I don't need eight kids. I can make do with six. How about only six kids?"

Only?!

I can't help but laugh when he says it like six is a massive compromise for him. Angel tries to smooth me over with sweet kisses and promises of doing all the dirty diaper work, but I turn around and run with him hot on my heels. Both of us are laughing uncontrollably, the sound carrying around the castle.

"You are crazy!"

"Crazy in love with you!"

30. The highest form of treachery

Nevaeh

"Angel, wake up!" I've been shaking this sleepyhead for ten minutes, and he still refuses to budge.

I woke up earlier than usual because my anxiety about today refused to let me rest. Without disturbing Angel, I slid off the bed to freshen up and took an hour-long scalding hot shower. But when I returned he was still in dreamland, hugging my pillow to his chest.

Changing into black cargo pants and a full-sleeved t-shirt, I give my mate five more minutes of being a lazy bum like me. When I go to wake him up, Angel swiftly yanks me down and rolls until I'm under him.

"Ugh, wake up, you stubborn man. I need you to do something for me." I gently coax him.

"And here I thought I tired you enough last night." Angel draws me in with the pretense of cuddling, but I know all too well he just wants more space to grope me.

My cheeks heat up at his mention of our late-night activities. Tracing the markings on his shoulders, I shudder remembering how I passed out after he made me come for the fourth time last night.

Things have naturally progressed in the bedroom since we confessed our love for one another.

These days, our nights and stolen moments during the day are filled with mind-numbing orgasms and memorizing every dip and curve of each other's body.

"We still have a couple of hours, sweetheart," Angel mumbles in his husky morning voice, which sends tingles to my nether region. Nuzzling his face into my neck, he breathes me in.

"Yes, but I need a different kind of braid today. Do you know the one where two braids start from the top of your head and then go down?" I try to explain what I saw in a magazine the other day, only for the sleepyhead to blink at me strangely.

"You mean French braids?"

"I don't care where they invented it! Will you please make them for me?" I scratch his scalp to butter him up. When I think he is finally melting, Angel drops his head in the crook of my neck and snakes his hands under my top to cup my boobs.

"Give me thirty minutes of cuddling and we have a deal." Angel doesn't wait for an answer and falls right back to sleep. Running my fingers through his hair and down his back, I recall our last council meeting.

Angel was very clear that we wouldn't have room for error or messes on our mission, and I didn't appreciate how he kept glancing at me during that speech.

I mean why would he single me out when Seiji is the one bringing all kinds of snacks and drinks with him like he's going on a picnic.

But of course, when I mentioned that, Seiji, my dramatic princess, acted all offended and even shed a few crocodile tears. He wept how it wasn't about his milkshakes but about *respect*.

And then he sang, 'his milkshakes bring all the boys to the yard'. Loudly. While fake crying.

I don't think the man knows he is tone-deaf. My ears are still ringing from the horrific performance.

Harvey was so close to tears that he begged Seiji to stop singing—*if you could even call it that*. Hazel almost threw her dagger at Seiji's head, which Grace snatched away at the last second.

I don't usually condone violence, but maybe a warning stab wouldn't have been the worst thing in the world.

Using a silent moment to myself, I let it sink in that going to The Forgotten Realm to capture Micah takes me one step closer to my revenge.

I know Angel understands my need to seek justice, but it doesn't stop him from worrying about how a personal encounter with my tormentor could affect me. The fact that he has witnessed all my emotional breakdowns, makes him all the more wary and protective of me.

A little less than an hour later, I wake Angel with kisses all over his face. The soft smile aimed at me convinces me to only ever wake him up like this after today.

As promised, Angel quickly freshens up while I wait for him to braid my hair. I don't have to wait long because he is quick and careful, like a professional at this point.

"Promise me you won't let your emotions cloud your judgment today and you'll be vigilant at all times," Angel says, putting an elastic on the end of my braid.

"Hey, when am I not careful?"

Fuck. I immediately regret the slip-up. I've handed Angel the perfect ammo to shoot my ego down to Hell.

"You had stitches from trying to make a *sandwich*, sweetheart."

I knew he was going to bring that up again!

"It was the knife's fault!"

Of course, it was my fault. I'm an idiot in the kitchen.

Angel thinks my constant denial is funny and laughs it up before kissing my head and ushering me out of the room. I knew he only kissed my head like that to stop himself from calling me an idiot.

Everyone is already waiting for us, everyone except August, who is staying with Seiji's parents for the day. The only thing I have to worry about leaving him with his pseudo-grandparents is how he will be in a food coma from authentic Japanese food by the time we come back.

The most mind-baffling thing that happened yesterday was Kiara, Angel's so-called mother, *ordering* me to leave August in her care while we were away.

Before I could tell her where to shove her idea of being in

the general vicinity of my son, Angel denied her and quickly dragged me away from the cunning woman.

I don't know what she wants with August, but I've warned the Nakayas about her visit, and they promise not to let Kiara or her husband anywhere near my boy.

Brushing Diamond's back, I admire the way his wings flap against the wind, making tiny particles of ash gather near his feet. Diamond's one wing is the size of my whole body. Imagine someone getting smacked by them. It would be like those cartoons; one smack and boom, they slide down like thin paper.

I've got to stop watching cartoons with August.

Everyone suits up in armor before grabbing their weapons. Grace straps a crossbow on her back and caps the quiver. I watch Seiji's whips disassemble and wrap around his arms, acting as extra armor.

Hazel is hiding yet another one of her daggers in her armor when Angel grabs it and hands it over to a warrior walking by. I already know that's not going to go over well with her. Hazel has a crazy obsession with having as many weapons on her as possible.

"But now I only have *nine* daggers. I can't leave with an odd number of weapons."

"You need *more*?" I utter in disbelief. "Where the fuck are you even stashing them?"

"I'll give you a full tutorial if you ask your *Angel* to give my dagger back."

I see my mate's stern gaze and don't bother convincing him. I'm not motivated anyway. Nine daggers are more than enough.

When Angel doesn't budge because I don't ask, Hazel hisses, "You need to work on your seduction. He's not whipped enough."

Angel catches her trying to sneak in another dagger and does his breathing technique before his non-existent temper gets the best of him.

Walking to my horse, I falter. Sure, I'm armored up too, but Hazel has nine daggers. Angel and Grace have their bows. Seiji has his whips, and Harvey has the shiny new sword Uncle Elijah gifted him for his coronation/wedding. But before doubts can slip in, I snap out of it.

I don't need a weapon. *I am the weapon.*

Harvey hoists Grace on his mighty red horse, who neighs when she rubs his stomach gently. It's no surprise the horse is just as taken with my sister as his rider.

Seiji whispers in his horse's ear before climbing on. Apparently, the Prince of Famine chose a horse that demands his rider to ask permission before every ride.

Just as dramatic as his rider.

A warrior circles the horse Hazel is taking with her to make sure he is saddled properly. The distracted demon almost bumps into Hazel but thankfully she avoids it by stumbling back at the last second.

Then the strangest thing happens. Hazel taking that step back should've meant coming in contact with Diamond's fire and recoiling from the burn... but nothing happens. I watch her tell off the warrior for not being more attentive before mounting her horse.

Scratchless. No burn marks.

Diamond whines in a way that demands attention but I'm not the one he wants it from. Why would he neigh for Hazel?

The horse stays distracted until Angel announces it's time to leave. With a kick, the horse starts to steadily climb the air. The cool air nips at me, forcing me to think over that strange incident at a later time.

A hollow feeling creeps in on my first flight. It feels incomplete without Papa cheering me on and warning Diamond about the consequences of dropping me.

Papa never trusted anyone else to look after me. It took him a long time to stop hovering over me every time I went out to play with Harvey or walked around the kingdom by myself.

Eventually, Papa eased out and immediately regretted it

when his precious stuff started to go missing, and I was terrorizing folks like he once did at my age. With every step I took, he wasn't too far behind me.

And now I have to live in our world without him.

It's not a home without the people who make it home.

Like Diamond can sense my inner turmoil, he neighs loudly, running zig-zag patterns among the clouds to distract me. Bending down, I hug the not-so-grumpy horse.

After crossing the portal, the journey is supposed to be an hour from the kingdom. Right on the edge of the human realm and Heaven is an abandoned cliff-side—also known as the only way into *The Forgotten Realm.*

The worst part is that one must dive off the cliff and into the ocean to transport there.

If I don't make it out, I want everyone to know I absolutely hate this idea, and my death is on Angel. He brought me here so I could have my revenge like a good mate, so it's his fault.

Every ancient lore we studied lacked any vital information on the realm except the one saying 'Even with it being a whisper away, not everyone with darkness within can handle the light'.

What is it with ancient people and encrypted messages?

The realm's magnetic pull slowly erases your will to leave the longer you stay, and without a known exit, it's no surprise not many get out. That place literally eats away all the light one might bring in and manipulates them into becoming a part of its never-ending darkness.

Good thing we have someone who knows everything.

Grace whips out her trusty journal to see if everything is on track. I remember her telling me Papa gifted her this enchanted journal when he noticed she was having a hard time organizing the abundance of information in her head. The book's enchantment helps her visualize her thoughts in writing and illustrations.

Her only warning before we jump is to make sure we don't stay longer than six hours, no matter what.

"Okay, we get in, find the sick moron, send his soul to purgatory, and get out. Understood?"

After Angel repeats the same thing for the fifth time, we collectively take a deep breath while standing on the edge and get ready to jump.

But before they can I startle everyone at the last moment. "Wait a minute." Turning to Hazel, my eyes trail to her legs.

"No, I'm not going to grow a fucking tail!"

"How am I supposed to know that when you never tell me anything?!"

She grumbles, tightening the strap of the black duffle bag on her shoulder and turning away from me.

Sighing in defeat I decide to poke her some other day.

I can't even turn to Grace for answers because my own sister, my same surname person, made a pact to keep the siren's precious secrets to herself years before I came into the picture. *Family betrayals sting the worst.*

Taking another deep breath, everyone turns to me, and only when it's clear I won't interrupt again, do we jump at the count of three.

Well, *they* jump. I don't have any plans on willingly jumping off a fucking cliff and into a deep-water body.

As I'm contemplating whether to wait here or go sit beside Diamond, I'm suddenly pushed from behind. Screaming all the way down, I use every curse word in my vocabulary at whoever committed the highest form of treachery by pushing me.

How did I not realize one of them stayed behind to make sure I jumped? I get my answer about who when *Harvey* jumps a second after me, swimming deeper into the water.

Wait till I get my hands on the piece of shit I call my best friend.

When I open my eyes again, I'm standing on solid ground and bone dry, except I can't see anything because of a thick fog surrounding me.

Sensing Harvey a step away, I jump on his back and choke him with my arms, cursing the traitorous cliff-pushing bastard. Angel struggles to drag me away from my hysterical best friend, who doesn't even attempt to get out of the chokehold since he's too busy laughing like a constipated cow.

Like I said, Family betrayals sting the worst.

Angel tightly holds me against his chest, whispering soothing words in my ear, hoping I will forget about knocking out Harvey's teeth. My mate is smart enough to not let me loose as he asks Seiji to clear the fog.

"Uh, I totally would only there's a tiny problem."

Hazel stalks through the fog and grabs Seiji by his collar. "Do not tell me your Divine isn't working."

"I wish I could." He clicks his fingers several times, but nothing happens.

"This is happening because of Anxo!"

"Wait, what—What did I do?"

"You didn't let me take my *tenth* dagger. I told you it's bad luck to carry an odd number of weapons."

"And you couldn't just... I don't know... toss one out?"

"Don't be ridiculous, Conquer. Why in the sweet hell would I do that?"

Without his powers, Seiji can't clear the fog. So Angel forms a human chain and starts leading us through the temporary blinds in hopes that the fog will clear out soon.

"Nothing has changed. We still have to find him in a limited time frame, so stay sharp and depend on your senses. It'll be fine. Remember, we've trained for something like this." Angel encourages us as we start moving, and I sense his relief when it gets thinner the longer we walk to the potential end of it.

Once the fog ultimately elevates, I take in the mysterious realm. Looking at it now, I can't believe how anyone can convince you to stay in this place for eternity.

Everything is black.

The sky? Black. The soil? Black. Guess the color of the trees? Surprise-surprise, it's black. The entire realm is empty except for the far-off hill, where we spot a couple of sheds. One of those is where our target is hiding.

This realm is straight out of a horror movie, where things behind you disappear into the dark abyss of nothing at every turn.

The only color I see is where people live in bright, colorful houses with small parks. The magic pulsing in this realm is so strong that it has made them forget their actual home.

On our trek up the mountain, Angel counts heads every three seconds to ensure we don't get separated. Good thing because I have the utmost faith in myself that I'd be the person running in circles trying to find the people I came with if he didn't hold my hand.

No one understands the struggles of being directionally challenged.

31. Knock-Knock little Death's here

Nevaeh

I squint to peek inside a window on the rustic two-floor log house at the tip of the not-really-there mountain.

The thick layer of dust on the window makes it difficult to study the layout, and since my Divine is currently taking a nap, it's more complicated to sense a presence inside.

I pity the warlock. While we still have our senses and strength to depend on, without his precious magic, the man is toast.

Hazel suddenly blocks my view inside the unkempt house by coming to stand before me and staring expectantly. I have no clue what the crazy siren wants until she waves a thick pair of fingerless gloves in front of my face, rolling her eyes.

So much attitude from such an innocent face.

I grab the gloves from her, assuming she'll turn around and leave, but she surprises me by staying. We do this a lot nowadays—sharing silence. I think it's comforting for her to know someone understands the ache in her soul without her having to put it on display.

Harvey returns from scanning the area, confirming we're not walking into a trap. Our time crunch might be an issue in this realm, but the main problem is our lack of knowledge.

We have no idea what kind of creatures are stuck in this realm and for what reason. Staying quiet and swift will ensure we get out of this place in one piece without encountering an ancient species trapped here for thousands of years and looking for food... i.e., *us*.

We march towards the house like it's our cousin's vacation house, and I'm about to kick the door down when Harvey pushes me aside to crouch in front of the keyhole.

A quiet click echoes through the air, and I discover my best friend—*even if a complete dumbass*—picked up a few things from those sly humans.

Hazel's eyebrows shoot to her hairline in surprise, "And here I thought you were nothing but muscle."

"Can we leave her in the water before going home?" Harvey pleads with Angel, who shakes his head with a sympathetic smile.

Hazel picking on people is my favorite thing ever. Especially when I'm not the target. The soul siblings start fighting over who will win in some random ass scenario that has nothing to do with our reality.

I want to go home sooner rather than never, so I push them apart and stride in. "Come out, come out wherever you are!" My voice sings through the house, followed by a crash.

Turning back, I hiss at Seiji, who is carefully stepping over the mess he made on the floor with a sheepish smile. The split second it took me to walk inside, Seiji managed to crash into the door—*don't ask me how*—and broke a vase sitting by it.

Why might one ask? Because he was busy enjoying his milkshake, that's why.

Angel breathes through his annoyance and inhales his anger. The nerve near his hairline twitches. I'm afraid one day it will explode if he keeps surrounding himself with the likes of us.

Asking for Hazel's bag, Angel pulls out a thick cloth and throws it over the mess so no one will slip and break their neck.

We take turns swatting Seiji on his head before Harvey pulls him up the stairs. They are as quiet as August is on the nights he sneaks into our room to climb between Angel and me after something spooked him.

I still don't understand why Micah chose this place instead of going to the numerous allies who would've helped him simply because they hated the Horsemen.

It's not long before Micah is dragged to me, kicking and

screaming. Where I would've loved a chase, Harvey binds him to a chair and doesn't resist the urge to pull the first few punches.

When Micah lifts his head with blood dripping down his cracked lips to see his captors, his gaze locks on me. Struggling to form words, he pales like a man who knows his time is limited.

"Don't look into her eyes, or that's where she'll start." Seiji shivers at the thought and plops down on the white leather sofa. Micah made the mistake of making this place look like the pearly gates of Heaven with all the white furniture. When I'm done with Micah, his entire place will be covered in red.

"You seem familiar. Oh, now I remember. Aren't you the warlock who dragged my son into that disgusting dungeon by his hair?" I don't pull the punch that cracks his nose, which makes him wail like a banshee.

It's has been a long time coming.

"Use your words, sweetheart." Angel interrupts my next punch.

"Why? My fists are much more capable."

A dagger appears before me, and my head snaps to Hazel. She's giving me one of her sharpest weapons—her favorite one. When the haunted look in my eyes reflects in hers, it's hard to tell which one of us is mirroring the other's pain.

Flipping the dagger, I relish in the genuine fear swirling in the coward's eyes, but once again, Angel decides to shit on my parade. "You promised information." He reminds me before I slip and give in to the intense need to carve this man from the inside out.

"Fine… only light stabbing then. Don't worry Micah, I'll take *excellent* care of you." Chuckling, I stab the dagger into his thigh. His scream echoes as I wait for Micah to calm down so I can drag the information Anxo needs out of him before actually enjoying my prey.

In times like this, I am forced to admit how comfortable I am with creating pain. Sometimes it scares me what I've become, but they did this to me. Every torture technique I know is their gift. Whatever I am today is what they made me.

They expected me to be a monster, so they turned me into one.

About half an hour later, Micah has a couple of broken bones, and I've retrieved everything Angel needs from this man. We have what we came here for. Locations of other high-ranking warriors—all except the dark queen herself. She remains hidden while her people pay for her sins. *What a leader.*

I know what the witch is capable of more than anyone, and I have this gut-twisting hunch that she's up to something... something I can't see even when it's right in front of me.

I'm about to ask Angel if I'm finally free to do as I please when a loud thud stops me. Turning away from Micah, I find Seiji flat on the ground with a banana peel crushed beneath his leg. Everyone bursts out laughing, and from the corner of my eye, I see Harvey recording the entire ordeal.

Using their distraction in my favor, I swiftly move my dagger to cut off all the fingers on the warlock's left hand in a single move. The attention immediately shifts back to the man screaming through the gag in his mouth.

He just can't shut up today.

"Nevaeh—" Angel tries to interfere, but I raise my hand, dripping with the warlock's blood to halt his approach.

"I've waited long enough."

I do the same with Micah's other hand, much slower this time to make the pain last longer. Next, I carve his chest and internally praise myself for the fine artwork.

'S-C-A-R-E-D Y-E-T?'

I knew the words would trigger Angel. He has seen those exact words on my thigh. The words that became a scar—*a permanent scar.*

The night he found me rocking back and forth on our bathroom floor still haunts him. I wanted to burn my flesh or slice that piece of my skin to erase the reminder of my time in that cell, but there was no way Angel would let me do that to myself.

That night, my mate saw just how broken Nevaeh Blackburn was. He witnessed me break down in his arms, and instead of leaving me on the floor, he gently collected my pieces and held on to them until I was ready to be glued back together.

When he saw how much that scar bothered me, Angel took me to Grace. My sister quickly whipped out a potion that could help, but it came with a price.

The medicine burned hotter than hell, and it took hours for the pain to become tolerable. The scar faded more and more each day until I was free of the mark and the memory it carried.

Grace had secretly started working on a rare potion the day she met Harvey. She wanted to be prepared in case the markings from Fates triggered Harvey or made his old bruises flare up. Fortunately, Fates took pity on Harvey and freed him of every scar that reminded him he was ever alone or broken.

Grace offered to make me more, but the pain you experience as the potion works is eerily familiar to how I got those scars. No amount of scar-free skin was worth revisiting that pain over and over.

Angel doesn't intervene anymore, but it doesn't stop him from standing right behind me in case I need him.

"You remember that night, don't you Micah? The night you carved my worst fears on me, asked me to beg for your mercy?" Grabbing his bloody cheeks, I squeeze until I hear his cheekbones crack. "Your turn to beg. Beg like I did. Ask me for mercy even when you know it won't save you. Beg or I'll continue to carve you like a piece of wood," I sneer.

"You are an... an abomination made to r-ruin my kind. I w-warned my Queen to let me deal with you, but she wanted you alive."

I can't say I don't admire his lack of survival skills because it gives me a chance to drag this on. He doesn't realize it, but the hatred in his eyes is only making this easier for me.

"Like you tried to *deal* with me that night?"

The silence behind me worries me if I've said too much, but if I don't lay it all out today, I won't get another chance to. I can't move on until I've put my past in the grave once and for all. I refuse to let the shadows of my past steal the light from my future.

Micah smirks with his bloody teeth on the display and the courage of a dying man. "I almost had you. I could've taken what I wanted if it weren't for the boy."

I grit my teeth, thinking about that night. Flashes of fear and desperation start bleeding into my present.

A shuffling sound behind me makes me glance at Hazel now sitting on the floor with all her daggers laid out. It makes my stomach warm to see she's waiting for my signal to unleash the rage hidden behind her calm exterior.

When I ask her for a spoon instead, she looks at me baffled before handing it over with a sly smirk.

I've been where Micah is, and all he did was enjoy the show like a coward, never once meeting my eyes. So I use the cold steel spoon to scoop an eyeball—*or two.*

I memorize the terror on Micah's face and the pain in his eyes, hoping they will replace the memory of his touch.

I pull the gag down, itching to hear him plead for his life before I end it because no matter what his last words are, I didn't come here to forgive. I came here to *forget.*

"I-I'm s-sorry... I s-shouldn't h-have... I will leave... a-anything you want... p- please... I-I'm so-sorry..."

With his last words, I step behind him to avoid the splashes of his blood when I slice his neck. Slowly. Hearing him choke on his blood is music to my ears before I cover his mouth with the gag to make the process more agonizing.

I'm sure I look like a maniac with a satisfied smile on my face and blood on me, but the memories of that night hurt a little less now. After what he tried, I don't regret a single thing I did to this filthy man.

"You're too scary sometimes. Even for me." Harvey breaks

me out of my head, nodding at me slightly. His relaxed grin assures me it's over now. I can finally bury this part of my past and never look back.

Harvey understands the importance of this moment because, after all, he was there that night. I will be forever grateful he gained consciousness when he did. He saved me from something that would've forced me in a direction where meeting Angel and having a family would've been a faraway dream.

As Angel strides toward me, I'm eager to be wrapped in his arms when I hear it.

Marching troops.

Motherfuc—

32. Welcome to the red house

Nevaeh

T he sound of metal clinking and boots stomping with unparalleled coordination makes my stomach sink. I squeeze my eyes shut when it finally dawns on me who they are.

"Please tell me I'm hallucinating, and I don't hear Heaven's warriors marching up the hill," I plead.

"You're hallucinating, and you—"

"I will kill you, Sharky."

Clapping his hands, Seiji wedges himself between Hazel and me to pull me away. "Hey, save that rage for the army coming to bury us here."

But how did they find us?

Angel kept today's mission as close-knit as possible because he didn't want the entire kingdom to panic over us going to The Forgotten Realm. No more than half a dozen high-ranking warriors know about our current whereabouts, so I don't understand how we are in this mess.

If Heaven's army is here for us—*without an exit strategy*— then this is a suicide mission. It's hard to wrap my head around Heaven sending their soldiers on a suicide mission just to target a couple of innocent kids.

Okay... we're not really kids per se and aren't all that innocent either, but this is still extreme.

Closing my eyes, I focus on the movements to estimate the number of skilled warriors marching to their deaths.

30... 45... 53. *Fucking shitballs, we're so fucked.*

Looking at the shocked faces around me, I answer the lingering question. "Over sixty warriors trained by minor gods of war and chaos. This is not good."

Suddenly Angel is repeatedly clearing his throat and expectedly looking at Hazel, who is shuffling on her feet nervously. The exchange momentarily steals my attention from our reality.

Why do I get the feeling that, for a change, I'm not the one responsible for this mess?

Throwing her duffle bag on the floor Hazel starts retrieving gun after gun from inside it. Skillfully ignoring the glare Angel has directed at her she continues passing out the human weapons until every hand in the room is armed. Grace and Anxo refuse since they already have long-range weapons on them.

I would much rather rely on my fists than these machines I cannot seem to figure out, but alas, desperate times call for desperate measures.

The weapons keep coming, and it takes me a second to size them up before I realize the siren has an enchanted bag. "Hey, we don't work with witches' you traitor!"

With a guilty grimace, Hazel flashes me a tiny smile, "It was before you." My glare only intensifies, so she adds, "I blackmailed and threatened her if it makes you feel any better." *It does.*

Hazel goes rigid when Angel bends so they're at eye level. Pointing his finger at the window, he asks her in a tone that doesn't leave room for excuses or deflection, "When did you piss off Heaven?"

Hazel struggles to keep her composure, but I know from experience that the moment Angel loses his carefully structured patience, she'll be in a ton of trouble.

Hazel opens her mouth to snap back, no doubt, but the look on Angel's face stops her. "Recently."

"How?"

She mumbles the words so quietly I completely miss them but it's impossible to miss the steam coming out of Angel's ears. "You *stabbed* Hermes?!"

Hermes: The ancient Greek god of trade, wealth, luck, fertility, animal husbandry, sleep, language, thieves, travel and blah blah blah.

I've heard he's the sleaziest of the bunch.

"He wanted to fix my *'fertility issues'*. Fucking creep. He's lucky I didn't cut his dick off to save the world from another one of his offspring."

I don't need the whole story. I'm on the siren's side.

I can practically see the wheels in Grace's head turning as she thinks out loud. "If you think about it—"

"You *really* don't have to."

Grace ignores Hazel and continues piecing Hazel's mess. "We've earned quite a few enemies in recent years."

"And I've heard almost all of them blaming a certain mouthy siren for their passionate hatred for us," Seiji adds, which earns him a stink eye from Hazel. For the first time, he has the opportunity to get Hazel in trouble, and he's taking full advantage of it.

"Come out, you demented abomination! We have a debt to settle!"

Uh-oh. I take it back. I still have a hand in this mess.

So that's Victor. Another high-ranking warlock I have a teeny tiny issue with.

"I'm actually very busy right now, but my mate would be happy to take my place!" I shout back.

"Seriously, you sell me out that easy? I'm offended, sweetheart." Despite feigning offense, Angel pecks me before turning back to Hazel. "I want a list of everyone you've pissed off and why, when we get home."

Seeing Hazel's frown, Angel adds, "I won't make amends if you had a good reason like Hermes, but I can't have people scheming behind my back just because they asked about your heritage or looked at your daggers a certain way."

Hazel's face sours and she grumbles under her breath before agreeing.

Walking over to the window, Seiji cracks his neck, "Grace?

grab my inhaler. I'm about to fuck some shit up."

"But you don't have asthma. In fact, you can't—"

"You don't understand dramatic effect, do you?" On his sassy remark, Grace backs up with her hands raised.

When Angel comes to stand in front of me, effectively hiding me from view, I get this insane urge to kick his knee from behind. I swear on everything in this dumb realm, if he asks me to hide behind him like some damsel in distress, I'm going to punch his pretty face!

A hand nudges me, and I look down to find Angel holding his hand out for me. Gently pulling me beside him, he asks, "Ready to kick some ass, sweetheart?"

The mischievous smirk on my mate's face promises chaos, and I'm here for it.

He's definitely getting extra kisses tonight.

Unstrapping her crossbow, Grace jogs up the stairs to cover the large windows and take advantage of the better vantage point.

Angel pulls out a soft cloth from Hazel's bag to wipe the blood from my hands and kisses me deliciously thoroughly before following Grace's lead to set up camp upstairs.

I shake my head to clear the fog my mate's touch always leaves me in. Clearing my throat, I watch the soul twins take cover behind the windows on the left side of the house while Seiji follows me to the right side.

Stealing a glance outside, I'm confused if these soldiers are simply idiots or extremely confident that they don't even bother surrounding the cabin. I pity the fool who taught these warriors such weak-ass battle strategies. Papa would've laughed until he cried if he was here.

"I can't believe Heaven is conspiring with the coven. What the fuck did we ever do to them?" I mumble to myself, not exactly expecting an answer.

"What did we ever do to them, you ask Grim Reaper's *unnatural* child?" Seiji looks at me like I've grown two heads. "Are you forgetting the war your dear father and uncle caused by *breaking* into Heaven, *stealing* Divine to *make* a daughter, and then naming her backward Heaven just to get that *'fuck you guys'* across?"

"That's history."

"History in which they lost. I think we've given them plenty of reasons to make a deal with the witches." Seiji gulps nervously, counting their numbers.

Victor barks just as the first round of *poisonous arrows* comes flying in our direction. "I should've killed you when I had the chance!"

Without warning Hazel aims through the window, shooting with such precision that the bullet lands perfectly between Victor's eyes.

Damn girl.

The thud of Victor's body hitting the ground breaks the eerie silence. In a blink Heaven's soldiers are charging forward, shooting viciously as they try to get closer to the weakly built structure of this house.

The way Victor's death has deepened their resentment gives away just how close Heaven has gotten to these snakes. With a warrior cry, one runs straight at the door and crashes against it with enough force to shake the foundation.

I thought I knew how far someone would go when they didn't have anything to live for, but watching these warriors run at the house to break our defense without caring about bullets makes my blood run cold. This troop knows their defeat is imminent but they're not walking away without drawing our blood first.

Just like we trained, Angel and Grace stand guard from the second floor over the railing, raining arrows on anyone who crosses the trashed doorframe. Harvey and Seiji switch their empty guns with whips and swords, working as a team to cover the left part of the house.

Beside me, Hazel is slicing men open before tossing me two Wakizashi swords that I quickly tuck into my belt. I still have a few bullets remaining before I'll need to draw the two mini swords. Together, we start clearing up our side of the room as more and more warriors barge inside, making us struggle to keep our pace.

With our combined efforts, it's not long before no more than thirty warriors are left. The boys are doing a great job of tackling their side when I take a second look and find Grace now standing above Harvey on the dining table, her crossbow dripping with blood.

A sudden pain in my left arm alerts me back to my surroundings just in time to dodge another strike. Somehow, I end up getting cornered by half a dozen warriors choosing me as their sole target by forming a circle around me.

Bloody Heaven-bound assholes.

In the middle of diminishing my circle, I catch a glimpse of a warrior creeping on Seiji from behind. Without overthinking it, I use the tiny gap between the soldiers hovering over me and shoot the warlock.

My lack of attention gives my opponents the perfect opportunity to gang up on me. I barely dodged the first attack, a sword grazing my shoulder, but not the one aimed at my thigh. Swallowing the blinding pain of my flesh slicing, I whip out the sharp wakizashi swords to slice the hand that comes for me next.

I'm twisting limbs and breaking knees when I see Harvey lowering Grace from the table and carving a safe path to the main door. Grace is in good shape, with just a small scratch on her shoulder, but Harvey on the other hand, has a deep gash on his forehead that's bleeding, and a cut on his shoulder that's halfway cauterized.

My desperate need to make sure Harvey leaves unharmed gets the better of me, and I send one of my swords flying at the sneaky warrior closing in on him.

When they safely make it through the door, Seiji takes over keeping guard. His whips make it impossible for anyone to get closer without getting their flesh torn apart.

With Hazel and Grace now covering the only exit, Harvey

turns to help me. I shake my head and try to speak between my unsteady breaths. "Angel first."

From the corner of my eye, I can see them make a safe passage for Angel to cross the room. We are in different corners of the house and him being farther away means it's easier for him to get trapped.

The constant slicing and getting stabbed starts taking a toll on me and I'm barely managing to hold myself up with a non-functioning leg. I'm struggling to pull out my mini sword from a skull when suddenly Angel is breaking through the circle around me.

As much as I want to scream at him for not putting himself first and risking his safety for me, I'm too drained to protest. Limping behind him backward, I cover our backs. The moment Angel is with me, Harvey and Hazel start raining bullets.

A foot from the door, I relax thinking it's over when unexpectedly a warrior leaps up from the floor. I'm not quick enough to gauge the attack when he impales me just below my collarbone with a sharp dagger.

The screams of my friends gasping in horror get muffled by the warrior cackling like a maniac and all at once it hits me without my Divine, if I die here then that's it. *No saving me.*

Shoving the fleeting dark thought out of my head, I blink past the black spots and watch Angel stab the warrior's neck with his arrow, and the cackling finally stops.

Crossing the room, Angel drags a half-dead warrior to our feet and Harvey quickly steps in to hoist him over his shoulder. I don't ask what they want with the soldier and simply move out of the way to lean against the door frame—*or what's left of it.*

When I open my eyes next, Grace is running to me, saying something I don't quite hear. Without warning, she grabs the handle of the dagger still buried in my chest and pulls the blade out in one swift moment.

I yelp, "Fuck woman. Have you never heard of giving a warning before you do something like that?"

"I thought I did! I'm so sorry, but the blade is clearly poisoned so I had to act fast."

I take a deep breath, pushing through the pain and dizziness that I now realize is due to the poison. Through clenched teeth, I assure Grace I'm fine and she can stop hovering.

Standing at the entrance of a house splattered with blood and filled with dead bodies, I remember promising Micah a blood ceremony for his death.

This is so much better.

Without wasting another breath, Angel strides to me, covered in blood from head to toe, and swipes me off my feet. I hiss when the cut on my thigh stings and gasp, "I can walk."

I don't miss the pain on Angel's face when he rests his cheek on my head, not caring that it's damp with blood. "Let me. *Please.*"

I scan everyone else and whine in my head about the differences between us.

Seiji is nearly unscathed, not a single scratch on him. I'm seriously jealous of his whips. They create the perfect barrier around him, and the few minor cuts he did have are already healing.

Hazel is scratchless. *No surprises there.*

Angel, on the other hand, has a gash on his head similar to Harvey, but not as bad. Other than that, he's in perfect shape, too.

Why do I always have to look like I just crawled out of a bloody ditch?

A wave of dizziness hits me again and I rest my head on Angel's shoulder and wait for it to pass. When the heartbeat beneath my cheek picks up dangerously, I open my tired eyes to find my mate's gaze fixed on my injuries.

"I'm okay, Angel. Just a little dizzy. I would tell you if I wasn't." I try to assure him, but I know he won't believe me until he checks every inch of my body with his eyes and hands. For someone whose mate is covered in decade-old scars, Angel hates seeing something as small as a mosquito bite on me.

The walk to our exit out of this realm doesn't take long, and once again, we are standing before a similar cliff.

Seiji is the first to dive into our experimental exit route, and *of course*, he complains about none of us having any regard for his precious young life. Harvey ushers Grace next and follows not even two seconds behind her with the unconscious soldier on his shoulder. Hazel jumps next, after making sure we weren't followed.

I can't stop a whimper from escaping when Angel adjusts me in his arms to wrap my thighs around his waist. Holding my face in his hands he asks, "Trust me, sweetheart?"

"With everything in me."

There's no hesitation this time. In the last five months, Angel has proved he's the only one for me. There wasn't a single day he didn't make me feel protected and loved by him.

"Thank Fates. I was going to ask you to jump with me, and it would've been really awkward if you said no." Angel grins like a Cheshire cat before his lips brush against mine. Taking my bottom lip into his mouth, Angel sucks lightly. He kisses me with a softness that weakens my knees more than they already are.

Walking over to the edge, he whispers, "Close your eyes, baby."

Hiding my face in his neck, I squeeze my eyes shut and try not to pay attention to the sudden whoosh of wind or the feeling of not being on the ground anymore. Wrapping myself in his warmth, I trust him not to let go.

I jolt when Angel bumps his forehead with mine, and I look around to see we are back on solid ground and out of that bland realm.

Angel carefully lowers me next to my horse so I can lean on Diamond before marching to the battered soldier with calculated steps.

When he bends to hold both sides of the warrior's head, I noticed the change in Angel's body language immediately.

The muscles in his back tense and the veins in his forehead protrude as he forcefully invades the warrior's mind.

"*Archangel Michael.* You're well aware we don't appreciate obedient dogs sniffing around our business, yet you don't seem to heed warnings, do you? This is my first and last warning to Heaven. Do. Not. Interfere. Unless you're prepared for a war we both know you won't win."

Once Heaven receives the message loud and clear, Angel tosses the warriors down the cliff.

Returning to me, Angel carefully helps me on his horse, before climbing behind me.

I'm surprised when Diamond obediently follows Angel's direction to follow behind him. Even when I'm not his official rider, it's good to know Diamond recognizes Angel as my mate and respects him as a Horseman.

"Rest sweetheart. I'll be here when you wake up." Angel kisses my forehead softly, and my eyes flutter shut, refusing to open again.

33. Tongues unleashed

Nevaeh

I'm two steps away from the staircase that leads to our warm bed and the shower calling my name when in usual fashion, something goes wrong.

The wrong thing, aka Angel's womb provider, comes barreling inside the castle with a scowl that does nothing to hide her wrinkles. With her claws out, she *demands* to speak with Angel privately, but to her utter displeasure, I don't move an inch.

As Kiara aggressively paces our living room, I watch Anxo act like her unhinged ramblings are just another Tuesday for him. Thinking ahead, he quickly asks the group to scramble and has the audacity to use my favorite set of emerald eyes to convince me to leave and rest. I compromise by sitting on the staircase while he deals with his crazy mother.

The hatred swimming in Kiara's eyes is unmistakable as she shakes with rage. Gesturing to the blood covering my mate, she spits out, "I knew you were aggressive and impatient, but I didn't think you'd turn into a *monster* for her!"

Angel's face falls, but he doesn't look half as surprised as I feel. Clenching his jaw, he turns his back to me so I can't see how much that comment hurt him.

How can a mother be this cruel to her own son? Kiara's brain is rotten if this is how she treats her family. I can't even imagine Papa raising his voice at me, much less intentionally saying hurtful things to hurt me.

"Look at you! Is this how you want to rule *my* kingdom? You will ruin everything with your recklessness. And don't even get me started on that lowly *werewolf* boy you've taken in. You can't just announce an heir like that Anxo! Who knows what his lineage is or who—"

"One more word about my son, and I'll bury you right here." Kiara stops to glare at me for interrupting her. "August is our *son*, so don't you dare insult him or my mate."

I've had enough of this. If she won't close her trap, I will gladly do it for her.

"How dare you talk to me in that manner. Don't you forget, I'm your mate's *mother*." She hisses and threateningly steps closer as if that will intimidate me.

"And?" Angel finally faces his mother head-on. "You don't even know the meaning of the word."

Kiara is stunned. It doesn't take a genius to figure this is probably the first time Angel has talked back. As much as I love this man for his patience and understanding, I hate when people like Kiara take advantage of it.

"Don't you dare talk to me that way boy," she seethes. Kiara braves a step towards my mate but takes that same step back when I stretch like I'm about to get up.

Coward.

"I apologize, Mother, but tell me—how else am I supposed to word my frustrations about your disgustingly unfair parenting? Or the way you constantly put me down and refuse to accept August as your grandson just because he doesn't carry my blood."

Her face doesn't hide her surprise anymore as she stands with her mouth agape, trying to form a response.

"I have excused your behavior time and time again, but I won't stand idly as you berate *my son*. Either you respect me and my choices, or I'll cut you off for the sake of my family's happiness."

Swoon.

I'm so proud of Angel for finally calling out his mother for her filthy actions and taking a stand… even if it means losing her altogether. I can only imagine how hard this must be for Angel, but his parents have left no other choice for him. What else is he supposed to do when all they do is crap over his life and berate him with every word they speak.

Looking back at the woman glaring at my mate, it's hard not to punch her. It shocks me when I don't see an ounce of guilt or sadness on her face even after Angel makes it clear that he will break all connection if she doesn't stop.

The only thing she's fixated on is how dare he speak to her in that manner. Why do people like her decide to become parents when all they have to offer is hurt and lifelong trauma?

Angel looks down to hide the hurt in his eyes at her reaction. Her desperate need for authority and power over her son is ruining what's left of their relationship and she still can't seem to care. It's exhausting to love someone who is determined to hate you.

Taking over the useless conversation, I decide it's time to end this so I can tend to my mate. We deserve to curl up in our bed and forget about the world for a few hours after the day we've both had.

Standing up, I dust myself off, "Alright, it's my turn now. Since you don't care about watching your mouth, it's better you talk to me anyway. First things first. Help me understand why you're still living in *our* castle with your good-for-nothing mate?"

Cue the dramatic gasp.

I scoff at her pathetic acting skills and get to the point. "I've been considerate enough not to force your hand, but since you like badmouthing my mate so much—*in front of me no less*—I want you to make yourself scarce. Meaning don't be in my line of sight if you want to live."

Immediately losing the attitude, Kiara pales. Balling her fists by her things she grits out, "You can't kick me out, I'm his mother! I'm the Queen of Conquer!"

"Tsk-tsk, what happened to that posh accent and the 70's dialogue delivery, Kiara?"

"Anxo, son—"

"Don't you dare address my mate directly." My Divine peeks

out after being repressed all day as my eyes flash gold, making her stumble back.

Turning to my mate, I kiss his jaw and ask him to wait for me in our room. I desperately want to follow him upstairs but I need to handle my monster-in-law for good.

Angel pulls me back by my arm before I can leave and the request is evident in his eyes.

Why does everyone think murder is my go-to solution?

Standing on my toes, I kiss him tenderly and promise I won't kill Kiara before nudging him to keep walking.

Standing before the woman breathing fire, I purse my lips to stop myself from laughing out loud. It's as if she is trying to burn me with her glare when I bend to match her height and smirk tauntingly.

"You're lucky Anxo still respects you enough not to let me claw your eyes out and feed them to you until you're shitting eyeballs for a week."

Kiara gasps and raises her hand to slap me. She has me confused with a different woman if she thinks I wouldn't stomp on her skull until she is a pile of bloody curry if she touches me. Grabbing her wrist before it can touch my face, I squeeze until her knees buckle and Kiara picks up on how easily I can crush her wrist.

Laughing humorlessly when I let go, I watch the pathetic woman scramble back in fear just before Khatri appears out of nowhere like he could sense I needed his assistance.

"Make sure she's out of the kingdom by morning and do it quietly. I don't want Anxo waking up to unresolved drama."

"It'll be my pleasure, Princess."

"It's *Nevaeh*."

For that, I leave the stubborn Warriorhead alone to deal with the hysterical former Queen.

Finally stepping into our room, I find Angel sitting with his head in his hands, mumbling to himself. I can practically see the dark cloud of despair hovering over his head. Angel looks up when the door clicks shut behind me and gives me the weakest smile I've ever seen, before nodding towards the bathroom.

After cleaning up, I put on a silk robe and a fresh pair of underwear before going to my mate.

Only clad in black sweats with his bare chest on display, I have to force myself to focus on Angel's mental well-being instead of drooling over the sight of his muscles and ridges on his stomach.

With his back resting against the headboard, Angel is staring off into space, and I can't take the looming sadness anymore.

Walking to him, I climb on the bed to straddle his lap. The sudden action surprises him enough to snap him out of his daze. Holding me close, Angel leans forward to rest his cheek on my chest. Some of his tension eases when I start running my fingers through his soft curls and kiss the top of his head repeatedly.

"I hate feeling like this," He whispers so softly I could've missed it if I wasn't holding my breath, waiting for him to say something.

"Like what?"

"Like a *monster*. Like a worthless man who ruins everything he touches."

The hatred in his voice for himself is something I never want to hear again. My heart squeezes painfully when he looks at me with solemn eyes, waiting for me to agree, for me to nurture his delusions. The expectant way Angel is looking at me is tearing my heart.

How can I ever think of him as a monster when all I see is a man worthy of so much love but too afraid to grasp it?

The anguish on his face slices at my heart. He needs to know nothing about what he just said is true. Lifting his chin with my thumb and forefinger, I stare into those beautiful eyes when I tell him the *truth*—not the bullshit his parents have fed him for years.

"You're not a monster, Angel. Not even close. Everything

you do is to protect your family and a kingdom that depends on you to do right by them. And sometimes... sometimes that means you have to spill blood, but that doesn't make you a monster."

"I'm not a good person. She knows the things I've done. She's right. I don't deserve any of this, all the good things. *You.*" Shaking his head, Angel buries his face in my neck to hide from the world.

Is that what Angel is worried about? The blood on his hands? Blood that came from protecting his people?

"Go on then. Spill every terrible thing you've ever done and watch how I will continue to stand by you," I urge him by gently kissing his head.

My sweet Angel lifts his head from my neck, his sorrowful red eyes barely holding back tears of frustration because I'm refusing to see his *so-called sins.*

He is trying to convince me—*Nevaeh*—known for the trail of bodies I leave behind, that *he* is the monster.

Somebody needs to remind this guy who his mate is.

Gently stroking his cheek, I urge him once again.

"Go ahead, Angel. Try to sabotage yourself, tell me what they made you believe was a monster's doing. Lay it all out in the open, but I'll tell you this now... I've been in love with you long before I knew you, and I won't stop after you tell me everything. I don't give a shit about what you did to ensure the safety of your people because *I know your soul.*"

Holding his face, I wipe the tears from the corner of his eyes. "After all the pain you've seen, you still find a way to remain compassionate, understanding and so kind that it takes my breath away. You can never be a monster, Anxo. You are my *Angel.* A little battered and bruised, but still my Angel. Even the real ones above aren't as perfect as you are."

With a tender kiss on his lips, I lean back, and my heart soars to see a hint of his precious smile peeking through.

"Just when I think I couldn't be more obsessed with you, you prove me wrong." He chuckles, his voice hoarse from holding back tears.

"Good. Let's keep it that way forever."

Smashing our lips together, I give into the desperate need to feel him closer. I've never taken initiation in the bedroom before, but Angel deserves some extra loving tonight. Our lips move together in perfect sync, tasting each other and touching every part of naked skin we can reach.

Spreading my fingers on his chest, I feel his heart pick up at my touch, and slowly lower them to his abs, tracing every curve and dip on his stomach.

When I pull away from our heated kiss, Angel groans. He tries to pull me back, but I move away to lick his jaw, slowly peppering kisses down his neck. I start with slow, wet kisses and grow more confident with every touch. Angel grunts when I bite his neck and tug his curls at the same time.

Starting my journey lower, I leave pink marks all over his chest and those beautifully carved abs, shuffling further down as I go. When I palm his bulge over the sweats, Angel hisses at the sudden contact, and his hips involuntarily buck up, pressing him harder against my hand.

Tugging at his sweats, I wait for him to give me enough space to slide them off before my hand finds his massive length over his boxers. Angel moans when he feels my hand on him, with only a thin layer separating us. I move to get rid of the buffer when he stops me.

Looking up, I see desire burning in his eyes, but he's still holding my hand in place.

"Did I do something wrong?" I ask timidly.

Don't tell me I messed up already.

"No! Not at all. But I uh... are you sure, sweetheart? You don't have to do anything you don't want." Angel grits out through clenched teeth and a tight smile, clearly holding himself back.

I move up to kiss him and let my need shine through my fervor so he can see how eager I am to please him. I want him to know I'm enjoying every little change in his breathing and the sounds of pleasure.

"I want to. I really, *really* want to. Let me make you feel good, Angel," I murmur against his lips and smile when he finally frees my hand.

Kissing him one more time because how can I resist, I settle between his legs so I'm face-to-face with his desire—a desire that is ready to rip the material off his boxers if I don't do something about it. I look at him, waiting for a nod before removing the final barrier, and his rock-hard length slaps against his stomach.

I'd be a liar if I said I'm not intimidated by the sheer size of this thing. It's enormous, covered in thick angry veins and a dark pink tip dripping clear fluid.

Out of instinct, I swipe my tongue on his tip to suck it clean, but the feral sound that follows is enough to encourage me to repeat it. Lightly sucking on his tip, I grip him softly, moving my palm up and down.

Angel groans at the movement. "Tighter, sweetheart."

My palm tightens around his length, falling into a rhythm he responds to. I change my speed and grip and listen intently to what he likes best.

When I fasten my pace with a tight clasp around him, the loudest groan yet signals I've found the best pace.

Moving my other hand lower, I palm his balls, playing with them until he is bucking and pushing himself up to feel more.

Time for some revenge.

Slowing down, I swipe my tongue over his tip, making him grunt. "You like that, Angel? Do you want my mouth?" I suck on his tip aggressively before suddenly stopping, making him growl throatily.

When I keep changing my grip with every stroke Angel finally catches onto my teasing.

"Sweetheart, if you don't put my cock in your mouth before I count to three, I'll take it away." He breathes out, doling out my punishment.

I want to win, but I don't want to stop pleasuring him. His

moans are addictive... just like his taste.

"You're cruel." I pout, continuing my slow strokes.

"You want to know how much I want this, my sweet girl? Is that it?" Angel grabs the back of my head to bring me to my knees for a hard kiss and I'm melting when he lets me go.

I immediately take his length into my mouth. He is too big to take all of it at once, but I manage a good portion before I start moving up and down, sucking as I go.

"So good, baby... so warm and pretty. Your mouth takes me so well," Angel whispers.

I'm sure Angel loves watching me ease him in my mouth. He hasn't once taken his eyes off me. I hum when his tip suddenly touches the back of my throat. It feels rough and a little uncomfortable, but the way his breath hitches, I don't dare complain.

His moans get louder, but I can still feel Angel holding back from accidentally thrusting into my mouth.

I want him to lose control and give himself to me completely. Letting go of my grip on his thighs, I lower them until I'm gripping his firm ass and urge him to push up.

Angel growls deep in his throat, holding my face in his hands, he starts to move me the way he needs.

"So perfect. My sweet girl is perfect for me, pleasing me so good." Angel chokes out before thrusting up, hitting the back of my throat every single time.

I focus on breathing through my nose when I start feeling so full with him stuffing my mouth like this.

"I-I'm going to come, sweetheart. Want me to pull out?" He asks, making me shake my head as much as I can and hum in denial.

The vibration from my mouth makes his rhythm falter, so I take over. Angel gets lost in his pleasure as I lead him to his release. It takes me three deep sucks before he is falling apart with a loud groan.

Thick, warm fluid clogs up my throat in spasms until I swallow. After lapping my tongue around him to clean him up properly, I help him pull up his boxers, seeing as he's lying motionless, trying to catch his breath.

Climbing up, I curl into his side, and he tucks me in closer. Turning to me with a dopey smile, Angel chuckles in a daze. "If your plan was to melt my brain, congratulations sweetheart, you did a great job."

Rolling on top of him, I trace his jaw and the red marks now littering his skin. "I did good?"

"You were perfect. I think I died and came back to life."

"I liked it too. I'm going to love you like that all the time now." Wrapping my arms around him, I rest my chin on his chest.

Angel stares at me with a grave look, "I don't think I'll live long if you do that all the time." He pulls me closer and kisses me like we haven't seen each other in hours. "I love you, sweetheart."

"Even when I melt your brain?"

"Especially then."

I pull back when I feel him rubbing my hips and his hand slip under my silk robe. "I wanted to make you feel good, Angel. I don't want anything in return," I breathe against his lips.

"But I want to taste you," He whines like a child being denied his favorite candy.

"And you can whenever you want, but you should rest now." I move to slip out of his hold, but he stops me.

"There's no way my girl is falling asleep without me tiring you to the point you can't keep your eyes open."

Leaving kisses on my neck, he bites down gently and flips us so he's hovering over me. My robe is on the floor in a swift motion, and Angel sucks a harsh breath through his teeth when his eyes fall on my naked body.

Without a warning, his teeth latch onto my nipple as he leaves his marks all over my chest. I'm a mess in seconds. His touch is always too much and too little at the same time. My own hands roam his back before drifting to his bulge, which is painfully hard once again.

"How?" I whisper to myself in shock when I palm him through his boxers.

"Have you met yourself?" Angel chuckles sliding off his boxers and lying on his back. Motioning for me to come closer, he orders, "Come sit on my face beautiful... and face my cock."

When I take too long because I'm not sure if I heard him right, Angel loses his ever-there patience and pulls me over his face by my waist. With his hand on my back, he bends me over until I'm facing his rock-hard again.

I go to ask him if he's sure about this, but when his mouth finds my clit, giving it a hard suck, I gasp and buck away from him.

"You're dripping sweetheart. Stay in place or the next time you move, I'll have to punish you." That's all he says before diving in without warning, and I jolt again, which results in a hard smack on my ass.

I moan breathily, which catches his attention, and he repeats his so-called punishment on my other cheek while devouring me. Once I'm able to see through the stars of his sweet torture, I focus on the beautiful, needy dick in front of me and take it in my mouth.

His appreciative moan sends vibrations through my spine, and the cycle of delicious torture continues. Every thrust of his tongue travels to my brain until I'm barely hanging on to my sanity.

That's what we do all night until both of us are too tired to lift a finger and fall asleep in each other's arms.

34. Fact: Cake has magical powers

Nevaeh

Hiding behind a fallen tree trunk covered with a patterned camouflage blanket, I carefully move forward to get in range to shoot Harvey.

When Seiji suggested celebrating August's birthday in a paintball arena, I never imagined it would be this fun.

A week back, as August and I were watching a movie together, there was a scene with a little girl celebrating her birthday surrounded by friends, balloons, and cake. When I peeked over at monkey, his eyes held such longing I just had to make it happen.

After a long day of ruffling through the paperwork we found on his pack, Angel found his date of birth, which coincidentally was coming up sooner than we thought.

We planned to have each of us present one idea so we'd have a variety to choose from, but let's be honest: no one stood a chance against Seiji.

The man stormed in with a PowerPoint presentation with background music and theme pictures. In his presentation, he showed the Griari Empire of ancient dragons.

The dragon realm recently built a public gaming arena to boost inter-species relations and apparently, it's the best in all realms.

Since Horsemen had a good relationship with the empire, Anxo was able to secure a private arena for us.

Hazel is fuming, stomping everywhere because she has been shot *seven* times by yours truly.

We have been battling for the top spot the entire game and I bet she regrets teaching me how to shoot after the second time

I shot her.

By now, I've shot Seiji four times, and Harvey five. The lovesick fool was so busy admiring Grace that he forgot the basic rule—never turn your back on your enemy.

How many times have I shot Angel? *None.*

Because I love him, and we don't shoot people we love.

I'm about to scare the living crap out of Seiji, who is hiding behind an ugly green drum when my little monkey appears out of thin air and blocks my path.

We talked about not shooting August at first thinking he might feel bad. But when he burst out laughing on his first colorful splash, it was clear he didn't mind being covered in rainbow goo.

Glancing at the *guns* in my hand, he shakes his head in exaggerated disappointment.

The little man stares me down accusingly like I've stolen his last slice of pizza. Doing his best to act stern, August places his hands on his hips with a miniature gun hanging off his back.

"What's with the look, kiddo? This isn't cheating; it's called strategy. No one said I couldn't take an extra gun." I try to convince him in a hushed whisper.

When we first got here and observed the setup in the middle of the woods, for a moment there, I worried it would trigger August about the night we escaped, but so far, I haven't seen any signs of panic or stress.

August's eyes narrow, picking apart my lie.

"Okay, fine! Maybe they said no extra guns... but... but I'm doing this for our team!"

August sighs and pinches the skin between his eyes. Outstretching his hand, August silently asks me to hand over my extra gun. I'm stunned by how eerily similar he looks to Angel when my mate is also tired of my shit.

"Are you sure you want to be an honest player, kiddo? We can beat Angel. And think how much fun it will be to watch Hazel sulk."

I try to win him over to the dark side because it's more

fun here but he keeps blinking at me as if I'm the one acting ridiculous.

"Ugh, fine! You're turning into a mini-Angel with all those morals. Here, take away my chance to crush these truckers and make them wish they never challenged me." I give up my extra gun, but not before I make sure he knows how much I hate it.

As if trying to remind me of our surroundings August throws his tiny hands in the air.

"Oh, I know it's just a game wisebutt!" I whisper yell, crossing my arms and abandoning both my guns to sit cross-legged on the ground.

August pads over to me to kiss my forehead, cupping my cheeks in his little hands before grabbing up my extra gun and skipping away. Shit, now he will reveal my stunt to the dragons keeping score.

I'm watching him hop away, getting shot by colorful paintballs and giggling with every blast when a gun on my back makes me stiffen. I slowly turn to look over my shoulder, and my heart leaps to find Angel behind me, pointing his gun at me.

"You're going to shoot me?" I gasp melodramatically, placing a hand on my heart and another on my forehead, fake crying a little to make it all the more heartbreaking.

A faithful lover turned enemy over a game of paintball.

How. Very. Tragic.

"Shut up, idiot. I came to kiss you before the game ended, but now I'm rethinking it." Angel laughs and quickly kisses me when a loud alarm goes off.

The team behind the game walks in, and I want to be clear that I don't have a problem with them. I mean, I didn't until this particular woman walked right into Angel's personal space like they were old friends.

"Hello again, handsome! We have the scores ready. You sure you don't want me to bump you up." She laughs in a high-pitched nasally voice. Her focus fixed entirely on my mate as if I'm invisible in her eyes.

Grabbing my hand, Angel brings it to his lips to kiss my knuckles. "Thanks, Lacy—"

"*Tracy*," She corrects Angel, her eyes stuck on my hand that he is now holding to his heart.

"Sorry about that. My husband has trouble remembering names that are not important."

Next to me, Angel fakes a cough to hide his laugh. Tracy's whole face turns red, but this is on her. Hitting on a man who is clearly with someone, especially in a realm where mates are considered sacred, is appalling.

Don't like the embarrassment? Check if the guy actually wants you before pulling out the flirting tricks.

She must've seen us kiss earlier or heard him introduce me as his mate when we came in, but the woman was too busy drooling over Angel and making jokes about how he was strong enough to lift her.

I can lift her, too. I'll even throw her. *Far-far away*.

When the dragon lady quickly scurries off without a goodbye, Angel turns to me with a smile so large I wonder if his cheeks hurt. This man loves it when I act like a crazy jealous girlfriend.

"Husband, huh? You know, now that you wholeheartedly accept the idea I'm going to wife you up real soon, sweetheart."

Not like I'm objecting.

Judging by the giddy smile as Angel leads us back to the group, I know he is planning the details of our wedding in his head. *Silly Angel.*

I burst out laughing when I saw everyone covered in bright pink—the color I was assigned.

Before the game, the guys were stupid enough to propose a girls vs. boys match. Of course, we won. As Seiji and Harvey grumble about their loss, Angel won't stop whispering how proud he is of me.

Fates, I love my man.

Yes, I shot my own team member too.

Why? Because it was fun and it made Hazel furious—a

bonus in my eyes.

The flirty blind woman returns to ask if we'd like a picture to remember the day by and of course we agree.

In usual fashion, Seiji rants about how neon pink is not his color but agrees to bear the shame of this picture for generations to come because he loves us.

Angel wraps his arm around my shoulders, pulling me close to his chest. August runs up to stand between us, grinning widely with his gun aimed at the camera. Harvey steps to my right, pulling Grace in front of him by wrapping his arms around her waist, while Seiji and Hazel stand to my left.

Just before the camera shutter clicks, Seiji cracks a joke that has us all laughing. I'm in awe of the result— the photo perfectly captures our joyful, carefree expressions, our eyes sparkling with happiness.

The woman leaves to make four copies of the photo, and we disperse to change out of the jumpsuits given to us.

Ten minutes later we find each other again and wait for Angel to finish his last-minute meeting with the king. He wanted to personally thank him for providing extra protection and being mindful of our predicament with Visha.

Hazel mumbles something that makes Harvey snicker and shake his head at her. She looks more relaxed than I've ever seen in a loose-fitted black denim jacket over a short white jumpsuit. Harvey stands tall wearing his trusty leather jacket as he pretends not to notice Grace giving him *sex eyes*.

Grace decided on a summer dress with sneakers. Earlier she asked Hazel to twin with her, and the siren snorted so loud I bet Uncle Lucifer heard it all the way down in Hell.

Just like he always does, Angel barged into the bathroom this morning while I was showering and left a short sky-blue summer dress that matched his shirt. He didn't leave without a few kisses too but who's complaining.

I came out of the bathroom to find him with his sleeves folded to the elbows and the shirt neatly tucked into his dark pants. I traced over his markings, all but drooling over him until Seiji ran into our room and pestered me to help him pick one of the four outfits he wanted to wear.

The fashion expert—*Seiji made me say it*—is sporting a light blue denim jacket decorated with symmetrical mirrors embroidered in colorful threads.

Looks like my positive feedback went straight to his head because Seiji is parading around like a celebrity waiting for the paparazzi to pop out.

For his birthday monkey insisted on wearing his favorite Disney sweatshirt with a dashing lion printed on the front. My little monkey is beaming with happiness, his dino clutched to his chest and I have to pinch myself to check if this is all a dream.

Seiji follows my gaze to where I'm admiring Angel's muscular back and huffs. "So, you're letting it go? That woman flirted with your man, and you won't do anything about it?"

Why do I feel he is trying to get a reaction out of me?

"Angel didn't pay her any attention, and she ran off when I introduced myself as his wife. There is no need to do anything." I purposely don't tell him how I was close to breaking her nose earlier.

Hazel pipes in, "Couldn't be me. If I had a man, and some bitch was trying to get all cozy with him, she would have three less fingers and way fewer teeth in her mouth after I was done with her."

I can't help but slightly agree, but I'm trying to be civil for Angel's sake. He is already stressed about mending fences with all the people Hazel has pissed off on our behalf. Causing a scene will only add to his stress.

The list Hazel handed over was four pages long.

Back and front.

I didn't even bother checking the number of people on it, but I did scan some of the reasons.

While some were genuinely creepy and were practically asking to be stabbed, the majority were Hazel offending *them* and then taking offense from their retaliation.

For example, when a centaur joked about how she was similar to his pet fish (the rare kind), she shot the tank to prove him wrong.

"Stop trying to instigate her, you troublemakers," Grace chastises Hazel and Seiji.

Grace is like the good tiny angel on your shoulder, and these two idiots are the devils with red horns and a pitchfork. In the movies, I love it when the little devil wins, but in reality, it's better to listen to the angel in white.

We spend our evening walking around the Griari empire and touring the nearby shops before picking a quiet restaurant to cut the cake and have dinner.

Huddled before the restaurant, everyone is bouncing with excitement, and Angel and I can barely suppress our emotions over August's first milestone with us.

I go to follow everyone inside when the familiar feeling of being watched stops me. To confirm it's nothing other than my paranoia, I scan every face in the crowd that turns in our direction but find nothing suspicious.

I begin to walk back to the restaurant again, but something in the air is making my skin crawl, even my Divine is starting to stir sensing the possible danger. Turning my head in every direction, I look for the source of the goosebumps on my arms when a silhouette running past the thick trees surrounding us makes me freeze.

I try to make sense of who or what I'm seeing but the shadow is camouflaging itself with the darkness around it, making a chill run down my spine.

"Hey, what are you still doing out here? The little guy is about to take a fist out of that cake." Hazel startles me, and the silhouette disappears faster than I can blink.

It could just be the shadows from the trees playing tricks on your eyes, Nevaeh.

"I thought I saw something."

She sighs, "Trust me, I get it. I don't like being surrounded by a crowd any more than you do, but I've checked everything inside, so stop worrying and enjoy your son's day."

Going inside, I see August buzzing like a monkey high on sugar. Grace asks him to make a wish before blowing out the candles. I bite my tongue at how ridiculous and creepy the human birthday ritual is but continue to sing the stupid song at the top of my lungs.

After handing Seiji a plate loaded with the biggest piece of cake, Angel gives me the last of it. Taking the plate to share with August, I'm halfway into my seat when a shaky whisper turns my body to ice.

"*Vove you, mama.*"

It takes me a second to understand and more to beg every person in the room with my eyes to tell me I'm not dreaming— that the little boy beside me didn't just say those words.

Right when the first tear rolls down Grace's cheek, reality sets in. Seiji's spoon slips past his fingers as he gapes at monkey to make sure he heard it right.

Clutching the back of my chair until my knuckles turn white, I search for Angel to confirm my mind isn't playing tricks on me again. With a slow, stunned nod, his glassy eyes take in the boy sitting with his head bowed.

August just spoke his first words out loud. To me. And he called me mama. *Mama.*

A small sniffle echoes in the silent room, breaking me out of my shock. When monkey wipes his nose with the back of his hand, my heart nearly stops beating from the hurt on his face... from my lack of reaction.

Carefully spinning August's chair, I crouch before him and hold his hands between mine.

"I'm so sorry baby, I didn't mean to make you cry. You just surprised me, and I just..." The crack in my voice betrays how hard I'm trying to keep the tears at bay. "Of course, I love you, kiddo."

Wiping the tears off his chubby red cheeks, I kiss the hands engulfed in mine. When he still refuses to look at me and continues sniffing, I hate myself for freezing.

The thought of him finally talking to me makes my vision blur, but I need to keep it together until I fix this. I don't want him to think I'm sad because of what he said.

"Remember our rule? If you're happy, I'm happy but if you start crying, I'm going to cry too. And you know I can't cry in public, I have a reputation to uphold." At least that gets me a tiny smile.

August finally looks up with those bright blue eyes that pierce through your soul and asks, "Vo-love me?"

Cupping his tear-streaked face, I kiss his nose, which makes him giggle as he tries to break free.

"I do. I love you monkey."

My reassurance calms whatever storm is brewing inside his head, and August leaps out of his chair and into my arms. I stumble back in surprise, but thanks to Angel and his preparation for literally everything, he is already standing behind me before I can fall back.

Grabbing my shoulders, Angel helps me up with the brightest smile on his face.

Glancing around the room filled with adoration and unshed tears, I take in my family as they shower August with love and kisses.

"I knew cake had magical powers!" Seiji cheers, making all of us burst into laughter, eyes shredding the tears we were holding back.

Angel engulfs me in a warm hug, peppering kisses on August's face, who giggles so hard Angel has to support my grip on the little guy before we all fall back.

"Papa, I talk now!" August squeals and I frame this moment in my memory forever.

After kissing his nose, which August tries to hide under his hand, Angel swiftly takes my lips for a heart-stopping kiss, which doesn't work well, seeing how we both can't stop smiling.

Lost in my Angel's eyes, it takes me a second to register the movement from the corner of my eye.

Seiji is about to stick his fork into my cake when my head snaps to him. Caught red-handed, I expect him to back off, but to my surprise, my famous murderous glare doesn't work. He is about to take a huge bite when I use my most powerful weapon.

Pleading with my eyes, I beg Angel to save my cake before the bratty princess can clean my plate.

One look from Angel and Seiji is running to hide behind Grace who generously offers him her share, much to her mate's annoyance.

"You know he is more terrified of you than me, right?" Angel doesn't even try to hide his amusement, softly caressing the back of August's head on my shoulder.

"Not anymore. That leech has crawled his way into my heart and isn't scared of my threats anymore," I mutter grumpily. *I'm losing my touch.*

"You love him." It's not a question. I don't have to spell it out for Angel to know how much these people mean to me.

"I do. It's so not good for my health or my reputation."

35. A living nightmare

Nevaeh

My steps feel light as a feather as we take the quiet route back home. This portal was hidden deep in the forest for privacy reasons. The serene ambiance is a good change after surviving the busy market where we celebrated August's birthday.

A whole day surrounded by the people I love did wonders to cement my new reality. I finally have it all. A home. A wonderful family.

But like every good thing, the warmth in my stomach doesn't last long when out of nowhere a heavy cloud of fear smashes into my chest.

I don't realize I've stopped walking until Angel calls my name over his shoulder, but I'm frozen in place. Adrenaline rushes through my nerves, preparing me for a danger I can't see.

Something feels wrong.

The dreadful instinct of evil approaching makes my stomach sink. When Harvey's eyes find me, his alarmed expression only confirms my gut feeling. Years of torment and constant fear have trained us to catch a threat before we can even see it.

"Hazel, put August to sleep. Now."

For once she doesn't make a sarcastic remark and sings a soft tune to spell August to sleep.

A faint cry from far away makes my blood freeze. Frantically moving my head in every direction, I try to pinpoint the sound but it comes to a still-stand, as if I spooked it.

Angel quickly starts huddling everyone towards the portal, sensing the same dread and discomfort lingering among the trees. Whatever it is, it's killing these woods with every breath it takes. This kind of destruction is unlike anything I've seen before.

The longer it takes to reach the portal, the more we feel a presence fast approaching with death and pain on its tail. Suddenly wild rustling and scratching resounds from every direction, making it impossible to judge its source.

Each picking a corner, we form a circle moving forward, but I can feel it in my bones that it won't be enough. It quickly becomes clear that there's no chance of getting to the portal without making ourselves an open target.

Conjuring his bow, Angel encircles us inside a clear shield charged with his Divine. Sensing my mate's worry, my Divine pushes me to free my restraint over it, and without overthinking, I let my Divine latch onto Angel's barrier to strengthen it.

Out of nowhere, a disheveled figure jumps out from behind a tree and charges straight at me. My heart jumps to my throat and I step back just before it collides against the barrier and bounces off it, landing on the ground.

I look up just in time to see two more figures crashing into the barrier. One after the other, dark shadows come barreling into the shield with such force that it cracks in some places. Angel quickly repairs the barrier with my Divine's assistance.

The first shadow is heaving and coughing up a lung as it pushes itself off the ground, and all air leaves my lungs.

"Is t-that?"

All I can do is nod at Harvey's stumped expression. Standing in front of me is a reminder of our past. Her clothes are ripped in places, and her hollow eyes stare at me with such hatred that it takes me back.

When my eyes fall on her shoulders I have to bite the inside of my cheek to stop myself from gasping. Arms carelessly stitched together like they were ripped apart more than once before someone pieced them back.

Twelve replicas of the girl I once knew.

I don't know what made me count, but the message becomes clear when I do. Visha ripped twelve souls from this world to get her own version of the future. This is her reminding me that she's always watching, lingering in the shadows, waiting for the perfect moment to finish what she started a decade ago. *To paint my world red.*

Whatever Angel sees on my face makes him intertwine our fingers and pull me closer. I lean on him and try to breathe, but my heart stops altogether when the limping figure opens her mouth—wider than normal—and lets out a loud wail that echoes in the silence.

I can hear her cries, but there are no tears or expressions on her face. The sound coming out of her mouth is as fake as the girl before me because I know she is dead.

Anisha is dead.

A strong rush of wind ripples the fake reflections until only one remains. Her wails of pain are muffled now but not entirely gone. I'm too stunned by what I'm seeing to try to make sense of how Visha did this.

I thought one over twelve supposedly dead creatures were good odds, but it's proving impossible to breathe freely without Anisha thinking of it as retaliation.

Risking a step back, I flinch when she once again slams against the barrier on my side. Every time I move—even an inch—whoever this is in Anisha's body, screeches and bangs her head on the clear shield until I stop.

It's like she doesn't want me to do anything but stand still and wait. Wait for what?

"Weapons out." Angel's orders through the link. Harvey materializes his sword as Seiji uses one of his whips to bind August to his chest while holding the other beside his thigh in preparation.

Before Anxo can devise a plan to get us out of here Hazel shakily whispers, "Anxo... the portal."

Glancing back at the doorway, I'm dumbfounded to see the portal *fading*. How is that possible? I blink rapidly to convince myself I'm seeing things again but it's true. Our only way out of this nightmare is disappearing in front of my eyes.

The lump in my throat grows heavy. Angel peeks over his shoulder and all color drains out of his face. I don't think even he could've seen this coming.

Squeezing his hand, I tap into the link. *"You need to get August out of here before it's too late. This thing is following my every move so if I distract it enough, you'll be able to get everyone out."*

With his jaw clenched tight, Angel's head snaps to me like he can't believe those words came out of my mouth. Checking back on the portal, Angel takes a minute to think over something before he breathes out, *"We don't have time to debate, so listen and follow for once. Nevaeh and I will distract whatever this thing is, and the moment you see an out... take it."*

Considering Anisha has her eyes set on me, I don't have any other option but to stay back but now my mate has made it clear he isn't leaving me behind.

At once, everyone starts protesting. I get that none of them wants to leave, but this might be our only chance at finding backup. It helps no one if all of us are stuck here.

Harvey is not even a part of the discussion. He took his eyes off Anisha long enough to beg Grace to follow Angel's plan before going back to watching Anisha like a hawk. Hazel doesn't even consider the option. She simply turns her back to me, signaling that she won't be leaving either.

That leaves two people who are smart enough to know which battles to fight and which to run from. Grace and August are the most vulnerable out of us, so there's no way we can let them stay back.

Turning to Seiji, I wait until his eyes leave the undead woman and come to me. He is shaken up, but I need him to do this before we lose the window.

"When Angel lowers the barrier on your side, I need you to take

August and Grace with you and run."

"I can't just leave you—"

Shaking my head, I don't let him argue. *"I can't move without putting everyone in danger and Anxo's shield is the only thing between me and that thing. Harvey is not thinking straight and Hazel is stubborn. I need you to do what I can't... protect my son. Make sure he's safe behind that portal and then come back with help, alright?"*

With eyes filled with helplessness, Seiji nods in promise and it eases a weight on my heart. Eyes still on Anisha or what's left of her, Angel and I lower the barrier behind Seiji in sync.

"Now!"

As soon as the barrier drops, Seiji starts running, one arm held tight over August and the other pulling Grace behind him. Angel holds up the barrier surrounding us while I send out my Divine to seek out those running and protect them until they cross the portal.

Visha's undead doll catches the movement, but before she can take off after Seiji, the portal collapses behind them, vanishing like it never existed.

"Portals don't glitch. And they surely don't disappear like that. Something strange is happening back home, Conquer." Hazel puts my shock into words.

To distract Anisha from blindly searching for the ones who left, Harvey moves closer to the barrier, placing his hand on the electrified wall protecting us from the rabid zombie.

"Anisha," Harvey's whisper seizes her attention. Vacant eyes waiting for him to come to her.

Harvey tries to step forward but I grab his arm before he can even think about stepping out of the protective circle. He turns back to me, eyes filled with unshed tears, but I can't let him go to her. He doesn't know who—or *what* she is.

"That's Anisha. She's—"

"Dead." Forcing the bile down my throat, I keep a firm grip on Harvey's arm.

The horrified look in his eyes slashes my soul. I know he

considered her a friend, a kindred spirit trapped in her own worst nightmare.

We didn't get many opportunities to become familiar with other prisoners, but we met Anisha doing chores around the coven. She was older than us and had survived a lot more than anyone one person could bear.

Watching Anisha made our resolve to escape stronger because we knew what would happen to our minds and bodies if we never got out.

After the night Harvey escaped, things got worse for us. The prisoners weren't treated as living beings but playthings for the coven. What happened to Anisha and the others was something I wanted to take to my grave. Harvey has enough guilt about his escape that I didn't want to add more, but with her standing here in front of us, the secret is out.

Suddenly Anisha falls to her knees, calling out my name in such agony the sting in my throat becomes unbearable. She's not her. This is not Anisha. I don't know what Visha did to her, but this is not her.

Anisha falls forward with her palms on the ground, breathing heavily and that's when I see it. A subtle movement inside her chest makes my blood run cold. My breath hitches when the skin on her chest stretches forward as if something inside her is clawing its way out.

What have you done, Visha?

Snapping her neck sideways like she's seeing things we can't, Anisha sniffs wildly before abruptly standing straight like someone is holding her up by a string. Blinking rapidly, her eyes turn soft, and tears fall down her slashed cheek when her eyes find me again.

"Nevaeh? Everything h-hurts. Help me."

Harvey tugs harder, but I hold on. My heart is breaking too, but no matter how convincing she is, I know that's not Anisha.

Because I was there. I watched as Visha ripped her apart limb from limb.

If Visha thinks she can manipulate me with the dead pieces

of my past, she is sorely mistaken.

Anisha's cries get harder to ignore, and my grip on Harvey becomes bruising. He is breaking in front of me, wanting to help someone he once knew and shared pain with, but I can't let him through.

Harvey's head snaps to me, and the anger in his eyes stuns me. "She's in pain. You have to help her!"

"Help me, Harvey," Anisha screams at the same time.

"Help who, Harvey? That's not Anisha! She is dead. I *watched* her die. This is just another one of Visha's mind games."

When Anisha sees that Harvey won't be coming to her after all, the softness in her eyes hardens into something sinister. Her body snaps like all her bones are breaking, as her wails melt into deranged cackles.

I don't get enough time to gauge her next move before Anisha is running at me with a speed someone as battered as her shouldn't possess. The pushback this time is so brutal I think it will finally get her to stay down, and give us an opportunity to run like hell, but she pulls herself up in no time.

Her shoulder is bent at an odd angle, and her forehead is dented on the left side like her skull is empty on the inside. With a loud cry, Anisha slams her head on the barrier and we stand there, stunned by her strength.

Hazel tries to move, probably thinking another distraction will help us find a way out, but in an instant, a replica of Anisha is in front of her, clawing at the barrier on her side. Only when Hazel shuffles back does the replica fade.

Her body starts vibrating dangerously and when her limbs twitch in a way that's too familiar, it finally dawns on me.

Visha has overloaded her with dark magic more than a vessel can handle, and it's clear Anisha's body is nowhere near strong enough to contain all of it inside her.

She is about to explode.

"Angel let me out, I have to get to her now."

"Not happening." Angel immediately refuses.

"You don't understand, she is about to blow up. Look at the way her fingers are twitching, Angel. Anisha is carrying enough dark magic to reduce everything to ashes for *miles*. Think about the Griari Empire, we aren't far from their border... this will *destroy* them."

Hazel steps forward in my support and tries to convince Angel. "Visha is trying to rewrite fate by erasing their existence. You can't be a part of that Anxo."

He doesn't budge but I don't expect him to. For Angel, his family takes priority over his duty.

"Fates will erase your markings for not stopping it. Not to forget your Divine... Uncle Elijah will have to strip us of our Divine for disrespecting Fates." The tick in his jaw is proof Angel knows I'm right.

We might be symbols of doom but even the Horsemen will face dire consequences for going against what's already written by the sisters of fate.

Angel is trying his best to hold the barrier, but the magic inside Anisha is far more powerful than the body it's trapped in. With every scratch, the darkness inside her creates another crack in the barrier.

Anisha makes another inhuman sound from deep in her chest, and we stagger back to put as much distance from the ticking time bomb as possible.

Black cracks start forming on her skin as the power inside her fights to escape the weak body and latch on to the barrier, eating away at it.

If I'm right and Anisha is holding an unnatural amount of dark magic inside her, then Angel's barrier won't hold against the explosion.

Not unless my Divine absorbs most of the impact.

Scanning the barrier, I look for the weakest spot. "Promise me you won't lower the barrier no matter what." The desperation in my voice makes it clear what I'm about to do.

Angel turns me around and pulls me into him, holding me tight by my shoulders. "Don't. Let me think. Just give me a minute and I'll come up with a better plan."

"There's no better plan unless we want to be part of a genocide. I know my Divine can consume that magic and still survive." I beg Harvey to back me up but like Angel, he is adamant on finding another way. "Trust me, I can do this. I've made it through before."

There was a reason Visha only used her harshest spells on me and not Harvey. Our Divine's aren't made for tackling dark magic. She didn't want to accidentally kill Harvey in the process.

Holding my face with desperation leaking through his voice, Angel whispers, "I can't lose you. Not you. I won't survive. Please don't make me do that, sweetheart."

The fear in his eyes makes it evident that even when he knows this is the only way, Angel's panic won't let him see logic.

"You won't lose me. We'll be fine. I promise we'll be alright." Pulling him in for a kiss, I hold his face. Angel relaxes into me, thinking I've given up.

Behind Angel's back I search for Hazel. The single affirmative nod from her is a relief. I knew I could count on her to think rationally and not get tied up in emotions.

Losing my grip on my mate's hair, I signal Hazel. At the same time, she tackles Harvey to the ground while I push back from Angel and make a run for it.

Ignoring Angel's anguished scream behind me, I cross the barrier and collide with Anisha.

A half-second before an earth-shattering boom, I call upon my essence to surround us. Waves of dark magic explode out of her body, and Anisha turns to ash. The force of the blast forces me on my knees, and I scream in agony as swirls of unparalleled power spread inside my chest.

My Divine absorbs every last bit of tainted magic before my head spins and I fall back, hitting my head hard on the ground.

When the darkness finally fades, I'm blinking up at a sky full of bright stars and steady planetary bodies.

How long was I out? And how did we get home?

I yelp when I try to sit up. The slightest movement feels like I'm melting into the ground. As the dark magic settles inside me, the burning in my chest gets stronger and I'm left wheezing for breath.

Carefully turning my head to the side, I see Angel slowly picking himself up from the ground with fresh cuts on his face and covered in ash. Only when I see Harvey help Hazel up, do I sigh in relief.

Mission successful. Everyone is alive and breathing.

Faded sharp ringing is all I hear when they come running to me. I can see them shouting, but the words seem too far away. Whatever he's looking for in the dark is only making Angel angrier.

Turning back to the sky, I take a deep breath that burns my lungs and makes me whimper.

Once the stabbing pain in my chest fades a little, I flutter my lids open to my favorite pair of green eyes hovering above me, tears lining his lashes and fear prominent on his face.

"I'm so sorry, sweetheart, but we can't wait. I need to take you to the medical bay *now*." Angel whispers hoarsely before carefully picking me up. I can't stop the scream that leaves me when his arms scrape the burns on my back.

It will take time for my Divine to gain its strength back after absorbing copious amounts of dark magic. The pain is starting to settle in my bones and I'm not sure how much more I can take.

Angel tries his best to avoid my burns, but it's impossible at this point, as the blisters cover most of my chest, arms, and back. I have to muffle my whimpers in his neck when each sound of pain coming out of my mouth makes Angel wince and apologize like he's the one hurting me.

Hazel runs ahead, screaming at people to get out of the way as Angel runs as fast as he can carrying me.

Years of torture have made my Divine resilient, I can already feel some of my wounds cauterizing. Good timing because I can barely breathe through the pain now.

"Call the healers!" Angel roars, his chest vibrating from the force, and I cry out when my arm rubs against his shirt.

Whispering a quick apology to me, Angel glares at the healer who asks him to lay me down. Angel continues to ignore the healer's request until Grace rushes in and scolds him for still holding me in his arms instead of letting the healers help.

A shiver runs down my spine, filled with pain when someone turns me on my side to check my back. Angel is immediately in front of me, stroking my hair and doing everything he can to ease my pain, even the tiniest bit.

"The portal collapsed, Anxo. How is that even possible? One minute, Seiji is running to call reinforcements, and the next I turn back to see the portal is gone. And not just that one. Every single portal in the kingdom—all of them collapsed at once."

I wait for someone to address what Grace said, but all I get is silence. The lack of answers is starting to bother everyone now.

"Why is she looking so pale?" I hear Seiji come in, but his voice is muffled.

"What's happening? Something is wrong, Grace, she looks worse." Hearing the panic building in his voice, I squeeze Angel's hand to comfort him.

Grace bends to whisper, "I don't want to reward your recklessness, but it was a good idea." She walks to the end of the bed and removes my shoes.

When Angel asks again, Grace remembers the man whose hair is turning grey, from constantly worrying about his mate. "She absorbed a lot of dark magic Anxo, what else do you expect? Thankfully, her Divine is resilient or this could've been a lot worse."

That *she chooses to say out loud?*

"I take my eyes off you for one second, and you run off to become the martyr!" Harvey reprimands me but stops when I whimper because it hurts so much.

Or maybe I fake it because I'm too tired for a scolding.

Kissing my hand, Angel shakes his head with a chuckle. Of

course, he can tell when I'm faking.

My mate doesn't need to tell me he is angry, his eyes do a pretty good job of that. "Why do you insist on giving me a heart attack every other day."

"To keep you on your toes."

"Well, stop. I hate it."

"But you love me?"

"With everything in me."

The thump of my heart slows, and my vision gets hazy once more. I relax on the pillow but force my eyes open to find Angel again. I try to muster enough strength to talk, but he understands me without saying it.

Angel always knows.

"Sleep, sweetheart, I'll be right here when you wake up." He caresses my cheek softly. I close my eyes with the image of Angel looking like someone finally put his soul back inside his body.

36. Error: friends not found

Nevaeh

Bringing the blanket over my head, I try to go back to sleep but the memories of last night keep flooding in, leaving me in a limbo between dreams and reality.

All I want is to bury my head in my pillow and pretend last night was just another bad dream.

Patting the bed on my other side, I shiver at the feel of cold sheets. That can't be right. I've never woken up alone since Angel and I started sleeping in the same bed.

Where is he?

The absence of my mate gives way to a strange budding ache in my stomach. I don't like not being around him. Even as I fell asleep last night, I was so sure I would wake up to my mate pacing the room like a caged animal, going mad with worry.

Before I go looking for Angel, I decide to clean up and my muscles crack like I haven't used them in months when I push off the bed.

My steps falter as I pass the bedroom window and see a dark storm brewing outside. Pushing the curtains aside, I take in the heavy clouds thundering in warning.

I know I complain about the sunshine and rainbows in this realm, but for once, the gloomy weather doesn't bring me the peace it once did.

Brushing off my paranoia, I rush to the bathroom, and the scalding hot shower helps relax my muscles.

The burns I was covered in last night are nowhere to be seen, and the only scars left on my body are ones that don't define me anymore.

Putting on Angel's hoodie and my own sweatpants, I leave

the wet mess of my hair for Angel to deal with. My first stop in the living room is useless. Even the kitchen is empty. Now that I think about it, the whole floor is quiet.

Too quiet. It's never this quiet in the Horsemen castle.

The absence of my family didn't bother me when I woke up, but the longer I don't find them, the faster the ache in my stomach crawls up to my chest.

Rushing up the stairs, I try to find the conference room, and for a change, it doesn't take me four tries. But I don't find it because of my sharp memory but the sounds of screaming and smashing echoing in the corridor.

When I push the doors open, my sudden arrival halts their argument. I'm shocked at the state of the room. Broken wood and pieces of glass littered around.

A council meeting is not a surprise after what happened last night, but the way some of them are avoiding my eyes is feeding my anxiety.

Seiji and Grace run over to engulf me in tight hugs when August suddenly pops up from behind me and crashes into the back of my legs. The boy knows better than to eavesdrop on meetings, so what was he doing here?

The uncertainty and anger lingering in the air force me to stand straighter and pull away from the hugs. I hate feeling on guard in my own home, but my gut twists in a way that warns me to prepare for the worst.

Before the tension in this room can choke me, my eyes search for Angel. Only after I spot him standing in a far corner, do I breathe out. Finding his eyes already on me makes me smile so big my cheeks hurt.

I wait for him to come to me, but he doesn't move. With every second Angel stays rooted in place, my smile slips off. The vacant look in his eyes is unexpected... *scary.*

Clutching my hand in a tight grip, Grace turns to glare at Angel. Her scowl takes me by surprise. Grace is not the type to glare at anyone, let alone Angel.

Pulling away from Seiji's arm over my shoulder, I caress

August's cheek before going to Angel. Every cell in my body is aching for his embrace, and I don't want to wait any longer. If he won't come to me for some reason then I will bridge the gap for both of us.

Showing me his palm, Angel stops my approach, and my heart sinks. This is the first time he has denied my touch and I don't like how the rejection makes me feel.

"Are you feeling better?" Angel asks. His tone lacks his usual warmth, but he's still worried about me, so whatever he is angry at me about can't be that bad.

I don't let the hollowness of his expression get to me. Angel is stressed. What happened last night must've increased his worry and workload.

He's just stressed, nothing more.

Titling my head, I finally ask, "What's wrong, Angel?"

The deafening silence in the room only shatters when an elderly demon pushes his chair back to stand.

The ex-Warriorhead for Conquer has always irked me. When his lips twitch like he is holding back from smirking, my irritation only tenfold.

The demon nods his head at Angel, but my mate completely ignores the gesture, keeping his eyes fixed on the wall behind me. "The votes were clear, son. You know what to do."

"Don't you dare Anxo." I flinch when Seiji suddenly growls beside me.

The instinctual step back almost makes me trip over August, who I didn't know was hiding behind me. Looping my arms around his shoulders, I'm about to bring August to the front when my eyes fall on the two suitcases standing by the door.

Angel clears his throat, "I see you're feeling better." My hesitant smile completely vanishes when he steps away from the wall and gestures to the table of councilmen.

"The council took a vote about casting you out, and the vote concludes it's in the kingdom's best interest that you leave. We believe your presence is risking the safety of our people. If you and August leave, the coven won't have any reason to keep attacking."

What does he mean I need to leave?

I know last night was bad but I helped, and I fixed the mess, so why would he kick me out?

'Because you're not worth the trouble. All you bring is chaos and hurt wherever you go. They're happy without you. Safer without you. They don't need you... never did.'

I hear whispers in my head and freeze. But something is different this time. The voice... that's *my* voice.

I thought Visha was finding ways to slither inside my head at my weakest moments, but it's been me all along. I'm the malicious voice inside my head, and as cruel as the words are... they are also true.

I've been the one ruining everything.

"They won't let us vote because we're too close to you. Not like these traitors here know anything about loyalty," Grace's voice trembles with hurt.

Some council members have the decency to look away, while others don't bother hiding their disgust. The lump in my throat becomes harder to ignore when I find Harvey and Hazel just sitting at the table, not saying a word.

Pushing off his chair, Harvey stalks toward me, and for a moment, I think he is coming to stand by me, but to my utter surprise, he brushes past me like I don't exist.

Harvey leaves the room without a second glance, and when tears start streaming down Grace's cheeks, I don't know who I'm hurting for more.

He will come back. Harvey will never leave like this.

When my eyes meet Hazel's blank ones, I still. Averting her gaze, she concentrates on the table in front of her. She's back to putting on a facade, I see.

I'm trying hard to figure out what I did for half the people I consider family to want to cast me out, but not a single reason jumps out. I've been loyal. I've protected them, picked their safety over my life every day.

Why am I still not enough?

"Why?" I ask in a hushed whisper to the man who's supposed to love me.

"I need to protect my people. This isn't our fight, and I've had enough of putting my people in danger for *you*." Angel says 'you' as if the word tastes sour on his tongue.

I thought I was his people, too.

'He lied. I told you not to trust anyone.'

Every word out of his mouth, every disgusted look thrown my way, every time he turns his body so I can't reach him, breaks my soul.

My eyes sting from holding back tears as I nod, fully accepting that it's his responsibility to keep everyone safe.

He's right. This was never their fight, and I did put them in danger, but he knew all this from the beginning, so why ask me to leave now?

A movement on my side catches my attention just in time to see the elder demon smirking to himself. His thrill turns into fake pity when he senses my eyes on him, but he's not fooling anyone.

August pulls away from me to stand beside the suitcases, his stuffed dinosaur clutched in his arms. The action makes my head spin. Two suitcases. *Two.*

As if he heard my thoughts, Angel confirms, "August will be leaving with you, considering he's your responsibility, not mine."

My head snaps to him in disbelief. I wait for him to take the words back. To tell me it's all a joke, and those bags are a part of some elaborate prank, but Angel doesn't blink, much less regard me.

As if my hurt caused by his careless words makes him uncomfortable, Angel goes back to staring at the damn wall behind me, essentially ignoring me.

I shouldn't have trusted him with my heart.

I can't bear the thought of dragging the boy in my mess and risking us falling right into Visha's clutches.

Steeling my spine, I match Angel's blank stare with my own. "I request you let August stay."

"Request denied. Now, get out." Angel hisses, and the foreign act makes me take a step back.

Where did my Angel go?

"Anxo, stop this right now! She'll be out there with no protection and a kid, you asshole!" Seiji fumes and I take another step back, realizing how firm his decision is if he doesn't care about what anyone else thinks.

"What about her rights? You can't kick her out of *her* kingdom." Grace steps forward, standing head-to-head with Anxo despite the drastic height difference.

"Horseman Blackburn will come back soon. We were handling everything just fine before *she* came along and destroyed our peace."

I was so close to pleading that it's borderline pathetic. But hearing Anxo talk about how I've ruined his life kills my will to beg or demand answers. This isn't about the dangers that follow me or the weight he has to carry so I don't fall back. Anxo *wants* me to leave.

"What has gotten into you? This is heartless, Anxo!" Grace is furious, and I've never seen her like this.

She shouldn't want me to stay, anyway. What happened yesterday will keep happening if I don't leave. Nothing Anxo said is a lie. Every attack this kingdom has faced in the past six months has been my fault.

"You take it back, or I swear to Fates—" Seiji is on Anxo before anyone can stop him.

"Stop it!" Silence greets my request. "Horseman Alarie is right. This isn't your fight... *never was.*"

I look into Anxo's eyes, those emerald eyes that never failed to fill me with love and warmth, offer nothing today. Eyes drowning in emptiness start to pull me along the longer I try to find my Angel in them.

I can't take the hatred and disgust anymore. My heart won't be able to survive more of his hateful words if I keep standing here.

Using the restraints I learned the hard way, I erase every emotion on my face. This isn't the time to break apart. I have a responsibility to find August a safe home.

A different, safe home.

Papa isn't here, my mate doesn't want me, and neither does my best friend or half of the people I call *family*.

I don't have a reason to stay, not when my presence is causing them despair.

Turning to August, I offer him a weak smile and assure him everything will be fine. I'll be damned if I let him bear the weight of my hurt. My baby gives me a dull version of his bright smile and grips my hand tightly.

Keeping my voice vacant, I address the room, "We are grateful for the shelter and protection, and I apologize for any pain I inflicted. You won't have to worry about seeing us again." I keep my voice firm and sigh internally when it doesn't crack like my heart does with every word.

My heart is beating in my head, and the throbbing is starting to blur everything, but all I can think about is if any of it was real. If I imagined it all.

Was it all in my head and never in my reach?

"Wise decision. Maybe after you leave, I will finally get some peace. And don't even think about lurking around, my warriors have a kill on sight for outsiders."

With those words, the last of my hope breaks.

I won't beg Anxo to let me stay when he doesn't want me here. I respect myself too much to stay here and face his hate constantly.

I won't beg for the love he has clearly forgotten.

Soft murmurs and sneers finally make it to my ears, and when I look around my heart falls to my feet.

Not only is my mate throwing me out like trash, but he also doesn't mind making me the primary source of entertainment for his people.

And here I thought he loved me.

Burning with embarrassment, I don't focus on Seiji screaming and begging Anxo to change his decision—even threatening—but all his attempts are brushed aside.

Conquer's ex-Warriorhead even claims Anxo is showing me mercy by letting me leave unharmed, after all the trouble I've caused.

I gulp the tightness in my throat when Anxo stands with his lips pursed as his warriors and elders berate me. He is acting like I'm his biggest inconvenience, not his mate. Not someone he said he would love until his last breath and made promises of forever, too.

Like I'm not his sweetheart.

Quickly composing myself, I wipe the corner of my eye. I feel the sleeve of *his* hoodie brush against my cheek, and I curse myself for wearing it today.

I want nothing more than to rip it off me, but it will have to wait until I'm out of this place for good.

I turn to leave when Seiji wraps me in his arms from behind. I don't turn, refusing to fall prey to my tears and make an even bigger mockery of myself in front of them.

"I don't care if he's Conquer. I'll beat the shit out of him if he doesn't come to his senses," Seiji whispers, his voice thick with emotion.

Taking a deep breath, I level myself before turning in his arms. "I need to leave Seiji," I keep my voice low so no one except the two surrounding me can hear. "The coven is after me... *us*," I glance at August, standing next to the door, waiting for me. "Everything is my fault—"

Seiji cuts me off, "It's not your fault. Something is wrong with Anxo. I don't know why he is acting like a complete jackass."

"He's just protecting his people."

As much as it hurts me to admit it, I know Anxo's primary motive has always been to protect his people. I just thought my little boy and I were also one of those people.

I might forgive him for making a fool out of me in front of

all these people but I will never forgive him for breaking my trust... for breaking my family.

"I'll come with you—" I stop Seiji and step back from him.

"No. You should stay here. I'll have my hands full with August, and I don't want to constantly worry about your safety, too."

Grace hasn't stopped crying since I walked into this room, and as much as I understand their concerns, I need to leave now. The staring, the snickering, the whispered underhanded comments are getting harder to ignore. And my soul keeps shattering with each glare Anxo throws my way.

"I'll take you to the portal," Anxo comes forward, but Seiji quickly stops him.

"The fuck you will."

"Only a *Horseman* can open them after they collapsed yesterday, so it's either me or..."

"I'll do it." Akihiko Nakaya, Horseman of Famine strides to me. I don't know how I didn't notice him before. I search him for signs of disappointment or hatred, but there's only regret. For what? I'm not in a state to find out.

I nod in answer. At this point, I will do anything to get this over with so I can be as far away from Anxo as possible.

I allow Grace to hug me one last time, and she makes it impossible to stay strong when she breaks down in my arms. Once I pry Grace off me, I turn to say goodbye to Seiji, but he storms off before I can.

Sighing under my breath, I grab the smaller suitcase with August's things and throw one last watery smile over my shoulder to Grace.

Grace calls out my name again, and I turn around to find her wheeling the other suitcase toward me. "You didn't take your bag."

With my hand over hers, I stop Grace from trying to hand over the bag. "Grace, I came here with nothing, I'll leave the same way."

The only reason I'm not leaving August's bag is because I

will never choose my pride over his comfort.

Suddenly August breaks free from my hold and starts running to Anxo. My breath falters as I watch him close the distance between him and someone he still considers his family and pure terror grips me.

Releasing my essence, I send it flying to August to shield him, unsure how the Horseman would react to *my son* running to him. It takes August a mere second to put his toy near Anxo's feet and run back to me, but I don't dare to breathe in that second, panic gripping me over his safety.

Looks like I'm back to my old ways.

A flash of hurt passes through Anxo's eyes. Instead of the toy near his feet, he keeps staring at my Divine circling August like my essence has offended him.

The realization that it took an hour to shatter the trust it took us months to build has me staggering back before I steady myself.

The emotion is gone as fast as it broke through Anxo's defenses, and the version of him that broke my heart and family shows his face again. I feel a pinch in my head that grows into a throb the farther I walk away, but I squeeze my eyes shut and wait for it to subside.

Leaving the castle, I don't look at anyone or anywhere as I follow the man walking ahead of me to the closest portal.

When I think I can finally let go, a small hand squeezes mine, telling me there's a long way to go before I can fall apart without scaring my boy.

I'm surprised when the portal opens to a house sitting in the middle of nowhere. Papa Nakaya says it's Harvey's old house in the human realm, and he has allowed me to use it until I can find something permanent for us.

How very generous of him.

I would've felt something other than numb, but the ache in my chest from this morning has dulled everything to the point that I don't feel anything. What would I even say to a man who calls himself my best friend yet didn't blink before turning his back on me?

Despite Harvey's choices, I'm grateful for the house. I'm in no shape to search for a safe place.

Besides giving me a key, Papa Nakaya doesn't stay longer, and I'm glad for it. When he reaches for a hug, I step away and walk into the house without looking back, slamming the door to that life shut behind me.

I'm always prepared to be left alone, so what happened today might be heartbreaking but it's not surprising.

I guess my fears were nothing but premonitions of the worst times to come. The voice in my head always knew I would lose him. It kept warning me, but I was too damn happy to pay any attention to it.

And now, the person I thought loved me snatched my entire world from under me, leaving me with nothing.

How naïve of me to think I could have it all.

37. No, that's not crying you hear

Nevaeh

I t's been a week. Six days to be exact, since I was kicked out.

This past week, I've done nothing but watch cartoons with August as he ate microwavable meals and snacks.

I'm glad Harvey has the same kitchen expertise as me because that means the pantry was filled with readymade meals. It took August a long time to get on a proper diet after we escaped the coven, and I couldn't have let some menial heartbreak mess up his schedule.

I was prepared for when August would ask why we weren't living in the kingdom anymore, but he never did.

I had a whole story mapped out about how the coven was looking for us, so we were playing a little game of hide and seek, but I forgot to consider August isn't as naïve as other kids his age. He never asked because he knows we were kicked out.

Now, every morning I put on a strong front and I spend all my time watching TV with August, making sure he feels safe and loved. I smile and laugh with him. I listen when August talks about his favorite colors. I make animals of gold smoke so my little boy doesn't feel lonely when he plays. I do everything to keep him occupied and entertained.

And when my son is sound asleep, unaware of his mama drowning in her pain, I let myself break down into violent body-shaking sobs to ease the constant ache in my heart.

I haven't slept more than five hours since we came here because my nightmares decided to make a comeback. The lack of sleep is starting to worry August, but I've promised him I can handle it.

I'll be okay. We'll be okay.

All I want August to worry about is what movie he wants to watch before bed. No matter how much he wants to help, I won't burden my little boy with my mess. He is a kid, and I will do anything to make sure he gets to be one for as long as possible.

When August finally falls asleep after yet another Disney movie, I tuck him into my bed again tonight. He has refused to sleep alone since we came here and it's like we're back to square one. Back to learning life all over again.

I'm tearing apart the kitchen trying to find where I left the coffee mug and somehow end up with a swollen forehead. I smacked myself with the cupboard.

Typical.

What little composure I have over my emotions shatters completely, dragging me back to the memories that hold nothing but loneliness and hurt. My knees buckle and I fall to my knees, muffling my cries behind my hands and screaming silently.

I'm done faking it. I'm done keeping myself together. Everything sucks and everything hurts. My brain has never felt this foggy, my body is begging for rest… and *he's* not here.

I'm banging my head on these stupid cupboards because he's not here. It hurts, but what hurts more is that he's not here to put his hand over my forehead to save me from the pain. My fingers are bloody from picking on them because I miss his hand in mine, miss having his rings to anxiously fiddle with.

I keep stumbling around this unfamiliar house and hitting my pinky toe on every hard surface because he's not here to stop me from bumping into things. I can't even breathe right when my anxiety gets the best of me because he's not here, demanding me to breathe for him.

He's not here, and I hate it.

These last six months made me addicted to his presence, and I never thought I'd have to live my life without him. I want my Angel back because I'm even more broken and bruised without him, and I was just starting to heal.

He was the medicine for my soul, and I want—no *need* him to come back, but that's the worst part.

No matter how much I need him, no matter how much I can't be without him, *he doesn't want me*. He doesn't need me and maybe never did, and that's something I have to learn to live with.

I have to sit back and watch myself drown, slowly getting worse, falling into the familiar hole of never-ending nothingness. One more push or even the slightest nudge would shatter me, and I know this time, I wouldn't be able to glue myself back together. Not on my own.

I don't remember passing out, but jolt awake when I feel a blanket over me and a tiny body snuggling into my chest right there on the kitchen floor.

A night filled with nightmares and crying is not an option anymore with August beside me, so I lay there, stroking his head as he sleeps, holding me.

Looking down at the innocent little boy, I once again shove my heartbreak as far down as possible. This kid deserves a better parent than a broken woman.

Fuck, Anxo and his entire kingdom.

I have what I need right here, and if he doesn't want me—*if he doesn't want us*—then that's his loss.

I will survive bloody toes and blue foreheads, but he won't survive his mate hating his existence.

I'm willing to nurture this anger and betrayal until I piece myself back together and take care of Visha for good. And then... I will close the book of my past, including Anxo and his every memory.

Fuck it all to purgatory.

38. Traitors among us

Anxo

Six nights ago.

I still can't shake the terror I felt when I carried my mate to the medical wing. The sight of my mate writhing in pain shook me to my core, and I truly experienced what being paralyzed with fear feels like.

Dragging a chair next to her bed, I can't help the anger that rises thinking about how, once again, Nevaeh took it upon herself to save us by putting herself in danger.

I'm more than relieved she's okay but I can't let her keep doing this. I refuse to watch my mate sacrifice her well-being over and over just to prove to that voice in her head that she's not evil.

That she's not a monster.

Sleep is the last thing on my mind tonight so I lean back in my chair and make myself comfortable. Nevaeh hates waking up alone and since I can't risk climbing into bed beside her, this is the next best option.

Closing my eyes, I thank Fates for keeping my family safe when the bitterness of my reality finally settles in.

If nothing else, the night has revealed my blindside and how our enemies might have taken advantage of it. I've been so busy tackling one problem after another that I lost sight of the big picture, but not anymore.

Grace links me that August is having trouble falling asleep, so I decide to quickly run back to the castle to tuck my little man in. He might've been asleep for most of it but August can sense the lingering distress on the adults and it's not helping him relax.

I'm back to my mate in less than ten minutes. Marching inside her room, I find the nurse who helped with August all those months back fumbling with the medicine Giana, our healer, left for Nevaeh.

My sudden arrival startles her. The nurse mumbles something about checking on Nevaeh before quickly disappearing out of my sight.

Long after the woman is gone, I still can't stop thinking about the tremble in her hands or how she flinched when she noticed me standing by the door.

I want to ignore the strange interaction and focus on my mate, but every little detail about tonight has been playing like a loop inside my head, begging me to sort them out.

Walking through my memories with a clear head does nothing to give me answers. So many things don't add up. Nothing makes sense after Anisha appears. And the biggest question remains, how did she find the location of our portal in the first place?

Portals only reveal to those who are connected to our realm, which is why Grace was able to stumble upon one and cross it. It can't be a coincidence for that *thing* to find one at the exact time we were close by.

No matter how hard I try to stall until morning so I can unpack this mess with Nevaeh, my head refuses to shut up. Finally having enough, I link Harvey to take my place and stay with Nevaeh while I go to retrace our steps.

I need to know exactly what happened last night.

Turns out Hazel and I are on the same page because I find her pacing the road behind Conquer that leads to the portal. A shared look has my gut churning. I have a feeling I won't like what we find.

Usually, by this time in the morning, the sun is starting to peak through the clouds, but today, a storm that's been brewing for days is finally making an appearance.

My heart is in my throat as I approach the portal that disappeared into thin air. A portal collapsing on itself is unheard of, and the hope I was holding onto that it was all a freaky coincidence shatters the moment Hazel points to where the portal has been tampered with.

From this end.

Despite my brain offering multiple rational explanations, my gut knows who's behind this. And when Hazel puts my nightmare into words, I stop breathing entirely.

Only Horsemen know these portals enough to disrupt their magic and force them to collapse.

Or Ex-Horsemen.

Ignoring how early in the morning it is, I link Khatri. The Warriorhead mumbles something in his sleepy daze but instantly becomes alert at my order.

"I need you to find my parents. Only take warriors you trust. Do whatever you have to, but don't let them leave the borders, Khatri."

I don't stop to question his loyalty. Dean trusted him with his life and around his daughter when Nevaeh was young. That says enough in my books.

Panic slams into me when Khatri links that my parents are nowhere to be found. The sudden realization that I've left my mate alone surrounded by unsuspecting enemies has me turning around and running to her.

"What is happening Horseman Alarie?"

"I will explain everything just don't trust anyone for now, okay? Ignore all orders from anyone other than my family —*the one I chose.* And make sure no one gets in and out of the kingdom without my say-so. I want all portals seized immediately."

My head is spinning, as I run back to my mate. I'm trying to wrap my mind around the new pieces of a puzzle I've found when abruptly Hazel's arm shoots out to stop me. My steps falter, looking at the group of elders and elite warriors waiting outside the Horsemen castle.

My frustrations win as I stalk to them, but before I can ask them to leave, the former second-in-command of Conquer requests an emergency council meeting.

I'm about to tell him to scramble out of my sight when Hazel agrees on my behalf. From the bottom of my heart, I want these people to scurry off. I have no interest in diplomacy or politics when my mate's life is in danger, but something is stopping me from doing so.

Reigning in my anger, I link Harvey to meet us in the conference room after Khatri takes over his place to stand guard over Nevaeh.

As soon as we're seated the ex-Warriorhead goes straight for the kill. "Horseman Alarie, I think we can both agree that the kingdom has been facing some serious troubles lately. And after last night, many of us are suspicious that Nevaeh might be the one responsible for it all. We have good reason to believe she is purposely putting our future leaders in harm's way."

Watching half the room nod along in agreement and present reasons why the future Horsewoman of Death should be cast out, makes the whole picture clearer.

Everything clicks in place and it finally dawns on me.

We're on the cusp of a coup.

This is why the coven always knew where to find us. Our own people were selling us out this entire time.

The discovery that the people I trusted were after my love was blinding. I never imagined the one's I've protected, for whom I have risked my life—more times than I can count—would betray me by targeting my family.

As much as I want to squeeze their necks until their last breath leaves them, I need to be smart about this.

Everyone who knitted this elaborate scheme to destroy my family right under my nose deserves worse than a quick death. I'm breathing fire as I scan the ones who agree with the nutcase my father chose as his Warriorhead and carve their names into my memory.

Soon I will carve this betrayal on their flesh.

Subtle nods from Harvey and Hazel are signs that my perfect life is about to blow up, and there won't be anything subtle about it.

I sit there and act like it's the perfect solution. I act like my heart isn't bleeding every time they call my mate a nuisance. I act like I wouldn't have to repeat these words to her if I have any chance of getting her to leave this kingdom.

I can't risk my mate and son staying in a place surrounded by familiar faces and unfamiliar betrayals.

I have to make her leave. Even if I have to tear my heart out and let her stomp on it to do so.

Present.

It's funny how one night can turn your life upside down. It's been seven days since Nevaeh left—*Correction*—seven days since I made her leave.

Broke her heart, her trust, and my family to pieces.

I will never forget the hurt I saw in her eyes when I refused her touch. The way her eyes held back tears, tears that *I* caused, is an image that will forever be engraved in my mind. I made a promise to keep her safe and ended up being the one to hurt her the most.

That day, I wanted her to call me names, yell at me, curse me, or even stab me, so I could feel a fraction of the pain I was forcing on her, but I forgot how loud that evil voice in her head could get.

I'm the one who proved her fears right.

I just know that voice made her believe she deserved it, that what I did was a long time coming, and now she knew better than to repeat her mistake.

Her mistake of falling in love with me.

Her mistake of letting me destroy her walls only to destroy her along the way.

Fates I wish she was here. I wish I could breathe in her addictive scent and feel complete with her touch, but all I can do is curse the night our world fell apart.

I tried to link her that day, to tell her I didn't mean a word I said, but she was too broken to realize her headache was my fault—*just like her heartache.*

Since the day I asked my mate to leave, I have spent every single minute trying to figure out a way to flush out the traitors and get my mate back.

If only I could figure something out.

I've never been this dysfunctional before. I want to get this over with so I can bring my sweetheart back home, back to where she belongs, and beg for her forgiveness, but everything is upside down, and I can barely think straight.

The worst part is how Seiji and Grace haven't talked or even looked my way since that day. They've locked themselves in their respective rooms and Grace has absolutely refused to see Harvey. It's killing the poor man.

The castle has never looked emptier. The living room resembles a ghost town. It was never this quiet even when it was just the four of us living here.

The door to my office suddenly bursts open with such force it rattles the walls. With no care for the dent I'll have to repair, Seiji marches straight to my desk and delivers a bone-cracking punch to my jaw before I can blink.

Okay, I deserve that.

"I tried to stop them." Harvey runs in, out of breath, to stand next to Grace, who completely ignores his existence and tries to hold Seiji back from throwing another punch.

"He's lying. *Again.* I told him to move, and he did," Grace retorts.

Harvey rubs the back of his neck and looks down, but I don't blame him. I can't even imagine what the rift between the new couple must be like.

"We want the truth. The whole truth. Now." Grace takes a seat in one of the chairs in front of my desk and makes herself comfortable. When the room remains dead quiet, she scoffs impatiently. "Is it because we hold no major position in the kingdom?"

"Come on Gracie, you know that's not it."

Banging his fists on my table, Seiji asks, "Then tell me how is it? Because the way I see it, the soul twins are clearly part of it while we are left out. Why don't I see them ripping their hair out, getting sick with worry over Nevaeh and August."

Hazel turns her back to me and stomps to the door. When I think she's about to leave, Hazel slams the door shut and stands with her back against it, making sure our conversation remains private.

Rubbing his eyes tiredly, Seiji takes the seat next to Grace. He makes no effort to hide his disappointment, but when his eyes level mine, I know Seiji is trying to understand what changed in those couple of hours.

"I've known you my whole life, Anxo. So don't you dare lie and say it didn't tear you apart to watch her leave. It's like you were trying to hurt her, to make her walk away by saying all that shit." Seiji and Grace share a look before Seiji breathes out, "Look at you man, you look like a pathetic heartbroken puppy. Anyone with eyes can see you didn't want her gone, so what the fuck happened? Why did you do that?"

Seiji might sound sympathetic, but his eyes hold a clear warning that this is the last time he's asking *nicely*.

Leaning back in my chair, I heave out a long sigh, running a hand through the stubble I haven't bothered to shave in days.

"We gave you a week to get your shit together, but all you do is mope around and stalk our warriors like a creepy ex-boyfriend. So, spill."

Seiji is clearly at the end of his rope, and my dramatic pause will only get me another purple bruise.

I have some seriously aggressive friends.

I massage my temple to relieve the constant throbbing before I tell them everything—from the fumbling nurse to the double-timing warriors. How the portal didn't really collapse and the coup of our lifetime.

I still can't figure out how we teleported back to the kingdom that night and neither can anyone else. Even the strongest beings can't cross our heavily spelled barriers without dying, so who did that?

"So that was your plan? Get Nevaeh to leave and then what? Sit around and wait for the traitors to come to you?" Grace interrogates us and Harvey and Hazel quickly look down to avoid her wrath.

"No, I thought... I thought—" I stutter.

"What have you figured out then? Who else is involved in this coup other than your treacherous parents? I still don't understand why they would do this. What's the end goal? And why only target Nevaeh, why not Harvey or Seiji? What about the coven, do—"

The questions Grace is throwing at us are precisely the ones that run through my mind every damn second, but I don't have the answers. I can't even say I saved Nevaeh by hurting her heart because all I did was delay the threat.

But I couldn't think.

My mind stopped working the second the amount of danger Nevaeh was in, settled into my bones.

I couldn't think of anything other than getting her far away from this place.

Blinking fast, I keep my head down and ruffle through the mountain of papers that now spot a few teardrops.

Fates, Anxo you don't have enough time to drown in your pain. I have to try to keep my head straight. There's too much work to be done.

"I don't have the answer to any of that. I just know Nevaeh wasn't safe here," I croak out, not daring to lift my head and pass a file to them so they can see I at least made arrangements to keep my sweetheart safe. "They still have protection. I have my best and most trusted warriors keeping guard."

Rubbing her temple, Grace sighs, "This is a mess. It would've been much easier to digest if this was the soul twins idea, but I can't believe *you* came up with this plan, Anxo. What were you thinking?"

The repeated mention of my epic failure is starting to grate on my nerves, and I'm getting sick of hearing it. My brain is way too jumbled to process my guilt and everything that's been happening all at once.

I'm trying to identify the traitors, maintaining two kingdoms, overseeing security, preventing the coven from attacking, and constantly defending my decision to adopt August. Everything that's been building up for days finally reaches its peak and I just... *snap*.

"That Nevaeh was going to die if she stayed here!" Banging my fist against my desk, I glare at the papers spread before me. "She was being targeted in her own home, and I had no fucking idea by who. I *had* to get her out of here. Did you stop to think what would've happened if I started sniffing out traitors while she was still here? What if someone—" Fisting my hair, I take a sharp breath.

For once, I have no idea what to do or where to start. I'm someone who always has a plan. I'm always ten steps ahead but this caught me completely off-guard. My own oversight has gotten me into this mess.

"I admit I don't have all the answers, but I wasn't going to gamble with my mate's life. You saw the lengths Visha was willing to go, and who knows what she has in mind next. Letting them stay meant telling Nevaeh that her home wasn't safe anymore, and I couldn't do that to her, okay?"

Grace opens her mouth to throw another logic my way when I say, "Can you tell me you would've done anything differently if Harvey was the intended target."

Grace bites the side of her cheek and sniffs. If just the thought of being in my shoes is hurting her then she definitely doesn't want to be in my head right now.

The pain of knowing I hurt my mate to protect her, only to massively fail at protecting her heart, is heart-wrenching.

I understand her frustration. It was torture to put my love for Nevaeh and August aside and approach this logically. And even if it hurts right now, I know removing them from the equation was my safest bet.

Looking my family in the eye, I try to convince them I'm doing my best because I really am. "I *needed* her to be safe before I could turn this place upside down."

Grabbing my hand, Grace links our fingers, silently telling me she understands. I know she doesn't agree with the way I went about things—*I don't either*—but knowing your mate is in danger messes with your head.

With a determined nod, Grace snatches the notepad from my desk and starts writing something aggressively.

Pushing off the chair, Seiji picks up a map before sweeping everything off the table.

"I've always wanted to do that."

Oh, no problem, Seiji. Live your dreams.

It's not like it took me *days* to sort those out.

"We need a plan." Hopping on the table, Seiji lays out the map and stares at it intently as if the piece of paper will give him all the answers he needs.

Hazel moves closer to examine the locations that Grace is marking on the map.

"I might have an idea." Grace mumbles, slightly distracted by whatever is running through her head. Fates, I've never been more grateful for her.

The need to have my sweetheart back is clouding my mind, and the guilt of hurting her is killing me so much that I can't even form proper sentences, let alone an elaborate plan.

"Of course, you do." Harvey boasts, but a sharp glare from his mate shuts him up.

"None of you are forgiven. I'm only doing this for my sister and nephew."

I have a lot of people to make things right with and not a lot of time.

Fates have mercy on me.

39. Conquer above all

Anxo

Sending a frustrated groan heavenward, I force my legs to keep moving.

My lack of sleep in the past two weeks is rearing its ugly head these days. Not having my sweetheart to hold in the dark of night has taken a significant toll on my health. The purple bags under my eyes are proof of that.

With every passing day, all my thoughts revolve around Nevaeh. Our memories together keep playing on repeat like a broken record, and each time, my pain returns with a vengeance when I remember how lost and numb she looked that day.

Now, my life is a never-ending cycle of loving her more than life but having to live it without her. The emptiness in my soul yearns to be with her. and my Divine keeps clawing at my insides because it's my fault she's not here.

After Grace forged a plan, I had to stand in front of the entire kingdom and announce that the Princess of Death was now a rouge. I had to publicly deny her right, her fate, and her connection to me.

The news caused an uproar. I watched angry, disappointed faces demanding me to take my decision back, and as happy as I was by the uproar, I didn't miss the ripple of excitement that buzzed through the crowd.

Standing on that stage, I watched the traitors try to hide their glee. They silently relished the fact that Nevaeh didn't have the kingdom's protection anymore. Those reactions solidified my will to continue the charade, and when Grace asked if I was ready for the final step, I didn't hesitate to pull the trigger.

Horseman Nakaya, Harvey, and I performed a discreet ritual that altered the original enchantment of all portals and barriers surrounding the realm. The ritual was to stop anyone with harmful intentions for the Horsemen from entering or leaving the realm.

We knew our plan went against every oath we'd taken, but it was necessary to protect the kingdom and our families from ones poisoned with treachery.

Exactly two nights after the declaration of my mate's departure, hundreds of soldiers marched to the portal in the middle of the night.

They were carrying enough weapons and manpower to destroy an entire realm, not just a princess. As much as that picture enraged me, I didn't overlook the lengths they were willing to go to cause a single scratch on my mate's beautiful body.

The Princess of Death has always lived up to her title.

Our ruse worked smoother than I could've imagined, so when the first line of warriors tried to cross, the power rippling from the altered portals reduced them to ashes.

Once the traitors realized they'd been lured into a trap, they tried to run back, but a defensive wall of Tetrad kingdom's new army was waiting for them. Every single traitor was captured and led to the dungeons where they would stay until their punishment was decided.

For the first time in Horsemen history, the loyalists and elders came to a unanimous decision. No formal proceeding or public execution. Death was the elected punishment for anyone found guilty of treason. Even the families of those warriors turned their backs on them.

Hazel helped Khatri with the interrogations and learned about all the mythic nations who had pledged allegiance to the coven to destroy us. One visit to each kingdom and more than half of them turned on their tails and ran, leaving the coven to fend for itself.

It's remarkable what a single visit from an out-of-control siren can achieve.

I was in the process of making contingency plans for the families who had lost their breadwinners after what happened when Khatri suddenly linked me and requested my immediate presence. His anxious tone had me pushing off my chair and rushing towards the dungeons at the ass crack of dawn.

Warriorhead Khatri has been of immense help in the past two weeks. Even when he has two kids and a mate to tend to, the man hasn't once complained about the extra workload.

Stepping out of the shadows, I find the man pacing back and forth with a subtle limp. The tense vibe circling him tells me that whatever he has found will result in another sleepless night for me.

"Why are you limping?"

"Apologies Horseman, I know it's early, but I figured you'd want me to inform you immediately."

Being deflective at five in the morning should be a crime.

"The leg Khatri... I asked you why you're limping."

When the man simply motions for me to follow him, I huff and walk behind him. Passing the dungeon gate, I nod at the warriors keeping guard before the door shuts behind me. The only sounds I hear now are prisoners complaining and crying.

Being surrounded by people who betrayed me has me sending out pleas to Fates that I can leave without my hands dripping with blood. Hazel needs to speed up punishing them before I lose my patience and do it myself.

Turning the corner, Khatri steps aside so I can see who he has shoved into our worst cell. Whoever it is, I can tell they've managed to piss him off, which is a hardship in itself because Khatri is always so *zen*.

A disbelieving grunt escapes me when I take two figures uncomfortably sitting on the long concrete bench in the middle of the cell. The sound snaps them out of their pity, and they immediately stand to dust their outrageously expensive clothes.

"You ungrateful child." Anger rising in her eyes, she steps closer to the bars. "How dare you let these guards treat us like lowly delinquents. I am the Queen on Conquer for Fate's sake. Get me out of this filthy cage, this instance, Anxo."

The audacity is *astonishing*.

My parents are in a dungeon cell. A cell allotted explicitly to traitors who intended harm to the kingdom and my mate, yet they think they can order me around.

The mysterious puppeteers are finally within reach. The ones who tipped off our enemies about our locations. The reason why every traitor babbles about being loyal to the ring, even when they were planning to assassinate my mate.

"Captured them a mile south of the cabin Princess is staying at. You can thank Grace for the *gem of elixir* she gave me before we left. It lowered his shield of fabricated reality long enough to give us a fair shot."

Now I know where that limp came from.

My mother meets my stare without a hint of guilt or shame, and I have to bite my tongue before I say something that will stop her from giving me the answers I desperately want. But I can't swallow the scoff filled with disgust for them.

It didn't take me long to accept their betrayal because when it comes to my parents, I always expect to be disappointed.

"Get us out of here, son. Immediately." My father orders me. On what ground, I have no idea.

Son. That word pinches at my nerves. Shaking free of their past betrayals, I remind myself I'm not here as their son. That boy died a long time ago; they made sure of it. Standing in front of the two traitors responsible for my family's pain, all I want before I order their well-deserved punishment is to know the reason behind their heinous deception.

Looking into the eyes of the two people who I refuse to consider family any longer, I ask, "Why?"

Kiara has the audacity to look bewildered. Like she has no idea what I'm asking.

"Your faithful followers failed. Time and time again, yet

you never stopped trying. Why is hurting my mate so important that you are willing to cross every line, sacrifice every moral?"

"What are you talking about, son... I would never—"

I cut off my father before he could spit out any more nonsense. "Lie, and I'll leave you here to rot for eternity."

Snarling, my mother leaves her husband behind to walk to the enchanted bars, but sure not to touch them.

Kiara Alarie. Always the one in charge.

I hate that I get that from her. The need to always be a step ahead, to make sure I'm capable of anything and everything if need be. The only difference between us is that while every awful thing I've done was for my family and my people, she plays with lives and ruins people for sport. She serves no one but herself.

My father—*Luke*—grabs his mate to pull her back. I'm afraid he will convince Kiara to keep her wits when Khatri decides to goad her.

"I think there's a misunderstanding Horseman. I don't think they did it. Think about it for a minute, what are the chances a retired Horseman and a has-been Queen would willingly go against the *Princess of Death*?"

Luke's head snaps to his mate whose eyes are burning with rage as Khatri keeps on adding adjectives to subtly insult them.

"I mean look at her, she's clearly not smart enough for a coup or stupid enough to go after Nevaeh, right?"

"I'm not smart enough? I've been picking up the slack of all those useless devotees, and you think I'm not smart enough?" Pointing at Khatri, Kiara finally loses grip on her anger.

Pacing back and forth, she pulls on her hair in frustration. Luke tries to hold back his mate but she has started mumbling, a sign that she's not in control of her emotions anymore.

"I've been planning for years... *years!* And that girl ruined everything." Kiara stabs at my heart with her finger, the green eyes I inherited from her filled with manic rage. "You have no idea how difficult it was to sneak that witch past Dean's defenses the first time."

No. There's no way *my mother* did that. She wouldn't.

I was expecting her to be cruel, hurl loathing curses at me and my mate, but in her incensed madness, Kiara has revealed her biggest sin.

My veins turn to ice and I freeze in place, just like my father, who fails to stop his mate from saying too much.

"I found the perfect place, the precise time when I knew Dean would be preoccupied. Everything was going according to plan, but that incompetent bitch do? She just let those two stroll out of her so called impenetrable dungeon. Visha ruined *years* of plotting and still had the gall to ask for my help."

She was the one.

The one who caused my mate and brother to suffer in that dungeon for a decade. She kept them away from their families in a place where they were beaten to the inch of death for years. She caused that. My own mother. A woman so heartless she didn't hesitate before sending two *kids* to their deaths, and for what?

From the corner of my eye, I see Khatri tense before he lunges at the cell, and I barely stop him from ripping apart the bars and burning himself to ashes.

My body fills with dread, and one thought keeps running in my head over and over again. How will I ever face Nevaeh knowing my mother is the cause of her every nightmare?

"Why?" My voice is void of any emotion.

Whatever little love I had for them, whatever respect I couldn't shake because, in the end, they were my parents, evaporated into thin air with her confession.

The nights I stayed up with my mate when her nightmares wouldn't let her sleep, or the times August couldn't tolerate being away from me because he was terrified of being hunted down started playing in my head on a loop.

I breathe through the pain when I remember the night Harvey broke down in front of me after finding out about his parents. I remember promising Dean that I'd get his daughter back before he died of heartbreak.

She did that. They did all that.

Their choices have been haunting my family for years. To think they did these horrible things and planned these elaborate schemes to hurt their oath family disgusts me.

"How. Could. You?" I seethe.

"Because it was supposed to be ours! It was our idea to combine the kingdoms! The Tetrad kingdom was *my baby*, and they took it! It wasn't supposed to be four dynasties pretending to be one in front of the world. I wanted all four of the kingdoms ruled by one. *Conquer above all.*"

My sperm donor exclaims as if anything he said would ever justify his actions. The way he thinks of his kingdom as *his baby* grates on my nerves. I'm a testament to how he treated his *actual* baby.

"You didn't even want the throne. You forced a teenager to take over your responsibilities because you were too busy roaming around the world," Khatri growls from beside me.

For the first time, I regret that they weren't around much. Maybe then I would've seen their true colors sooner.

The woman I am ashamed to call my mother chuckles manically, "That's where you're wrong. We were busy destroying the other Horsemen one by one. Once they were all out of the way, we were ready to take what was rightfully ours."

I'm speechless by her logic. They are admitting to doing everything a leader takes an oath *not* to do.

"Oh, don't look so glum, son, you can have it all after us. The Tetrad kingdom is yours... At least it was before you walked in with that abomination and called her your mate."

I can't control it anymore. I throw my head back and start laughing my head off. Khatri has to keep me steady with his arm around my shoulder when I'm about to fall to my knees because I'm laughing that hard.

After weeks of nothing but stress and grief, a burst of genuine amusement fills me because everything they just said is... *absolutely stupid.*

Their logic is flawed, their intentions are malicious, and their so-called hard work to destroy their kingdom is revolting.

Sobering up, I'm in utter disbelief to see they are still waiting for me to get them out of the cell. After what was just revealed they deserve to rot in here.

"You ruined my kingdom from within, but I have faith in myself that I can mend it again. You were treacherous to the throne, but I can try to be lenient and order a quick death as a thank you for birthing me." With every word out of my mouth, I watch their hope shred to pieces. "*But you hurt my mate.* You destroyed her childhood. You're the reason for her nightmares."

I tuck my hands in my pockets when I'm triggered to use them and take a step back. "I will never forgive you for what you did to my family."

Turning to the new sets of footsteps, I watch Harvey and Hazel stomp toward the cell with anger and disgust rolling off of them. "I can't touch you. I don't want that weighing on my conscience, but I know some people who will happily take turns."

Every prisoner in the dungeon goes still. Shocked their previous leader and his Queen are about to be treated exactly like traitors should be.

When the soul twins enter the cell, I turn my back on my parents and don't look back. "Keep them alive. There's a father desperate for revenge and we won't deny him his right."

Walking away from the dungeon, I feel the weight of my responsibilities slowly slide off my shoulders. Yes, it took us more time to flush out the silent enemies than I expected, but in the end, the kingdom is once again a safe home for my mate and kid.

Now, I can finally go and beg her for forgiveness.

By the time I reach the Horseman castle, warm rays of sunshine are peaking through the blanket of dark clouds that had swallowed the realm whole since the day my mate left. It's as if every part of this realm was trying to complain about

Nevaeh not being here in their own way.

I'm rearranging my office while thinking of ways to make it up to my mate when the door bangs open. I'm getting tired of patching the dents on my wall because my family doesn't understand the concept of knocking—or how to open a door like a normal person.

"Okay, I have good news and bad news, which one do you want first." Hazel slumps in the chair before my desk, brushing her wet hair behind her shoulders.

I can see she came straight here after cleaning the blood on her that belonged to my folks.

Stop. Don't dwell on that, Anxo.

I collapse in my chair too, drained from yet another night of work with no rest. "Good news, please. I want to hear at least one thing is going according to plan."

"Your folks will need more than plastic surgery to fix their faces."

Who's going to tell her the difference between good news and good news *for her*?

"Now the bad news: the warriors posted on the portal that leads to the dragon realm caught a warlock trying to pass through. The fact that he didn't turn to ash on entry doesn't raise much of an alarm, but it's an issue anyway. He's sitting in Khatri's office as we speak."

Groaning, I throw my head back and curse my luck. It's Okay. My grand apology will have to wait another day.

Forgive me for wasting another day, sweetheart.

Before I can stand, Harvey pushes me back into my chair. When did he walk in, and how did I not notice him walk behind me? I'm losing my marbles.

"Sit your ass back down." Hazel is suddenly inches from my face. "The only place you're going is to apologize and beg that glittery mini reaper to come back. The next time I see your stupid face, and you're alone, I will carve your skin and wear it like a jacket, Anxo."

I gulp audibly and swallow my protests, at the sight of the

menacing gleam in her eyes.

I have so many unstable people in my family that I can start a psych ward.

"We can handle whatever the witch is here for."

"Technically, he's a warlock—" Grace walks in, and quickly shuts up when Hazel shifts her glare to her, "but let's call him a witch."

Hazel takes over ordering and making plans on my behalf since I'm dead on my feet and way too emotionally compromised to worry about little details.

I feel unbelievably foolish for not involving them in my chaos sooner. Maybe I could've avoided some of the hurt I put on my sweetheart.

"Not happening. I'm not going anywhere with him," Grace shakes her head profusely.

"Darling—"

Stuffing her fingers in her ears, Grace stomps out of the room. She was kind enough to forgive Hazel and me, but Harvey is a different story. She allowed him back inside their room last week, but the poor guy was still sleeping on the couch.

I think Grace is more terrified of losing her sister than angry at what we did, and letting Harvey comfort her right now would mean losing the anger and anxiety that's been keeping her from completely falling apart.

Before I can apologize for the hundredth time, Harvey stops me. "Not your fault, brother. It was my decision; hence, I deserve the consequences. Stop worrying about us, and just get our two troublemakers back. Anyway, I have a brilliant plan to melt Grace. I will be more than forgiven before you're back."

Seiji snorts at the confidence, "Yeah, right. Do tell brother, what's this brilliant plan of yours?"

"Books."

"Books? That's your plan? To give her a damn book? Fates, men are useless."

"Not *a* book. I'm not that stupid. *Books.* Like an entire

library. I'm building Grace the biggest library in all realms and getting first editions of all her favorite ones."

Like Nevaeh would say: *holy fucking shitballs.*

Harvey smirks to himself, seeing the stunned looks on our faces before sauntering out to finish his apology mission.

Shaking off my nerves, I stride to the door myself to plan my perfect apology, but before I can cross the threshold, my feet freeze in place. When I look over my shoulder, Seiji is already watching me expectantly, his arms crossed as if he knew I wouldn't leave just yet.

"I just—what if she doesn't want to come back? What if I ruined us beyond repair?" Saying it out loud makes the dread in my stomach crawl to my throat.

I deserve this after the hurt I've caused, even if the reason behind it was their safety. I know Nevaeh will understand, but that doesn't mean it will lessen the pain she went through because of me. Any punishment she decides will be worth it, as long as I get a second chance.

"Oh, she'll come back. Just explain everything. *Thoroughly.* I bet the paranoia princess thinks you made her leave because you don't love her anymore, so make sure she knows you do."

I don't think I've ever heard Hazel give advice.

And good advice? That's new.

Before I can comment on the rarity, Hazel continues, "And don't forget to mention it was a once-in-lifetime stupidity thing."

More good advice with a sprinkle of insult? I should probably take her to a healer.

"Before I go, I... uh, I just want to thank you guys... for not giving up on me."

"That's what families do. We stick together." Seiji smiles at me and I realize how much I missed having him around.

"No matter the fuckups," Hazel adds.

40. Truth doesn't change the way it hurts

Anxo

This apology better be the best anyone has ever seen, or I might just lose the love of my life. Begging for forgiveness with an empty hand is a rookie mistake I'm not making.

As soon as I cross into the human realm, I make a beeline to McDonald's and order everything my mate and son like on the menu. With bags full of hot junk food in the passenger seat, my next stop is the grocery store that's an hour away from the cabin.

I'm not even slightly ashamed for leaving the store with two large bags filled with enough sugar and spice to last my little family weeks. It still feels too little for the size of apology I'm hoping for, so I make yet another pit stop at a charming flower shop and find a bouquet that screams 'I'm an airhead, please take me back'.

I spend around three hours running around the human realm, buying everything I know my mate likes. By the time I drop the last bag in the trunk of my car, it's filled to the brim, just like the backseat *and* the passenger seat.

Maybe I went just a little overboard.

I wish I could buy some courage on my way too because now I'm standing in front of her door with arms overflowing with apology gifts, yet I can't seem to knock.

I'm sure Nevaeh knows I'm here, but how the door hasn't been thrown open by my excited mate makes me want to jump off a cliff. I know I'm responsible for my own misery, but her dismissal doesn't hurt any less.

Taking a deep breath that I almost choke on due to the dozens of scents overloading my senses, I prepare to face the consequences.

With a mental promise that I won't leave without earning my apology, I wrestle with the bags coming up to my shoulders and knock—with my head since my hands are full. The door doesn't open, and the possibility of me dropping her precious fries and ruining them starts to make me panic. That will be her final straw.

Nobody messes with Nevaeh's junk food and lives.

When the door slowly creaks open, I sigh in relief. The little crack is barely enough for August to peek his little head through and the moment he sees me, those big blue eyes widen in surprise.

I wait for the excitement to come, but instead, August forces his face to show indifference and goes to shut the door in my face. *Ouch.*

Thanking Fates for my quick reflexes, I wedge my foot between the door right before August can lock me out without giving me a chance to apologize.

The little guy is *pissed.*

My kiddo huffs when I refuse to leave. Folding his arms over his chest, he tries to look intimidating so I won't dare cross the threshold.

Boy, I really messed up.

Fumbling with the bags, I drop to my knees but make sure I'm far enough from the door so August knows I won't come in until he allows me. Wholeheartedly.

"I get it. You're angry and disappointed and you have every right to be." I wince when August's glare doesn't let up. Hazel really outdid herself teaching him this.

"I hurt you, and I hurt Nevaeh. I promised to protect you from the world, but I failed kiddo—" I stop when he sniffs the air before pointing to the bag with nuggets.

Quickly handing over the bag, I stomp the urge to scream in joy when August loses the stink eye.

"I couldn't protect you both *and* fight the bad guys at the same time, so I had to send you away. I'm so sorry, monkey. But now the bad guys are gone and we can go back. I'm here to take you home."

August takes his sweet time picking apart my words for any traces of lies, all while stuffing his face with nuggets. Oh, how I missed watching him devour food like we don't feed the hungry little beast.

I look him over from head to toe, slightly relaxing when I don't see any physical signs of hurt. I'm grateful that Nevaeh took such good care of him, but as proud as I am of her, my insides twist in guilt for leaving her to do it all by herself.

"Home, Papa?" August asks curiously, and I don't miss how his eyes light up at the idea.

He called me Papa. That means progress, right?

"Yes. I just have to apologize to Mama and make it all better and then we can go." As soon as the words leave my mouth, his shoulders slump.

Oh boy... don't tell me he thinks it's impossible.

"Hey, have some faith in me, buddy." I separate the bags with his things before handing them over. August eagerly grabs at them, barely paying me attention over his favorite snacks. "Now go play while I beg for forgiveness. And learn from my mistake, never hurt the women you love."

When he leans in for a kiss, I don't hesitate to smack a big one on his forehead. My heart melts listening to him giggle as he skips inside the house.

August left his post at the door, and I was quick to take advantage and rush inside. The click of the door behind me sounds miles away when my sore eyes finally settle on her figure in the kitchen.

Seeing her after two torturous weeks, I expected my heart to mend at the sight, instead, what I see breaks it further. Nevaeh looks dead on her feet. Her cheeks are flushed and sunken, making her cheekbones sharper. She looks thinner, reminding me of the night I found her in those woods. Alone, injured, and barely holding on to life.

The hair falling down her back is still wet from the shower, dangling in a knotted mess. I know how much Nevaeh hates brushing through her wavy mess and always waits for me to do it for her. I will braid her hair and tackle those waves every day of my life if she agrees to give my stupid self another chance.

Just one more chance, baby.

My feet move toward her involuntarily, but I halt my approach as soon as her sharp eyes fix on me. Taking in my untidy and unkempt appearance, her brows furrow, seeing firsthand how our time apart has *ruined* me.

Nevaeh steals a quick glance at the bags of snacks and flowers in my hand. Her eyes start to soften slightly but before I can think my small effort might be able to sway her anger a little, she blinks twice as if erasing the image from her mind and turns her back to me.

"I'll pack his bag. You can take him back in half an hour."

My heart cracks open at that. Of course, she doesn't want to come back after what I did. What else did I expect after I broke her heart for fate's sake.

"I'm here for both of you," I whisper, afraid of saying the wrong thing. The rest of my words get stuck in my throat when I'm close enough to see the deep purple shadows under her eyes.

Her sluggish movements and rigid posture remind me of how she was before she felt safe enough to relax around me. I loathe myself for hurting her to the point where she is willing to let August go for his safety but won't even think about coming back with me.

I'm a grade-A dumbass.

"I screwed up." Her hands dropped the bowl she was washing, the sound dulled under the weight of my sudden acceptance. "I know I royally screwed up and broke your trust. That day, I made you feel unwanted and discarded, as if you meant nothing to me. But I know you can feel my truth sweetheart. You have to know my entire existence craves you."

Dropping the bags and flowers on the sofa, I carefully place the fries on top of it all. Dropping them in the middle of my apology would only make her want to kick me out even more, and I can't afford that.

Nevaeh leans against the counter, and it's clear how hard it is for her to hear me out.

With every word, I take small steps and look for signs that she wants me to stop. "The night of August's birthday, it was so easy for you to sacrifice yourself for us, and it… it scared me."

Another step, another truth. "I've seen you hurt too many times and I've held you through your pain and it has only made me more terrified of losing you because I know if anything happened to you, I won't survive. My life means nothing without *you*."

My planned apology was down the drain the second I laid eyes on my beautiful girl. Now, my brain has stopped working entirely, and I'm leading with my heart. I hope I can prove how sorry I am and how much I want her back.

"Remember the nurse you never liked? And Mason? They were part of this massive coup along with several high-ranking warriors and elders. They wanted to k—they wanted you out of the way. I found out about it the night you got hurt."

Nevaeh looks directly at me for the first time since I arrived. The moment our eyes meet, I want nothing more than to trap her in my arms and beg her to come back until she forgives me.

When my sweetheart starts breathing fire, I realize I probably shouldn't have brought up Mason or the nurse. I can practically see all the ways she plans to *talk* to them.

Fates, I hope her fire won't get diverted at me.

"Hazel and I went back to the portal when you were sleeping, and it was clear someone had messed with it from inside the kingdom. I was running back to you when they forced us into that stupid council meeting, but once they started talking it all made sense. They were why we kept getting ambushed and blindsided. The reason why I almost— almost lost you."

I twist the rings on my fingers like she does when nervous.

If she forgives me today, I'll let her twist my fingers until they break if she wants.

"I just couldn't think straight. I was scared out of my mind thinking of all the ways I could lose you. I didn't know who to trust, or who to turn to. Dozens of warriors, some I trusted most were working against us, and I just... I couldn't breathe. I kept thinking you were surrounded by people who wanted to hurt you."

Her hand reaches out to comfort me but she retracts it at the last second, thinking better of it.

Ouch. Again.

Fates, I'll do anything to hold her hand again.

"So, when the council proposed sending you away, I jumped on the chance. Harvey and Hazel agreed too because that was the quickest way to get you somewhere safe. I know it was rash and cruel, but how could I ever forgive myself for selfishly keeping you beside me, in harm's direct way when—"

My tongue freezes right before I can come out and say the rest. My past, the people I'm related to, and what they did hold the power to break us.

What if she decides to end us? What if she decides she can't be with me because of what my parents did to her?

"M-my parents... they did this. Everything. Nevaeh... they were helping Visha. *Like they did nine years ago.*"

Her sharp inhale slashes at my heart. When she looks away from me to stare at the countertop, I'm waiting for her to kick me out. To yell. To hold me accountable for what my parents did, for not seeing it sooner.

I'm holding my breath until Nevaeh's pinkie brushes against mine before she reaches out to hold my hand.

The simple initiative boosts my confidence, and I step behind her. I give my sweetheart a chance to shove me away, but when she doesn't, I cautiously wrap my arms around her middle and pull her back into me.

"They're alive?"

I stop breathing altogether, at the rage floating in her

question but when Nevaeh looks over her shoulder to assure me, I realize it's not directed at me.

It's for *them*. She's not boxing me in the same category.

"Yes."

"Okay."

That's it?

The moment Nevaeh leans back into me, my vision blurs with tears. I don't dare move my arms from where they belong. "I'm so sorry for everything, baby. I'm sorry for all those stupid things I said that day, sweetheart. I swear it broke me just the same to hurt you like that," I croak.

Nuzzling her neck, I plant small kisses all over the slope of her neck before I miss the opportunity and relish the sensation of having her in my arms once again.

Fates missed her. I missed holding my sweetheart.

"You're infuriating me, Anxo." Her words sober me up quickly, and I wince at her rising temper.

I convince myself it's a good thing she's angry. It will be good for her to release some of this pent-up frustration. I'll gladly let her get it out of her system now than hold it against me for days, or fate forbid *months.*

"I don't want your apology. I don't want logical explanations or how you did it for me. Fates, you're such an asshole. At least have the decency to say more hurtful shit, so I can keep my anger going b-because... because I don't want to forgive you. Not yet."

My whole body stills. My arms tighten around her; I refuse to be apart any longer. I'm not leaving her.

Not today. Not ever.

"I'm good with my fury and heartbreak so you can take your stupid apology and fuck right off," Nevaeh seethes, and I hold her tighter when her voice breaks.

"I'm *so* sorry, baby. Please give me a chance. Just one more chance. And if I hurt you again, you can put me in a grinder. Chop me to pieces and dump my body in the ocean. Better yet, ruin my filing cabinet. That will *really* hurt me.

Whatever punishment you decide, I'll accept without a peep. Just please... please come back home to me."

Still wrapped around her, I kiss her neck every few seconds. I can never get enough of my sweetheart.

Nevaeh accidentally snorts but quickly slaps her forehead for ruining her passive front.

I'm glad my apology is somewhat working when slowly her snickers turn into sniffles, and before I know it, she is breaking down in my arms.

I can't even soothe her because hearing her cry makes my throat close up, and soon I'm crying with her. Nevaeh grips my arms around her waist when she feels me shaking behind her and my tears on her neck.

Fates we are a mess.

"I d-don't want to let you in, only for you to abandon me again. I get it okay? I get that you thought it was best to ensure our safety, but you could've talked to me instead of kicking me out like that. That was a dick move."

My sweet girl hiccups, trying to talk through her hurt. Her fears are more than justified, but she has to know if it wasn't for her safety, I wouldn't even let her go the bathroom by herself, let alone live in the middle of nowhere.

Holding her close, I kiss the tears off her face. Wiping her cheek on my sweater she wipes off my kisses, but it's useless because I keep adding more.

Judging by how hard she's trying to hold back her smile, I know my cheeky girl is doing it on purpose.

My sweetheart loves attention and kisses.

After making sure she's not crying anymore, I kiss her forehead and pick her up to sit her on the counter. With my hands on her thighs, I make space for myself to stand between her legs and pull her close. Massaging her hips, I can't stop thinking about fattening her up once again. I don't like how much lighter she feels now.

Nevaeh plays with the collar of my sweater, and the feel of her soft fingers skimming the skin on my neck makes it hard to focus.

"As much I would've loved to show the world the consequences of hurting my mate, we needed more than revenge, baby. Trust me, no one walked out unscathed, but I had to make sure every single traitor was dealt with before they did more harm to my family... *to my heart.*"

Nevaeh looks away, blushing, but the hurt in her eyes is unmistakable. Cupping her soft cheeks, I kiss her forehead, then her nose, and then pepper kisses all over her face until my beautiful mate is giggling and trying to pry her face from my greedy lips.

I've won battles against the world and myself to be where I am, and ironically, the only person I would kneel for is the one who makes me feel on top of the world. Nevaeh could ask for my last breath, and I would give it to her.

Without my sweetheart, I'm nothing. A planet discarded from its galaxy. A star collapsing on itself. A rock in space floating with no direction. She's what makes life worth living.

Holding her face, I say, "It was never your fault, Nevaeh." I press our bodies together, hating the slightest bit of space between us. "I was not protecting my people from you, sweetheart; I was protecting *you* from *us*. *We failed you.* I should've seen anyone's malicious intentions for you, so I never had to hurt you like I did."

Nevaeh ducks her head when her eyes brim with new tears. With my index finger under her chin, I make her look into my eyes when I apologize again for hurting the love of my life. "I'm truly sorry and deeply ashamed of every word that left my mouth that day. I hate myself for hurting you. Can you try to forgive me, sweetheart? Please? I don't expect it to be now, but maybe in a week? A month? I'll wait however—"

Nevaeh surprises me by leaning in and crashing her lips to mine. Her arms loop around my neck and her fingers grip my hair to bring me closer.

I freeze for a second before the surprise fades, and I kiss her back with every fiber of my being. I pour all my love into the kiss. My lips caress hers softly and passionately, letting her know how much I missed her.

When she pulls back, I follow her to keep us connected because, at this moment, I need her more than I need air. My refusal to let her breathe makes my sweetheart laugh into the kiss, and finally, seeing her smile after the hurt I imposed helps shed some weight off my heart.

Playing with my hair, Nevaeh whispers, "I thought you hated me."

I don't use my words to reassure her this time. Sucking her bottom lip into my mouth, I kiss the doubts out of her. "Still think I hate you?"

She shakes her, "No, but you're not forgiven yet. I have terms, Angel." My sweetheart says cheekily and I kiss the tip of her nose. It's funny she thinks I won't give her anything she asks. My mate just needs to call me her Angel, and I'll give her the world.

It crushed me when she called me 'Anxo' and 'Horsemen Conquer'. My will nearly shattered, and I wanted to scream *'Mission abort'* before picking her up and running to my room to lock us in.

"Accepted."

My eager acceptance makes my beautiful mate chuckle. I have no shame admitting I need this woman to survive. She's the source of my happiness, my lifeline, and I would choose death over a life without her.

"You have to hear them first, Angel."

"I will do anything to keep you safe and content by my side, sweetheart. Everything I have is yours."

The past weeks, I had almost convinced myself that she would never look at me with those soft eyes again. The way she smiles blurs my vision. I bury my face in her neck and wipe my eyes on her shoulder.

Nevaeh smiles brightly, taking my face in her cold hands before squishing my cheeks and listing her demands. As she goes on with her list, it makes me smile like a goof because they seem thoroughly rehearsed. My insides feel warm to see she had hope of us finding our way back one day.

"I need back rubs. Every. Night."

"That and so much more."

I'm not letting my woman go to sleep without her being 200% sure of how much I love her.

"Extra cuddles."

"Absolutely."

"No more pouting when I steal your clothes."

Like I have any issues with how adorable she looks in my clothes. I just like to tease her about it. I would never admit it, but I bought twenty more sweatshirts for myself just so she could steal them.

"Wouldn't dream of it."

I kiss her nose and wait for more. I can tell she is hesitant about this, but I see no reason for her to be.

"You can never leave no matter what happens or who we face. Promise me you'll never leave me again."

"Sweetheart, the last two weeks have been the worst time of my life. I can't imagine going through life without you ever again. If you don't believe me ask Seiji, he'll tell you in detail how miserable I was without you."

I tell her about how Seiji and Grace barged into my office and all but forced me to accept their help so I could focus on getting my woman back.

She laughs, enjoying the stories of how miserable I was, and shows me every bruise on her gorgeous body that she had to endure because of me acting like an idiot.

Nevaeh is talking animatedly, her hands flying in every direction, telling me how she lucked out by having a stocked kitchen and a secure house, and I nod along until she stops abruptly. "You! You did it, didn't you?"

Her outburst takes me back, and I immediately start counting everything I've done wrong in my life.

"This house! The precooked meals! You knew I suck at cooking and the... and the house in the middle of fucking nowhere—no threats—and the closet magically had soft new hoodies! You... *you sneaky bastard!*"

She jabs an accusing finger against my chest, right where my heart is. I'm not sure if she's angry or happy because her smile is confusing me, but when she bursts into tears, I officially panic.

Wiping her cheeks, I apologize over and over again. Falling into my chest, she sobs on my shoulder, breaking my heart with every hiccup.

I know I can't erase all her pain with a single apology, but I can keep reminding her how much I love her. Rubbing her back, I kiss her forehead until she calms down.

"I love you," my sweetheart croaks hoarsely.

I squeeze her in my arms, which makes her sigh in content. I love her little sighs when I try to mold our bodies together by squeezing the ever-loving crap out of her.

"I love you, sweetheart. It's time to kiss your lonely self goodbye because I'm not leaving your side, not even for a second from now on." Wiping the last of her tears, I cup the side of her face that isn't pressed against my shoulder.

"You are not coming inside the bathroom when I pee. That's weird, Angel"

I simply hum and let her believe that.

As much as I love her in my arms, I know she is tired, and judging by her fatigue she has barely slept in the last two weeks. We have a few hours before the plan is set in motion, so I carry my sweetheart to her room, where August is waiting for us to pull our crap together so he can finally go home.

With August snuggling to my right and Nevaeh almost climbing over me from the left, I rub her back and watch her slowly fall asleep while August catches me up to speed on his adventures.

Nevaeh was right. Our son is turning into a mini sass queen... just like her.

I can't believe my four-year-old called me out for being *rude* and *mean* to his mama. While Nevaeh let me off easy, August on the other hand, made me apologize in ten different ways and twenty different bribes.

It's a good thing I'm rich because my son has expensive taste.

We take a well-deserved nap for almost five hours when a sharp pinch in my head interrupts our little sleep fest. I groan in annoyance, having to separate from my babies, but I don't get to bash Harvey's head in for ruining my time with my family because he shuts the link immediately after asking me to return home.

I hate my responsibilities sometimes.

41. So suddenly we are okay with warlocks?

Nevaeh

I watch Khatri's wife huddle her two girls to the portal with my sleeping toddler in her arms.

Uncle Elijah, the King of Hell, is waiting on the other side to provide a temporary safe harbor for anyone not participating in the coming war.

Khatri's youngest, Aurora, gives me a big wave with one hand while her other is clutching August's foot. Her big sister, Skye is actively helping others and leading the crowd through the portal safely.

I don't want to jinx it, but I see myself working alongside the fiery teenager someday. Skye might be young, but she is a warrior through and through. Someone worthy to take over after her father as the next Warriorhead for death.

"Something on your mind, Princess?" Khatri comes up beside me, leaving Angel to communicate last-minute changes to our troops by himself.

"Just worried."

"About the war?"

I snort very unprincess-like. "No. That I can handle, but sending August away? It's tearing me on the inside."

Khatri pauses to send a reassuring look to his mate, before turning to me. "August has alpha blood running in his veins, a royal one at that. My wife and Aurora might be rouges by technicality, but their wolves have accepted your son as their alpha. And let me tell you something about wolves: they are very primitive. Enough to sacrifice themselves if it means protecting their alpha."

Nodding to myself, I let his words sink in. He's right. Between Uncle Elijah, Skye, and his mate August will be perfectly safe.

Angel didn't ask my opinion for the first time when he ordered Amelia, Khatri's mate, to take August with her. He refused to even entertain the idea of our little boy staying in the kingdom during the impending attack.

We had to rush back to the kingdom when Harvey linked Angel. I thought coming back to a place that made me feel like an intruder would be difficult, but with Angel's hand in mine and August in my arms, I was already home.

On the car ride to the Horsemen castle, Angel briefed me on how Hazel has been secretly feeding false information to the coven spies lingering outside our realm's boundary. According to her rumors, the Horsemen have never been more vulnerable.

While they were anticipating the attack soon, it was a surprise when Harvey found groups of primary troops trying to break through our barriers in the middle of the night. Regardless of the sudden timing, Angel assured me we were prepared.

More like *Grace* is prepared. According to Khatri, Angel has been more or less useless since I left.

Oh, how that made my heart flutter.

It's no news that the entire supernatural world is holding its breath and waiting to see how this war will change the power dynamic in our world.

I know the coven is hoping to come out victorious, but Visha has no idea how sick we are of her mind games and petty backstabbing strategies.

I can't wait to close her chapter for good.

After addressing the warriors and boosting their morale, Angel rushes me to the War castle. We have yet to armor up, and if his prediction is right, there's not much time before the coven will be knocking down our door.

I can't remember how many times I've dived straight into

action without worrying about anyone or anything, but now that I have so much to lose, the mere thought of something going wrong is *petrifying*.

My train of thought halts when Angel stops abruptly, making me crash into his back. Turning to me, he is quick to kiss me until I'm breathless.

"I can't have you distracted today, sweetheart. So, tell me what's bothering you. Lean on me, baby."

The way his eyes are flooding with so much love and concern melts my defenses, and before I know it, my verbal diarrhea is taking over.

"What if something goes wrong? What if everything goes wrong and I never see you again? What happens if we lose? What if Visha goes for August next? He's a kid, Angel; he can't fight. And if we all die, who will protect him? He doesn't have anyone else. What if—"

Soft lips press to mine, effectively cutting off my nervous rant. Wrapping my arms around his waist, I grip the back of his shirt to ground myself.

"Everything will be fine." Angel kisses me again when I open my mouth to object. "The coven will be defeated by dawn, August will be home by tomorrow night and we'll be hosting an enormous victory celebration soon after. Once we win this —*because we will*—you and I will start fresh. Our second chance at life will be spent loving each other every day, building our own home, and you, my gorgeous mate would give me a dozen babies to run behind and love on."

I laugh at the dozen kids. Maybe three or four, but that's it. No more.

"I want that too. All of it. But now that I have everything I ever wanted, I'm terrified of losing it all." Resting my forehead on his, I hope to steal some of his optimism.

"You won't. We're The Horsemen of the Apocalypse for Fate's sake, no one can defeat us. Now... I need you to summon that devil inside you and wreck everything. This kingdom is counting on your crazy today."

Angel chuckles, and I smile back automatically, watching his dimples pop out. Giving myself a moment to admire my pretty Angel, I take in the way his eyes crinkle at the ends when he smiles. *Gorgeous.*

His smile is my favorite thing about him. My heart skips when I'm the reason behind it, and my soul sighs in relief like making him happy is the sole purpose of my existence.

"There's that smile I live for. Now give me a kiss." Angel moves in for his kiss but misses when I throw my head back and laugh my heart out. Grabbing the back of my neck, he brings me back, his warm hand covering my entire side profile.

"Nevaeh!"

And once again, Seiji interrupts us at the precise moment things are about to get good. He's lucky I love him, or I would've killed him the fourth time he did this.

"I'm starting to think he does this on purpose," Angel mutters.

"It's Seiji. *Of course*, he does this on purpose."

As much as I want to swat him, the moment I see Seiji bouncing on his feet, waiting for me, I run straight into his awaiting arms. When we collide, he sighs in relief and his tears get the best of him.

"I'm gone for two weeks, and you turn into a teary marshmallow?"

"I missed you too." Seiji mumbles, squeezing me once more before tugging me to walk inside the castle.

"Hey, where's my hug?" Angel pouts.

"I had to tolerate your mopey ass for two weeks, and now you want a hug too?"

"I wasn't mopey," Angel grumbles under his breath, and Seiji snorts at the false claim.

Diverting us from the subject of him being miserable without me, Angel gets into Horsemen mode. As we walk, he takes inventory of what happened while he was away. "Noncombatants?"

"The last batch left for Hell ten minutes ago. Our best

warriors are guarding that portal." Seiji answers question after question with precise details.

Harvey, Grace, and Hazel are already stationed at our northern border, where most of our portals are since the plan is to contain the damage to that side. It's an advantage that every castle has a waterfall in the backyard because it's one less side to worry about.

"Heaven?"

"Didn't show up."

I have never seen a smugger smirk before. Angel is more than pleased that Heaven didn't take his warning lightly. It's not the first time Horsemen have directly challenged Heaven, but last time Papa was here, and just his name was enough to make them reconsider.

It doesn't escape me how different my mate is when it comes to his family compared to the kind of leader he is. Though compassionate and patient with our people, Angel has a reputation for not giving out second chances to those who threaten his kingdom.

I'm linking with Harvey to discuss the battle plan and where he wants me when Grace nudges into our link and *squeals* how she can't wait to see me.

I love my Honeybunch, but the woman has no clue what her high-pitched excitement does to our sensitive ears. Harvey has to find her on the field to shut her up with a kiss before our ears start bleeding.

"Horseman Nakaya?"

"Dad is handling the south side. War and Famine Warriorheads are guarding the western gates. Khatri volunteered to cover the east wings so we could focus on the front and—"

A shadow moves past me to reach Seiji, and on instinct, I grab and push the person against the wall before he can touch anyone. With my hand on his throat, the *warlock* chokes from the pressure.

A warlock in my home? *He must have a death wish.*

"Tell me one good reason I shouldn't snap your neck right this second."

"Nevaeh. *Don't*." In a blink, Seiji removes my grip and drags the warlock behind him.

"Hey idiot, you're supposed to step away from strange men of enemy species, not get closer!"

Ignoring me like I'm the one acting strange, Seiji stands like a wall between me and the man I'm trying to stab with my eyes. The warlock in question straightens up and tries to step in my direction before I stop him.

"Woah buddy, stay right there before I burn your brown ass to a crispy black."

Seiji shelters the man by stepping in front of him again, and my glare softens when it meets his cautious gaze. The warlock is just as tall, if not an inch taller than Seiji, so the cover is not practical but it's a statement nonetheless.

Gritting my teeth, I back down. As much as I hate how Seiji is protecting this warlock, I don't want to hurt him unintentionally.

"*That* is a warlock."

"*He* is Jackson."

I scoff, but Seiji continues, taking advantage of the fact that I'm not in attack mode anymore. "He came to warn us yesterday. Told us everything about the coven's battle strategy."

I can see how Seiji is choosing his words carefully. Ignoring the sting of him choosing a stranger over me is all I can do at the moment.

"That just proves he is treacherous to his own kind. So why the fuck should I trust him with my family?"

Jackson's jaw ticks. *Ah... so I've hit a nerve.*

The warlock steps away from Seiji's protection and boldly move of standing directly in front of me, away from the one person saving him from my wrath.

Okay, he gets a point for being brave.

"I was the one who teleported you back to your kingdom

the night Anisha attacked. I followed Anisha after the Queen blasted her with black magic but then lost her trail. I only found you again because of the explosion."

Excuse the fuck out of me.

Taking in my stunned expression, he glances back at his protector, who encourages him. Seiji is practically dancing in his head at how Jackson has managed to take me by surprise.

Seiji pleads, asking me to keep an open mind when all I want to do is to bash this man's head in. Less now that I know he helped us at a crucial moment, but he is still a warlock, and his one good deed doesn't change what I think of his kind.

"Then where were you all this time?" Angel asks, and I'm glad he is just as suspicious. I don't want to be the only bad guy here.

Trusting a witch? *Not happening in this life.*

"I was on my deathbed. The spell I used to teleport the four of you took a lot out of me. I only recently gained consciousness, and then followed the siren to a portal."

Ah fuck, now I have to give the guy more points for literally saving my family and risking his life. *Shit.*

Squinting at him, I smirk when a drop of sweat rolls down the side of his face. "Why are going against your kind?"

Jackson ducks his head in apparent shame, but I need to know he's not like the witch-bitches I grew up with.

"After what they did to you and all the others, why wouldn't I? And I'm not the only one who hates her ways, but no one cares about your opinion when you're nothing but a rule-following warrior under a tyrant."

I hate that I can sympathize with him for feeling oppressed due to lack of power. I know everything he is saying is true, but what makes me hesitate is that he is one of *them.*

The ones who destroyed me and my best friend. People who terrified my son enough to leave invisible scars on his little heart. Their hands might've only hurt the three of us directly, but they ruined so many lives in the chain effect of their actions.

I haven't seen my papa in years because of what *they* did. Harvey lost both his parents because of *them,* and August lost his parents, his pack, and his destined life because of *Visha.* Grace and Angel have mates who they will have to carry emotionally for the rest of their lives.

What happened might be in the past, but it altered the entire course of my life.

Do I have it in me to put my trust in the hands of someone related to those who hurt me? But then again, I didn't even think about holding what Kiara and Luke did against my mate.

I can tell Seiji sees that even when I'm grateful for Jackson's help and his newfound allegiance to the Horsemen, it's not enough to make me trust the warlock. Trusting him would go against my every instinct, and I need more than one favor to take that step.

"I have news. Big news," Seiji sputters.

When the pregnant pause becomes pregnant itself, I clear my throat and raise my brow at him to spit it out.

"Not the time to be dramatic, Princess."

Taking the warlock's hand in slow motion, Seiji *intertwines* their fingers and makes a show of *kissing* the back of Jackson's hand.

The blank expression on Jackson's face melts into a gentle smile, and I'm left there standing, gobsmacked.

The meaning behind the action makes me shaky. I turn to Angel and instantly feel better about being blindsided because he is just as bewildered.

Smiling bashfully, Seiji shrugs before uttering the word I know he has been dying to say.

"*Mate.*"

"Oh shit. Fuck. Mother—" Angel covers my mouth and waits until I'm done cursing every word I know.

Hopping in excitement, I jump on Seiji. "Why didn't you lead with that, you drama queen!" We laugh like two maniacs and jump in each other's arms, forgetting about our mates. "Fates, I'm so happy for you."

I've told these people to stop messing with my badass reputation time and time again, but the number of happy tears I've shed since I met them is embarrassingly high.

Angel clears his throat, and I know it's my sign to return to his side. Seiji starts tearing up, and Jackson immediately takes over, whispering in his ear until the waterfall stops. I all but melt in Angel's arms, watching them interact like they've known each other forever.

Smooth mocha skin, deep brown eyes, and a jaw that could cut me in half. Jackson surely complements Seiji on the outside. They make a damn fine couple.

Seiji reintroduces us in a different context, and this time, it's much more pleasant. I behave like a woman who *occasionally* swears and nothing like the crazy one who was cussing for ten minutes straight.

Before Seiji and Jackson leave us to take their respective positions at the front line, I watch with pride swelling in my chest, as Seiji puts on his face armor.

The mask is a deep black color, and the delicate patterns carved into it are filled with melted emerald stones. The armor covers half of his face from his hairline to his chin.

Throwing a final wink my way, Seiji is ready to leave but I call out Jackson's name at the last second. The warlock turns to regard me curiously, probably thinking I'm about to threaten his life again.

"Try not to die, okay? Us Horsemen don't take it well when our family is hurt."

With glassy eyes and an appreciative grin, he nods once before walking towards the battlegrounds, hand in hand with his mate.

Another name on my ever-growing list of family.

42. Showdown motherfuckers

Nevaeh

With a half-gold face armor carved and embedded in tiny gems, the Horsemen of Conquer, rustles through an old cabinet, after helping me strap my body armor.

Whipping out a small box, Angel wipes the dust on it before showing me what's inside. A choked gasp leaves my lips when I see what he is holding.

"Dean got it made not long before he left. I think it was a reminder for him to not lose hope."

In his hand is a face armor that looks like plain glass, but the instant Angel holds it to my face, the glass adheres to my right profile. My lips part in surprise when he turns me to a mirror and I watch the armor light up with hundreds of small, intricate, glimmering gold veins.

I've seen similar patterns on my Divine when it circles me —*like it has a life of its own*—but seeing them come alive makes a sense of belonging run through me. After years of fighting against my Divine, I finally feel what it's like to be one with it.

Diamond impatiently stomps his horseshoe when he sees me on the rooftop with my mate as if asking us to hurry the fuck up so he can join his brothers in battle.

Angel's pure white horse with majestic golden wings and accessories follows Diamond's call and spreads his wings wide to show us he's ready for some action.

From this high point, I see the exact moment the first invading force crosses our portals and descends into the battlefield. Our warriors are alert, anger of enemy feet on our sacred ground radiates off them and a similar need to show the world what the Tetrad kingdom is capable of fills me.

A loud clap of thunder makes my head jerk to the sky that's bleeding red for the first time. Heavy black clouds hide the twinkling stars behind them as if protecting them from the gruesome sight.

A roar of rage and the blur of someone slicing through Deviants catches my attention. Leaning against the railing, I watch his crimson face armor hiding the blood I know must be splashed on Harvey's face.

Standing in the middle of what once was a field filled with rare exotic flowers, Seiji lashes his whips on the ground before letting them fly across and dig into the flesh of anyone who dares to come near him.

I'm not surprised to find Jackson steadily levitating above his mate, protecting both Harvey and Seiji from dark spells thrown their way.

A loud screech from a were-dragon reminds me of the creatures hovering above us. I turn just in time to catch one tearing out a gargoyle's neck with his teeth before tossing the body to the ground.

With a loud command I didn't expect from my petite sister, I watch with pride as Grace commands her team of skilled archers to aim for the third portal opening just on their south.

A group of were-dragons are positioned atop every tower to assist the archers bring their targets down.

I remember calling Hazel *crazy* the first time I saw her in battle mode, but I'd like to add *batshit* to it as well.

A hoard of warlocks circles the siren, and like she is performing a dance routine not standing in the middle of a battlefield, Hazel moves gracefully enough that slicing our enemies looks like they are made of *butter,* not flesh and bones. What proves me right is the sinister smile playing on her lips. She is covered in blood and guts but smiling nonetheless.

Batshit. Crazy. Siren.

I have this unexplainable feeling that Papa would absolutely love her. He has a unique way of appreciating the crazy in other people.

I notice witches are heavily using Deviants in the first layer of confrontation. It's convenient since Deviants lack the moral compass or survival instincts to not run into the field like rabid dogs hungry for blood.

I was surprised when Angel told me how many empires and dynasties turned their backs on the witches to save their own asses after our siren visited them. Well, most of them because djinns, gargoyles, and—*not so surprisingly*—werewolves were stupid enough to bet on the wrong side.

I had expected Visha to realize the barriers around the kingdom were purposely lowered to let them pass through, but maybe I've been giving her a little too much credit this entire time.

Sheathing a sword behind my back, I'm buzzing with excitement when the last of Visha's soldiers crossover because it's time for the actual game to begin.

The enchanted shield surrounding the kingdom is abruptly raised, turning the portal gates untouchable. The sudden change causes a wave of panic and dread to crash into our enemies.

Now their only way out is by *death*.

I watch my worst nightmares unfold into an opportunity served on a silver platter. The scene before me reminds me of the days I felt so helpless that I couldn't do anything but watch as they tortured and killed all those prisoners.

This coven still holds power over me long after I've escaped their clutches, but after today, I refuse to carry the guilt of not being strong enough to help more people like me. People like Anisha. Like my little monkey.

"I get to avenge them all today," I whisper with my eyes on the bloodshed below me.

Sensing Angel behind me, I don't think before leaning against him. Pointing to the raging battlefield before me he says, "Everyone not on our side is yours to feast on. Stab them, slice them, shoot them, curse them. Tonight, you do whatever your precious heart desires."

Tugging me to Diamond, Angel helps me climb on. "This is your chance to avenge yourself, Harvey, and our son. Avenge every tear your father shed waiting for his daughter to come home, every lie they told to break your spirit, every drop of tear that mixed with your blood. Make them pay their dues, sweetheart."

Brushing off the tear that trickles down my cheek, Angel cups my face and pulls me down to kiss the half of my forehead that's not covered.

"You look so hot when you ask me to rage."

Dropping his head, Angel laughs and double-checks my armor seeing how Diamond is getting too impatient to stay in place. Squeezing my calf, Angel asks for my full attention. "If I see more than five bruises on you at the end of the night there will be punishment."

"Ohhh, daddy behavior."

"I adore your ability to be so innocent yet so filthy."

With a teasing wink that makes my insides tickle, Angel backs up. "Now go unleash Death."

With a loud neigh, my beautiful morbid horse cuts through air and his enemies. His mighty wings knock down multiple witches to the ground on his glide. A pale Death's horse with flames consuming his wings and legs steals everyone's attention, and Seiji takes excellent advantage of it.

The grass beneath our enemy's feet turns black before burning to ash. Creating a tornado, Seiji traps a group in an unforgiving rush of wind before extinguishing the tornado along with every last breath of oxygen. Hundreds of warlocks, witches, and gargoyles fall to the ground, coughing up blood as their lungs beg for air.

Harvey moves in next before they can predict him. The 6-foot-something man climbs his red horse, and in the blink of an eye, their size grows until the duo resembles a walking mountain. They crush every soul that falls, turning them into a thick red sauce with a white seasoning of bones.

Gross. But creative.

One thing about Horsemen is that we're invincible together. Challenging us is considered nothing short of suicidal because when we join forces, even the mightiest mythics tremble in fear.

We're the Horsemen of the apocalypse.

Our Divines are connecting on a level I've never experienced before. With our newfound proximity, I feel my power amplify until it's hard to breathe. The rush of power surging through me feels exhilarating yet equally terrifying.

To prevent myself from unleashing something beyond my control, I've always restricted my essence.

To avoid unleashing something beyond my control, I have always restricted my essence from reaching its full potential. Built invisible walls around my Divine, but now, with every slice of my sword, I feel it crumbling.

With every crack, the knot in my head tightens farther and farther until it snaps hard enough that my Divine explodes inside me. I can't hold back the grunt of pain that leaves my lips as I struggle to reign in my essence.

Diamond races to the middle of the field and throws me to the ground not-so-gently. I go to snap at my horse, but he thinks the moment I'm losing control of my power is perfect timing to drop me off in the middle of battle and take off. I push my palms against the ground to stand up, but my body is stuck.

This surge of untapped power running through my veins is what Visha has feared all these years. I can feel my Divine prepare to finally relinquish all control but I'm not sure I'm ready for it.

The ground shakes beneath me and I struggle to rise with the barren ground soaking my power, craving magic only I can offer. My head falls back, breathing through the burn in my lungs and an agony-filled roar leaves my lips.

I've been fighting for control my entire life, and this is the moment my Divine decides to give up. Should've known bad timing was my thing by now.

A crack under my foot makes my eyes snap open and I watch my essence shoot to the ground and disappear. Gold cracks spread through the field in a blink, and like the veins have a mind of their own, they snake over to my enemies and climb them until nothing but mangled bodies drop to the ground.

Wherever my Divine snakes, wounded warriors on my side heal before my eyes, ready to fight again. Warriors assumed dead now stand unscathed since the Angel of Death is Hell-bound. I.e., an ally. He gave his word to Anxo that he wouldn't record any souls we lost today.

Archangel Azrael, the first-generation Angel of Death, recently celebrated his grandson's coronation.

Elias Azrael, who I'm sure is looking up and enjoying the show, sitting beside the first son of Satan and the current King of Hell, *Elijah Lucifer*.

It should've been Lucifer's grandchild running Hell too, but unlike the rest of the supernatural world, it took our original King of Hell a few centuries to realize he wanted a mate by his side too. It was something he desired but didn't dare to ask until he was the only one immortal and unloved... and he couldn't take all the lovey-dovey couples around him anymore.

That epic love story is another reason Heaven has been extra pissy with Hell in the last few centuries. Let's just say I was the *second* person Hell stole from Heaven.

Since Diamond ran off on his own to headbutt and fry the enemies of his kingdom, I take off in the direction of my partner in crime. The sound of a sickeningly sweet whistle raises my amusement, and I let my Divine, wrapped in shimmering gold, crawl on the dark soil, engulfing everyone it touches.

Following the sharp whistle, I feel giddy because I know exactly what this particular tune does. Her whistle has dragged every witch, gargoyle, djinn, and werewolf within a twenty-foot radius to her. They don't even know that they are walking straight into a trap since their bodies have no control over their movements anymore.

Breaking through the circle around Hazel, I come face to face with my partner. Volunteering to cover the left side, I kneel and lay a palm flat on the ground. The puppets to the siren's hypnotic magic choke when entrancing gold veins wrap around their bodies, and spikes come out, digging into their skin.

I'm finishing my share when Hazel starts cackling like a madwoman. "You're living up to my nicknames, huh? *Glittering Death.* Oh, and those bags under your eyes? Nice touch. Really sells your unhinged act."

"Unhinged? *Me?* Someone get this woman a mirror!"

In between our banter, we lure and strike our next group in perfect rehearsed patterns.

With every Deviant Hazel and I cut in half, every werewolf Harvey tears apart with his bare hands, every gargoyle Angel and Grace pierce from the sky, and every djinn Seiji whips to purgatory, our enemies start reducing to nothing.

But I've had enough of fighting Visha's followers. All I want is to find the soulless monster responsible for this bloodshed, who continues to force her coven and so many others into facing the consequences of *her* sins.

Ever since I charged into the field, my eyes have been searching for Visha, so when I finally find her sitting on a levitating throne made from the corpses of my warriors, it's clear why I didn't see her before.

Visha smirks, struggling to move the mangled side of her face, and waves at me with her arm that's covered in burns. *The consequence of excessive dark magic.*

When I first saw her, it wasn't as bad, and I thought a dark witch like her would know her limits, but as the years went by, I took pleasure in watching her lose herself and relished the way it destroyed her body.

Visha growls at her warriors to do better, to fight on her behalf as she continues to just sit there, causing so much pain. I witness her soldiers sacrifice themselves while she maintains her haven, and disgust rolls off me in waves.

The image of an 11-year-old girl scrubbing her throne makes me blink rapidly to get rid of it but I fail.

I remember accidentally dropping the filthy cloth, and Visha broke my arm in half by stomping on it with all her might as my punishment. I remember the way she looked down on that vulnerable little girl and treated her worse than the dirt under her shoes.

Visha was gifted with clairvoyance yet she failed to see the real monster was living inside her all along. She only used her gift, power, and position to cause harm.

Visha called me her doom and I guess she was right.

"Go get her."

Hazel snaps me out of my head and whistles to beckon my horse. She understands the burning need for revenge crawling inside my veins, and steps in to help.

After what *he* put her through, Hazel deserves a good payback story too, and I vow to make sure she's the one to drive her dagger through his heart. She deserves to be the last face he sees right before he loses his pathetic life.

Walking backward, I promise her through our link that one day it will be her turn, and I will hold down an entire army so she gets her revenge. Hazel, as always, simply shakes her head and reminds me to keep my bloodlust in check.

Catching a glimpse of Diamond as he runs towards me, I grab his fur and climb on his back in the middle of his stride. Diamond steps on air, and we take off to where Visha has created a makeshift throne for herself.

The moment she notices me fast approaching, Visha orders the four warlocks shielding her, and they don't hesitate before hurling balls of fire at me. *Rude.*

Diamond absorbs the attacks without flinching, and before I can start worrying about how much he can take, the two warlocks flinging fireballs at us fall to the ground like sacks of potatoes.

Whipping my head back just in time, I see Angel aim and

shoot another arrow wrapped in his essence at anyone who dares to come for me.

I can't help but think how poetic this is. Angel is the one who helped me glue the pages of my past together so I won't keep finding ways to rewrite the book of my life, and now he's here, helping me reach the final chapter so I can burn the damn book for good.

Blessing me with his sexy smirk, Angel yells at the top of his lungs when he could've just as easily used our link.

"No one messes with my wife!"

"Not. Your. Wife!" Everyone around him snaps in sync.

"What a bunch of jealous A-holes." Muttering in our link, Angel aims at the last warlock in my path but not before giving me a look that screams, 'I'm not going to tolerate not being married to you any longer'.

Tapping into our link, I tell him *soon* before focusing on Visha. My proximity heals the warriors she was using as her makeshift throne, and they fall to the ground, landing perfectly on their feet, and joining other warriors to watch me reach the finish line.

The last two warlocks try to flee when they see their death fast approaching, but two perfectly aimed arrows pierce through their hearts, and just like that the last of Visha's soldiers fall to the ground.

With no one left to fight on her behalf, Visha conjures her darkness. It's weak but I can see she's not ready to give up. Dark magic seeps out of her pours, leaking in the air.

Collecting her unbridled magic in her palms, Visha throws it in my direction. I turn Diamond away just in time to make sure I'm the only target for Visha's last attempt at survival.

My chest burns from the harsh impact. I feel the magic digging into my bones before my Divine takes over. Inch by inch my essence breaks down the darkness inside me, turning it into something I can feed on. With every blow Visha throws, I grow stronger with the dark magic and my Divine working together.

With every blow, Visha steps back and her hands start trembling. She knows this is her own fault. She made me this. She taught my Divine to be friends with the darkness inside me.

When her eyes grow wide, I follow Visha's gaze and look down at my arms. Covered in gold veins, my skin is crawling with raw untamed magic begging to be released. When Visha sees her attacks are doing the exact opposite of what she intended, she takes off.

Now, she will experience what it feels like to have your powers snatched from you. What it feels to be helpless, to be at the mercy of someone who hates your existence.

Running through the clouds she dodges the arrows my mate aims her way to slow her down.

Patting Diamond, I say, "Time to hunt."

Diamond takes off after Visha, who is no match to his speed and within seconds I'm in front of her. My horse leaps forward and I grab Visha by her neck and lift her in the air. Like a caged animal, she does her absolute best to thrash around to make me lose my grip and fall to a quick and easy death.

After everything she did to me, all the innocent souls she burned alive, chopped to pieces, how naïve is she to think that I will let her die that easy?

"Please," Visha croaks pathetically. Ignoring her pleas, I pat Diamond who is agitated by her presence.

"Now you're begging?" I huff. Visha digs her nails in my arm but that pain is nothing compared to what I'm feeling in my heart.

"I begged too, didn't I? Spent hours by your feet, pleading, screaming for mercy, hoping that you'd show some sympathy but you never did. We were kids," I spit out. "*Kids.* And you whipped my best friend in front of me, sliced me open in front of him, and *never* showed mercy, so why should I?"

Visha grunts like she could care less, and the lack of remorse fills me with rage.

"You've reached your end, and I'm here to collect." A single tear rolls down my cheek, but that's all I'll allow. She's not worth more.

"You know something your precious visions didn't tell you, Visha?" I look her dead in the eyes and relax the pressure on her neck so she can feel the weight of my words. "I can take your Divine."

Visha stops struggling instantly, her limbs fall by her side in shock and horror-filled eyes look back at me.

The entire world stops beneath me, and a collective gasp of shock echoes in the now silent field. This isn't something I've shared with anyone other than my family, and the fact that the world will witness me do it will be controversial.

No matter how she interpreted them, Visha's visions were never wrong. Despite her best efforts to prevent those visions by killing me and the ones blessed by Fates, Visha forgot that no one can change what's already written in the books of Fate.

The vision she saw of me destroying her entire coven was always going to happen. If I didn't make it out of that dungeon, someone else would've been responsible for her fate, but in every universe, every dimension, every realm, her future ends with a pathetic death.

Visha, the once mighty queen, starts struggling harder when her thick brain finally processes my words, and she realizes a quick and easy death is not in her cards.

Her shock is justified since only The Almighty God or the King of Hell has the power to take away someone's Divine. Even Fates can only write magic in someone's life journal but can't erase it.

Our Divine is a large part of our identity, and it's considered the highest form of humiliation in the supernatural world to be stripped of your Divine because, essentially, it takes away your right to our world.

"Wait—stop. If you k-kill me, how will you s-save your family from *him*?"

My grip tightens on her neck, but I can't help but falter at the confidence. A coy smile appears on her lips when she sees

I'm baffled.

"Who?"

"A threat no m-man has ever faced, a power beyond your knowledge, and a... and a future you can't run from." Visha recites as if the words are carved into her memory.

A power beyond your knowledge?

"I can help you destroy him. Spare my life, and I will tell you e-everything about him. Everything that's about to come." I can hear the manipulation in her voice, and I'm amazed Visha is still fumbling to save her life when there's no chance of it ever happening.

I've seen this before. Visha has a knack for figuring out someone's deepest fear and using it for her benefit, but not this time. I've had enough of her manipulation.

Even if danger lurks around my family, we can deal with it just like we dealt with her. Let's see who has the power to stand against the literal causes of the final apocalypse.

"Your games don't work on me anymore."

With that, I close my eyes and take a deep breath, expanding my lungs as my Divine reaches out to push past her flesh. Her screams of agony are high-pitched, and they make me want to cover my ears, but I continue reaching inside her forcefully and pulling out her Divine, not even trying to be gentle about it.

When I open my eyes again, her entire body is covered in burns, strings of her glowing essence are pouring out of her, and disappearing where my palm is slowly squeezing the life out of her.

Her screams get louder once the last of her Divine is ripped from her. A witch losing her Divine is painful, but a human enduring torture designed for a supernatural being is like someone reaching inside your chest and pulling your heart out. Slowly.

My essence circles her like a predator, absorbing every bit of her Divine before eating away at her soul when I should be sending it to purgatory.

But I'm not a reaper yet; so the rules don't apply to me.

With one last squeeze, Visha slumps forward and I let her go. Hearing the loud thud and the crack of every bone in her body, I closed my eyes and finally let the tears fall past the relieved smile on my lips.

I'm finally free.

43. Purgatory has awful reception

Nevaeh

Taking Grace's hands in mine, I let my Divine brush over her skin and heal her superficial cuts.

Seiji circles me like my essence, enjoying his front-row seat to my eyes glowing gold, and my powers coming out to play. Jackson, on the other hand, is standing ramrod still with his lips parted.

With every passing second, Seiji shuffles closer. If I were to move my right arm even an inch, it would bump his nose. *Silly man.*

Once Honeybunch is all patched up, Seiji lightly shoves her out of the way and takes her place with his hands held out. The idiot is bouncing on his feet in excitement while I stare at him blankly.

He knows he doesn't need my help, right?

Angel snickers against my neck, holding me to his chest like I'm his comfort teddy bear. "You're already halfway healed, airhead. Don't bother my mate for silly scratches."

"Ugh, fine. Jackson, bring your juicy ass over here, pumpkin!"

Shaking my head, I chuckle as Seiji pulls his mate in front of him, who is clearly too shy to ask for help.

Even when Grace is now fully mated to Harvey, she is still essentially a human... with a longer lifespan and better health, but it takes her a tad bit longer to heal. Hence why I offered my services. And now that Jackson is also family, he deserves the same special treatment.

Once Seiji hits his quota of gushing over my essence, he complains how unfair it is that only the Horsemen of Death was given the 'badass smoke effect'.

Tuning out his whining like we always do, everyone gets to work on helping around the kingdom.

We succeeded in containing most of the battle to the northern side, so the damage shouldn't take more than a couple of days to fix, especially with the centaurs and their construction crew already drawing up plans and discussing a timeline.

I guess this is what happens when you go to war against a superior species. The wizards have less than a dozen covens left with castles as empty as a ghost town, while we'll be up and running in less than two days.

Seiji aids the earth fairies in ensuring the ground regains fertility. Every last drop of blood is pulled out of the soil, and a fresh batch of grass graces the empty, once barren land. By the time the morning sun peaks out, it's starting to look as if we never had a war to begin with.

I pass a group of kids dancing and cheering on my way to clean up. Their happiness and joy are contagious, and I'm glad we hid any signs of a brutal battle before the regular folks returned.

Removing what is left of my armor, I clean up in the War castle before we all go home to rest. I'll need my energy for when Uncle Elijah comes by to drop off my little monkey.

Despite Angel's thousand protests that Hazel needs rest too, she decides to stay back to talk to the second-in-commands and get a gist of how things went on their end. Leaving her stubborn ass, I drag Angel to the Horsemen castle because the siren might not need it, but I feel like I can sleep for three days straight.

My steps falter, and I gasp in horror at the awful sight. "They broke my favorite fountain. Angel look! Fuck, I loved that ugly piece of art. Ugh, I feel so orange!"

Sighing loud enough, I bet people on the other side of the kingdom heard, Angel tucks me into his side.

"*Red*. You're angry, so you feel red."

"But I hate orange, so I should feel orange, right?"

"Right... I'm sorry, sweetheart. My bad." He deadpans.

"It's okay, I still love you."

Lifting on my toes, I kiss his jaw before walking past the hideous fountain that's broken into a thousand tiny pieces. No one needs to know that I asked Khatri to *accidentally* target a certain showpiece.

Walking up the stairs, I can practically hear my comfy bed calling out to me. Daydreaming about cuddling my mate and falling asleep in his arms, I don't watch my step and crash into someone's back.

"Oh, for fuck's sake! Watch it, you mammoth of a man, don't you—" My words get stuck in my throat when I peek past Harvey and find a certain man standing in the middle of my living room.

"Looks like I'm a few hours late." The man sheepishly rubs the back of his neck and drops his bag on the floor with a thud. "In my defense, reception in *purgatory* is total shit."

Grace is the first to shake her shock and run to the man. He engulfs her in a tight hug without hesitation and laughs when Grace immediately starts sobbing. They embrace each other like they've been apart for ages.

"That was mighty irresponsible of you, Dad. Do you know how worried I was? And didn't I tell you to keep me updated? God, why are you always this reckless!" Hearing an earful from his daughter, the man apologizes and shushes a crying yet smiling Grace.

How this woman can feel this many emotions at once still baffles me.

Looking at him now, I notice the difference between the real man and the blurry images of him engraved in my head. He hasn't aged much in the last decade. With his Divine slowing his aging to half, he looks more twenty-six than thirty-seven. But there's no mistaking the maturity in his actions and features.

The light stubble is new. I don't like it.

It makes him look like a man who just crawled out of a place where shaving was not a priority, and I have this urge to ask him to go shave it off. The differences between what was in my head and my reality are so vast I can't help but panic.

What else have I been imagining wrong?

I curse Harvey in my head when he moves to stand beside Grace and leaves me exposed. *Dumbass.*

The laid-back man curiously regards my best friend, squinting his eyes before they widen comically. His wide evergreen eyes bounce to Grace, Harvey, and then Grace again, silently asking his daughter for a logical explanation as to why he is suddenly standing before his missing Horseman.

When Grace introduces her mate by his name, the older man completely goes off the hook. Both men try and miserably fail at holding back tears while engulfing each other in a bear hug.

What a bunch of crybabies.

I don't realize I've snorted out loud instead in the safety of my head until the man's soft eyes brimming with tears snap to me. *Shit. Fuck. Shit.*

Harvey backs up, shaking the man by his shoulders. Laughing with tears freely falling down his cheeks, Harvey nudges the man I've been aching to meet toward me.

Hearing a muffled cry next to me, I turn to find Seiji bawling his eyes out, hiding his face in Jackson's chest, who is also failing to keep his composure.

Okay, so suddenly, everyone is drowning in tears except me. Wait, Angel—*Yeah, no.*

My mate stands behind me, rubbing my shoulders and clearing his throat. This is stupid. I should be the one comforting him since he looks to be on the verge of an emotional breakdown.

When the big man with deep evergreen eyes and a ripped denim jacket starts in my direction, I step back on instinct. The way his face twists in raw hurt makes me regret that step instantly. My chest aches with every tear he wipes to regain some composure, but for some reason, I can't take that step forward.

The man braves another step forward, and that's when I realize I'm pressed up against Angel tightly.

I strain my neck to look behind me, and the minute Angel sees my panic, he turns me around in his arms and gestures something behind my back.

Closing my eyes tightly, I focus on the fact that I can't see him anymore. He doesn't even look the same for fucks sake. Why didn't I think of that before? Of course, he wouldn't look the same; it's been a decade!

Calm the fuck down, Nevaeh, you're crazy is peaking out.

Angel breaks my daze by kissing my forehead, "Hey, you're okay. Everything is okay. Just take a deep breath for me. Can you do that, sweetheart?" Nodding my head repeatedly, I focus on breathing until I don't feel like I'm standing on the edge of panic.

I feel a pressure in my head before Angel links me. *"You know him Nevaeh. No need to be cautious, I promise."*

I think I'm going to pass out.

What the fuck is happening to me? Where did this sudden rush of fear come from?

"He looks different."

"Time does that," Angel reassures me.

"Time changes how you feel too. What is he feels different about me now?"

"Why don't we ask the man how he feels before jumping to any conclusions, okay?"

Sorting my thoughts as much as possible, I grab Angel's collar and stand on my toes to whisper in his ear. His heart skips beneath my palm when he hears my first question. Holding my face, he kisses my forehead again before turning back to face everyone.

The man is clutching the back of a chair to restrain himself from instinctively approaching me, and I really appreciate it.

My stomach bottoms out before Angel even asks my

question. The absolute fear of the answer I'll get is making it impossible for me to unfreeze myself.

"Did you know we found Nevaeh?"

The man's face crumbles with hurt as if he is cursing himself for not knowing sooner. "No. I heard about the war, and that The Tetrad kingdom was involved, so I came to help." Rubbing the back of his neck, he admits, "But I forgot to ask the *when* part."

I snicker quietly behind Angel's shoulder, but the man hears me perfectly fine. His desperate eyes find me, lips quirking up the tiniest bit.

That's so like him. He came running to join a war but didn't ask what it was about, who was involved, or even when it was happening.

Angel purses his lips to hide his amusement, but my next whisper makes him stiffen and grab my hand, clutching the back of his shirt.

"Do you plan on leaving again?"

"Never," the tired man croaks immediately.

I breathe out a relieved sigh. I'm so damn tired of losing and rebuilding myself every time someone leaves. I don't care how selfish and cruel it might sound, but I have to protect myself. I don't want to lower my defenses for someone who's going to leave and never look back.

I never imagined my paranoia would hinder the first time I saw him again, but when your fears are louder than your own voice, there is no hiding from them.

I have lived with these fears for years, and now, as I watch them unfold, I want to crawl back into my head where it's safe. Where I won't have to hear him say he doesn't want me anymore.

What would he think of me if he knew everything I have done to survive? What if he's only here for Grace and his kingdom, and not for the long-lost daughter?

My worries, questions, and fears start to overwhelm me to the point I don't notice him running at me until I'm wrapped in a hug strong enough to crush my bones.

Papa. *My papa.*

The hug is tight to the point of suffocating. It's good that between Angel, Seiji, and Harvey, I'm used to being squished by giant men on a regular basis.

Papa wraps his arms around my shoulders and holds me protectively. I don't realize I'm holding him just as tight until my arms start to shake and my knees give out.

Sobbing like a child reuniting with their parents after getting lost in a crowd, I bury my face in his chest and let him support me while I empty a decade's worth of longing for my father's embrace.

I've spent countless nights filled to the brim with doubts that he abandoned me. I feared that he didn't want me enough to save me from those monsters. But here I am, in my father's arms, as he continues to thank the universe for bringing me back to him. I did most of the work, but sure, Papa, let's thank the *universe.*

"Heaven comes Hell, kiddo, no one's touching my family ever again," his voice is thick with emotions and his words hold a promise; one that will destroy realms before he lets it break.

Today, the final remnants of the voice that made me question everything disappear because now I know my papa didn't loathe me... he loved me. He didn't forget about me even when he forgot himself.

I reluctantly step away before this whole day turns into us just crying on each other's shoulders. Papa halfheartedly lets me go, but not before wiping my tears and softly kissing the top of my head.

"You need to stop crying *trouble.* You know if you start crying, I'll cry too, and I can't do that. I have a reputation to uphold."

With tears streaming down my face, I swipe under my nose and chuckle. "You can't call me trouble anymore. I'm a grown woman now. Very decent and docile."

The five members of my so-called family present gasp in sync, not even hesitating before they betray me.

"*Decent?* Stop lying, monkey." Harvey butts in.

Before I can smack my dumbass of a best friend, Seiji joins him, "And *docile?* Bitch, you made a grown man *pee...* by *staring* at him!"

For fucks sake! Couldn't they wait at least one day before telling Papa his daughter is a minor nightmare?

Traitors. All of them.

"I think she meant *deranged* and *dangerous.*" It's good that Angel is hugging me from behind and essentially holding me hostage because my derange is creeping out.

Winking at me subtly, papa mouths 'That's my girl' and gives me secret thumbs up.

Papa raises his brow in question when Angel kisses the side of my head and comes to stand beside me. I wait for a reaction but Papa maintains a blank stare.

"So... uh this is Angel—*Anxo Alarie.* Shit, you already know that. He's my mate..." I trail off, turning to look at my Angel before continuing, "And soon-to-be husband."

The smile that blossoms on my Angel's face is worth risking my entirety over. This isn't the first time I've called him my husband or husband-to-be, and every single time I do, I fall in love with him a little more by how pleased he looks by that title.

An obnoxious fake cough interrupts me admiring my mate, and I turn to find Papa squinting at Angel.

It's weird to see him show any kind of negative or angry emotion when I've always seen him cracking people up with his cheeky attitude.

Clearing his throat, Papa asks in a deep voice, that I'm guessing is meant to be threatening. At least for someone who hasn't known him for years. "So, you're the mate?"

"Yes, sir." Angel bites back a smile.

"And you know who I am, right?"

"Dean, I've known you—"

"I'm trying to threaten you, boy; go with it."

"Of course, sir. Continue."

It's hilarious watching Papa pretend to scare someone he clearly adores. Angel stays quiet and allows Papa to finish his 'You hurt my daughter, and I will use my scythe on you' speech.

These two are adorable.

"I will find myself another Conquer the day you make her cry... or get her pregnant."

"Wait, no—" Angel immediately let go of me to grab Papa by his shoulders. With desperation oozing from his voice, he shakes Papa, "Come on, man, I can't *not* have kids. And they'll be your grandkids..."

"Exactly why I don't want them. I'm barely thirty-seven, which means no grandpa bullshit." Turning to Grace, he repeats, "That goes for you too. *No babies.* None. Nada."

"Old man has lost his fucking mind."

A flying centerpiece hits Harvey straight in his chest. Bending forward, he curses Papa and *pledges* to have a kid in the coming year and to teach them to say 'grandpa' as their first word.

This idiot. That's exactly what Papa wants.

Ever since we were kids, he knew reverse psychology was the best way to get what he wanted out of Harvey and the hot-headed dumbass always fell for it.

Who's going to tell Papa, Harvey was already eager to jump the baby train.

Before Papa can fill Angel's head with more baby nonsense, a loud bang from behind startles me. Hazel strides in, tucking her dagger away and muttering about incompetent assholes under her breath.

Stopping to take in the scene before her, she grits out, "Oh, for Lucifer's sake, please don't tell me I walked straight into mushy stuff. Listen, it's been a long ass week, and if I have to stand around you babies tearing up, I'm going to lose my shit —" Hazel stops abruptly when her gaze finds Papa.

With confusion burning in her eyes, she turns to ask me, "Is he your…"

"Papa? Yeah, that's him." I can't stop the way I slightly bounce on my feet in excitement.

Sharp dark eyes turn to slits as the siren directs her glare at my father. "Oh, look who decided to show up. Care to enlighten us on what made you *finally* share your divine presence with us mere peasants Mr. Big Bad Grim Reaper?"

I wait for Papa to answer her, but he keeps grinning at Hazel like she isn't trying to stab him with her eyes.

And why is he smiling like an idiot?

Grace and I forgot our anger as soon as we saw Papa but Hazel is not afraid to tear him a new one even when she never met the man and wasn't personally affected by his absence. She saw how much his absence hurt us and that's enough for her to demand answers.

Suddenly Papa throws his head back and starts roaring in laughter. I watch with wide eyes as he loses his ever-loving shit and nearly falls to his knees because of how hard he is laughing.

"Oh, Heaven is going to love this," Papa murmurs with a mischievous look in his eyes and wipes the side of his eyes. "I see there are some new additions to the family." He smiles at Jackson before fixing his cheeky gaze on Hazel. "And aren't you a little hellfire… *mate.*"

Wait what?!

Papa slowly walks closer to a frozen Hazel, who's watching him eat the distance between them with a calculative look.

My mouth falls open when Papa allows his dark essence to seep out of him and circle Hazel eagerly. He watches in awe and chuckles when Hazel gasps when his Divine brushes the exposed skin of her arms.

I'm about to warn him about Hazel's no-touch rule when both their eyes flash black for a fleeting second before returning to normal.

"No. Fucking. Way." Hazel quietly exclaims, her eyes not straying from Papa, her mild excitement and nerves settling as the black essence floats back into Papa.

Hearing Hazel curse so casually, Papa's eyes practically start shooting hearts at her. I've never seen a couple who screams *'made for each other'* the way they do.

A loud, hysterical laughter breaks my focus from the uh... couple? to Seiji, who is rolling on the floor, dying of short breaths. "Of course, they are mates!"

Epilogue
Perfect ending or a new beginning?

Nevaeh

With a content sigh, I shuffle back to sit between Angel's legs, my back against his hard chest. Resting my head on his broad, naked shoulder, I breathe in the freshwater scent of the waterfall before me.

After weeks of endless meetings and piles of paperwork, Angel woke me up this morning with sweet kisses and told me today would be just about us.

It turns out that sunbathing on the roof of the Horsemen castle while enjoying the breathtaking waterfall before us was the perfect way to rekindle our romance.

Once the madness that unfolded in the supernatural world after the Tetrad kingdom defeated the Cresent coven settled, the King of Hell decided it was time to tighten his reins on all his creations. Within a week Uncle Lucifer established an elite force to monitor inter-species conflicts and help deescalate them.

And not even two days after we had finished rebuilding the kingdom, Elias Azrael, the Angel of Death came for a visit. As the elected head of *The Diablo Towers,* the supernatural peacekeeping force, he wanted us to know that the Horsemen almost making the witches extinct was not ideal.

He didn't exactly come to reprimand us, and let's be honest even if he did, it's not like they can say much when it comes to the Horsemen. We are not obligated to follow their rules, but Angel was happy to participate in any grand plans that Diablo Towers had to make our world safer and more harmonious.

Anxo assured the Archangel that the Tetrad kingdom

wasn't planning to wage any more wars and that world domination was not in our five-year plan. When he left, it was clear by his relief that Elias didn't want to prepare for doomsday a week into his new job.

I think it's safe to say my first year as a free citizen has been chaotic, to put it lightly. After rebuilding the kingdom and dealing with the repercussions of the war, it's good to feel this blissful calm with no lingering threats.

Beside me, Angel tips his head back, enjoying the sun shining on his beautiful skin and tanning it the perfect shade of gold.

My eyes follow the path of the small drops of water still clinging to him from when he stood below the waterfall. I watch them roll down his firm chest to the hard ridges of his stomach before disappearing down the V just above his swim shorts. The sight is so tempting I have to brace myself before I slide down his body and trace that V with my tongue.

When I can't take the distance anymore, I turn in his arms and slowly crawl between his legs until I'm straddling him. Angel's arms immediately trap me between them, urging me to settle in closer.

"Are you tired of me already?"

The warmth in Angel's eyes quickly melts into something dark, fueled by lust.

"You haven't kissed me in twelve whole minutes. I don't like how you're not obsessing over me." His grip on my hips tightens and I'm not ashamed to admit the tiny bikini I'm wearing dampens dramatically at the sight of his crooked grin.

Tsking, Angel shakes his head in mock disappointment. "How rude of me. Come here sweetheart, let me make it up to you."

Gently cupping my face, he pecks my lips before peppering feather-light kisses to my eyelids, cheeks, and chin. Finally, his hand grabs the back of my neck to catch my lips in a passionate kiss that makes it harder to suppress my need for him.

"So pretty," Angel murmurs against my lips.

My fingers having a mind of their own, trace his spine before tangling in his curls. When his warm tongue strokes mine, I tug on his hair to keep him in place. The pull makes Angel groan, his hips bucking up on instinct. When his hardness hits my throbbing core, I can't stop myself from grounding on his evident bulge.

A sound escapes the back of my throat when our grinding creates a soothing friction for my ache, and Angel takes that chance to devour my mouth with his tongue. With a hand on my hip, he helps me set a rhythm that serves us both.

I pull his hair and use the little gap between to gasp out, "More Angel, I need more. *I need you.*"

His warm mouth finds my neck, teasing me by leaving slow wet kisses and sucking softly. I'm a second away from begging him to stop this torture when he senses my impatience.

His hands on my hip grip me firmly to hold me steady as he covers my collarbone and upper chest with kisses.

Growing frustrated with my bra, Angel tears the bikini top before tossing it away. My nerves light up with fire when his mouth finally wraps around my breast, sucking and biting my nipple.

When I stop grinding, too overwhelmed with thinking what's about to come, Angel spanks my ass hard enough that my hips start moving against him, desperately.

"One more." I can never imagine being like this for anyone but him. With Angel, I'm at his mercy to do whatever he wants. Hearing my plea, Angel chuckles before alternating between my ass cheeks, using the smacks to motivate my hips to grind harder.

Five more bittersweet stings and I'm panting from the lack of oxygen in my lungs and the lack of his fingers inside me, but thankfully, I don't have to ask for more.

After thoroughly giving my breasts his attention and leaving marks all over my chest, Angel leans back to admire his masterpiece. The hand previously gripping my boobs in a death grip snakes to my bottoms, cupping me through the unwanted barrier between us.

With his eyes fixed on mine, Angel looks for signs if I want to stop, but he won't find any.

I want this. I want him. *Desperately.*

Leaning forward, I catch his lips in a needy kiss full of clashing teeth and sucking his bottom lip into my mouth. I rub myself on his palm, making my decision loud and clear.

Grinning at my eagerness, Angel pushes my panties aside before his fingers dive into me with one quick thrust. The pace never falters even when his face is buried in my neck, sucking and biting at the skin to push me closer to my release. My walls start to throb painfully, seeking the orgasm his fingers are nudging me towards.

Wrapping his free hand around my throat, Angel pushes me back until he can see my flushed cheeks and the hickeys covering my chest. Bringing my lips an inch from his, Angel demands, "Come for me, baby."

The growl in his words is enough to push me over the edge. I'm pretty sure I'm screaming something, but all I hear is my heartbeat in my head.

Slowly coming back to the present, my body falls limp and I slump over his shoulder. Angel keeps moving his fingers in and out of me in gentle movements to stretch my orgasm, only for it to trigger another smaller one.

Angel chuckles when I grumble about him finally pulling his fingers out of me. With my head resting on his shoulder, I gape when he brings the fingers that were just inside me to his mouth and suck them clean.

I thought I was done for the day, but the renewed faint throbbing between my thighs says otherwise.

Pushing my head off his shoulders, I hold his warm cheeks to kiss him. I taste myself on his tongue as his hands run all over me, softly massaging my muscles.

Taking control of the kiss, I let my hands slip down to trace the lines heading south, and that's when Angel realizes just how far I want to go.

"More, sweetheart?"

With our bodies pressed together, I can see how hard Angel is trying to hold back, but there's a lick of hope and anticipation in his eyes until I whisper a soft, *please.*

Angel quickly turns us around to hover over me and gently lays me on the towel he had spread on the floor. Kissing my nose, he asks, "Want to go back to our room, sweetheart? I don't think this is how you imagined your first time."

I smile at his worry, "No, this is perfect. Everything with you always is."

I never wanted the candles and rose petals on the bed, anyway. I'm perfectly content, wrapped in my mate's arms and surrounded by him in every sense of the word.

"And what about you? You're okay with this, right? It's your first time too."

Angel chuckles and ducks to bite my cheek. "I get to devour you, baby. This is already a dream come true."

I giggle and get comfortable when Angel asks again if I'm sacrificing some fantasy because of the heat of the moment. Resting his doubts to bed, I bring him in for a sweet kiss and wrap my legs around his waist.

Angel breathes into the kiss, and I feel his heart running a mile a minute. Good to know he is a little nervous, too. Sitting back on his knees, Angel removes his trunks and throws them near my bottoms, the ones he tore to pieces like a caveman.

Fuck. I know I've seen him before, and I've had him in my hands and mouth, but thinking about him *inside* me is a different story.

"There's no way that will fit."

I don't realize I've said it out loud instead of the safety of my crazy mind until Angel throws his head back with a boisterous laugh that rumbles in his chest.

It takes him a minute to calm down, and his smile is nothing short of amazement when he looks down at me. "You were made for me, sweetheart. I promise it'll fit."

Hovering over me, Angel cages me between his arms. His

greedy hands explore my curves, and I lose myself in the sparks his touch brings, but when his hard-on rubs my clit, the nerves kick in.

Angel doesn't let me clamp up or overthink about the potential pain. Massaging my hips, he kisses me passionately and I'm distracted long enough that I only react to the little sting when he is already half inside me, slowly sliding in instead of forcing his way.

I whimper when Angel fully drives in, and his thickness pulses against my walls. I'm vibrating with need, which only makes me lock around him to keep him in place. I don't ease up until I hear a groan mixed with a growl on top of me.

Thinking he is in pain, I look up only to see nothing but pleasure on Angel's face. Resting his forehead on mine, Angel fights the urge to move. His green eyes are darkened with need and I don't realize I'm squeezing around him until Angel hisses.

"You're killing me, sweetheart," Angel rasps before slowly pulling out. Sealing our lips together, I moan when he pushes back in with one long thrust.

The pain slowly fades, only coming in short spasms every time Angel thrusts into me, but the pleasure overcomes the slight sting. With every breath Angel takes next to my ear, I lose the ability to think about anything else but him.

My arms loop around his back, gripping his shoulders tighter with every thrust. Angel speeds up, adding more power behind each movement until he is thrusting in and out of me hard enough to make every inch of my body vibrate.

I want to drag myself away from this intense feeling and not move a muscle at the same time. With his damp forehead resting on mine, Angel lifts my right leg over his shoulder to get closer.

"Look at you. So perfect, sweetheart. Such a good girl, taking me so perfectly. You were made for me, weren't you, baby?"

I lose my head when Angel hits a spot that drives me so

wild, I start chanting, 'Don't stop' and 'Keep going'. Judging by the smirk that refuses to leave his lips, Angel is enjoying making me fall apart for him.

I'm afraid I will split in two if he goes any harder, but that doesn't stop my mouth from asking him for more. Desperate to not have even an inch separating us, Angel lifts both my legs over his shoulder so he can press his chest against the back of my thighs.

The change in position makes me scream out in pleasure, and I'm suddenly grateful we're alone in the castle.

"Eyes on me, sweet girl. Look at me when I make you scream my name."

Fuck. Angel's dirty words are my weakness.

I open my eyes with great strength because his dick pulsing and pushing in and out of me in such desperate thrusts makes me want to squeeze them shut from the intense sensation.

The moment our eyes connect, I feel a sharp sting in my chest. My palms get warmer, and the need to bring his face closer becomes unbearable. Holding both sides of his face, I let the sudden rush of warmth flow from me to Angel, making him moan into my mouth.

When I break the kiss, a beautiful sight awaits me.

My gold essence is circling my mate. The shimmering golden smoke is dancing over his skin, making him look even more angelic. The patterns on Angel's skin twirl and shift to add another story to his life and Angel's eyes flash a powerful shade of gold that makes my heart skip.

His essence, the shade of pale sunrise, comes to play and brushes on every part of my skin Angel is not touching. Even when our Divines have joined the moment, Angel doesn't let his intensity falter or keep his hands from clutching onto me.

"My sweetheart. My mate. Look at how much I crave you. Even my Divine can't get enough of you."

When his thumb suddenly presses on my clit, my eyes fall shut once again, and I gasp in surprise. The next time I open my eyes, I feel mildly disappointed to see everything back to normal, as if I had only dreamed of our Divine fusing together.

"I can feel you squeezing, baby. Will you come for me? Let me feel you coat my dick in your sweetness."

If I could talk, I would warn him just how close I am, but my breath hitches when he unexpectedly pinches my clit, throwing me off the edge with nothing but his name on my lips.

His uneven thrusts don't stop, prolonging my release, and just when I'm coming back to earth, Angel starts rubbing my clit in slow, lazy circles.

"Too... much," I croak. My hand blindly finds his wrist to hold onto, but I don't make him stop.

"Want me to stop, sweet girl?" Angel asks smugly. He knows I have no intention of stopping him. His thrusts get harder, but his rhythm is uneven and sloppy, so I know he is close too.

"No—*ah fuck!*" I breathlessly moan as he thrusts two more times before hitting that sweet spot again. The second time I cum is much stronger and Angel follows me this time. I feel his warm release fill me up and stretch my orgasm to its limit.

After carefully lowering my legs, Angel falls on top of me. It's hard to catch my breath with his dick still buried deep inside me, but Angel refuses to move. I'd be lying if I said I wasn't gripping him just as tightly, not wanting to be empty of him yet.

Nuzzling his head between my breasts, Angel kisses the one closer to his mouth, making me shudder at the feeling. I run my fingers through his hair, scratching his scalp softly while the other lightly traces his back, healing the scratches I made.

As long as I'm around, I refuse to let him feel any pain. He has scared my demons away and tended to my pain— emotional and physical. Angel makes me feel confident in myself. Makes me believe I'm worthy of being loved and appreciated by him, so the least I can do is heal his wounds for the rest of our lives.

Angel clings to me like a warm, heavy blanket. His soft breaths tickle my skin. Giving my boobs one last kiss, Angel takes my lips for a soft kiss.

Leaning on his elbow, Angel softly brushes my hair out of my face. "I swear to love you for as long as I breathe, and long after that."

There was a time when the adoration in his eyes as he talked about loving me made me shy away, but now I revel in his eyes on me. Now, I want to be showered in his kind words and sweet kisses all the time.

Giving back is easy with Angel. The way he loves me, not reciprocating is practically impossible.

"I love you more."

His smile brightens when I say it back, and he leans to kiss me again, only to stop short when I wince.

That doesn't feel too good.

"It hurts that bad, huh? I'm so sorry, baby; I got carried away being inside you for the first time. I should've been more gentle."

His face morphs into guilt, whereas I'm thinking how to tell him that even if he went ape shit crazy, I wouldn't have minded. *Not one bit.*

I bite my lip, thinking about all the ways I can have him now when Angel breaks my train of thought.

"You dirty-dirty woman, you're thinking about doing it again, aren't you."

"Maybe," I shrug innocently.

Chuckling, he smacks a loud kiss on my lips. "Come on, let me give you a warm bath first. It'll help with the tenderness."

Angel lifts me slowly with my legs clutching his waist and arms around his neck. Snatching the towel from a chair beside him, he wraps it around us. The towel is big enough to cover our naked bodies and the fact that he is still inside me... long after we are done.

He is totally obsessed with me.

"You're not sore?"

"Nope."

I huff and bite his neck. "No fair."

Angel picks up the towel that was under me and neatly folds it with one hand. On the way to our room, he throws the towel in a bin along with my ruined bikini set.

"So, when's the wedding?"

Seiji's sudden appearance startles us, and I shriek loudly. Angel grips the towel tighter so we don't accidentally flash him.

"How do you keep showing up out of nowhere?" Angel grunts at our intruder for ruining our peace after such strenuous activities. Maybe Angel needs another round if he still has the energy to be irritated.

"I was thinking of chocolate whiskey cake with salted caramel drizzle. Naturally, I'll be in charge of decoration because let's be honest, I'm the best at... well, everything." Completely ignoring how Angel is on the verge of murder, Seiji continues to list details about *our* wedding that *he* has been planning since the *second* day we met.

I interfere before Angel decides today is the day he finally kills our Price of Famine.

"Princess... I'm kind of *naked* under here."

"Oh, yeah, understood. I'll leave you guys alone. But everyone will be here soon for brunch, so no more hanky-panky!" He shouts, running the other way.

As soon as Seiji disappears, I pepper Angel's neck with kisses so he'll drop the urge to throw stuff. What actually works is reminding him of the relaxing bath he promised me.

Was that all we did in the privacy of our bathroom?

Maybe. *Maybe not.*

An hour later, I walk down the stairs with Angel's fingers intertwined in mine, excited for weekend family brunch.

After Jackson was officially inducted into the kingdom, Seiji moved into the Famine castle with him, so a weekend brunch was the perfect excuse to stay close.

It was a shock to his parents when Jackson was introduced because Seiji waited until *after* the battle to tell the kingdom and his parents about finding his mate.

He wanted everyone to know firsthand that Jackson wasn't anything like the others of his kind we dealt with. When the warlock took our side and killed people of his own kind because he knew what was right, he easily won everyone's trust and love.

On the day of his move, I even baked a cake for the couple, but it somehow *exploded.* I had to clean a lot of icing from so many places. And before I could try again, Angel banned me from the kitchen, and everyone backed him up. It was a minor incident, so banning me was a bit dramatic.

It was just *cake*... that *exploded*... and might've hit Harvey in the face... it was also a little bit rock solid.

Like I said, a bit overdramatic.

But it's been fun watching Seiji and Jackson grow closer. Since Jackson is so quiet and emotionally mature, it's interesting to see him come out of his shell while simultaneously grounding Seiji. They are polar opposites, but they fit together so perfectly it feels like they've known each other for years instead of weeks.

Talking about couples, the other new couple has become the kingdom's most favorite gossip topic.

We all know Papa is essentially a goof, so he loves embarrassing Hazel and riling her up every chance he gets with his antics. They both play pranks on each other all the time, and it usually ends with one of them drawing a weapon, but not being able to do anything because of their bond.

Because of these two, the Tetrad kingdom has its own drama/comedy show, and people love it. Especially when Hazel comes on top of their *friendly* feud. Papa was a troublemaker growing up, so there are a lot of elders who enjoy his ass getting roasted.

Walking into the dining room with Angel, I look for monkey first. Finding my boy, I ruffle his hair and bend to kiss his head. "Breakfast?"

"Yes, please."

"Pizza?" I whisper.

"Duh," his reply makes me chuckle, and I secretly serve him a slice without Angel noticing.

Monkey might still be rigid around strangers, but he has grown out of his shell in our time here. He is spoiled with affection, and I can see how much he loves being the constant center of attention.

They don't see it yet, but I know the signs of a sassy kid, and this little werewolf spends way too much time around me not to have an attitude.

After August came back from staying with Uncle Elijah and his mate, he wouldn't stop blubbering about how much fun he had. The King of Hell fell face first for my toddler's charm... which reminds me I need to have a serious talk with Papa about his friend.

It's high time Uncle Elijah stopped sending over presents. I mean, what is my kiddo supposed to do with an ancient sword *twice* his size?

"Sweetheart, finish your juice, please," Angel pushes my glass closer without looking away from his conversation with Grace. When I make a face at the glass full of green things, Harvey quickly swaps his empty glass with mine before anyone can see.

"This is why you're my favorite best friend."

I knew it was coming. Harvey swats my head as soon as the words are out of my mouth. "I'm your *only* best friend."

Harvey adds an extra spoonful of pasta to my plate to make up for the disgusting juice he saved me from.

I love my dumbass.

"Thanks for sharing." Hazel snatches the cupcake from Papa's plate, who turns to glare at his mate, but before it can turn into a fight, Jackson drops a new one before Papa.

Grace and Angel were very happy when Jackson joined them as the peacekeepers in our group. With additional troublemakers, we needed extra peacekeepers.

"So good, mama." August looks up at me with a smile before he goes back to humming as he eats.

At this moment, surrounded by the people I've come to love as family, teasing and laughing with and at each other, instead of letting myself surrender to this peace, I'm waiting for that one pull that will unravel this flawless vision of my life and force make me go back to the darkness I was once used to.

I'm hoping with every fiber of my being that this dream won't end because even if all of this is a lie, it's a lie I want to live forever. To have this peace forever, grow old and closer to my dysfunctional family without worrying about losing it all.

But every great story has to tackle a few bumps before the happily ever after, right?

Acknowledgment

Dear Reader,

As I write this I'm overwhelmed with gratitude for this incredible journey of writing my debut book. The path to this moment was filled with hours of rereading my own words, struggling to learn how to correctly market my book and the sheer determination to see my dreams come true.

First and foremost, I want to thank my family for trusting me enough to quietly support me until I was ready to come clean about my secret project. My siblings who never miss a single social media post and love flaunting my work. I couldn't have done this without you all.

My heartfelt thanks to all the fellow authors who encouraged and welcomed me into their world with open arms and said no to gatekeeping.

Last but not least, to you, dear readers—thank you for embarking on this adventure with me. Your support means the world to me, and I hope this book brings as much joy to your hearts as it has to mine.

With sincere gratitude, Leona Reed.

About The Author

Leona Reed is a self-proclaimed introvert perfectly content in a world of books and daydreams, where stories are endless and reality takes a backseat. When she's not creating swoon-worthy book boyfriends, she's crafting snarky one-liners and even snarkier characters. Writing romance is her happy place —and she's more than happy to take you along for the ride.

Printed in Great Britain
by Amazon

52204386R00270